# Death Wish
*Alexa O'Brien Huntress Book Five*

# Trina M. Lee

# *Death Wish*

## *Trina M. Lee*

Published 2012

ISBN 978-1478359036

Copyright © 2012, Trina M. Lee

All rights reserved. No part of this publication may be reproduced, stored in a retrieval system, or transmitted in any form or by any means, electronic, mechanical, recording or otherwise, without the prior written permission of the author.
Manufactured in the United States of America

Editor
B. Leigh Hogan

Cover Artist
Michael Hart

Published by
Dark Mountain Books

This is a work of fiction. The characters, incidents and dialogues in this book are of the author's imagination and are not to be construed as real. Any resemblance to actual events or persons, living or dead, is completely coincidental.

# *Chapter One*

Feeding the bloodlust was the only way to control it. It was a sad but true reality. The euphoric high led to an inevitable crash and burn. I could either accept that or fight it until I lost all control.

When the bloodlust got bad enough, I made my way to a seedy part of town and browsed through the selection of pimps, johns and gangsters. The harsh truth was there were far more of them than one might assume.

I lingered in the darkened doorway of an abandoned building, watching my chosen victim. He was a known thug with a reputation for collecting debts owed to one of his drug-dealer pals. I could only imagine how many knees he'd shattered in his time. He seemed like fair game to me.

I was about to make my move when I felt it. My senses blazed. I became keenly aware that I too was being hunted. Now that was interesting. No sooner had I reached out metaphysically to locate my stalker than I was knocked to the ground. My head hit the pavement and pain shot through my skull. Stealthy. They didn't usually get so close before I felt them.

"I didn't think it would be so easy." My attacker snarled down into my face. His breath was rancid. He stunk of death and old, rank blood. "If fucking had a smell, you would be it."

So gross. I lashed out with blast of raw energy. It launched him through the air and slammed him against a parked car. I was on my feet in a leap, ready for more.

"If that's a line, pal, I ain't biting." My hands grew warm as power pulsed through me, waiting for release.

He was faster than I expected. His speed was impressive, allowing him to dodge the psi ball I'd tossed before he barreled into me like a bull on a rampage. I braced for it but didn't have time to avoid impact.

My back hit the wall of the abandoned building hard enough to knock the wind from me. He fought to get his hands around my throat. The vampire then banged my head against the hard, brick structure. A growl spilled between my lips, and I bared four vicious wolf fangs.

"So you've got a little bit of fight in you. Well, let's see it, hot stuff." He tightened his grip on my throat, choking off my air supply.

He was still mocking me when I slapped him with another surge of power. It threw him on his ass, giving me time to follow up with a kick to his face. I leaned over him, holding a psi ball ready.

"Want to tell me what that was all about?" I hit him with the roiling gold and blue ball. The resulting shriek was music to my ears.

"Someone wants you dead, bitch."

The vampire couldn't have found a better way to break my focus. Finding his moment, he took advantage of my confusion. He brought both hands together and smashed them like a giant fist into my face. I tasted blood and saw stars. I hit the ground hard as he threw me down.

"So what else is new?" I muttered, picking myself up.

Someone sent this jackass after me? Maybe I shouldn't have been surprised, but I was. I didn't go looking for trouble, but it always seemed to find me. I couldn't let this guy make it back to whoever sent him. Not in one piece anyway. I needed answers.

We squared off, each successfully blocking the other's attacks. He didn't seem to have much in the way of metaphysical ability, but he threw a hell of a punch. I didn't have the staying power a vampire had; I would tire before he would. I struggled to focus my concentration. It was difficult with a flurry of fists he threw in my face.

I misjudged his next move, and he gained the upper hand. All of a sudden, I was flat on my back looking up at the starless city sky. Fangs grazed my throat, spurring me into action. Gathering my power close, I directed it with enough force to make his head snap back. He crashed through the pane of a nearby bus stop shelter. The sound of shattering glass drew little attention. Nobody in this neighborhood cared about an altercation unless it involved them.

## Death Wish

My would-be killer's attitude changed abruptly. As he got unsteadily to his feet, we both noticed the giant shard of glass jutting from his stomach. That had to hurt.

A scream tore from him as he jerked it free. Blood poured from the wound. It was unlikely to be fatal. He was undead, so it would take more than that to kill him. Still, it seemed to be enough to get him rethinking this entire situation.

I advanced on him, and he began to back away slowly.

Hell no. He was not running away from me.

He turned to bolt as I threw myself at him. We went down hard with him taking the worst of the impact. I was done playing. His lack of offense made it easy to center my focus. I grasped his energy, feeling his stone cold heart as if I held it in my hand. And then, I squeezed.

The shriek that burst from him hurt my ears, but it brought a smile to my lips. I shoved enough power into him to make it burn. With a hand on his throat, I forced him to meet my eyes.

"Who wants me dead?" I demanded, fangs bared. To show him I was serious, I pushed another burning wave of power into him.

He struggled to speak through the blood that filled his mouth. There was a wild glint in his dark eyes. Maniacal.

"Who doesn't?" The bastard laughed despite the fact that I was slowly crushing him to dust from the inside out.

"Last chance to start talking," I hissed. "What did they offer you to take me out? Give me a name, and I let you walk."

"Liar."

Knowing his time was up, he brazenly spat blood in my face. It wasn't worth trying to get anything further out of him. With an angry shout, I envisioned his black heart in my mind, and I crushed it. Power went out from me into him, joining us for just a second before his body burst into dust and ash.

After brushing myself off the best I could, I risked a glance in the side mirror of a nearby car: a bloody lip and nose, bruised cheek and black eye. Not bad. It would heal by morning if not sooner.

My body ached, but all I could think about was what the vampire had just said. There was a price on my head. I replayed those words, searching them for a lie and finding none.

Sudden paranoia had me listening extra hard to the sounds of the city. I'd had the wrong people take a dangerous interest in me in the past, but this was a first. A hit. On me? The idea was incredulous. Wasn't it?

A deadly chill stole over me. Someone out there had a price tag with my name on it.

## Chapter Two

It was past dawn by the time I got home. I felt Arys's cold vampire energy long before I reached my front door.

He was a vision of naked splendor, lying in my bed with his head propped on a mountain of pillows. Arys dropped the book he held when I entered the room.

"What happened to you?" His midnight blue eyes were intent upon me, taking in my cuts, bruises and bloodied attire. Small, silver rings shone in his ears, nose and lower lip. With his sexy mess of black hair, he looked both bad ass and beautiful.

"Where do I begin?" I sat on the edge of the bed and started peeling off my clothes. "I tangled with a vampire who informed me there's a price on my head. Is that news to you? Because it sure as hell is to me."

"Tell me you killed him." Arys's watchful gaze was heavy upon me as I struggled out of my clothing.

"Hell yes I did." I kicked the jeans across the floor, wincing as pain shot through my ribs. Damn vampires. I crawled into bed beside Arys, collapsing gratefully into the soft mound of blankets. I should have dragged myself through the shower, but I was too exhausted.

"Too bad you couldn't beat a little more information out of him first." Arys pulled me close and pressed his lips to my forehead. "Anyone who fucks with you is going to be wearing their insides on the outside when I'm done with them."

His soft kisses were a gentle caress down the side of my face until his mouth claimed mine. The touch of his tongue was hot against my bottom lip. A rush of power burst through me as our energy joined with a jolt of electricity.

"You have to be careful." Arys spoke between kisses, his hand lost in my long blonde locks. "It's got to have something to do with what Maxwell knew about us. Others are figuring it out."

I realized the book he'd been reading was his own journal, the one he'd given me for my birthday. I hadn't read very much since receiving it a few weeks ago despite Arys's nagging at me to do so. It was hard to take in too much at once. Since Maxwell had revealed that Arys had known about me long before I'd been born, things had changed. Arys was more neurotic than I'd ever seen him.

He feared what he'd been told, that his darkness would destroy us. I didn't want to believe it, though somewhere deep inside I knew it to be true. Two different witches had warned us at very different times about the dangers of our connection. Yet, I knew there was more to it; something was missing…

I snuggled in against him, reveling in the way his body felt alongside mine. "You're the calm and cool one. I'm the nutcase. Don't go changing that on me."

He chuckled, a low sound that made me smile. "You're right. I'll let you be the crazy one since you do it so well."

I pinched him playfully, satisfied when he made a pained noise. He lightly bit my earlobe, moving to graze my neck with his sharp fangs. I closed my eyes, content to be in his arms. Wrapping me tighter in his embrace, Arys's energy was warm and comforting.

When it became clear that sleep planned to evade me, I sat up and grabbed the old leather journal from where Arys had abandoned it on the bed. He'd closed it so I couldn't tell what page he'd been reading. I'd only made it through a handful of pages myself.

I propped myself up against the pillows and rested the book on my lap. Arys remained close, his face buried in a pillow and an arm across my waist.

"You're never going to finish that, are you?" His voice was muffled, and his eyes were closed, but I knew he was alert. He wasn't as relaxed as he appeared.

"I will. I'm just not sure when. It feels weird, reading your personal thoughts and feelings from so long ago. It's hard to wrap my mind around it all."

I flipped the journal open to the first page. I'd read it so many times already, but I often came back to it. The words were faded but legible.

## Death Wish

*October 14, 1849*

*I saw her again in my dreams, the wolf. I wish I knew her name. All I know is that when I see her, she is mine. She haunts me. The image of her lingers long after I wake. I have yet to see her true form. In these dreams, she is always wolf, but I know that's not her true face. She is human, too, but whom she is, to me, remains a mystery. I've known the love of many women. Yet something about this wolf makes me feel like no other woman has. Alive. And somehow, complete. I don't know who she is, but I know I must find her.*

To know that Arys had seen me in his dreams more than a century ago was mind blowing. I still couldn't quite comprehend how that could happen.

The only witch I knew who had known about things of this nature was dead. However, Lena believed that Arys and I were meant to be together, two beings cut from the same magic cloth, destined to unite.

I could almost hear her voice: *Sometimes this is the natural order of things; as hard as it might be to believe, it's meant to happen. A bond like this lasts to the death.*

She had given us a warning though, one I'd never forget. A bond like this could drive one absolutely mad. Lena had made me promise to be careful. I'd never guessed then how deep it went.

I knew why I kept coming back to that very first journal entry. It was because Arys had seen me as a wolf before I'd ever been born. It was confirmation that everything with Raoul, the attack and my change to wolf, had been meant to happen. That was hard to swallow. During my childhood years, playing with my sister as a clueless, happy child, all of this had been there, waiting to happen. The loss of my innocence, my misplaced love for the man who killed my family, it was my destiny. And, I hated that.

"Stop torturing yourself." Arys made a half-hearted attempt at swiping the book from my hands. "I gave it to you so you could find answers. Not so you'd drive yourself crazy."

"Cut it out. This journal is fragile. Don't wreck it." I turned the page, giving him a teasing glare. "I am finding answers. I'm just not happy with some of them."

I skimmed through the next page. It was a detailed account of a gruesome night out. Arys and Harley had been busy boys back in those days. The first time I'd read about how they had seduced a young woman and driven her into a sexual frenzy, I'd been disturbed. I didn't want to read it again. Still, I couldn't help but linger over a few especially creepy parts.

*Harley brought her to the brink of climax, enjoying her pleas for more. She oozed sexual energy, and we devoured it. I bit her wrist, letting the blood flow over my tongue. It stirred my every hunger to life. I longed to be inside her, taking all of her. Body and blood. But, Harley had had enough play. Now, he wanted her to scream.*

I shuddered and turned the page before I could read anymore. My own memories of Harley were not fond ones. However, they were nothing compared to the depravity that lay within these pages. Arys and I shared one another's memories, thus everything he had written about his sire brought those horrific memories from my subconscious to the surface where I was forced to relive them as if I'd been there.

I distinctly preferred to keep those memories safely entombed beyond the reach of my conscious mind, so maybe Arys was right, maybe I never would finish reading his journal.

"Did you get some kind of perverse pleasure out of recording your debauchery with Harley? It makes me want to scream."

"Yes. I suppose I did. I also get some perverse pleasure from your reaction to it."

There was no humor in his eyes. It was my own fault. I'd been dumb enough to ask about his past, and he'd answered. I easily forgot how dangerous Arys was. He was part of me in so many ways, and yet sometimes, I felt like I didn't know him at all.

"Fantastic," I muttered. Shrugging off the feeling of unease creeping over me, I kept flipping pages.

Bypassing previously read tales of blood play and wicked games, I paused where I'd left off. It had been several days since I'd read the journal. I was starting to think it would leave me with more questions than answers. Only one way to find out.

## Death Wish

*November 17, 1849*

*I had the strangest dream that I was a wolf. I awoke confused and startled. As a vampire, I know that can never be. It's she, inside my mind again. I'm sure of it. I need to know whom she is before it drives me insane. I don't dare speak a word about her to Harley. Not yet. I need to find her.*

*I need answers. Alice has been called a charlatan, a fraud, but I've seen enough to be sure that she knows things. Answers from Alice won't come easy or cheap.*

I glanced down to find Arys watching me intently, likely waiting for my expression to change as I read. I stroked a hand through his soft, ebony hair.

"Why don't you tell me these things yourself, Arys? Then you can censor the parts I really don't want or need to know."

"You need to know all of it, my wolf. Just read it."

I was skeptical. "I really need to know about all the fun you and Harley had driving women into a sexual frenzy while you killed them? I doubt that."

Arys snickered, and it sent a shiver down my spine. "You don't want to read it because it gets to you. You start to remember, and you like it."

"Screw that." My response came too fast, and my pulse quickened. I hated it when he was right.

"Keep reading. The worst of it never made it into that journal anyway."

"That's reassuring."

It wasn't. I did not want to read more about Arys's murderous activity, but I did want to know more about Alice and what, if anything, she knew about us.

*January 4, 1850*

*Alice is either a liar and a thief or a woman who knows too much. She read my palm, an act that seemed very contrived and only for show. Then she started talking, and I almost wished I'd never gone to see her at all. She confirmed what I already knew, that the wolf is mine, somehow. Twin flame. That is the term she used. The wolf is my twin flame. I had never heard of this before. I asked if she meant we were soul mates. The shriveled old hag laughed as if I were a fool.*

*Twin flames and soul mates are often confused though never the same. According to Alice, soul mates are two different people meant to be together, but twin flames are part of one another, created as one and split into two. Two separate beings, two separate souls, and yet we are one. Alice claims that twin flames rarely ever exist in the same lifetime. They aren't meant to. Yet if they do somehow unite, it is for a reason. A spiritual purpose. Of course, I asked why. Alice was unwilling to part with more information without parting me from more money. I concluded that she had little else to share. Perhaps I will go back. Perhaps I never will.*

*If Alice speaks the truth then I will likely never know my wolf. I don't even know her name. And, for some inexplicable reason, that pains me.*

I read the entry a second time and then a third. Twin flames. I had never heard the term before. I flipped ahead to the next entry, but it was about an argument with Harley, something that meant nothing to me right then. My mind was stuck on the twin flame revelation. Too impatient to keep reading in the hopes of finding more information, I jumped out of bed and ran upstairs to fetch my laptop. This question required the internet.

Arys raised his head, an inquisitive expression on his face as I jostled him about while getting settled with the computer on my lap. "What's up, love?"

"How could you not have told me this before?" I tapped my fingers impatiently on the keyboard as the laptop went through the motions of starting up. "This can't possibly be true."

I typed it into Google, grateful for once that the search engine corrected my spelling. My fingers were shaky on the keys. I skimmed through the search results. For something that I'd never heard of before, a surprisingly large number of websites were devoted to the topic of twin flames.

As I made my way through the sites that looked the most promising, a strange feeling began to twist my stomach into a knot. Most sources were quick to tell me that a twin flame and a soul mate were not the same thing. Twin flames were much like a coin. Each side was just half of a whole. Neither could exist without the other.

*Death Wish*

I went cold inside as I read on. The yin yang was used to explain twin flames more frequently than anything else: Light and dark. Night and day. Life and death. Each side possessed a little of the other.

I devoured everything I could find on the subject, analyzing it all with my own personal bullshit filter. What it all boiled down to was that a twin flame union was rare and usually unsuccessful. Both halves often struggled with the immense power of their bond. It usually destroyed them. Emotional turmoil and conflict would follow the twins always, as they could never hide anything from one another. The truth was always there, deep down inside.

My lungs froze when I read that last part. Our shared memories fit that description a little too perfectly. I shook my head and tore my gaze from the screen. This could not be real. It was just too much to process.

For over a hundred years, Arys had lived with this knowledge, wondering if he would ever know me. How many times since we'd met had he wanted to tell me, knowing I would never believe him? When did he know for certain that I was the one?

It was hard to swallow. I was shocked, in disbelief. Yet, I knew it paled in comparison to whatever Arys had been feeling these past few years, knowing what we were to each other while I'd lived in sweet ignorance. It must have been hell for him.

He watched in silence as I scrolled through page after page, all of them telling me the very same thing. Could this be why I was now marked for death? Maxwell had put it together before I'd killed him. How many others knew what Arys and I were?

I gestured to the unbelievable words on the screen. "You should have said something, Arys."

"Don't you think I wanted to? It killed me not to blurt it out the first night we met. Or, every night thereafter."

"If I recall correctly, you accused me of purposely entrapping you. You bastard." I crossed my arms and glared. Let's see him explain that one away.

Arys watched me intently as he spoke, shrugging unapologetically. "It was so hard to accept. I'd lived all these years believing I would never know you. Once we spoke with Lena, and she basically confirmed what Alice had told me, I couldn't deny it anymore."

"Uh huh." I regarded him thoughtfully. "Yet, you still waited almost an entire year after that to give me the journal. You could have told me yourself."

"And, have you refuse to believe it? No way." Arys's lips curved into a playful grin. "You're hotheaded, Alexa. You're difficult to talk to sometimes, especially when it comes to your power and your well-being. Letting you read a hundred year old journal was more dramatic and left you no room for argument."

Mischief shone in his eyes. All it took was the right look from him to ignite the flames of desire within me, and he damn well knew it. It got him what he wanted, more often than not, but not this time.

"So what's your excuse for pushing me to be with Shaz, then, if you knew I was always meant to be yours? Are you going to blame that on me, too?"

Arys's smile faded. Tearing his gaze from mine, he stared across the room as if seeing something I couldn't. "I was afraid for you, of what this will do to you. I still am. This thing that unites us, it could destroy us. I thought if you chose him, if you and I were apart, maybe you'd be better off."

The fact that he wouldn't look at me made me want him to look at me that much more. What would I see in his eyes? A tremor of fear shook me. Arys wasn't alone in his concerns. I knew his fears were justified. He thought his darkness would consume me, and judging by the past few weeks, it was starting to. Still, it wasn't his fault.

"Well, according to pretty much every site on the good ol' world wide web, we are part of each other, and there is a reason for that. We have a purpose. It has to be worth the risks."

"A purpose that is unknown to us and means nothing if our power destroys you." Arys's tone was bitter. "You're in danger, Alexa. I can see it happening, and I know it's my fault. If I hadn't bound you by blood, you wouldn't be a slave to the bloodlust. It's like I've infected you with parts of me you were never meant to have."

His guilt-riddled energy felt abrasive and cold. It wasn't like him, and I found it irritating. "If you hadn't done it, Harley would have. Either that, or I'd be dead."

Arys looked up sharply with a flash of anger in his eyes. "I know. I hate that it had to come to that. He wouldn't have it any other way. He never could accept you as part of me."

Nothing in Arys's expression changed, but I knew how sensitive a subject this was for him. Harley had turned him, effectively ensuring Arys never died a human death and guaranteeing that he would live to see my lifetime. As twisted as that sordid little situation had been, Harley had played his part, to our benefit.

The fact that I'd killed him made Harley a touchy subject. Arys's true feelings for his sire became evident the night he'd stormed into The Wicked Kiss and grabbed me by the throat while snarling about how my magic pussy had seduced him.

Remembering it made my temper flare. It was long over and not worth dredging up. Arys loved me, I knew that. Yet that night was evidence of how, even that which bound us, could also divide us.

"Well, I am a part of you, Arys, and we are both part of something else. I just wish you had told me sooner. It would have saved us a lot of trouble."

He closed the laptop and shoved it aside before reaching for me. I went gladly into his embrace.

"I never meant to keep you in the dark, Alexa. I thought I was protecting you, letting you choose your own path instead of allowing it to be chosen for you."

I smiled at his wishful thinking; it was endearing. "Our fate was chosen for both of us. Now, let's figure out what the hell we do with it before it kills us."

# Chapter Three

I stood in the small upstairs bathroom with a blow dryer in hand. My long blonde hair hung almost to my waist in damp chunks. I pulled a brush through it absently, lost in thought. When my hair was dry enough, I applied a light dusting of dark grey shadow to my eyes.

I gazed at my reflection, searching my blue eyes for someone I recognized.

My eyes were deep brown, or at least they were supposed to be. The undead power coursing through me turned them Arys's drowning blue again.

The mascara wand shook in my hand as I brushed it over my lashes. I was jittery from the blood hunger and power churning inside me. I took a few deep breaths and focused. Steady.

I wore dark slacks and a tight black shirt, casual and easy to move in. The summer night would be warm, but I brought a knee-length leather jacket to hide the dagger at my waist. I wanted to be ready for anything. If someone was going to take me out, I sure as hell wasn't going to make it easy for them.

After a quick trip through the Tim Horton's drive-thru, I was equipped with an extra-large coffee and the desire to kick some ass. I hit the button to open the sunroof and headed for the highway. I was on my way to see Brogan, Lena's daughter. She had called because someone had been snooping around her store, asking questions that triggered her suspicions. Naturally, I was curious myself.

Arys had been reluctant to let me go alone. My argument had been that he couldn't accompany me everywhere. We were going to find out who wanted me dead, but in the meantime, I wasn't going to hide at home. Besides, I'd be spending the rest of the night with Jez and Kale. I'd be as safe as I could get.

The warm summer breeze ruffled my hair, smelling faintly of rain. It was a gorgeous night. A pale orange streak hovered low over the horizon as the sun's final light faded. It would be a perfect night to run as wolf.

I usually ran with Shaz and Kylarai, as well as the rest of our local pack, on nights like this. It was as close to pack as we came these days. Several pack members were understandably uneasy with my ties to the vampire world. Considering the danger I was currently in because of it, I couldn't fault them for that.

I took Whitemud Drive to the south side of the city where Brogan's magic shop was located. Since her mother's recent death, Brogan had taken over the store, a fascinating place called Toil and Trouble. The place went unnoticed if one wasn't looking for it, but to those who practiced magic or sought magical guidance, it was madly popular.

I pulled into the parking lot a half hour before closing. It was empty other than two cars, one of them being Brogan's little red Honda.

Toil and Trouble was in a busy part of town. Plenty of people passed by on the street, both on foot and by automobile. I watched them all carefully before getting out of my car. I held my power tight inside, ready to use it.

The Dragon Claw sat on the passenger seat. It was a hell of a weapon to carry in public with its ten-inch blade. I slipped the jacket on and slid the dagger into the sheath hanging from the studded belt slung around my hips.

I exited the car and crossed the small parking lot to the door. I reached out psychically, feeling the environment. A myriad of energies swarmed the area as people passed through. It was heavily human and fragmented, as if very few had lingered. Nothing set off my internal alarm.

Inside, the store was brightly lit, momentarily assaulting my eyes. A chime indicated my arrival. Brogan looked up with a smile from her place behind the counter.

Her dirty blonde ponytail bounced as she waved before turning back to the customer she was helping. My inquisitive gaze roamed over him. Young, late teens or early twenties. He was decked out head-to-toe in Goth attire. The black liner was heavy around his eyes, and spikes adorned his throat and wrists. His dyed black hair was long and disheveled.

I surveyed the rest of the store before stepping up to the counter behind him. Only one other person was inside, an older woman with a clean-cut appearance. Her brown hair was twisted into a bun. With glasses perched on her nose, she thumbed through a book on the far side of the shop.

I waited patiently while Brogan spoke to the guy about his purchases. With another glance at the lady reading, I psychically touched her ever so slightly, sensing what kind of power she had, if any. She didn't react; she had no idea I was feeling her out. Nothing.

Turning my attention to the Goth guy in front of me, I did the same to him. And, I was stunned. Power didn't roll off him the way it did with some, but once I reached for it, I couldn't miss it. He was a natural alright, clearly born with this power. He was pure human, a witch. A potentially dangerous one.

He didn't seem to suspect that I was psychically analyzing him. Or, if he did, he didn't let on. He was engrossed in conversation with Brogan. Peeking around him, I tried to get a look at what he was buying without being too obvious.

Brogan was busy wrapping a black glass chalice in bubble wrap. "Are you sure this is the one you want?"

"Yes, that's the one." He seemed anxious, like he wanted her to hurry up.

A few crystals lay on the counter, each a different color. Brogan reached to wrap those next. A scrying mirror and an amulet of some kind completed his purchases. It was hard to get a good look at either. Something was carved onto the amulet, but I couldn't make it out.

"Remember, if you have any questions at all, don't hesitate to call or email." Brogan beamed a friendly smile at him and received a half-hearted shrug in response.

She met my gaze over his shoulder, and I lifted a brow in question. Only then did he turn to look at me. Fear shone in his eyes as he looked me over. It took me a second to realize that he was reacting to my power.

I imagined I felt dark and deadly. To me, his energy felt human, but it went deeper than that. It tapped into the unseen, the force that made us all so much more than mere physical bodies. I knew my energy hadn't felt human like that in a long time.

## Death Wish

I forced a smile and stepped back, hoping to seem less threatening. He must have thought I was a vampire – I felt like one to everyone else – so I made sure he saw clearly that I wasn't sporting any fangs. Well, at least not until the wolf came out.

Brogan pushed his change and the bag filled with his things into his hand. Flustered and rushed, he took the bag and shoved away from the counter as if he were afraid I might chase him.

"Have a nice night, Gabriel," Brogan called after him. The door chime sounded, and he was gone.

"Sorry about that," I apologized with a grin. "I think I freaked him out."

Brogan glanced at the woman browsing the bookshelf and lowered her voice. "You feel like you've sprung a leak and can't contain yourself."

I shrugged and leaned on the counter. "It's one of those better safe than sorry kind of nights. I'm tapping a little more than necessary tonight."

"Understood." Brogan nodded knowingly. "Let me see what I can do for this lady."

With a friendly smile pasted onto her face, she slipped out from behind the counter and approached the woman. I lingered where I was, checking out the items stocked near the cash register. I was curious about Gabriel and his intentions with the things he'd bought.

After a few minutes with Brogan, the woman chose a few books and stepped up to the counter. I smiled politely and moved out of her way.

I picked up a crystal from a box near the cash register. Turning it over a few times, I admired its smooth surface. The crystal started to hum, a strange sound I could feel more than hear. I quickly dropped it and rubbed my hands together as if that would remove the strange sensation.

Once Brogan and I were alone in the store, I said, "That kid, Gabriel, how old is he?"

"I'm not sure. Eighteen or so." Brogan's hazel eyes narrowed, and she glanced toward the exit where Gabriel had disappeared. "He's so young but so skilled. I don't think he has any idea how dangerous that could be."

"Power makes him a potential victim. Let's hope he stays off the radar of the real big bads." I didn't elaborate. We both knew what that could mean.

Brogan looked worried; her brow creased in a frown. "I do worry about him. I hope he doesn't do anything to get himself in trouble. He's a regular here. I try to watch out for him. My mom always believed our abilities should be used for helping others, but she also warned me of how dangerous that could be." There was a distant look in Brogan's eyes as she remembered her mother.

"He'll be alright." I was in no position to make such claims. The kid was so young and walking in such a dark world. The last thing he needed was to turn out like me: blood hungry and working for the bad guys.

My thoughts strayed to Lena. Guilt over how she had died still plagued me. Maybe it wasn't directly my fault, but someone killed her in an effort to get to me. It was hard to accept.

"Your mother was so good to me. I'll always be sorry for what happened to her."

I reached to brush a hand over Brogan's in a quick gesture of offered comfort. Our skin met briefly, and my power reached out to taste hers, rich and earthy but pure and untainted by the darkness that fed the undead power burning in my own veins.

I pulled away quickly, before I could call her power to me, as I always tended to do with Kale. The urge was there, independent of me. I refused it, forcing it back down inside.

"I'm sorry. I'm kind of running at full capacity tonight. Anyway, you wanted to talk to me about someone?"

"Right." Brogan turned the sign on the door from open to closed. "There was a woman in here earlier, kind of sketchy. Right away, I got a strange vibe from her. I can't always tell, but I think she was a werewolf. She was asking questions. Most of them were about you."

"Me?" Maybe I was going to find the person behind the hit sooner than I'd anticipated. "Tell me about her."

"She played it cool, browsed around. Started by asking questions about the store, mundane stuff. Once she got me talking, she slipped in a few casual questions about The Wicked Kiss. She wanted to know who owned it. Asked if I knew them. That kind of thing." Brogan moved about the store, turning off lights and extinguishing scented candles. "I kept my answers short. I could tell she was trying to figure out how much I really knew about you. I told her I didn't want to talk here but maybe after I closed the store for the night."

I gazed around the store, thinking over what I'd just heard. The store was so cozy and quaint. Honey-colored hard wood floors created a sense of warmth. It was a relatively small building though it held a lot of items. Glass-topped cases lined one wall, filled with jewelry, amulets and silver daggers. The bookshelf was a large, floor-to-ceiling model stacked with spell books of all kinds. Toil and Trouble stocked everything from herbs to candles to voodoo dolls. The assortment was both impressive and intimidating.

"She arranged to meet with you?"

"Yep." Brogan produced a business card from her back pocket. "She told me to call this number if I couldn't make it. Otherwise, I'm meeting her at the Starbucks down the street in an hour. Or, so she thinks."

The card was white and plain, having only a name and a phone number. Zelda Fitzgerald. It was laughable. Not even a clever attempt at a fake name.

I stared hard at the card. I knew that name, not just because Zelda was F. Scott Fitzgerald's wife. I strained to remember something else, but I couldn't quite put a finger on it.

"Brogan, can you tell me what she looked like?" As I stared at the name printed in neat black letters on the card, I was swept back in time. I did know one person who had taken an interest in the Fitzgeralds. Just one. And, she was dead.

"Tall with long, curly hair. Brunette. I think her eyes were dark. Jeans and a t-shirt. Nothing that especially caught my eye." Brogan's ponytail fell over her shoulder as she inclined her head, studying me. "Do you know who she is?"

"No. I mean, I don't think so." I shook my head, unable to believe what the borrowed name on the card told me. It was impossible; it had to be. "So, I guess she'll be surprised when I show up in your place."

"That's the plan."

I held up the card. "Can I keep this?"

"Of course." With a bright smile, Brogan nodded enthusiastically. "Don't hesitate to let me know if you need anything. I'm always here to help."

I forced myself to smile, hoping she wouldn't see the shadows in my eyes. "You got it."

My exit was hasty. The card in my hand held the faintest trace of energy. It was so miniscule I could barely feel it. It taunted me. She had touched it. Zelda Fitzgerald. I knew who she was, knew it with every part of me, despite the odds being stacked so strongly against the possibility.

*The Great Gatsby* was part of the school curriculum. To me it had been a bore, even more so when the teacher made us watch the movie version as well. But for some, it had sparked an interest in the Roaring Twenties and those who made the era what it was.

One person in particular had developed a fascination with that time that had existed so long before she did. Someone who had the soul of one far older than her teen years. Someone who had died the night Raoul attacked my family.

\* \* \* \*

I arrived at the coffee shop early. I wanted to stake the place out before walking inside. As far as coffee shops went, this one was very public and busy. It was as safe a place as any. When I was satisfied that I wasn't going to get jumped, I went in and chose a table that allowed me to watch the door.

I had a death grip on my frappuccino cup. As each minute ticked by, my nerves grew increasingly frazzled. Would she still want to talk when she saw me instead of Brogan?

At exactly one hour past the closing time of Toil and Trouble, in walked a leggy brunette. Her dark gaze landed on me, and I was dumbfounded. My stomach twisted, and a fresh surge of adrenaline crashed through me.

She jerked to a halt, shock registering on her face. It was gone in a flash. She recovered fast. Forcing herself into motion, she approached me with a shaky smile.

"Hey, Lexi. Long time, no see."

Nobody called me Lexi. In fact, I hated the nickname. Only one person had called me that, and she died ten years ago. Yet, there she stood, no longer the kid that lived in my memories. All grown up and somehow alive despite everything I had believed, it was her: my sister.

Shock. Absolute, total and utter shock.

I stared in disbelief. Her hair was the same deep chocolate brown as our mother's. It fell in curls over her shoulders. Clad in dark jeans and a trendy jacket, she was tall and lean; I'd always been the short one.

I met her brown eyes, so like my own, and found wariness, confusion and possibly even hope in their depths. How could this be? She was dead. Raoul had killed her along with our mother and father. Yet there she stood, waiting for my reaction.

"Juliet?" Her name felt foreign on my lips. I couldn't recall the last time I'd said it.

"In the flesh." Her voice wavered ever so slightly. "It's been a long time."

I had to remember to breathe. Stunned as I was, it almost hurt to suck in a ragged breath. "How? He killed you. I know he did."

She shook her head, and something close to sadness passed through her eyes. "No. He killed mom and dad. I probably should have died, too. I was in a coma for two weeks. I woke up surrounded by strangers. And, you were long gone."

The events of that night played out in my head. I'd been attacked, lying there in a pool of my own blood. My family lay dead, strewn throughout the house. My dad and my sister had been in another room. I never saw their bodies with my own eyes.

"I thought I was the only one who survived. I couldn't hang around after that. After what he turned me into." This was too much to take in. I just kept staring at her, waiting to wake up from this dream.

Juliet slid onto the seat across from me. She sat stiffly. Her face hardened, and her tone became brittle. "You didn't go far though. Not from him. How could you do it, Alexa?"

I was confused. Juliet seemed to know a lot more about me than I would have guessed. "How long have you known I was alive?"

"Long enough to know that you slept with the man that did this to us. How could you? After what he did to mom and dad's marriage? After he murdered them?" She spoke calmly, but there was venom in her words.

The weight of her accusatory stare grew heavy. She may have been my sister, once, but she was a stranger right now, one who had no right to question me. Not unless she was willing to spit out some answers of her own.

"I didn't know about mom's affair with him until last year. I never knew he was the one who attacked us that night. He kept it all from me. And now, he's dead."

She studied me hard, finding truth in my response. Her face softened. "You're powerful. More than you ever were as a kid."

I shrugged. "Things change." The initial shock began to fade. I couldn't allow old memories to break down my defense. I didn't know if I could trust her.

"They certainly do."

An awkward silence settled between us. I wanted to ask her so many questions, but most of them she would never answer.

"What are you doing here, Juliet? Why now?"

Her full lips twisted into a frown. "I'm sure you have a lot of questions. So do I. For instance, why are your eyes blue? And, why do you work with a demon?"

I was channeling a lot of power in my anxious state. It was instinct to keep it coiled tight and ready inside me. Apparently, I was tapping a little too much if my eyes were still blue.

So, she knew a lot about me. I couldn't help but feel that was unfair. She hadn't been bothered to reveal her existence, but she'd clearly put in the time to learn about mine.

"My eyes are still brown. Usually." I offered nothing else. I had no way of knowing how much she knew. I wasn't about to tell her. "I don't suppose you want to tell me where you've been all these years, or why you never bothered to get in touch."

Juliet smiled, an amused little quirk of her lips that triggered memories of that same smile on the little girl I'd known her to be. It was familiar and safe but also possibly misleading.

"I suppose that's fair." Juliet was calm and collected. Nothing about her indicated she was as nervous as I was. She was just so suave. "I was taken in and raised by a government organization. They wanted you, too, but by the time they came for us, you were gone. They gave me a place to call home, and now I work for them."

She paused to allow me to take that in. I leaned back in my chair, crossed my legs, then uncrossed them. I was restless, and it showed.

"So what do you do for this organization? And, why wait until now to tell me you're alive? That information would have been really nice to have, Juliet." Her name felt so odd in my mouth, though it shouldn't.

"I clean up messes. Tie up loose ends. Gather information. That kind of thing." She held my gaze, unflinching. "I'm sorry. I wish I could have told you sooner."

My little sister grew up to be a killer just like me. That truth held something horrifying, something that broke my heart.

"So you're some kind of black ops. Espionage, covert operation and assassination? Mom and Dad would be so proud."

"It's not so different from what you do. Is it?" Leaning back in her chair, Juliet crossed her arms over her chest and regarded me with the fierce intensity of the wolf. "I work for the Federal Para-Intelligence Agency. It's classified. Our business is national security on a paranormal level."

A chill crept over me. I didn't like the sound of this. "You're telling me a paranormal government group grabbed you after the attack, and now you're part of their team? You never wanted to leave?"

"Sounds crazy, huh?" She nibbled her bottom lip, the only nervous gesture she'd exhibited so far. "Almost as crazy as being taken in by the man who murdered our parents. And then, sleeping with him."

My cheeks burned with both embarrassment and fury. With my anger, my power flared. The lights dimmed in response. Not good. "I understand how that may look to you. I've spent the past year wishing I'd been the one to kill him. But, I don't owe you an explanation."

We stared intently at one another. I could feel her wolf staring out at me, sizing me up. I was torn, wanting to touch her to make sure she was real and to shake her for daring to judge me.

Juliet's gaze dropped to the coffee stained tabletop. "This is hard for me, too. I've really missed you. You were supposed to be with me, all these years. By the time the FPA tracked you down, you were working for Shya."

The FPA had clearly done their homework on me. She knew a lot. Too much. It didn't sit well with me.

"What do you know about Shya?"

"A lot." When Juliet looked up, there was a cold, calculating glint in her eyes. "He's an FPA error that won't disappear. He has his own agenda, which seems to involve manipulating anyone and anything with serious power to get what he wants. Including you."

"You don't have to tell me that Shya's up to no good. He's a demon. Why would the FPA ever expect anything else from him?"

"He was bound by a deal, one that he carefully constructed with a loophole. He got his hands on some classified information and went AWOL. We were keeping an eye on him, but our informant has gone missing. We assume he was murdered."

The blood drained from my face. I hoped it wasn't noticeable. The realization sunk in with a mind-numbing smack. Veryl, my jackass boss, had been that FPA informant. And, I had murdered him.

"Informant?" I tried to keep my tone light, unaffected. "I imagine that's a job that comes with a pretty serious risk factor."

She shrugged. "Sure. I doubt his link to the FPA killed him. He wasn't one of our guys. Just someone that would slip us info every now and then."

I wanted to kill Veryl all over again. He had to have known the FPA had my sister. He must have also known that they wanted me. And, he'd made sure to keep me for himself. At Shya's command?

I took a deep breath and fought back the anger that threatened to overwhelm me. "If you're talking about Veryl Armstrong, I killed him."

Juliet paused, then nodded, short and curt. "Oh, I see. Why?"

"He was blackmailing someone. At least, that's the official reason." Wow did I ever wish I had a glass of whiskey. My nerves were shot.

"And unofficially?"

"I wanted to. Veryl kept a lot of secrets from me, like who'd attacked us. He had a bit of a God complex."

"Hmm." Amused understanding shone in her eyes. "That explains why we haven't been able to reach him. Look, Lexi, I'm here because of an investigation. One of our agents was found dead a few weeks ago. Abigail Irving. The FPA thinks you might be involved."

I was speechless. I stared at her, flustered, and tried for the best damn poker face I could muster. It took a minute to make my tongue work. "Who?"

I had known the night I killed her that Abigail Irving would haunt me. I never dreamed it would be like this. Veryl was one kill I'd proudly admit, but to anyone outside my inner circle, Abigail was "Speak no evil."

Her gentle smile faded. "They've got you on a watch list, Alexa. They don't trust you. Because of the power you have, you have the potential to be dangerous."

I laughed then; I couldn't stop it. Her statement wasn't funny. Actually, it was downright threatening, shocking in that slap in the face kind of way. "I'll take that as a compliment."

"I'm not going to say anything about you being the one who killed Veryl." Juliet reached into her pocket and withdrew a cell phone. She tapped the screen a few times and put it away. "Remember how I'd cover for you with Mom and Dad when you'd sneak out your bedroom window? And, then that one night you got caught. Climbed into your room, and Mom was sitting on your bed in the dark."

"She scared the hell out of me. Grounded me for a month."

"Me, too. For lying for you."

The memory rose up like it was yesterday. We shared a laugh, giggling girlishly like the teenagers we used to be, before everything changed and our world was doused in blood. Tears flooded my eyes, and I blinked them back, fearful they would be crimson. I didn't want Juliet to see that side of me.

"I missed you, Lexi."

I laughed, but it was painful. "I missed you too, Jules."

"I'm not accusing you of anything. I'd like to turn a blind eye to the whole thing. But, you work for an enemy. Be careful. I would hate to see us end up on opposing sides." Juliet's warning hung ominously between us.

The hits just kept coming this week. Since I was already screwed six ways from Sunday, I figured I'd ask the question dancing on the tip of my tongue. "Should I be worried?"

Juliet tapped her fingernails on the tabletop in an erratic pattern. With a stiff set to her shoulders and a bleak nod, she said, "If you killed Abigail Irving, then yes."

## Chapter Four

The band Crimson Sin was playing at The Wicked Kiss. The addition of live music had really improved the place, giving the club an edge that a DJ spinning top 40 songs couldn't. Although, the vampire bar didn't really need any extra edge.

Sipping a whiskey on the rocks, I watched the activity from my favorite table while pondering the events of my evening so far. The business card with Juliet's fake name on it burned a hole in my pocket. The urge to pull it out was strong; I just couldn't stop thinking about our reunion. It was surreal.

The dimly lit booth was positioned perfectly to allow me a clear view of the entire club as well as both entrances. It was also far enough away from the dance floor and stage to provide the illusion of a laid-back setting.

"I can't believe I let you talk me into this." Jez pursed her ruby red lips and eyed the front entrance. "I'm still pissed."

I shoved my nagging thoughts of Juliet aside and focused on the angry leopard sitting across from me. "You have every right to be pissed. But, how long do you plan to drag this out? Either forgive him or cut ties with him completely. It's not fair to torture Kale like this."

Jez frowned and twirled the little umbrella in her drink. Her long, golden hair fell in wild curls down her back. With piercing green eyes, she shot me a dirty look. Jez was the only naturally born Were I knew; our usual sterility made children near impossible.

"I haven't even begun to torture Kale," she scoffed. "It's the least he deserves after what he did to me."

I sighed, nodding in agreement. I understood where her anger stemmed from. Kale was one of few people Jez truly trusted, but he'd blown that trust to hell. Kale had recently returned to his old killing ways. Unable to control himself, his bloodlust had targeted Jez.

"You don't have to do this, but you have to do something." I glanced at the door as a trickle of anxiety crept over me. Jez wasn't the only one nervous about Kale's arrival.

The scowl on Jez's pretty face looked out of place. A sultry smirk was more her style. "If he's late, I'm out of here."

I shook my head but didn't bother replying. She just wanted to be snarky; we both knew damn well Kale wouldn't be late.

Butterflies took flight in my stomach as my anxiety shifted from one thing to another. I looked back and forth between the front entry and the doorway at the rear that led into the back hall. Lined with private rooms, the back hall was where vampires took their willing victims for some fun and games.

"Why are you so nervous?" Her green eyes narrowed, and she watched me speculatively while sipping from her pink cocktail. "You know he'll try to fuck you before he kills you. Me... I don't stand a chance."

Frowning, I shook my head and leaned back in my chair. "Not cool, dude."

"Sorry." She shrugged but offered no real sense of apology. "It's true though. You guys have a weird relationship. So complicated."

I clutched my glass, seeking false comfort. My original intention had been never to drink at The Wicked Kiss. So much for that.

My nerves were getting to me; I was freaked out not just by Kale's impending arrival nor even the hit out on me. I felt Shaz here, too, yet he was nowhere to be seen. Which could only mean one thing: he was lost in the role of blood whore. Again.

Things had gotten disturbingly twisted between me and my wolf mate in recent weeks. We had both made mistakes that apologies and regrets would not fix. Shaz and I had been through a lot together. We had known each other for years, since we were new wolves adjusting to life with a dual nature. So much had changed since then.

Nausea caused my stomach to turn at the thought of Shaz offering himself to a vampire. He got off on the rush. I knew firsthand how powerful it was. Most certainly addictive. One look around the place made that obvious. Because it was Shaz, his obsession was that much harder to swallow. I was the only reason that he'd ever experienced the wild ride of the vampire's thrall, and I blamed myself.

Jez leaned across the table to touch the back of my hand lightly. "Don't go getting all drunk on me now. I need you to fight Kale off if he's developed a taste for leopard."

Her gentle touch was a friendly gesture of support. I didn't have to give words to my emotions. I appreciated her attempt at humor and forced a strained smile.

I stared into the golden whiskey. Lovely poison. I drank more often than I should, and though it didn't affect me the way it did humans, it was still a source of escape. Of course, I'd much rather be losing myself in the promise of ecstasy found only in the kill. Tonight, whiskey would have to do.

Minutes before midnight, Kale swept through the front entry. With the grace and presence that five centuries had gifted him, he sauntered toward us. Dressed head to toe in black, complete with his trademark leather duster, he was painfully alluring. More than one human female sought his company as he made his way through the club.

I struggled not to choke on my whiskey when his sugary sweet energy reached me. "See, Jez. I told you he wouldn't be late."

Kale reached our booth and immediately slid onto my side, across from Jez. I pressed myself farther into the corner than was necessary, feeling awkward and nervous.

"Hello, ladies." Kale's gaze slid over me, lingering for just a moment before turning to Jez. No matter how many times I looked into his mismatched eyes, I was always enamored. The right one brown and the left a startling blue, heterochromia had endowed him with an eerily beautiful feature.

"You're anxious tonight, Alexa." Kale observed. "It's enticing."

Enticing was the last thing I wanted to be to a vampire whose control was precarious at best. "I just found out there's a price on my head and my dead sister is actually alive."

A frown creased Kale's brow. "Seriously? That's intense. Who would be stupid enough to think they can take you out?"

"Ahem," Jez loudly cleared her throat, drawing our attention. "Can we play 'Who wants to kill Lex' later? This little shindig is supposed to be about me."

Kale turned his attention to her, and I released the breath I'd been holding. They stared at one another, Jez with fire in her eyes. She was going to be stubborn about this.

"Jez," Kale began, speaking loud enough to be heard over the music but keeping his tone gentle. "Thank you for agreeing to see me. I wanted to apologize to you, face to face. I have no excuses. I'm sorry. I wish I had never hurt you."

There was a dramatic pause as Jez considered his apology. She tossed her curls and twirled the little umbrella in her drink, all the while staring him down with that haughty cat gaze. I struggled to keep from rolling my eyes, but it wouldn't be Jez without a little drama.

"That's the best you can do? You almost killed me, Kale. You know, like dead. I trusted you." Leaning back in her seat, she dropped the umbrella and crossed her arms. "And, you should know I don't trust very many people."

Unaffected by her attitude, Kale nodded. "I know. I'm honored to have had your trust, and I fully understand that I've destroyed it. But, I am sorry. You know you mean a lot to me."

"Prove it."

I sat in amused silence, a half-empty glass in my hand. Poor Kale. She was really intent on putting him through the ringer.

In part, he was humoring her, giving her what she wanted so this whole thing would blow over. But, I knew Kale, and if he didn't genuinely care about their friendship, he wouldn't be here. Being the amazing guy that he was, he was willing to do anything it took.

"What do you want from me, Jez?" His expression was playful, but his manner was serious. "Want me to get on my knees and beg your forgiveness?"

A slow grin spread across her lips. "Knock it off, Kale."

However, he was already standing up. I was shocked. "Jez. Isn't that a little much? You're not going to make him do that, are you?"

"No, that's fine." Kale rose and went to her side of the table. "If Jez wants me to beg, then begging she'll get."

"Hey now," she protested with a giggle. "I did not ask you to beg. Don't be ridiculous."

He gestured for her to stand, and I cringed. I couldn't believe he was doing this. Despite Jez's protests, I could see the flash of pleasure in her eyes.

It was hard to sit there and bite my tongue when he knelt before her. He grabbed her hand, holding tight when she tried to pull away. A few people at the nearby tables turned to stare, but Kale paid them no attention.

"Jez St. Claire, you are the little sister I never had. You're one of the only people on the planet I would do this for. You have no idea how filled with regret and guilt I am over what I did to you. I hate myself for hurting you. And, I am truly sorry." With true repentance in his eyes, he gazed up at her.

The depths of Kale's love for Jez captivated me. Not only was he willing to humiliate himself in public, he acted as if it were the least he deserved. I groaned inwardly, hating myself for swooning over this. I flashed back in my mind to a night of warm summer rain and Kale. It had been less than a month ago that we'd made love outside The Wicked Kiss, but it felt like forever.

Jez dragged out her response, staring at him until the tension hummed. After making him wait for what she felt was a reasonable amount of time, she nodded. "Thank you, Kale. I forgive you. If you ever try to kill me again, I'll have your balls for breakfast."

And just like that, Jez abolished the grudge she'd been holding for weeks. She pulled Kale to his feet for a hug, and the tension between them slipped away. He resumed his seat next to me, winking a puppy dog brown eye at me.

"I can't believe you did that." I laughed, shaking my head.

"Honestly, I expected her to really torture me, so it wasn't too bad." Kale shrugged it off as if he hadn't just made himself her bitch.

"So, it's been a while since the three of us did something. I mean really did something." Jez leaped in like the last few minutes had never happened, let alone the last few weeks. It was mind-boggling. "We need to hang out. But, not in this place. It's disgusting. We should go to a concert or a movie."

I'd given up on figuring Jez out long ago. She was a firecracker alright. From being pissed at Kale to excitedly planning an outing, she was lively in a way that made her infectious. No wonder the vampires here were so drawn to her.

With my back to the corner of the booth, I nodded as necessary while she prattled on. There was a pleasant tingle in my limbs as the alcohol coursed through my bloodstream. My anxiety eased and I relaxed.

Kale was alluring at such close proximity. Just a year ago, he hadn't set me off like this, but as my power had grown, so had my hunger for him. Some might say that the two weren't related, that plain old, physical lust afflicted us, but I knew the source of my desire was something bigger.

"You know what we should really do?" Jez continued, pausing only to sip from her drink before going on again. "Road trip. Seriously. We have never done anything like that. Let's go somewhere. Oh! Let's go to Vegas! You have some ass to kick there, Lex. It would be a blast."

"Vegas? Oh hell no." I shook my head despite my mild intrigue. "I can't begin to imagine the kind of trouble we'd find there."

"Then let's not imagine. Let's go. Pick a date."

Kale laughed and relaxed in the booth beside me. Just inches kept us from touching. "Knock yourselves out. Most road trips aren't exactly vampire friendly."

"They can be." Jez shrugged off his protest. "We can hit hotels during the day. Really damn expensive ones. It would kick ass."

What was she doing? Kale and I on a road trip together would be all kinds of bad news regardless of whether or not she was there too. Not to mention the fight with Arys that would ensue. I hadn't considered leaving town at all recently, although a chance to get away didn't sound like a totally bad idea.

Las Vegas had made me curious in recent months. Arys had ties to the city through his sire, Harley, the most powerful vampire in Sin City, or at least, he was.

"Besides," the feisty leopard went on. "You guys need to spend more time away from this place. Both of you. It's a menace to your mental health."

"Can't argue there." I tossed back another mouthful of whiskey. A vacation from this place sounded like heaven.

Right on cue, the rear door separating the back rooms from the rest of the club opened, and Shaz strode through. My stomach plummeted in a nauseating free fall when *she* appeared at his side. They didn't touch, yet there was an unspoken intimacy between them. I was going to be sick.

I knew very little about her, the vampire Shaz had become acquainted with. She was a tall, leggy thing with long black hair. I got the sense that she wasn't an old vampire but not brand-new either. I didn't even know her name, but I hated her more than I'd ever hated anyone or anything. Even Raoul.

It wasn't just her. It was everything she represented. This world…my world. And now, because of me, it was Shaz's world, too. He'd promised me that he wasn't sleeping with her, but that had been weeks ago. Things change, and I didn't have the guts to ask.

Besides, a sexual element always tinged such encounters; the absence of intercourse didn't mean it wasn't sexual. Of course it was. My own personal proof of that sat beside me, a dark dream in leather. The carnal tension had been running high between Kale and I long before our night in the rain. It was only a matter of time until Shaz made all of my mistakes.

Worse than sexual tension was the chance of emotional entanglement. That was the fear that gripped me as I watched them from across the room. I held my glass in a white-knuckled grip, willing myself to react. I was frozen.

Feeling the weight of my stunned stare, Shaz met my gaze across the distance. We shared a moment of horror, and then he looked away. So, he hadn't expected to see me. Should that make me feel better?

The chatter at my table fell quiet as my companions followed my gaze. I watched Shaz whisper something to the vampiress who immediately turned my way. He was trying to get away from her without making a scene. I could tell by the tension in his shoulders as he pulled away. She stopped him with a hand, ensuring I was watching before she slid a hand into his platinum hair and laid one hell of a kiss on him.

The glass in my hand shattered into several little shards. Whiskey splashed the table and covered my hand. Blood welled up from the cuts I'd sustained, but I barely noticed. I was already fighting my way out of the booth.

I snapped. Rather than throw Kale out of my way, I leaped across the table, hitting the floor at a run. Jez's voice was quickly lost in the crowd as she called my name. The wolf inside me exploded in a territorial rage. I was suddenly all fangs and claws, ready to kill.

The crowd was thick, and I shoved people out of my way with more force than necessary. Both Shaz and the vampiress looked up at my sudden approach. Fear flickered in Shaz's jade green eyes. He reached as if to stop me, but I threw him back with little more than a thought.

The power exploded inside me, overflowing to wash throughout the building. It was magnificent. The vampiress had no chance to brace against it. Using my bloody hand to guide the force surging through me, I drove her to her knees. I was lost in the hypnotic rush of life and death, as the vampire and werewolf power I possessed became one writhing, demanding entity.

I saw nothing but her. The rest of the club ceased to exist as I stared down into her frightened brown eyes. I wanted her to hurt. In response to that thought, she screamed. I envisioned her insides on fire, and her shrieks became deafening.

A wicked smile pulled at my lips; it didn't feel like mine. "Don't you realize who you're messing with? I will break you." My voice was exceptionally calm, almost detached.

She cowered before me, grasping her head in agony. I could feel it, her true death. I could have it. The power went out from me with surprising ease. It was almost disappointing that I could kill her so easily.

"Alexa, please." Shaz lingered nearby, his voice an annoying reminder that if I loved him, I couldn't destroy her. He'd put up with too much from me in the name of love.

I growled, shooting him a dark look. I didn't release my hold on her though. No, I wanted her to know she'd gone too far. Her heart was there, in my mind. I could feel it, ready to burst at my command. I had killed more than one vampire this way, and every time it got easier.

"I don't know what you were thinking, putting on a display like that, but I am not the one you want to fuck with." I put pressure on her heart, squeezing until she coughed blood. In my mind, I was inside her as surely as if I'd held her cold, dead heart in my hand. With a hand beneath her chin, I forced her to meet my eyes. "You won't get another warning. Next time, we finish this."

I dropped the livewire running from me into her, releasing her from my deadly hold. She collapsed completely, spitting blood and whimpering. Only then did I notice the entire place had fallen silent. Even the band had stopped.

Several vampires were on their knees, blinded by pain as a wave of heavy energy swept over the crowd. Shya's words echoed in my head. *"You have immense power over vampires and werewolves. You are both and yet somehow neither, all at the same time."*

I hadn't believed that then. I was starting to now. As I looked down at the suffering vampiress, it was startlingly undeniable. Shaking from the pressure of conducting so much energy, I needed some air, so I turned and headed for the front door. However, I carefully avoided eye contact with those I passed.

Shaz said my name, but I didn't stop, and he didn't pursue me. Jez ultimately caught hold of my arm and stopped me in the lobby. She held firm, refusing to be shaken off.

"Hey, are you alright?" She produced a tissue from her purse and gestured to the blood dripping from my nose. "That was pretty fucking intense. You dropped Kale like a sack of bricks."

I accepted the tissue and wiped my nose. It wasn't bleeding much, and I felt fine. "Is he ok? I didn't mean to."

"Yeah, he's ok. Or, he will be, anyway." When she couldn't keep me inside the building, she followed me outside. "I felt something, too. It kind of scared me."

I turned to her sharply. Jez didn't readily admit fear to anyone about anything without a damn good reason. "Why? What happened?"

She shrugged and walked farther away from the entrance and the people that mingled there. With a longing look at some of the smokers enjoying their cigarettes, she feigned casual. "When you dropped Kale and the others, I could feel this pull inside me. Like you were pulling the cat out of me. Forcing the shift."

"Sounds like what I did with Zoey, when she was stuck in wolf form."

"Well, it didn't feel so great. It didn't hurt, but it freaked me out. How about we don't have a repeat of that, hmm?"

I turned toward the parking lot, focusing on the earth at my feet to ground my unbalanced core. I was riding a high so intense I walked on clouds. "Sorry, Jez."

Her presence was comforting. Jez was special to me. The circle of people I could trust was small, but I was madly grateful for every one of them.

"It'll be ok, Lex. I know you're hurting more over this Shaz stuff than you would ever let yourself admit. There are no easy rides in love. It's complicated agony. But, it's worth it."

I couldn't help but stare intently at her. That didn't sound like something she'd usually say. "Is it really though? Or, is it just not knowing when to let someone go?"

"Don't talk like that. We both know that's not what either of you want."

No, it wasn't what I wanted. What I wanted was to go back to a time before Shaz had gotten involved in any of this. It was too late for that.

The night air was muggy; it did nothing to provide the cooling relief I longed for. If only it would rain.

My breath caught when Shaz's car sped past us as he peeled out of the lot. He and I needed to talk. We'd been dodging this issue for weeks, and that mistake had caught up to us. I didn't want to delve deeper into it, but I knew if we didn't, we wouldn't grow past this. And, it would destroy us.

# *Chapter Five*

The urge to go after Shaz was strong, but he was long gone. It was anyone's guess where he was going. I wanted to punch something, but the claws protruding from my fingertips prevented me from even making a fist.

My wolf wanted to take over, to shield me from the pain by escaping my human body. If I could just lose myself in the forest, it would all cease to exist. If only that were true...

I paced in the parking lot, unwilling to go back inside the club. It was probably best if I vacated for the rest of the night. I had a lot to deal with. Jez leaned against a nearby car, watching me silently. Restless and distressed, I didn't know what to do with myself.

"Just what were you trying to do in there?" Kale's voice rang out behind me seconds before his honey-dipped energy slid over my skin like a forbidden caress. "Blow the roof off the building?"

"I don't know," I said with a shrug. "I snapped. I couldn't let her challenge me that way. Not in my city and most definitely not in my club with my wolf. It just happened."

"Well next time you lose it like that, direct your focus. Save the rest of us from having to take an undeserved hit." He joined Jez where she stood against the car. With a look that was supposed to be serious, Kale studied me. "You're an accident waiting to happen, Alexa. Too wild and unruly. It's dangerous."

I didn't buy his serious expression because of the playful lilt to his tone. Whatever I'd done to Kale inside, some part of him had liked it.

"Maybe that's why someone wants me dead." I felt pinned under the weight of their matching stares. "Sorry. It shouldn't have happened."

"Nobody is going to hurt you. You just proved why that wouldn't be easy." Jez shrugged casually, but her shoulders tightened, and her body language became defensive. Wary.

Kale's gaze dropped to my bloody hand. His pupils dilated and a memory blazed between us. "I'd like to meet the person willing to take you on after what you just did in there."

"I don't know." With a shake of my head, I scanned the area. I couldn't be too careful, not until I knew who was gunning for me. "This is just more trouble I don't need. It seems to find me no matter what I do."

A sudden, unnatural wind picked up, tossing my long blonde hair around in total disarray. The air rippled, and Falon appeared out of nowhere. It spooked me and I jumped. He eyed me with grim amusement dancing in his silver eyes.

The fallen angel looked over us each with scrutiny before dragging his judgmental gaze back to me. "You really aren't the brightest crayon in the box are you, wolf?"

I bristled at his tone, and my guard went up. After what had just occurred inside, I was in no mood to take lip from the asshole angel.

"I have a name, you son of a bitch." I met his gaze evenly, showing no fear. What the hell was he doing here?

Tall and chiseled with fair hair, he looked like any model in a men's fashion magazine. He was good looking, but it was a surface beauty. His wings were absent, hidden beneath some form of illusion that drove my curiosity crazy. Without them, he lost a lot of his intimidation factor.

"Alexa," he said my name slowly, dramatically emphasizing every syllable. "Do you have any idea of how stupid you are?"

I sensed Kale's sudden tension, but I didn't dare take my eyes off Falon. The twenty feet or so separating the fallen angel from me became much too close for comfort. I wanted to claw his eyes out but wasn't dumb enough to try.

"What are you doing here?"

He continued as if I hadn't spoken. "Only an idiot would draw attention to themselves by calling power like that without good reason.

Might as well walk around with a neon sign over your head that flashes the word, dumbass."

I seethed with hatred for this infuriating creature. "I had my reasons, none of which do I owe you as an explanation. Where do you get off coming to my place of business to judge me?"

Falon's laughter cut through the night, as malicious as it was melodic. "Your place of business is little more than a den of sin and sacrilege. Don't flatter yourself."

"Fuck you, you pathetic demon lapdog." I spat the words without thinking, letting my anger guide my sharp tongue. "If Shya sent you, tell him I have nothing to say to him through you. If he didn't send you, then you really don't need to be here."

I blinked, that was it. I never saw him move, but he was suddenly so close we almost touched. Glaring down into my face, Falon fixed me with ice-cold eyes.

"You attract the attention of everyone with any ties to power when you do that shit. That power may be yours to command, but it comes from a place bigger than you can imagine. Use it wisely."

I had never felt any source of power or metaphysical wonder from him. It was there, I knew, but hidden. I didn't feel it now either, but I saw it, there in the depths of his eyes. So cold and broken but immense, like the mountains and the sea, larger than I could dream. The promise of destruction was there, and I knew with deep-seated certainty that Falon's power was something I never wanted to see.

"Don't talk to me like I'm a child, you pretentious bastard."

His cruel grin restored some of his intimidation factor, but nothing about him indicated that he'd ever been anything better than he was now. "Shya is so wrong about you."

Dismissing me entirely, Falon swept by me to get a closer look at Jez. She perched on the edge of the car, frozen in place. She stared at him like he was scum, but the anxious vibes she gave off betrayed her.

"And, what have we here?" Ignoring her scathing expression, Falon studied her with curious intrigue. He seemed a little perplexed. "Of all the mixed bloodlines I've seen, never have I seen one quite like you. Fascinating. Where has Shya been hiding you?"

Jez stumbled over her words as she attempted a stuttering response. Kale came to her rescue. Laying a friendly hand on Falon's arm, he smoothly captured the angel's attention.

"Jez prefers to work the streets, clean up the trash. That kind of thing. Now, what brings you here?" Kale's interest was authentic. He clearly knew how to deal with Falon.

Falon cast a last lingering glance at Jez before turning his full attention on Kale. "The dreamwalker," he spoke in low tones. "I need you there tonight."

I was still stuck on what he'd said about Jez being of mixed blood. How could that be? Her face was a mask of ice, carefully constructed to reveal nothing.

"Dreamwalker?" I said, only half-listening. I was watching Jez as she forced a nonchalant expression.

"Yes, dreamwalker," Falon sneered. "As in, someone who can walk in dreams. Now there's a power that even a botched crossbreed like you doesn't have."

I snarled and lunged toward him. Kale effectively placed himself in my path, stopping me with both hands on my shoulders. Falon enjoyed my fury, which only ticked me off more. It was my own fault for letting him get under my skin. Something about him just stripped my composure away. Lately everything seemed to strip my composure away.

Kale guided him away, quickly asking questions to keep things neutral. It wasn't worth getting pissed at Falon. Between the target on my back, the mysterious FPA and the Shaz situation, I was overflowing with pent up frustration and the excruciating need to hurt something. Taking it out on Falon wouldn't ultimately help me feel any better about anything.

Running a hand through my hair in vexation, I looked around the parking lot.

Something didn't feel right.

The light from the street lit up the entrance. Traffic passed by like usual. Nobody in the lot struck me as particularly suspicious.

Closing my eyes, I breathed deeply of the air, picking through the myriad of scents. I could pick out little more than car exhaust and cigarettes from the nearby smokers.

The sudden awareness of being watched set my senses on fire. My eyes snapped open, and I did my best to survey my surroundings without appearing as if I was. In case of a psychic attack, I focused my energy on reinforcing my shields. I saw nobody as I turned in a slow circle. But, someone was watching.

"Lex?" Jez's voice was breathy and low. Wary.

The power of the earth vibrated beneath my feet. It was mine to call, though I was already buzzing with undead energy. Theoretically, I could create a shield strong enough to block a penetrative non-living physical object, like a bullet; unfortunately, I had yet to successfully do it.

Slipping into the wolf's alert and intuitive mind frame, I moved with a casual gait, feeling out my watcher. This dilemma left no room for fear, only readiness.

I'd started to think, perhaps, they were only going to observe, but then I felt it. My sixth sense took over, and I reacted. The arrow sliced through the air toward me. I held it tight in my grip before I fully comprehended that I'd caught it inches from my face. It was a crossbow bolt; the tip was sharp and deadly.

Everyone froze for a heartbeat. I stared in disbelief at the bolt in my hands. Then I snapped into motion.

Following the direction where the shot came from, I threw a ball of power that exploded like lightning at the dark end of the parking lot. A moving blur was all I saw of my unwelcome company as they fled in the opposite direction.

I gave chase, running as fast as two legs would carry me. It was fast but not enough. Not this time. I saw no sign of whoever had taken a shot at me as they disappeared out the other side of the alley that hugged the back of the club. The last thing I wanted to do was walk into a possible trap, so I turned back.

I clutched the crossbow bolt tightly. It had all happened so quickly. Mere seconds. I guess the idea of a hit out on me wasn't so incredulous after all.

Kale was on my heels, so close we almost collided when I turned around. Falon and Jez were where we left them, watching us. Jez's face was ashen, her jaw dropped in surprise. Falon's expression wasn't so easy to read. Stone cold and closed off, his silver eyes locked onto the weapon in my tight grip.

"Oh my God, Alexa. Are you alright?" Jez was on her feet, braced for a fight.

"Yeah," I said with a nod. My heart was pumping pure adrenaline, but otherwise I was fine. "Whoever it was, they're long gone now. Idiots. A rooftop shot would have been smarter."

Kale looked longingly in the direction my would-be killer had fled. "We should go after them."

"No." I turned the crossbow bolt over in my hands. It was heavy and sharp. Pretty damn deadly. "I don't want you guys involved in this. They've targeted me. Let's keep it that way."

"I can't believe you caught that thing." Jez shook her head in wonder. "That was impressive."

Falon smirked, but his eyes betrayed nothing. Whatever he was really feeling about what he'd just seen, he wasn't sharing. "Ah yes, the wolf caught a flying stick. Fascinating. I'd be more impressed if you'd caught it in your teeth like a frisbee."

If I hadn't just stared death in the face, I would have been pissed about that comment. As it was, the asshole angel wasn't worth the energy. I waved a hand dismissively in his direction and turned my attention to Jez.

"You should take off, just to be on the safe side. I'll give you a call later."

"Are you sure?" She frowned, clearly unhappy with my request. "I don't want to leave you after something like that."

"It's cool. I'm not staying. I just don't want to endanger anyone else tonight."

She looked uncertainly from me to Kale and then began edging away from us, toward the beat up, white Jeep at the end of the lot. "Be careful, ok?"

"Promise."

"The dreamwalker, Kale," Falon interjected. "Sooner than later." With that he was gone, leaving me alone with the vampire.

I watched Jez's taillights disappear down the street. This was turning out to be a less than stellar night. Kale continued to glance toward the alley behind the club. I knew he was itching to hunt down the person daring enough to take a shot at me. I couldn't let him do that.

"Don't even think about it, Kale. I can handle this. But, not tonight. Going after them could mean running straight into a trap. I want to do this right. On my terms. Not theirs."

We stared at one another, and I was painfully aware of how close we stood to the very spot where we'd made love in the rain. However, I was also aware of the weight of the crossbow bolt in my hand and what it represented. My skills and instincts had served me well tonight, but would they keep me alive every time? I had to hunt down the person behind the hit and soon. The next shot might get lucky.

"You should get out of here." The power rolled off Kale in tantalizing waves. "Want to come along to check up on the dreamwalker? Maybe we can do a little brainstorming. Figure out who could want you dead bad enough to take such a risky shot."

He expected me to say no. My common sense insisted I should. But, I was angry, scared and starting to shake.

"I'll come. You drive."

I waited until we were in his slick, black 73 Camaro before I grilled him for more information about the dreamwalker. Once we were moving smoothly through the late night downtown traffic, I used my many questions as a way to avoid further speculation on the near death experience I'd just had. "Whom exactly are we spying on and why?"

"We're not spying, Alexa." Kale laughed derisively. "That sounds so Hollywood-action movie. Just keeping watch."

"Spying." I corrected, grinning when he flipped me off.

A smile danced along his lips when he shot me a playful glare. "You're a pain in the ass. Anyway, it's a seventeen-year-old dreamwalker. We've been watching him."

"Is he dangerous?" I'd heard mention of dreamwalkers, though I didn't know much about them. I was tempted to run a search on my phone but decided to wait rather than show my ignorance.

"He could be. Right now, he's just your typical teenage boy."

"Why is he being watched, then, if he's not a threat?" It sounded sketchy. There's no way Shya or anyone else would waste the time and effort if there weren't more to this kid.

"To make sure he doesn't become one, I guess. Or, a victim." Kale didn't offer more in the way of explanation.

He navigated the city streets while I let my suspicions breed. I had been a teenager when Shya and Veryl had started pulling strings in my life. Whatever the demon really had planned for this kid, it couldn't be good.

The house we rolled up to was a basic two-level, middle-class family home. We parked on the opposite side of the street. It was late. I didn't expect to see a damn thing. However, a light was on inside the living room, and the glow of the television could easily be seen.

"He doesn't sleep much," Kale said, staring across the street. "Most dreamwalkers don't. Usually, I find him playing videogames, surfing the net or screwing his girlfriend. Only once have I come by when he was asleep. It was pretty weird."

"Weird? Like how?" I could see the silhouette of a person sitting near the TV. "Where are his parents?"

"Oh, they're upstairs. They have no idea what their son can do, I'm sure. Most people give dreamwalkers some kind of diagnosis like insomnia or some such thing. Really, it's just that they fight sleep because every time it means walking in the dreams of someone else." Kale shut the engine off and turned to me. "It was weird because I could feel that he wasn't really there. Even though his body was there, his energy was just gone."

Fascinating. I'd definitely have to learn more about dreamwalkers. Especially if Shya had an interest in them.

"So why exactly are we here? I mean, what reason is there to come by and stare at his house? It's strange."

"No reason really. Just to make sure we know where he is. To make sure nobody else does."

"That translates into, so he doesn't somehow get away from Shya. Or, perhaps so he doesn't get picked off by someone else." I nodded, as a sinking sensation settled in my gut. "I get it."

It was disturbing to me on so many levels, most of all, because I knew the same thing had been done to me. Maybe Shya had no reason to have me followed now or maybe he had just changed his methods of doing so. Regardless, I was still very much under his thumb, and as I stared at this innocent kid's house, it was devastatingly undeniable. Shya was the puppet master pulling our strings. What would he do if we cut the ties that held us?

"So what makes this kid special enough to be worth watching?" I asked, my tone thick with skepticism. "Can he kill people in their dreams? Control them? What?"

"Yes, all of that and more. The potential is there. Whether or not he knows how to use it remains to be seen." Kale met my eyes then, his gaze heavy and intense. "There are incredible downfalls to being a dreamwalker. He can never sleep without entering a dream that belongs to someone else. What he chooses to do there is in his hands for the most part. You want to talk about spying, what better way to sneak a peek at an enemy than by taking a walk through his subconscious?"

And, that right there was exactly why Shya wanted this kid. The poor bastard. Seventeen years old, and his life was already over. And, he didn't even know it yet.

"Poor kid," I muttered. "He has no idea what's in store for him. I don't like being on the opposite side of this, the one watching."

I went cold inside. I acted like I had some control in my partnership with Shya, but that was merely an illusion he allowed me. A sinking sensation threatened to swallow me. Every moment I spent watching the silhouette of the teenager inside playing videogames made it worse.

"I don't think I can do this anymore," I blurted, weariness in my voice. "I just want to hunt some scumbag vampire that gets off on killing kids or something. You know? I don't want to watch people get sucked into the dark by a demon. I can't help Shya do to others what he's done to me. And, to think of how many years I never knew that he was always there, behind the scenes."

For the first time since Kale and I had met several years ago, I wondered if he had ever watched me like this. How close was he to Shya? I didn't really know. Over the years, I had often had Kale at my side during a hunt, a constant shadow.

I visibly shuddered. Goosebumps rose on my arms, and I rubbed them uselessly. It had to be the paranoia talking. Kale would never do something so shady. Our friendship was authentic, not based on a lie.

After several minutes passed, Kale broke the strained silence. "You have your own role to play, Alexa. Only you can decide what that is. Being associated with Shya doesn't make you anything like him. He's not a silent force in your life anymore. You're not a caged animal. Don't let him make you think you are."

"You're right, I know that. The past month has been overwhelming. I'm still adjusting." I blew a lock of hair out of my face. "But, thank you. You always know what I need to hear."

Kale was quiet for a moment, contemplative. "Hey, thanks for getting Jez to see me. I know you had something to do with that."

I shrugged as if it was no big deal. In actuality, I'd had to beg, threaten and cajole Jez endlessly before she'd agreed to meet him. "It was easy. She just needed a push."

A few minutes passed in silence. It was a comfortable quiet though. I was relieved. It was starting to feel the way it used to with Kale, easy-going and relaxed. No need for strange tension and awkward moments. I was starting to think we could get past the events of last month.

I hesitated for just a second before deciding I had to share this. "The FPA is investigating the death of Abigail Irving. My sister is one of their agents. Not only did she survive the wolf attack, she claims Shya split us up. He got me and the FPA got her. Now, she's hunting me, and I think she knows it."

That got Kale's eyes rolling. "Don't worry about the FPA. If they come for you, then they come for me, too. We shared that kill. You're not taking the fall for that one."

I was surprised at how quickly he shrugged it off. "You're not concerned? I have enough people after me. I don't need the damn government pinning me for a murder. Oh hell no."

"Your focus should be on the hit and finding out who you have to kill for it." Concern lay heavy in his eyes when he looked over at me. "I can't imagine who would want to take you out, but please promise me you'll be careful. I think I'd die if anything happened to you."

The discomfort we'd both been successfully battling settled over us like a heavy blanket. The love that could never be. Our story would have no happy ending; it was impossible. And yet, we were so inextricably, emotionally entangled.

I found it hard to meet his eyes and searched for any reason to break contact. "I guess this means I'm really big time now. Is this some kind of rite of passage or something?"

"Take this seriously, Alexa. We need to find out who's got it in for you. Don't be reckless or careless. That just makes it easy for them."

"I know. I appreciate your concern. Really, I do." Guilt settled in to taunt me for my suspicious thoughts a few minutes prior. How could I think he would be capable of double-crossing me?

"You know I would do anything for you."

"Don't get yourself killed for me. I mean it, Kale. I can handle this. I'll deal with it somehow. But, I don't want anyone I love getting hurt because of me."

Strained silence settled over us as we both sat with the awareness that this was as close to acknowledging our feelings as we were going to get. Everything we could say had already been said. We had to move on.

## Chapter Six

Nearing sunrise, I made the short trip down the highway from Edmonton to Stony Plain, my small but cozy hometown. Despite the insanity of my evening, my biggest worry right then was the lack of communication from Shaz. I'd expected to hear from him by now. It was driving me nuts. I couldn't leave it this way. We had to talk.

When I saw my empty driveway and equally vacant house, my hopes took a nosedive. I parked in front of the house but didn't turn my car off. Instead, I pulled out my phone and called Shaz. Holding my breath, I listened to the ringing in my ear, knowing he wasn't going to answer. The call went to voicemail, and I hung up. He was purposely avoiding me.

With a sigh and a few choice curse words, I turned the car around and made Shaz's apartment my next destination. The five-minute drive was spent attempting to come up with the right thing to say. So, when I turned into the parking lot and saw his empty parking space, I was both surprised and crestfallen.

My mind raced, conjuring up all the possible places he could be. None of them made me feel any better. Slamming a hand against the steering wheel, I turned to my phone in desperation and called Arys. It was close enough to sunrise that he should be home.

"Hello, beautiful wolf." Arys's voice was low and seductive. "I assume you're looking for the pup."

"Yes." It was good to hear Arys's silky smooth tone. Even through the phone, it sent a happy tickle down my spine. "He tore out of The Wicked Kiss earlier. We had a bit of an incident."

There was a pause, and I expected Arys to start grilling me for details. So I was blown away when he said, "I know. He's here."

That was the last place I would have guessed Shaz to be. "Um, what the hell?"

"Don't analyze it. Just come by. See you soon."

I stared at my phone long after he'd disconnected the call. I wasn't sure how I felt about Shaz going to Arys. It was just so unlikely. I didn't know what to make of it.

By the time I stood on Arys's front step, I was a mess of nerves. I tried to swallow my unease, knowing how obvious it would be to them. There was no shaking it; I fully expected to be the bad guy here.

The sound of their voices reached me when I pushed the door open. Any other time that would have been a welcome sound. I dropped my shoulder bag on the counter and crossed through the small, rarely used kitchen to the living room. Arys's house was small but cozy. He had the blinds tightly drawn to keep out the sun, but a tall flood lamp bathed the room in a warm glow, creating the illusion of early evening rather than early morning.

Arys was the picture of comfort in a recliner, clad only in a pair of red and black checker pajama pants. Shaz stood stiffly in the center of the room, as if he'd stopped mid-pace. Our eyes met, and something crumbled inside me.

The carefully constructed neutral expression he forced did nothing to hide the pain and anguish in his jade gaze. He had promised this wouldn't break us, but it was, I could feel it.

"Hey," he said, and that one simple word was loaded with emotion.

So many things threatened to spill forth in a torrent of rushed desperation. It took a moment for me to sort my thoughts. "We need to talk."

"Look, Alexa. You had every right to do what you did tonight. But, I don't want to see a repeat of that." Shaz paused, running a hand through his hair, a nervous gesture. "And, I don't want to see that agony in your eyes every time you look at me."

"You should have killed her," Arys interjected. He shot me a direct look, one that clearly stated he expected me to do just that. "It wouldn't hurt to make an example of somebody."

Choosing not to address Arys's comment, I kept my focus on my white wolf. It broke my heart to look at him, feeling this wall growing between us.

"You have every right to make your own choices, Shaz. I can't stop you from being with her or anyone else. But, I don't want to watch you lose yourself in that world. You don't belong there."

"I know," he agreed, his steady gaze wavered. He looked down at the floor, studying the carpet at his feet. "There was a time when I believed that you didn't belong there either."

"I don't." My stomach was floaty and twisted. I felt ill. "I don't want to."

"But, you do. I saw what you did tonight. It proves more than anything that you belong in that world."

The silence was deafening. Arys looked back and forth between us but said nothing. A series of memories swarmed me: Shaz and I when we were both still so new and raw as werewolves. Back then, we had sought comfort in one another, and I'd believed it was the worst life was going to get.

"I just want you to be happy."

Shaz looked at me sharply. His eyes flashed with anger. "I want us both to be happy. But, you had to go do something stupid, and then I did something just as stupid. This isn't the way it was supposed to be."

It wasn't. Life in our small town had allowed us both to harbor picket fence dreams. With the forest blanketing the edge of town, Stony Plain was perfect for us, but I'd always known that idyllic life would never be mine.

"I know." I stood there with them staring at me, feeling put on the spot.

Without budging from his comfy chair, Arys drew our attention with a raised hand. "I think you two are making this out to be a bigger issue than it needs to be. It's a less than pleasant situation driven by human nature. You have to let it go. And, staying away from The Wicked Kiss wouldn't be a bad idea. For both of you."

A muscle twitched in Shaz's clenched jaw. "Let it go? Seriously? This coming from the man who is probably the most jealous, possessive one of the three of us. Funny, Arys."

Arys smiled, a sensual flash of fang. "This isn't about me. You're both hurting, filled with remorse, jealousy and forbidden desires. Well... welcome to life. Never has a pair of devoted lovers walked this earth without facing their share of trials and tribulations. Why do you think wedding vows have all that for better or for worse stuff? Get over it or give up. There are no other options."

Couldn't argue with that. I knew he was right. That damn vampire was almost always right. I'd never admit it too readily, though.

Shaz nodded his platinum head and shuffled his feet. "I'm not willing to give up." To me he said, "Are you?"

"No." I didn't have to think about it. "Not a chance."

"Alright then." Arys nodded approvingly and gestured to each of us with a hand. "I now pronounce you both over it. A month of the two of you brooding is more than enough. Precious wasted time, you know." Casting his dark blue gaze on Shaz, he added with a grin, "Now kiss your woman and make it official."

A boyish smile graced Shaz's lips, and I adored him just a little bit more. He was so special. My emotions surged when he obeyed Arys and crossed the room to pull me into his arms.

His kiss was tender but restrained. I could feel his uncertainty, the same fearful doubt I felt. Scents of The Wicked Kiss lingered faintly on him, but beneath that was the heady aroma of wolf and Shaz. It transported me to a place where the forest embraced us and the moon was our only master. I longed for the pure simplicity of the wolf's world.

Arys demanding that we just get over it wasn't going to make this all disappear. Still, he'd made a point. Love was hard. Fight for it or fail. I was going to fight.

I became increasingly aware of Arys's intense stare, but Shaz seemed oblivious. He nuzzled the side of my face, his breath warm against my ear. "Don't let me lose myself in that place, Lex. I can't live that way."

It was something eerily similar to what I'd said to him not too long ago. Asking Shaz and Kylarai to kill me if I rose after death as a maniacal, blood-crazed vampire had been my way of ensuring I never had to live lost entirely to the consuming darkness. Yet, I was already halfway there.

"I won't let it have you." I held him tight, my arms around his neck as I hugged him close.

The creak of leather was loud in the quiet as Arys shifted his weight on the recliner. He waited until we looked at him before speaking. "I won't lose either of you to The Wicked Kiss. It's vile and filthy. Stay away from it. I mean it. It's Sinclair's problem now."

There was no room for argument in his tone. Since Harley had first come to town almost a year ago, The Wicked Kiss had been nothing but a blight. I'd spent more time there than anyone should in their lifetime, and I wasn't even a patron.

"That place is pure evil." Shaz's words were muffled in my hair. He held me like he'd never let go. "I'm not myself when I'm there. I hate what it does to me."

"It needs to be burnt to the ground." Arys's offhanded remark set off warning bells for me.

"Don't do anything stupid, Arys." I pulled away from Shaz so I could look at Arys but didn't release him entirely. I clasped his hand in mine, fearful of letting go. "If The Kiss was destroyed, everyone who frequents it would find somewhere else to carry on their business. I don't want that."

I saw the hard set to Arys's jaw, and I was sure he was going to fight me on it. So when he didn't, I knew he either planned to argue later or go ahead and torch The Kiss whether I approved or not.

"Alexa's right." With an exasperated sigh, Shaz thoughtfully rubbed his chin. "The majority of the vampires there are less than twenty years old. It's a safe hunting ground for them while the death toll stays far lower than if they were hunting on the streets."

"Besides," I felt deflated as fatigue crept in. "It's better not to have to worry about them in great numbers wreaking havoc on the streets. Too many other things out there are a far bigger threat."

"You both really have been spending too much time there," Arys observed with a frown. "It's warped your brains. Those willing victims are just junkies like the pup."

"Hey!" Shaz protested.

Arys continued as if he hadn't been interrupted. "If keeping humans from harm is your goal, allowing them to become addicted to the rush of the bite is hardly the way to do that. Everyone in that place gets off on giving, taking and fucking."

I made a frustrated sound that was mostly a growl of expletives. "I get it. The place is seriously bad news. I still believe something can be done with it. Even if it takes turning it into a church, I will change that place." Arys smirked, and I pointed a finger at him before he could open his mouth. "You stop being right. And, don't get used to it. That streak will run out eventually."

"Hey, I don't give a damn about that place or the people there, other than the two of you. It's a den of weakness and addiction for everyone that delights in the naughty backroom playground. It's a candy bowl of pills with something for everyone. Up, down or sideways."

The Wicked Kiss had a way of seducing even the most strong-willed. Vampires readily got their fix of fear, blood and violent sex while humans got off on the rush of screwing a vampire and playing in a dark world that would only consume them. Adrenaline can be just as addictive as anything. Why skydive or bungee jump when you can let death taste you?

I didn't want to encourage destructive behavior among the human clientele, but I had to ask myself, if they weren't finding a thrill in the vampire's bite, would they be on the streets sticking dirty needles in their arms in a desperate attempt to find that rush? Which was the lesser of two evils?

"I don't care. I'm not making any snap decisions. It's fucked up, but who's to say what those people would be doing if they weren't consorting with vampires?"

"Fine," Arys said, stretching like a lazy cat. "You call the shots. I really want nothing to do with the place."

With thoughtful intrigue, I studied him. "You don't want much to do with anyone or anything outside your personal little bubble. Do you?" I was thinking about how Arys had refused to work with Shya.

"Not particularly. I prefer to look out for number one, and that doesn't include demons pulling strings in the underworld or vampire junkies in tacky nightclubs."

"Then what does it include?" Shaz suddenly looked exceptionally interested.

Arys smiled, secrets dancing in his eyes. "Wouldn't you like to know?"

There was a lull in conversation. The perfect moment for me to tell them what had happened outside the club. I still had the crossbow bolt sitting on the passenger seat of my car.

"So, uh, there's something I should tell you both. Someone took a shot at me tonight." I launched into retelling all of the events of my evening. As I spoke, I could feel the atmosphere in the room shift.

This was the first time Shaz had heard about the hit. He paled but said little, nodding thoughtfully as I spoke. Arys's temper quickly flared, and a muscle in his jaw twitched.

"You shouldn't have gotten involved with the dreamwalker, Alexa. You can do nothing for him. Hell, you can't even keep yourself out of trouble."

"What?" I stared at him, unable to believe what I was hearing. "That's what you focus on out of everything I've said?"

Arys looked annoyed. "This is demon stuff you're messing with. Shya isn't going to put up with any shit. If he wants the kid, he'll have him. You have bigger problems, like almost taking a bolt to the head."

"I can't help but wonder what things would have been like for me if Shya and Veryl hadn't lured me in. I can't stand by while they do it to someone else. Don't make me feel bad about that." It wasn't worth arguing with him, but my feelings on this were valid.

Arys scowled. "I don't want to lose you. Why must you hold that against me?"

"You know I don't. But, this is my life, and I'm tired of having it manipulated by others. I can make my own decisions. They may not be the best ones, but they are mine to make."

"The dreamwalker's life is not yours to save." Arys's tone was low and smooth but deadly. "You won't be any help to him or anybody else if you're dead. Or worse. I don't control you and neither does Shya. If you want to run around alone taunting people to take a shot at you, go right ahead. Maybe fucking up a few too many times will cure you from your insane obsession with death."

"Don't be a dick, Arys," I warned. I looked at him through wolf eyes, staring intently until he shrugged and crossed his arms over his chest.

We faced off across the living room, adversaries in the heat of the moment. Arys brought out my feisty, defensive nature like nobody else. I think we both enjoyed the conflict; we fed off the fire.

"So, if you guys are done," Shaz broke in. "Well, even if you're not done, I'd like to state for the record that I think finding out who has a hit out on Lex is more important than arguing about whether or not she can take care of herself. I think she's more than capable."

"Thank you," I said quietly. His support meant a lot, but it would have meant more if he hadn't just been getting his rocks off with someone else. It wasn't fair of me to think like that.

Arys smirked and Shaz gave him a derogatory look. It still astounded me how much Shaz had changed since we'd first met. I tried to pinpoint exactly when he'd matured from a frightened teenager to the

Alpha wolf he now was. Had one specific event brought it forth, or was it always there beneath the surface? The years had gone by so fast. So much had changed, including us.

"I can't let myself be intimidated by an asshole with a crossbow. I caught that damn thing, Arys. Inches from my face." I refused to let him plant the seed of worry. "I know I'm not invincible, but I have power, and I'm finally learning how to use it."

"We'll find out who it is," Arys declared. "But in the meantime, all I ask is that you be careful. Don't be so reckless."

He was hiding something, some thought or fear. There had been a time when Arys considered my ties to the human world to be little more than an inconvenience. What had changed?

The vampire looked between Shaz and me, contemplating. "As long as you're here, pup, there's something else you should know."

"What?" Shaz was immediately suspicious.

I shook my head and shot Arys a warning glare that he ignored. Keeping his gaze on Shaz, he told him all about the journal and the twin flame revelation. Hearing the twin flame information repeated didn't make it any easier to swallow. If anything, it was harder because I was coming to accept it as true.

My white wolf looked devastated. He sat heavily on the end of the couch, staring at the floor. "So it's not just circumstance. You're really part of him."

I knew what he was thinking. He was wrong. I exchanged a look with Arys. He must have seen the helplessness in my eyes.

"Don't miss the point, pup," he said. "Alexa and I are halves of a whole, but we were never meant to exist together. Not without a reason. And, the odds of us finding out what that reason is before our bond destroys us are slim."

When Shaz looked up, he had a heartbreaking weariness in his eyes. "I think I knew. Somewhere deep down inside, I knew it would be him."

"It isn't like that." I went to him, grasping his hand desperately. "I always said you balance out what he does to me. It's true. I need you."

I truly did. Shaz had always been my source of comfort, my wolf, the one who made me feel like I belonged somewhere. I had always felt that he was just as much a part of me as Arys was.

"I am a danger to her, Shaz. It's you that grounds her." Arys's expression betrayed nothing, though his tone held a somber note. "We're bonded outside the natural scheme of things. If I'd remained mortal, I never would have known her. But, you still would have."

Shaz let out the breath he'd been holding. "This is a lot to process. It's just so… huge." He turned intense wolf eyes on Arys. "Why the hell did you wait so long to tell her?"

There was silence as the two of them stared into one another. Shaz always rolled with the punches better than I did. Now that he'd accepted what we had told him, he wanted to know more. He stared expectantly at Arys who wore a mask of guilt.

"I wasn't sure I'd ever tell her," Arys admitted. "But, some people know about us. And, it's changing her. Keeping it to myself wasn't going to stop that. I only wished it would."

I wasn't surprised to hear that. "You've got to stop that shit, Arys. You can't hide anything from me. It's always going to come out."

"I know. Try to see it from where I'm standing. I never knew if I'd find you, and now that I have, I don't want to lose you." To his credit, he had the decency to look chagrined.

His tendency to hide information and criticize my decisions was at the heart of most of our arguments. Seeing the raw emotion in his blue eyes made it hard to be angry.

"I understand. As hard as this is for me, I got the better deal. I can't imagine what it's been like for you."

Arys gazed at me with those entrancing eyes. There was a seductive pull to his energy. It was manipulative, getting under my skin like a metaphysical itch.

A frown graced Shaz's youthful face. "It's always about you, Arys. You already had her, and that wasn't good enough so you blood bonded her. You made her what you are. And now, it's devouring her. You're a real piece of work, pal."

Arys tilted his head to the side and regarded Shaz with bitter amusement. "Watch your mouth, wolf. You were right there encouraging her to accept the blood bond. It was to keep her safe."

"Safe from everyone but you." Shaz was fearless, rising to challenge the vampire with his cold stare.

"Wrong!" Arys hissed. In a flash, he was up off the recliner, in Shaz's face. "Everything I am was already inside of her. You saw signs of that before I ever bonded her. What we share isn't about blood. It's beyond life and death. My darkness tempts her, but you keep her wolf alive. You keep her human. But, you're too busy whoring at The Wicked Kiss to see that."

Shaz growled and bared fangs. I shoved my way between them, forcing them apart.

"Cut it out! Finger pointing doesn't do a damn bit of good. I'd like you both to keep in mind that I am not an object. I don't belong to anybody. I am my own entity, a person joined to you both in different ways but owned by neither. Got it?"

Grudgingly, they each nodded. Arys didn't believe it. I could see it in his eyes. He believed I was his to claim, and maybe if I'd been in his place, knowing what he knew for so many years, I'd have felt the same way. Still, I wasn't above handing out an ass kicking to either of them.

Swiping his dropped keys off the table, Shaz headed for the door with an angry stride.

"Shaz, wait." I hurried after him and grabbed his arm, trying to make him look at me.

He shook me off and flung open the front door. "I can't do this right now."

"Please? Don't leave. Not like this," I pleaded. Fear gripped my heart as the wall between us grew.

"Sorry, Lex. I just need some time alone."

I turned away when he disappeared through the doorway. I felt ill every time he left my side. I couldn't shake the fear that one day it would be the last time. I didn't want to have that vision etched in my memory forever.

## Chapter Seven

I returned to the living room to find Arys settled back into the recliner. He beckoned to me with a crooked finger.

"That went well." Crawling onto the lounger, I squeezed in beside him. "Why the hell did Shaz come to you of all people?"

His bare chest was slightly cool to the touch. He hadn't fed recently. I ran my fingers over the hard expanse and down to the thin smattering of hair that disappeared below the waistband of his pants.

"He came to ask me for help." Arys paused, letting me wrap my brain around that before continuing. "I'm glad he did. It took balls for him to come to me."

"Agreed. Can you help him? I mean, what can we do?"

"What drew him in was the rush of the power and the excitement of the intimate nature of being bitten. That started with us." Our eyes met and we shared a look. "Shaz's problem began when he started seeking out the same thrill without us. We had no way of knowing what was going on with him. He's too damn stubborn."

I nodded knowingly. "He didn't want to admit that he got off on being with you that way."

"There's not a damn thing anyone can do for him until he's ready. If he wants my help, Alexa, you need to be aware of what that might mean. If he were to come to me, if he were to ask for it…"

Arys fell quiet, letting me put the rest of that sentence together. I shook my head. I couldn't think about this right now. Sleep began to call my name, tugging at my eyelids. I didn't realize I was drifting off until Arys touched a hand to my face and I jumped.

The chair jerked as he closed the foot extension. Gathering me in his arms, Arys brushed a kiss across the bridge of my nose. It tickled and I laughed sleepily.

"Bedtime," Arys declared. "You don't sleep enough."

"There's no time to sleep," I mumbled into his shoulder, my arms clasped around his neck. "My sister is alive, and I'm being investigated for murder by the FPA."

"You're just full of surprises tonight, aren't you?" Arys carried me down the hall to his bedroom. Spending the day in slumber buried in the fluffy marshmallow that was Arys's bed didn't strike me as a bad idea. As sleep crept in further, the worries of earlier slipped away.

After gently laying me against the mountain of soft blankets and pillows, he stripped my clothing off and drew a satin sheet up over me. Arys shed his pants and crawled in next to me. The touch of his naked flesh against mine brought a sigh to my lips.

It didn't take long for sleep to claim me. Unfortunately, it was restless and disturbed. It was just past three in the afternoon when I couldn't take the tossing and turning anymore. Arys remained in the slumber of the undead. He didn't really need to sleep. Not often anyway. I think he just enjoyed the luxury of it.

Once I tired of staring at the ceiling, I slipped from the bed and padded down the hall, through the living room to the kitchen. I dug through my shoulder bag, looking for Arys's journal. I didn't like to leave it at home where it could be found by anybody who might decide to bust in and paw through my stuff.

I paused to check my cell phone for messages: one from Jez and one from my best friend and beta wolf, Kylarai, but nothing from Shaz. I'd hoped to find a text, something to let me know things were cool. So much for that.

I slipped my phone back into my bag, grabbed the journal and headed back to the bedroom. Arys stirred slightly, reaching to touch me as I settled back in beside him.

The pages felt so fragile. I turned them with care, skimming through as I went. There was more on Alice. It didn't tell me anything I hadn't already figured out. Harley's name caught my eye several times. Morbid curiosity drew me to an entry I'd previously skipped over.

Once I turned my full attention to Arys's memories, recorded decades ago, I got caught up in his words. Everything else fell away but that night captured on the pages in my hands.

*Trina M. Lee*

*December 5, 1849*

*They were lovely really. Like usual, Harley's choice. He has a weakness for virgins. Personally, I prefer a woman who knows what she's doing and can appreciate the things I do to her. The virgins...they tend to scream. A lot. Of course, I have found virgins to be very quick to beg. And, that I just can't get enough of.*
*It was easy enough to lure them home. It always is. The right word or gesture, and they're more than happy to sneak away from a party before their companions notice their absence. Harley can sniff out a virgin anywhere. He claims virgin blood to be the nectar of the gods, but I find it to be a little too pure for my tastes. These women though, they were divine. A blonde and one with deep scarlet hair who was surprisingly eager when I had her spread-eagle on the chaise lounge.*
*Once Harley's shy little blonde began shrieking, things really became interesting. Everything had been going splendidly. My little virgin temptress writhed beneath me as I pleasured her with my mouth. She begged for more, and I savored the heat of her womanhood against my tongue as I fed on the burning energy of her desire. It was intoxicating, a prelude to the moment when I would taste her blood.*

I had to pause, to focus on taking a breath. I realized I'd held mine while reading. The words sprang to life, pulling me into the scene as Arys's memory of this night crashed into the front of my conscious thoughts. I was seeing it through his eyes, reliving it as if I'd been there myself.

*Screams rang out and my innocent beauty became alarmed. I assured her that there was nothing to fear. Drawn into the lull of my manipulation, she pulled me close, offering herself to me. Harley would have his victim screaming for hours if he could manage it. I wasn't ready yet to make mine fight for her life. All in good time.*
*Tight and warm, her body was resistant when I took her. The pained sounds she made as I filled her sent ripples of pleasure throughout me. Her soft whimpers gradually became cries of joy. I was drowning in the waves of her excited energy, drinking it in. I itched to bury my fangs in that delicate throat of hers. Patience is not a virtue I*

*possess. I waited, hoping to time the moment with her climax, preferring to take all that she had to give at once.*

*I sensed that she was close. My control snapped, and I bit deep into her neck. She screamed. Blood gushed from the wound, and I drank of it greedily. The spell was broken. Free of my thrall, she thrashed violently. I bit her again, pinning her arms above her head. I drank hungrily; her blood coated my tongue deliciously. Though aware that she was in a fight for her life, she couldn't help but respond to my careful manipulations of her body. Buried deep inside her, I felt her inner muscles clench as climax shook her and euphoria claimed me.*

I could taste her. She was mine, and I couldn't wait to taste her death. To be the bringer of it, the master of all that she was. I heard the shallow gasps for breath but didn't recognize them as my own. I ceased reading as the memory took over.

Arys had drained her completely. Her screams had accompanied those of her friend, and the vampires took their fill of blood and sex. She begged Arys for her life, pleading and promising. It only encouraged him. Her pleas were like fuel on an open flame. Arys killed her, and he loved every second of it.

The scent of her was thick in my nostrils. Fear, lust and blood all entwined in one storm of sensation to overwhelm me. I was suddenly beside myself with need.

"Alexa?" Arys's voice was a distant echo, as if he were far away. "It's not real, Alexa. Don't lose yourself in my past."

I wasn't seeing him anymore. He had faded along with the rest of the bedroom as I spun headlong into a memory that wasn't mine. I saw the candlelit room with the cream-colored chaise lounge and the shrieking woman upon it. She was young, eighteen perhaps. She fought hard once she broke free of Arys's powerful mesmerism. Some victims would smile happily as they died under his thrall. But others, they fought until that very last breath.

There was a rush of white noise, almost deafening in my ears. I was lost in my kill, Arys's kill, and my sense of reality shifted. My four fangs filled my mouth, and I reached with clawed fingers for a victim that wasn't really there.

I'm not sure how long Arys shook me, trying desperately to get me to come back to him. "Come on, Alexa! You're not part of that world. I was. I need you in the here and now."

I mumbled something incoherent. Harley's devious laughter echoed all around me. I heard his victim wailing. I wanted him to make her stop, to just shut her up. I couldn't take much more. The screams, the blood and the erotic flavor of terror, it was all driving me into a frenzy.

I was caught between myself and Arys. Feeling his hunger for her and his deep-rooted satisfaction as he drained her life away conflicted with the need I felt to be the one he claimed in such a powerfully intimate manner. My vision swam, alternating from Arys's past to the present. I had always been a part of him. Even then, when I had yet to be born.

Arys's voice was firm when he demanded, "Do you want her? Or, do you want to be her?"

It took a few moments before awareness hit me. I was lying flat on my back with Arys straddling me, holding my arms pinned above my head. It became clear what he was asking. He was offering me release from the grips of his horrid memories.

I was flushed with desire for both body and blood. I couldn't form a response. My mind was a mess of blood stained images. I don't know what Arys saw in my eyes, but he didn't wait any longer for a reply. True to his nature, he made me the victim.

He slipped a hand between my legs, finding me ready. An evil light shone in the depths of his eyes, and a smirk tugged at his lips. "Hell, if I'd known that journal would make you so hot, I'd have given it to you months ago."

"You did this to me. You made me a monster." I was rambling without thought, saying whatever danced onto the tip of my tongue.

Arys leaned in close, his lips brushing mine as he spoke. "You were always meant to be a monster. I just make you enjoy it."

His kiss was gentle and soft, so contradictory to the tension I felt emanating from him. Nudging my legs apart with a knee, he positioned himself between them so that I was comfortably pinned beneath his weight. Every time I closed my eyes I saw her, the redhead sprawled out before him, bleeding and begging even as she enjoyed his touch.

"Look at me." Arys's demanding tone startled me. "I want to see terror in your eyes before I bleed you."

I almost choked on the stifling sensation that flooded me. Fear. Arys had frightened me during such an encounter only once before.

That same time he'd also threatened me. Once again, the promise of pain in his words made me ache for him.

Burying his face in my hair, he pressed his lips to my neck and breathed deeply of my scent. He was encouraging my fear with the taunt of his fangs against my vein. I tensed, uncertain. The thick swell of his erection against me was both exciting and intimidating. I felt him draw on my energy, feeding on my bloodlust, fear and desire.

Arys slipped inside me with a rough thrust, forcing a cry from me. He groaned as the power rose up to engulf us. His mouth was warm on my skin. I could feel him shaking with the strength it took to keep from biting me, to hold out for the right moment when it would throw us both headlong into the abyss that sought to claim us.

There was a change in him, a shift in our dynamic that made Arys the aggressor. He often was aggressive, but never did I truly feel like a victim with him. Not until now. He peered down into my eyes, and all I saw was the predatory gaze of the wolf looking back at me. My wolf. It was an unsettling reminder that Arys had as much of my monster inside him as I had of his.

"Please, don't," I heard myself say. I wasn't sure what I was asking him.

With every slick stroke of his body into mine, my panic began to subside. The energy binding us grew and writhed, wrapping us in its magnificent hold.

He showered me with kisses on my lips and along my jaw. "You know me. You always have."

Conflict filled me as anguish over his words warred with comfort. Until I really knew what that meant, I could find neither solace nor regret in his words.

I gripped him with claws that cut deep red ribbons into his flesh. Every time he filled me, he brought me closer to the edge. He was aggressive, as if he couldn't possibly get deep enough. We were as close as we could physically get, and still it wasn't the union I ached for. Despite the fervor in which he made love to me, his kisses were soft caresses. But, only until his patience ran thin.

With a hand tightly entwined in my hair, he forced my head to the side and bit deep. My heart thundered in my ears at a deafening level as my blood poured into Arys's mouth. I had a moment of clarity, and I wondered if my life would end in his hands. Maybe not today but one day. If our destiny was to destroy each other, that might only be fitting.

I gasped for breath, unable to fill my lungs. Time felt non-existent. I had no conscious awareness of what time it was or how long it had been since I'd dropped the journal. All I knew was the pleasure and the promise of Arys's mouth on my bitten neck and his body declaring me as his.

He drove me headlong into the flames of passion that threatened to consume us. I was free falling through the throes of climax while my heart stuttered in an erratic beat. The metaphysical energy we'd called pulsed around and through us. It was too much for me. I couldn't breathe nor could I escape it. It was inside me, part of me. And for a moment, I thought it would kill me.

Blood trickled from my nose. My head felt as if it would burst. Arys's name was on my lips, but I couldn't speak. He sucked at my bloody neck. When he raised his head, my blood was smeared on his lips and teeth. Realizing that the power we'd drawn was more than I could safely conduct, Arys stripped it from me, effectively freeing me from its deadly hold.

I clung to him as I sucked air into my lungs. There was a hum in my ears, and tingles shot through my limbs. The bite on my neck throbbed in time with my racing pulse.

"Are you ok, love?" Arys pressed the side of his face to mine. "That was intense. Too intense for you."

My voice was raspy with the wolf. "I'll be alright. I might get a hell of a headache though."

Arys rolled over beside me but stayed close, pressed to my side. After tugging the bloodstained pillow from beneath my head, he pulled me into the safe confines of his embrace. I snuggled in against him, my head on his chest while he lazily stroked a hand through my disheveled hair.

"That's been happening to you a lot lately. The nosebleeds and headaches. I don't like it."

I wiggled my fingers, watching as the claws retracted. There was blood on my fingertips. "I'm fine, Arys." I felt better already. Besides, he was in worry mode lately; I wasn't going to feed it.

He wanted to say something more. I could feel it. After a long moment of contemplation, he gave in and spit it out.

"I don't think it's fine. I think it's starting to become more than you can handle." His hold on me tightened possessively. "It's dangerous."

I swallowed hard, willing myself to relax. My mortal body had been the subject of concern before, regarding the power we shared. My body bound me to the earth and to the wolf, but his undead energy was never meant for a living being. Together Arys and I were life and death, a nearly unheard of combination.

The full extent of what we were capable of was still unknown to me. I'd already decided that I wasn't ready to become a vampire. It would happen upon my death, something I planned to avoid as long as possible.

"Hey, what happened to enjoying the afterglow?" I asked, setting his worry aside.

He grinned, but I could see that it was forced. My intent wasn't to downplay his concerns. I simply didn't want to think about them right then. After a violent, messy expression of love, I wanted nothing more than to allow the illusive peace that came after to sweep me away. Reality could wait.

# Chapter Eight

I didn't come to the office much anymore. Since I'd killed the man who had run it, I'd had little reason to return. Back when I'd been hunting idiot vampires that drew the wrong kind of attention with their kills, this had been grand central, where we all came to regroup and to unwind.

Now, it was just a building that housed many memories. The kitchen was where I'd found Jez in a pool of her own blood the night Kale attacked her. My office down the hall was where Kale and I had succumbed to temptation for the first time. And, the main office at the very end of that corridor was where I'd killed my former boss, Veryl Armstrong.

I closed the front door hard when I came in, announcing my arrival. Noise from the kitchen greeted me. Lilah looked up suddenly, mild surprise creasing her brow.

"Alexa. Hi. How's it going?" She asked, closing a cupboard so fast it slammed.

I found it odd that she hadn't sensed me before I'd come inside. I was getting better at cloaking my energy. Good to know. If Lilah couldn't detect me, would Shya? I'd have to find out.

Lilah was a demon, one I didn't know nearly enough about. All I did know was that she was some kind of big bad in the underworld. Or, she had been. A curse held her trapped in a corporeal form, a vampire. Her demon power was limited, but it was still deadly. I'd seen her vanquish other demons with merely a word.

"It could be worse." I shrugged. "You?"

"Ditto."

## Death Wish

"I just came in to get the rest of my things since I'm not spending much time here anymore." I headed down the hall to my office, aware of her silent steps behind me. A chill crept up my spine. I resisted the urge to turn around.

"Falon told me what happened last night. Close call." Lilah hung back in the doorway, leaning against the frame. Her long copper colored hair fell in waves over her shoulders. Dressed all in black, her hair looked more like fire than usual.

I opened a desk drawer and started pulling out pens and notepads. "Not close enough for whoever was asinine enough to take that shot."

"They don't know who they're messing with." Lilah flashed me an encouraging smile.

"So I take it you haven't heard anything about who it may be?" I was acutely aware of her pale orange eyes on me as I tossed small desk items into my shoulder bag.

She paused, considering my question. "I have heard there's a werewolf asking a lot of questions about you."

I dropped my gaze to the desk drawer as I scooped out office supplies. What could Lilah possibly know about Juliet? "So I've heard."

"Let me know if you need any help tracking her down. I've got eyes and ears all over this city." Her expression was stone cold. Her smile had vanished.

"Thank you. I appreciate that." I had no intention of letting on that I was way ahead of her. If she didn't know it was my sister, I wasn't about to enlighten her. I couldn't shake the feeling that there was something more she wanted to say. I was curious but not enough to prod her.

I gathered up the knickknacks scattered about on the desk: a small stone wolf statue, a magic eight ball that had been a gag gift from Kale and a shiny green chunk of jade. Lena had given me the jade, along with many other crystals and charms over the years. I rubbed a finger over its smooth surface before dropping it into my bag.

I made sure to grab all personal effects from the room. Even the smallest bobby pin couldn't be left behind. Demons could do very scary things with personal belongings.

It was going to be easy to leave the office behind. My place here had ended the moment I'd killed Veryl. Things were changing. I was changing. Gone were the simple days when my biggest kill was a careless vampire or a twisted werewolf.

As I exited my office for what was likely the final time, Lilah moved to let me pass and took her last chance to spit out whatever was on her mind. "Hey, Alexa, when you came here that night to kill Veryl, did you take anything from his office?"

I froze. I had a split second to decide between a lie and the truth. "Yes. I grabbed some files from his computer." The truth came out steady and strong. I had nothing to hide. The way I saw it, I had a right to any further information Veryl had stashed on me.

"Oh." Relief flooded her features. It was gone before I could make sense of it. "That's all? Are you sure?"

"Absolutely." Now my curiosity was piqued. "Is something missing that shouldn't be?"

She shook her head quickly, her tight smile plastered back in place. "Not missing. Most likely hidden."

A lot of things could be said about Veryl, but nobody could ever say that the bastard wasn't clever. He knew his time was running out, and he'd planned ahead. What could he have hid that would have Lilah so worried?

"Would you like some help?" I asked, ignoring the text message alert that rang out from my bag.

"I've got this. But, thanks anyway. You should be kicking some vampire ass for info. I don't want to keep you from that." With a grin that didn't quite reach her coppery eyes, Lilah turned to go. "Have a good night."

I watched her disappear down the hall into Veryl's old office. The door closed behind her, loud in the sudden quiet. I dug my phone out, finding a message from Jez with photos asking me which outfit looked better.

I sent her a fast reply though my mind was otherwise occupied. Whatever Veryl had hidden from Lilah, it had to be important. My curiosity was insatiable. I wanted to know what it was.

My cell phone rang in my hand, scaring the crap out of me with the theme from *The Twilight Zone*. Arys had obviously been messing with my phone again. It was better than last week's Rick Astley song. Nothing like being rickrolled by a vampire. Real funny.

Shya's fatally smooth voice greeted me. "Alexa, would you mind coming by tonight? I have something for you."

"Is this something I actually want?"

"It's something you need to see. If you don't want it, you can walk away."

"Fine."

I had planned to stop by The Wicked Kiss despite Arys's order to stay away. I never was very good at taking orders from him. Thanks to the demon, Arys would get his way regardless of my personal rebellion.

\* \* \* \*

An ear-splitting shriek echoed throughout the house. I winced, resisting the urge to cover my sensitive ears. Watching a demon be tortured wasn't my idea of a good time.

The sound of flesh sizzling was followed by another scream. Holy water on demon skin was clearly not pleasant. I cringed inwardly and paced away from the ugly scene. The scent of sulfur was thick on the air. It was starting to give me a headache.

Shya stood off to the side, overseeing the proceedings. He was careful to avoid any potential splash back. Falon, the asshole extraordinaire, was taking a little too much joy in wielding the bottle of blessed water.

The entire fiasco had nothing to do with me. I still wasn't sure why I was there. Shya seemed to take perverse pleasure in making me witness these events. I glanced at him, noting the intensity in his red eyes as he stared at the man tied to a chair in the middle of his living room. It wasn't really just a man; it was a demon. Whatever he'd done to piss off Shya, it must have been big.

A peal of wicked laughter poured from Shya, and my skin crawled in response. Average height and build with a shock of blue-black hair, on the surface Shya was very much a fine-looking Japanese man. Lies. He wore that face, but he was a demon, and those red eyes ensured I never forgot that.

"I knew you'd slip up," he spoke to the man struggling in the chair. "You've gotten lazy. You can't be trusted anymore. It's time to send you back."

"No!" came the frantic response. With eyes wide and the stink of burnt flesh wafting from him, the bound demon panicked. "Torture me, tear my limbs off. I don't care. Anything! I can't go back!"

I lingered as far from the action as possible. The wall at my back was glass from floor to ceiling. I wished I could simply step through to the other side and escape the stifling atmosphere. A fire burned in the hearth adjacent to me. Nobody else seemed to find it uncomfortable, but on a hot July night, the fire was ridiculous.

"One job, Brook. I asked you to keep tabs on one person, and you failed. I have no further use for you." Shya held up a hand, holding off Falon's assault while he glared daggers at their hostage. "You've become a liability."

"I'll do anything. Please! You know how he is. It wasn't my fault!" The demon's eyes were solid black as he gazed up at Shya pleadingly. The desperation and fear emanated from him in thick waves that assaulted my finely tuned senses. Demon energy was heavy and oppressive. I wasn't a fan.

"What do you think?" Shya turned to Falon with an inquisitive expression.

Falon's silver wings stretched out behind him. A pure angel had white wings, but he was tainted. From shoulder to floor, they were still massive and gorgeous, far more beautiful than the black wings Shya possessed. Currently, Shya's were absent from sight, either by sheer illusion or demon magic, I didn't know.

Falon fixed Brook with a hard stare as he fondled the bottle of holy water. "Send his ass back to hell."

I stiffened at the malice in his tone. Everything that came out of Falon's mouth made me shocked that he'd ever been an angel. He was his own special brand of evil.

"Oh come on, Shya," Brook begged. "You can't let a goddamn fence rider decide my fate. He's not one of us." His anxious gaze landed on me where I stood trying to be invisible. "Might as well let the werewolf choose if you're going to let an undecided angel do it."

There was a sudden commotion as Falon advanced on Brook. Forcing a drop of holy water into his open mouth, Falon stepped back with grim satisfaction, watching the smoke rise from the face of the wailing demon. The whole scenario sickened me.

Shya turned to me with a look I couldn't quite interpret. "That's not a bad idea."

"Oh, no." I shook my head vigorously. "I can't do that. Please, don't bring me into this."

## Death Wish

Fear clawed its way up my throat, choking off my words. Shya scared the living hell out of me, but I was digging in my heels on this one. Just weeks ago I'd watched Shya and Falon kill a preacher. Whatever they were up to, I wanted no part of it.

"Look at her shaking like a frightened little girl," Falon scoffed. "You can't be serious, Shya. She's here for one thing, and this isn't it."

I was not shaking. Falon's derogatory attitude had me biting back an ugly retort. I did agree though. I wasn't here for this.

Shya looked amused. "Fair enough. This has taken long enough. We have other business to get to." To Brook he said, "You're lucky I'm in a good mood today. Consider this your last chance. Next time you let me down, I'll see you burning in the pit where you belong."

Brook sank back in his chair in relief, the heavy silver bindings on his wrists jingled with his movements. Silver didn't work on vampires or werewolves the way Hollywood would have one think. It did, however, work on demons.

Falon took his sweet time freeing the demon from his bonds, but I began to breathe a little easier. Shya's large modern home was sweltering, and I couldn't wait to leave. I didn't know if he really lived there or if it was merely a prop, but it was a nice place. Pricey. A second floor overlooked the main floor where we stood. The high ceilings and wide, open rooms made the place feel huge.

No sooner was Brook freed than he sprung out of the chair and unfurled his big black wings. His face bore the marks of the holy water. Battered and burnt, he glowered at Falon before disappearing in a burst of black smoke. The stench of sulfur choked me.

"Go," Shya ordered Falon, his head inclined slightly toward a door on the opposite side of the living room. "Get the wolf."

"Wolf?" I sputtered. "What's going on?"

I hadn't sensed anyone else in the house with us, but the moment that door swung open, I could feel it. Something wasn't right with Shya's basement. A chill crept up my spine. Instinctively, I wanted to flee the house. Whatever Shya had going on down there, it was bad.

A series of bangs and curses rose from the stairwell. Falon appeared in the doorway with a bloody, beaten man. He smelled like wolf, but I didn't recognize him. Falon dragged him across the room and flung him at my feet.

Shya ambled up beside me, his arms crossed over his chest. Eyeing me, he nodded toward the man on the floor.

"We've got a little problem here. This wolf has made some serious trouble recently. Enough trouble to get him killed. But, since he claims that you're the one who turned him, that decision falls into your hands."

Shocked didn't begin to describe my reaction. "What? I've never turned anybody."

"That's a lie." The man knelt before me, sullen and angry. "You attacked me on the street. Some guy pulled you off me and I ran."

*Oh, shit.* It hit me like a bitch slap in the face. I remembered him. That night Arys had found me at The Wicked Kiss after he'd warned me to stay away. It had been more than a warning. He'd outright threatened me, but I'd gone there anyway to seek answers from the one person I knew who had them, Harley. Arys and I had a shouting match in the parking lot before I'd ended up at a bar drowning my sorrows and ultimately losing control on a stranger outside. And, here he was.

"You're right. That was me." I stared down at his face, trying to see it in my memory. I couldn't. He looked back at me boldly, refusing to show fear. "I'm sorry."

His left eye was swollen, and his clothes were bloodstained. Falon had given him a good ass kicking. That lit a flame of anger inside me. If he was my wolf then he was mine to punish. Where did a fallen angel get off laying hands on my wolf?

"What happened to him?" I directed the question to Shya, but I locked eyes with Falon. "What did he do to earn himself a beating before I even knew about him?"

"He went to the human authorities with his story. He begged for their help." With a shake of his head, Shya looked at the wolf with utter disdain. "My man on the inside turned him over to me, but not before he wolfed out on two cops. I would have killed him immediately if he hadn't said your name."

"How do you know my name?" I was uneasy. Wolfing out on cops was not something to brush off.

The wolf looked between Shya and me uncertainly. "Everyone knows who you are. It wasn't hard to get some information on you once I started digging around. I knew what you looked like."

"Why the hell would you go to the police?" I demanded, my voice rising. I was having a hard time grasping all this. I wasn't sure how much more I could take tonight. To Shya, I said, "And why the hell do you have a fire burning? It's July."

Shya merely smiled, a vicious grin that shone with amusement. I kept my attention on the wolf before me. I couldn't believe what I was hearing. This was definitely not what I'd expected to find here tonight.

"I didn't want to hurt anybody. I thought they could help me before I did something I'd regret for the rest of my life. It was stupid. I get that. I just wanted help."

He was unapologetic, but I saw desperation in his eyes. He had learned the hard way.

I couldn't fault the guy for panicking and seeking a way out. I hated to ask, but I had to know. "Shya, what happened with the cops who saw?"

"They've been dealt with. They don't remember seeing a thing. However, if such an incident had occurred in front of a whole crowd, it wouldn't have been such an easy fix. Mind control and memory manipulation does have its limits."

I stood there in the agonizing heat, trying to think through the onslaught of questions forming. Shya watched me expectantly.

"Kill him." Falon spoke up from where he stood near the open attached kitchen. "It's not worth the risk of keeping him around. He's just one werewolf."

The way his tone changed on that last bit rubbed me the wrong way. I had a feeling there was a hidden jibe there.

"It isn't your call to make," I snapped, my words ending on a growl. I glared hard at Falon who leaned back against the kitchen island, casual and unaffected.

"No, Alexa. It's yours." Shya swept an arm toward the wolf on the floor with a grand, dramatic gesture. "Claim him as your wolf or leave him to us."

Trepidation filled me. I didn't want anyone's life in my hands. Not like this. I gazed down at the wolf, my wolf, and I felt a territorial obligation to him. "What's your name?"

"Coby Haines."

"Well, Coby Haines, this is your lucky day. I'm not going to decide your fate. You are. Are you ready to die now? To escape the wolf in the only way possible? Or, do you want me to claim you as pack? You'll be mine to protect, and in return you'll keep a low profile."

A snort of derision came from Falon. I ignored him. Shya was quiet, but I could feel the weight of his watchful gaze upon me, judging my choice.

Coby cast a careful glance at Falon, then Shya before settling his gaze on me. "I'm not ready to die. I just want help."

"You'll get it." The way I saw it, I owed Coby. For the past few months, he'd been out there, changed because of me, and I hadn't even known. What he did was thoughtless, but he deserved a chance.

"Come on. Let's go." Taking Coby's hand, I pulled him to his feet and steered him toward the door. "I assume I can leave now, Shya. Unless there's anything else."

Shya's amused smile never wavered. "Have a nice night, Alexa."

The eerie sensations floating around inside Shya's house spilled over outside. The entire property felt cursed, like it writhed with something black and bottomless. The house was outside of town, down a dirt road east of the city. I assumed Shya had several reasons to live in a secluded area. Everything about the place, including Shya himself, set off my personal warning bells. I was hasty to get away.

Coby hesitated near my car. He looked back at the house for a moment as if torn before grasping the passenger door handle. If I were him, I would second-guess getting into a car with the person who turned me, too.

"Are you going to get in?" I dropped into the driver's seat and started the car. I was in a hurry to leave. "It'll be a long walk back to town." Well, it would be on human legs.

I opened the windows and the sunroof, drinking in the night air. It was delectably cool in comparison to the insane heat inside.

"I have nowhere to go. Not anymore." Coby got into the car but continued to glance nervously out the window.

"Well, you're not staying here. I'll drive, you talk."

I snuck a look at him. He had to be in his late twenties or early thirties, dressed casually in jeans and a t-shirt. With light, ash brown hair and a five o'clock shadow, he was ruggedly attractive. He turned hazel eyes on me that were all wolf.

His wolf looked out at me, and I knew how close he was to losing it. He was still so new, but I wasn't worried. Wolves were my comfort zone, even those who could barely hold it together. I held his gaze, enforcing my dominance without moving a muscle. I saw it in him when he accepted the unspoken hierarchy. His wolf backed down, and Coby visibly relaxed in his seat.

"Look," I began, giving the Charger a little more gas than necessary in my haste to peal out of Shya's long driveway. "I wish there was something I could say. I know an apology isn't going to cut it."

"Save it. I don't want an apology. I just want help. No offense, but I really don't want to end up like you, attacking people on the street."

That stung but he spoke the truth. When I'd been newly turned and in his place, I hadn't wanted to end up like me either.

"Fair enough."

An awkward silence descended. My fingers were tight on the steering wheel. I was at a loss for words. I imagined a part of him wanted to tear my head off for what I'd done to him, but he seemed mostly resigned to accept it.

"I know how hard this is in the beginning. Everyone smells like prey, and the simple act of the sun setting sets the wolf loose sometimes. It gets easier. Really."

The silence was making me uncomfortable. If he wasn't going to talk then I was.

"There's a pack in a small town outside the city, in Stony Plain. We run together every full moon. Many of us live normal lives, keep normal jobs. But, we have each other's backs. You're more than welcome to join us."

"Normal jobs?" His tone was skeptical. "I thought I was going to kill my co-workers. I couldn't stand to be around them. That smell. So strong and …"

"Human?" I supplied. "Yeah, that takes some getting used to."

"I lost my job. Then I lost my apartment. And now, I wait to lose myself every time it happens. Every time I can't fight it off." He stared out the window, saying what he'd probably never said to anyone else but longed to. "I'm starting to see things differently. We're still human, but we're more than that, too. Just tell me one thing. Tell me we'll never be as inhuman as they were. Back at the house."

I had once consoled myself with the assurance that as long as there were vampires and demons, I was minor league on the monster scale. I'd been so wrong.

"I wish I could tell you what you want to hear. I can tell you this though: Embrace the wolf. That part of you is more special than you know now. But, don't let it control your actions. And if you want to stay sane, stay away from vampires and demons."

Gravely serious, Coby turned to study me. I got the feeling he was trying to put his finger on what was so different about me. Most werewolves could feel that I wasn't entirely the same creature.

"This is all so surreal. I feel like I'm living in a horrible dream, and I can't wake up."

I could relate to that. I knew Coby wanted some kind of reassurance, but I had offered all I could. He would have to go through the motions day by day and let the puzzle pieces fall into place. That was the only way he'd accept the wolf and what it meant. Some people never did accept it. They didn't last long.

"I have an extra room in my house. It's a big house. If you need somewhere to crash for a while… There's a forest on the edge of town. It's safe and a comfort to have so close by. You're welcome to stay."

I expected Coby to turn down my offer. He looked positively miserable when he muttered, "Thank you. I'd really appreciate that."

I hoped he couldn't tell how uneasy the entire situation had me. It wasn't every day I had a demon throw a werewolf at me and tell me he was mine to take care of. Yet, I was an Alpha wolf. I would step up to the plate to protect and guide him. As surprising as this was, it was my responsibility. I cringed to think of what Shaz and Kylarai would say when they found out about this. If only that was my biggest problem right now.

# Chapter Nine

It was well after three in the morning by the time I got Coby comfortable in Raoul's room. The master bedroom seemed like the best place for him. It was on the top floor of the house, two floors above my room, and it was equipped with an en suite bathroom.

I stood awkwardly in the doorway with an armful of blankets. Since Raoul's death, I rarely went near his old room. Too many memories.

"Help yourself to anything you want from the kitchen," I said in what I hoped was a friendly tone. "I'm not sure the selection is the best. I can get groceries. There's a list on the fridge that you can add to."

I was rambling a little. I fully expected to be at the top of Coby's least favorite people list. Nothing I could do about that, so I was going to overdo it on hospitality.

"I appreciate that." Coby wore a mask of weariness. His shoulders slumped as he sat heavily on the side of the bed. "Don't trip over yourself trying to make me comfortable. I'm fine. Thank you."

My smile was so tight it hurt. It must have looked incredibly forced. "I'll be downstairs."

We shared another long, uneasy silence. I jumped into action, depositing the blankets on the bed. I uttered a quick, "Goodnight," and vacated the room like I was being chased by a swarm of bees.

I busied myself in the kitchen making green tea. It felt too empty. Something was missing. Shaz. It was his favorite room. He was a master in the kitchen.

It dawned on me that I hadn't heard from him all night. Leaving my mug next to the kettle, I dug my phone out of my bag. One missed call, but it was from Kale. Shaz hadn't called or so much as text messaged.

With a tired sigh, I punched in Kale's number and waited. He answered on the third ring. The noise of The Wicked Kiss was loud in the background.

A woman's voice whispered low but close to the phone, followed by Kale's low chuckle. "Alexa, hey. Are you alright? I was a little worried when you didn't answer your phone."

"Really? It sounds like you have your hands full. Shouldn't the club be closed by now?" My tone was harsher than it needed to be. Kale, on the phone with a woman in his lap, was not my ideal conversation.

"The doors are closed for the night. This is the after-hours crowd." The sound became muffled as he moved to a quieter location. "Sorry. I wasn't sure you'd call back tonight. I wanted to talk to you earlier about a theory I had, but this isn't a good time."

"Um, right." I held the phone with one hand and poured hot water into my mug with the other. Did Kale have an idea as to who was after me? "Well, maybe we can talk tomorrow then."

"I'll stop by the club after dark. I have to make a stop at the dreamwalker's house first. It shouldn't take long." His voice dropped as if he didn't want to risk anyone overhearing him.

I stirred the tea bag around in my cup and frowned. "Why so early? Isn't that more of a middle of the night kind of thing?"

There was a long pause before he answered me. "Usually. It's better if I don't say too much. I shouldn't have brought you there the other night."

"Why not? What's going on?" I demanded. "If he's in danger I want to know about it, Kale."

"You have to trust me on this one, ok? I'm not going to let anything happen to him. But, you have to stay away from this. You have enough things to deal with as it is."

I scoffed and took a sip of my tea. "You don't know the half of it."

"What does that mean?"

"Never mind. I'll explain later. I'll see you at the club then."

After I hung up, I stood there sipping my tea and pondering what was going on with the dreamwalker. I didn't trust Shya or his interest in any of us. After watching Falon torture that demon, I was more suspicious than ever.

I wasn't going to get to sleep any time soon, so I got settled on the couch with my tea and Arys's past. Though Coby was two floors away, I could sense his presence. Oddly enough, I found it comforting.

I steered clear of entries involving bloodshed and mayhem; so much more lay within the aged pages. Arys had a side that I didn't see much of, but it was fascinating.

*April 18, 1855*

*It's been three years since I've seen Harley. Still, I feel him everywhere. The tie that binds is breakable only by final death. So many times, I've considered giving myself to the sun. And, every time I know I'll never do it. Not for him.*

*Once again, we are apart, and I am finally able to think clearly. I plan to enjoy every minute of it. It won't be long before he makes his way back to me. He always does. It's been so long since the night he turned me, but it always feels like yesterday.*

*I prefer to be alone, to play the game my way. I feel like I'm waiting for someone who will never arrive. Passing the time grows difficult, so I seek out other outlets for the growing frustration. Painting. An art form I barely noticed before has now come to mean so much. That thoughtless process requires something deeper than words, thought or basic emotion. I stare at a blank canvas until the space between it and myself ceases to exist. For days, even weeks, I lose myself, surfacing from the powerful pull of creation to find something new and wonderful staring back at me.*

*Or someone.*

*The first time I saw those dark eyes peering back at me from the canvas, I wept. Pale, ashen fur cloaked her. A vicious predator, she stared out at me with fear and accusation, demanding I find her. I destroyed the painting. Set it ablaze. I won't bring her to life again. I can't bear it.*

The unmistakable sound of footsteps outside pulled me from Arys's past straight to my feet. Adrenaline swept away my wonder at his artistic flare.

It was still dark, though dawn was just over an hour away.

The noise came from the back patio. A heavy tread, paced back and forth from one end to the other. I moved slowly toward the stairs that led up into the kitchen. The sliding patio doors would be locked, but that wasn't going to stop a vampire who wanted in. And, since this wasn't Hollywood, no invitation was needed.

I paused on the stairs, listening hard. I reached out metaphysically, trying to get a feel for whoever lurked outside. Vampire, definitely. It was tough to get a read on him or her. There may have been more than one.

I glanced toward the upper floor. Coby was likely asleep, unaware of the potential trouble. The heavy pacing gait continued, and I knew it was a trap. I was being lured out.

Knowing this was just what they wanted, I crept silently to the patio door, threw open the blinds and flicked on the outside light. There was nobody there.

As silly as it was, I checked the lock anyway. They were toying with me. But why bother? Why not just kill me? Or try to.

I waited, knowing that my unwelcome visitor was going to make his move just any moment now. To act too quickly would be a mistake on my part. I expected an attack of some kind. I anticipated the moment when a vampire would crash inside and try to kill me

I was in no way prepared for the patio to burst into flames.

The heat and force of the sudden ignition threw me back. Seconds later the double glass patio doors shattered. Thousands of deadly shards landed where I'd just been standing. A few pieces cut through my pants, biting into my flesh.

Throwing myself through the kitchen into the front room, I reached the door in time to find it engulfed in flames. They'd covered the entire perimeter. Coby and I were trapped inside.

"Coby!" I screamed his name as I ran down a floor to the living room to check the north facing windows, finding a haze of orange.

I snatched Arys's journal from where it had fallen and shoved it into my bag with my phone and car keys. If I wanted to make it out, that would be all I could take with me.

Again, I screamed for Coby. I was frantically searching for a way out. It didn't take long for the fire to find its way inside. Smoke filled my lungs and burned my eyes as the shriek of the smoke detectors assaulted my ears.

I slung the strap of my bag across my chest and ran for the upper floor. I crashed into Coby on his way down. He reached out to steady me on the stairs as I lost my balance.

"We have to get out." I coughed as the smoke rolled in thicker. My eyes burned and watered, blurring my vision.

Flames crawled through the kitchen toward us, trapping us near the front door, which was already a mass of crackling fire. There was nowhere to go but up.

Without a word, Coby pulled me along behind him, back up the stairs to the master bedroom. He slammed the door shut behind us while I ran to open the window. I gulped the burst of outside air into my burning lungs. Before long, the fire would reach us; it was moving fast.

A cold spark deep in my core informed me that Arys was near. I would have wept with relief, but we still had a fire to escape. Coby joined me at the window, surveying our only option.

"We have to jump," he declared. "And, we have to do it before that reaches us."

I followed his gaze to the wall of flames eating their way through the main floor of the house and climbing toward us fast. The heat was already scorching us where we stood. We were high enough for the fall to be risky, but we didn't have another alternative.

I felt Arys's touch on my mind. His worry was as strong as his rage. I had no time to engage with him.

Not if I wanted to live.

Briefly, I considered the shift to wolf. We'd be stronger that way, but Coby was too new. I couldn't know how he would act as a wolf. Besides, the neighbors would have called 911 by now. We would have to jump, now.

"You first." Coby's hand was firm on my back, urging me to go for it.

I hesitated for just a moment. Casting one last look back around the bedroom, where I'd spent so many nights back when the wolf was new, I saw Raoul's house for the last time. It had never really felt like mine. Why should it now?

It was the home of many memories, both good and bad. Friendships had formed inside that house. Hearts had broken. Hell, I lost my virginity in the office downstairs. But, I had no time for nostalgia. My time in Raoul's house was finally done.

I took one last look into Coby's hazel eyes, wild with panic. He was new. He didn't belong here. For some reason, that made it easier to let go. I climbed up into the window frame, steadied myself the best I could, and jumped.

For that one heart stopping second I was airborne, all I felt was relief. Relief that my entanglement with Raoul was over. The house and everything it represented had reached its final end.

However, pain quickly followed as I hit the ground with a bone-jarring thud. I followed the momentum and rolled away from the house.

Coby was right behind me; an anguished cry escaped him as he landed. I took a moment to clear my head and assess my injuries. I seemed to be ok other than my aching lungs and a twisted ankle.

I was barely on my feet when Arys materialized from the darkness beyond the glow of the flames.

Blood spatters decorated his pale face. His eyes were pure wolf. He ran his hands over me, searching for wounds I didn't have. The fire was reflected in his eyes, flickering amid the terror in those icy blue depths.

"Are you alright? Did he hurt you?" Arys's voice was rough, laced with the growl of the wolf.

"Who?" I gasped, turning to check on Coby who stood stiffly, pain contorting his features. "Who did this?"

"Vampire." Arys confirmed. "I tangled with him out front, but the neighbors came out. I had to let him go."

Sirens shrieked in the distance. They would arrive in time to contain the fire to my property. They may even save the garage where Raoul's Jaguar was housed. However, they could do nothing to save his home.

With shaky hands, I pulled my keys from my purse. "Please, get my car out of here before it's ruined. Go before the cops get here."

Arys's gaze flicked from me to Coby. I couldn't answer his unspoken question. Not yet. So, I shook my head and pressed the keys into his hand.

"I can't leave you." He shook his head, his face masked with stubborn refusal.

"It will be sunrise soon. You don't have a choice." I kissed him quickly and then shoved him away. "Go."

He slipped away as stealthily as he'd appeared.

## Death Wish

The heat from the fire was unbearable. I caught Coby's hand in my own and led him away from the house. We staggered onto the front street in time to see the back end of my car disappear. Seconds later, two fire engines raced around the corner to battle the flames that ended one of my nightmares while birthing another.

Coby pulled his hand from mine but stayed close. He looked at me with eyes that were all wolf. *Shit.*

"You've got to hold it together," I said, keenly aware of the neighborhood watching us. "Force the wolf back down. You have to."

His energy was explosive, alive with fear and pain. "I don't know how."

I couldn't do a damn thing to help calm him; I was a wreck myself. "Try. You can't let them see you like this."

The fire engines stopped in front of the house. They were quickly joined by an ambulance and two police cars. A fireman shouted at us, asking if anyone else was inside. I shook my head no. No one was inside except the memory of the girl I used to be.

Paramedics added to the commotion. They headed toward us with shouted questions that I couldn't process.

All I could think about was the parts of me that would go down in ashes with that house.

The large framed photo of Shaz and me that Kylarai had given me for my birthday was gone. Along with it were my laptop and the cross necklace I'd received from Kale.

The laptop was of little concern. I was no idiot. The files I'd swiped from Veryl had been on the hard drive, but they were also safely stored online just in case of a disaster like this.

The loss of Kale's cross cut the deepest. It was old – old enough to have belonged to his mother. I should never have had it.

As the paramedics drew near, I glanced frantically at Coby. He stared back at me with human eyes. I was grateful for that small blessing.

The sudden commotion made my head spin. People were on us with questions and first aid gear before I could utter a word. It took a few tries for me to explain clearly that we were fine, just a little banged up. I did all I could to stall when three paramedics ushered us toward a waiting ambulance.

"We're fine, really. We don't need to go to the hospital." I tried, but I knew they weren't buying it.

A female medic with a gentle smile but serious eyes gripped my arm. "We have to take you in. Just to be safe. If you're fine, you'll be released right away. Your friend is looking pretty rough."

I cursed Falon beneath my breath. It was his fault Coby looked so battered and bruised. At least these people thought all of that came from the fall out of the bedroom window.

Two men waited to assist us along at her command. I had no choice but to go along with this hospital song and dance. The sooner we went, the sooner it would be over.

"Fine," I relented. "Let's get this over with. I have shit to do."

I couldn't pull my gaze away from the burning house as the ambulance took us from the scene. The flames had reached the top floor. They reached for the sky, hungrily devouring the dwelling.

I did my best to ignore the paramedics as they tended to us. I waved away an oxygen mask as it was thrust at me. I was sore from the fall, sad from the loss of my house and more than a little pissed off.

Three attempts on my life in just a few days. Three failed attempts. I had to find the source of this insanity and make them sorry they'd ever heard my name.

Coby received more attention than I did. He allowed them to tend to his wounds and fit him with an oxygen mask. I wanted to be left alone. I managed to get close enough to Coby to whisper the warning, "Don't let them take your blood."

We were fine. Our bodies were already healing whatever injuries we'd sustained. Even Coby's shiner would be gone in a matter of hours.

The sooner we could bail out of the hospital, the better.

Yet after the ambulance ride, we sat in the ER for two hours waiting for more than a passing nurse to ask how we were. There were several other people waiting, most of them in worse shape than we were. I clutched my bag, finding comfort in the few meager possessions I had inside.

Arys's touch on my mind was gentle, tentative. I could feel the worry he tried not to convey. I needed to be with him. The safety I felt only in his arms was the only thing that would get me through this nightmare.

"Let's go," I said after another thirty minutes had passed. "We're not close enough to death to be a priority. I doubt they'll even notice we're gone."

*Death Wish*

Coby said nothing, just nodded, ready to follow my lead. I headed for the door and never looked back. I had a vampire to kill. If one of us had to die, them or me, it sure as hell wasn't going to be me.

# *Chapter Ten*

I stepped outside, squinting against the sunlight and reached for my phone to call a cab. A flash of platinum hair caught my eye from across the parking lot. Shaz was moving fast, slipping between vehicles at a near run. For the first time since the fire started, I wanted to cry.

His jade eyes burned with worry. I fell into his arms, and he lifted me off my feet, hugging me close. He rubbed his cheek along mine, a gesture filled with affection. A few hot tears rolled down my face.

"Are you ok, Lex?" He spoke softly. "No, of course you're not. I can't believe this happened. I can't believe it's gone."

"Did you see it?" I buried my face in his neck, breathing deeply of his scent. God how I'd missed this, just being with him without feeling the wall that had been built between us.

"Yeah, I saw it. It's just rubble. Only the basement is left. They were still hosing it down when I drove by."

His scent was soothing, calming the wolf inside. His presence meant the world to me. But, I never would have expected any less from him.

Eventually I had to pull back enough to gesture to Coby and make the necessary introductions. After what had just occurred, the news that I had turned Coby in a fit of bloodlust really didn't sound so shocking. Shaz took it in stride like he did everything else. Offering a friendly hand to our new wolf, he played the Alpha role to perfection, even going so far as to invite Coby to stay at his place.

It went without saying that I would stay with Arys. It was the safest place for me to be. Having Coby with me was an unfair risk to him. He would be better off with Shaz.

## Death Wish

By the time we got to Arys's house, I was in dire need of a shower and sleep. I left Shaz to handle introducing Coby to Arys and headed for the bathroom. Through the living room and down the hall, their voices followed me as I went. Arys didn't sound nearly surprised enough to learn that I'd turned Coby.

I closed the bathroom door on their conversation and peeled off my soot-stained clothing. The heavy scent of smoke clung to my hair and skin. My face was smudged with soot. A brief glimpse in the mirror revealed heavy circles beneath my eyes. I looked pretty rough, and I wasn't feeling so hot either.

Arys's bathroom became a sanctuary. The oversized tub with jets was perfect for two. He had a bigger selection of shampoo and conditioner than any woman I'd ever known. I turned on the water and stepped into the hot shower spray with a sigh. The tears burst forth, rolling down my face to mix with the water that cascaded over me. I let them come. Alone, I had no need to put up a front. I was hurting. And, where the hurt ended, the craving for vengeance began.

After scrubbing myself clean, I stood there with the water as hot as I could stand it. I must have been in there for a long time because the door opened and Shaz slipped inside.

"Lex? Are you ok in here? You've been in here for almost an hour."

The hot water was beginning to cool anyway so I turned it off and stepped out to find Shaz holding a large fluffy towel. He wrapped it around me before pulling me tight against him. I would have sobbed if I hadn't just cried myself out. Instead, I closed my eyes and drank in the comforting sensation of being in his arms.

"I'm so glad you're here," I whispered, my throat raw and sore.

He smoothed a hand over my wet, tangled hair. "I'm just sorry I wasn't there with you when it happened."

For a long time, we just stood there holding one another. Shaz pulled back before I was ready to let go. He grabbed a hairbrush off the counter and began to pull it gently through my tangled mess of hair.

"Do you have any idea who set the fire?"

He broke the silence. Our eyes met briefly in the mirror. He looked so haunted.

"A vampire. Nobody I know personally from the sounds of it. He must be working for someone else." The simple act of Shaz running the brush through my hair was comforting. So much passed between us with that gesture. "I'm going to find out who it is."

"You should get some sleep. You look tired." Shaz finished with my hair and pressed a warm kiss to my forehead.

"Stay with me?" I was both hopeful and fearful.

"Of course. I'll take Coby to my apartment and get him settled in. Then I'll come right back. Promise."

"Be careful," I warned. "Just in case someone's watching those close to me. There are some scary-ass daywalkers out there."

He kissed me again, his lips soft on mine. I hated that it took a horrible event to chase us back into each other's arms. "But none of them compare to you. I'll be back before you know it."

He left me in Arys's room where I made a halfhearted attempt to find a change of clothing that belonged to me. I had to have a few items lying around. I gave up and settled on one of Arys's t-shirts and some silk boxer shorts.

I was sitting on the side of the bed, staring into space, when Arys entered the room. We looked at one another for a minute before he began to pace alongside the bed. I wanted him to hold me, to grab me tight the way Shaz had. I knew why he didn't. He was keeping up that front, the one I had abandoned in the shower when the tears had flowed.

"Thank God you're alright." His voice broke, the one sign that steady, cool Arys was shaken.

"I guess I'm stuck here with you for a while." I tried to lighten the mood. It was impossible. "Didn't I have some clothes here?"

"I think so. Probably in the laundry room."

"I guess I'll have to go shopping. I'll squeeze it into my schedule between finding the asshole that issued the hit and tearing their fucking head off." I growled, unable to contain the rage that threatened to overwhelm me now that I'd cried myself out.

"It's got to be someone you know. Someone who has a reason to want this. It could be just about anybody." Arys mused as he moved about the room, turning off the bright overhead light and replacing it with the warm glow of the bedside lamp.

I climbed in amongst the mountain of pillows and blankets. As tired as I was, I couldn't relax. "Should I be insulted by that? I'm going after them. Tonight. I'll torture a name out of somebody."

## Death Wish

"I'm coming with you." Arys slid into bed beside me still half dressed in silk lounge pants. He sat stiffly against the headboard, edgy and ready. I doubted he would sleep at all today.

When he finally touched me, he simply stroked a hand down the side of my face. A shuddery breath escaped me. In Arys's touch, I found a deeper connection than I could fully comprehend. The direct contact was rejuvenating. Our energy danced, two entities that must always entangle into one.

A warm tingle spread through me, bringing with it a burst of power that reinforced my growing need for retribution. I captured Arys's hand and slid my fingers between his. The power burned through us, low and steady. Strong.

"I'm not going to make the mistake of thinking this will be easy," I said, giving his hand a squeeze. The power surged in response. "But, I'd say it's about time we show this city what we can do."

Arys gazed deep into me with a deadly calm. A grim smile tugged at his lips. "I couldn't agree more."

Soon, Shaz returned. He stood in the doorway, watching me with an expression I couldn't read. Arys vacated the bed, going so far as to leave the room. He understood better than we did how much we needed this brief reprieve from the issues in our relationship. How much we needed just to be together.

"Come on." I patted the bed beside me and smiled. "Don't leave me all alone in this giant bed."

He hesitated for only a moment, pausing to strip off his socks, hoodie and t-shirt, before joining me. The wolf within reached out to him before the woman did. I found peace in the presence of his wolf. The wolves didn't give a damn about vampire nightclubs, human mistakes or hitmen. They knew only the call of nature, the lure of the moon and the beauty of the night. That's all our wolves wanted.

Shaz snuggled in close. Slipping his arms around my waist, he rested his head against mine. The silence was deafening. It was nice. If only my thoughts would quiet down.

I breathed deeply of his scent, savoring it. I focused on every detail from the warmth of his body against mine to the softness of his hair on the side of my face. We lay curled together the way we had so many times before.

But, things had changed. For one, we hadn't made love in almost a month. The house where our friendship had formed had just been destroyed. I couldn't help but wonder if that friendship was just one more part of us that we were bound to lose.

Arys was right. Shaz was part of me, the one who kept me grounded and sane. But, Shaz was also on his own journey, fighting his own battles.

"I miss you."

My words burst forth on a wave of emotion. I turned my head so I could press my lips to his temple. I lingered there, feeling his pulse beat. The bloodlust lay silent inside me. Whether subdued by Arys's presence or merely by the recent traumatic experience, I didn't know. I didn't care. I was just happy to be free of it.

"I love you, Lex," he whispered the words into my damp hair. "Please don't ever forget that."

"I know." My voice was a low murmur like his. I was afraid to speak too loud and destroy the hush that had fallen over us. "Arys is right, Shaz. About you and I. We would have been together if he had died a human death. I fell for you before I ever met him."

Shaz's breath came hot against my cheek, followed by his lips. "He was already a part of you. You just didn't know it yet."

I turned my face so his lips met mine. Could he feel the slight tremble as I kissed him with everything I had? "So were you. And, you just don't know it yet."

No further words were necessary. His grip on me tightened possessively. I pulled the blankets up around us like a marshmallow cocoon and settled in for a few hours of fitful sleep.

The scent of coffee roused me just before sunset. I flung out a hand, seeking Shaz but finding only the empty expanse of bed beside me. I sat up, immediately awake. If I had dreamed, I had no memory of it.

The sound of voices reached me. Shaz and Arys spoke in low tones. I swung my legs over the side of the bed, pausing to listen.

"The only reason I haven't killed her is because it would piss off Alexa," Arys said. "She should have already done it. She spared the bitch. For you."

"I know that," Shaz replied, his tone calm and even. "You think I'm proud of myself for that? It means nothing, me and Bianca. She's just… she's nobody."

So, the bitch had a name. Bianca. It brought a bitter taste to my mouth, and I hadn't even said it aloud.

"What she is, is convenient. Just like Kale is for Alexa. You each seek to hide your weakness from one another when you should be seeking strength in what you share." Arys was flippant, believing his words to be unarguable.

"You know, Arys, this belief you have that the three of us can live happily ever after… It's such bullshit." Shaz's tone was sour. I could easily imagine the matching expression he likely wore.

Arys didn't respond right away. I froze, perfectly still, waiting to hear him address Shaz's valid claim. That thought had crossed my mind as well. There was no room for three in forever. But, choosing between them was something I'd selfishly refused to do. As long as we were all keeping silent on the harsh reality beneath the deceptive surface of our three-way tie, I wasn't willing to be the one to speak first and break the illusion.

Now, Shaz had done it for me.

"She loves both of us," Arys spoke softly, sounding lost in thought. "She needs us. You more so than you're willing to believe."

"She can't be with both of us. Not in the long run. It will come down to you or me. Or possibly neither. Can you handle that? Do you even let yourself think about it? Or are you so lost in the fantasy of finally finding her that you're blinded to reality?"

I bit my lip, unable to accept the words spilling from Shaz. I was expecting Arys to react with anger. He didn't.

"Of course I'm not blind to reality," he said solemnly. "I've been aware for a long time that you may be the one she chooses. You offer her security. I offer her pain. But, it's too late for one or the other. She is joined to us both. If you can't accept it, you'll have to be the one to walk away."

Shaz didn't hesitate before he retorted, "Goddamn you're a conceited bastard. I know Lex. She may love us both, but she knows how fucked up this all is. That's why she runs to Kale. He's her escape. From us. From being caught in the middle of something bigger than she is."

"Settle down, pup. She has a purpose, and you are part of it. You both need to stop seeking with others what you should be finding with each other."

"It's not that simple."

"Why isn't it?"

That was my cue to announce my wakefulness. It didn't take much for those two to go from chatty to snarky and aggressive. Better to stop that before it started.

I made my way down the hall, making noise as I went. They both looked up expectantly as I entered the kitchen. Shaz held out a steaming cup of coffee, which I gratefully accepted.

"Did you sleep well?" He asked, gesturing to the soup and sandwiches on the table. What a lifesaver. He knew just as well as I did that Arys's house was no place to find decent food.

"Surprisingly well, all things considered." I sipped from the steaming cup, closing my eyes as I savored the caffeine making its way through my system. Such a simple joy.

I made short work of the coffee and sandwiches. I was ravenous and stuffed myself while ignoring the shocked look Arys wore.

"So," he began when I had finished. "What's the plan for tonight?"

I shrugged, glancing down at my lack of proper attire. "I don't have much of a plan. Find something decent to wear. Go pound some information out of any vampire I can get my hands on. Somebody has to know something."

"I washed your things. You don't have much here. It'll do for tonight." Arys pointed toward the laundry room off the front porch. "I'll come with you to hunt down some info. Shaz is going to The Wicked Kiss to see what he can find out there."

I knew what that meant: Shaz was going to see if Bianca knew anything. I had already considered and then dismissed her as a suspect. She wasn't behind the hit, but there was always a chance she knew who was. The thought of Shaz going right back to her didn't sit well with me.

"I see. Well," I fumbled for the right words, or even a good poker face, but came up short. "Ok then. I'm going to call Jez and Kale. Maybe they can help."

I busied myself with the few clothing items I was fortunate enough to have left at Arys's. Along with the sooty clothes I had left in the bathroom, I had a whole outfit. A pair of yoga pants, a black tank top and even a set of mismatched bra and panties would get me through until I could hit up a store for a few things.

Thankfully, I had started leaving a toothbrush at Arys's house ages ago. As for makeup, it was meager. The black eyeliner and lip balm in my bag didn't give me much to work with. Nothing was going to erase the stress from my features or hide the darkness in my eyes. I was hunting tonight. Pretty could wait.

When Shaz was leaving to check on Coby, I could barely bite my tongue. Knowing he was going to seek out Bianca tonight was driving my wolf into a frenzy. Or, maybe that was just me, the woman, the vampire and the wolf. Insanely jealous.

He left me with a tender kiss and the promise to touch base with me soon. I had several messages on my phone to return, including one from a panicked Kylarai. She was understandably upset about the fire. However, that made telling her about Coby go much smoother.

"I'm so glad you're ok." Her voice wavered. Her worry was heavy on the line. "What can I do to help?"

"Stay safe. And, maybe expect to have a few girls' nights in the near future."

"If you need me at your side, Lex, don't hesitate to say so. I'm your beta. I mean it."

I didn't want to bring danger to Kylarai's door by involving her. "I promise I will bring you into this if I need to. Until then, it's safer for you to avoid catching the wrong person's attention."

It was hard to put Ky's mind at ease. She was so used to looking out for us. She couldn't protect me anymore. Not from Raoul when his deceit came back to haunt me nor from the vampires that wanted me dead now.

Arys was waiting near the door when I finished on the phone. My car keys dangled from his index finger. On the surface, he was completely composed and in control. His dilated pupils and excited energy indicated otherwise.

"How are you feeling?" He asked casually. What he really wanted to know was, if the bloodlust was rising, could I handle it?

"I'm fine." I led the way out. A faint layer of soot covered the Charger. Otherwise, it looked fine. I went to the trunk, checking on the Dragon Claw; I kept the blade hidden in the spare tire compartment. Safe and sound.

The scent of smoke clung to the interior. It would need a good detail job. I opened the windows to let the night air circulate through. Arys was quiet in the passenger seat. I could feel him silently studying me.

I had to see Raoul's house. The car was in motion, heading for the golf course neighborhood before I could change my mind.

I didn't get out. I just sat there, staring at what was left. It was worse than I'd imagined.

Black. Everything was so black. The heavy aroma of fire lingered to taunt me. The walls were still standing but just barely. The entire front picture window had blown out, allowing us to see the mountain of rubble inside.

It would be an insurance nightmare. Just another thing to deal with. I couldn't hunt and kill that problem.

"Alexa?" Arys stroked a finger down the back of my hand. "We should go. We need to find out who is behind this."

My hands clenched the steering wheel. My gaze was riveted to the destruction. It was never really mine, but it had been my home. Or, the closest thing to it.

## Chapter Eleven

I met up with Jez at The Wicked Kiss. She was a vision with a mane of golden curls tumbling over her shoulders. She made jeans and runners look like runway wear with her leggy frame.

Jez was ready to play the willing victim if it meant getting answers. She was riled up and ready to kick some vampire ass. I was happy to leave her to it.

The place was vampire central; the people there knew things. Somebody was going to talk. While Jez and I asked a few questions, Arys kept watch from a distance.

What made it eerie was that I couldn't always feel his presence. I was certain I could force my way through whatever shielded him, yet that was just further evidence that we could use the power we shared against one another.

It was past midnight. I couldn't help but notice Kale's absence. I'd left a voicemail for him earlier, and he hadn't returned my call. So, where was he?

My thoughts strayed to the dreamwalker and a strange, sickly feeling settled in my gut. He was just a kid, a teenager with his whole life ahead of him. A life that would become dark and twisted if Shya had a hand in it. Whatever Kale was up to over there, he was either running late or something had happened.

I couldn't assume anything. I didn't know enough. It wouldn't hurt to take a drive by the dreamwalker's house, right? I wrestled with the decision, wondering how much longer I could wait before I just had to go.

I watched Jez move through the crowd with a seductive gait. It didn't take long for her to draw attention. The vamps would be falling all over themselves to get a taste of her pure Were blood.

I tried calling Kale again. This time the voicemail picked up immediately, indicating his phone was off. It was never off. I was afraid he was on another bender. Kale on a bender was dark, dangerous and more than a little terrifying.

Arys glided through the crowd, making his presence unmistakably known. Both humans and vampires in the vicinity paused to take note of him. It was impossible not to. Tall, dark and handsome, he exuded supremacy.

The atmosphere shifted as he moved through the club. Tension thrummed through the room. Apprehension and fear rolled off many of the vampires present. How many of them could I trust? The one that issued the hit could be here right now, and I wouldn't even know it.

"Have you seen Shaz yet?" Arys asked upon returning to me. He seemed pleased by the reaction of the crowd.

"No. He's probably in the back. With her." My tone dripped venom.

"He's here trying to help you. Cut the boy some slack."

"You did not just say that."

"I did. He doesn't love her. He loves you."

I did my best to glare at him. He held my gaze, crossed his arms over his chest and shrugged. I clearly missed a portion of the conversation they'd had while I slept. Still, it was reassuring that Arys was so sure. Guy code and all that junk.

"I need to take off for half an hour." Changing the subject entirely seemed like a good idea.

"Alone? Not gonna happen."

"I just need to do a quick drive by. I want to check on the dreamwalker. I think he might be in danger." It occurred to me that telling the total truth was not going to help my case.

"Hell no. The minute you rush off and do something reckless is when they will get the shot they need to take you out. Don't make it easy for them." Jaw clenched and brow furrowed, Arys was damn sexy when he was annoyed.

"It hasn't been easy for them so far." Arguing with Arys was useless. I knew that. Instinct told me to get my ass to the dreamwalker's house. I had to follow that.

"Alexa." That one word, my name on Arys's lips, was thick with warning.

I fought back the urge to snarl at him. I didn't have the right. He was rightfully concerned, and though I hated it when he tried to dominate me this way, I knew I'd feel the same if I were in his place.

"Come with me then," I relented, "but I have to go."

I fought a battle with myself the entire way there. I couldn't shake the bad feeling that Kale's absence instilled in me. Perhaps it was arrogant of me to think I knew Shya had less than savory plans for the kid. It sounded hard enough to be a dreamwalker. He deserved to make his own choices.

It was too easy to get sucked into this world. I couldn't say I would have chosen it for myself. Then again, it had always been meant for me. I didn't know what to think anymore.

I'd half expected to find Kale's car outside. There was no sign he had been here.

The house was dark. That was the first thing I noticed. The light from the TV was absent, giving the place a vacant touch. The air was rife with negative energy. It hummed, thick and menacing. I had to go in. Something had gone on here.

Arys didn't protest when I told him to wait in the car. It allowed him to watch the house while I went inside.

Slowly, I swung the car door open. It was late. Lights were off in most of the neighboring houses yet none of them felt tainted by the inky swell of residual energy the way the dreamwalker's house did.

I reached out metaphysically, feeling out my surroundings. By doing so, something else could easily be feeling me as well. I couldn't both reach out and shield myself. It was a chance I had to take.

The lingering energy burned when I openly let it in. It was a blazing hot sensation that scorched. Shya. Faded and slowly dissipating, his energy was still strong enough to hurt. Goosebumps rose up all over my body and pressure began to build in my head. I couldn't let his power flow freely through me. I just couldn't take it. I had to block it out. I shielded hard, unable to shake the not so subtle reminder of just how powerful the demon was.

The house itself appeared normal, except for the side door, which stood slightly ajar. My wolf was leery. I drew closer, and the scent of blood reached me. I was both horrified and intrigued.

I sensed nobody inside. Nobody living anyway. I was envisioning the absolute worst when I carefully pushed through the open doorway. My keen eyes quickly adjusted to the darkness.

There was blood everywhere. I choked on the scent, struggling not to breathe more than absolutely necessary. It was fresh and tantalizing, taunting my bloodlust. It was only apprehension that kept the hunger at bay.

I stood frozen near the doorway. I could feel the echo of death all around me. The last thing I wanted to do was touch or upset anything, but I wanted to take a quick look around. Shya had done this. Why kill the kid's entire family? And, where were the bodies?

I crossed through the kitchen to the back hall where I could go either upstairs or into the living room at the front of the house. I did neither, pausing instead to study the framed photographs hanging in the hall.

The dreamwalker was an only child from what I could tell. With a shy smile and short, trendy, dirty blonde hair, he looked like any other teenage boy. Normal. Nobody was normal though. Not really. He should have been focused on girls, school and the future. Instead, he was plagued by a gift that doubled as a curse. It had stolen everything from him. Would he trade it all if he could? Would I?

I had never laid eyes on this kid. I didn't even know his name. Still, I felt we were kindred. Born human but never really meant to stay that way. Nobody had tried to save me. I didn't think I could save this kid, but I felt obligated to try.

"I knew you were stupid, but you are reaching a whole new level of idiocy." Falon's voice rang out, shattering the dead silence. A moment later, he materialized on the staircase.

A little shriek escaped me, and I muffled it with a hand. "You asshole! You do that again, and you're going to get a face full of claws."

Falon's face was a mask of judgment. Though he glared at me with haughty self-righteousness, satisfaction glimmered in his pale eyes. "You're not supposed to be here."

"What happened?" I returned Falon's glare tenfold. The angel was unpredictable and creepy, but he didn't scare me the way Shya did. The way I saw it, Falon was the last person capable of judgment. He was the ultimate fence rider, and his opinion meant nothing.

"You need to leave, Alexa. I have things to do here. Try not to drop any tainted DNA on your way out." He waved his hands at me as if shooing a bug.

I stood my ground, scowling back at him with all the venom I could muster. "I want to know what happened to the dreamwalker. And, where is Kale?" I was adamant, refusing to be intimidated when Falon's massive wings flared out as wide as the staircase would allow.

"You'll have to ask Shya. I'm sure he'll have questions for you as well. For instance, why you're here sticking your nose in business that is none of yours."

With my hands on my hips, I scowled at Falon as if he were something I'd found stuck to the bottom of my shoe. "What do you do exactly, Falon? From where I'm standing it looks like you're the help."

Fury flashed through his eyes, and I smiled. He descended the rest of the steps in near silence. The grace of his gait gave the illusion that his feet never touched the floor. He stepped close, in my personal space without touching me, and towered over my small frame, forcing me to look up at him.

"Better watch your mouth, wolf. Don't assume to know a damn thing about me." Falon spoke low and soft. The underlying menace in his tone was vague, but it was there. "Did you think these situations just disappeared on their own? I'm capable of things you can't even begin to dream of. You'd be wise to remember that."

"You may have never been human, but you're not better than me." I shot back, uneasy by his close proximity but unwilling to show it. "The fact that you're here right now proves that. You're fallen. I think that makes you just as tainted as the rest of us."

He grinned, flashing even white teeth. There was no humor in his silver gaze. "Oh you stupid little twit, you have no idea."

Fear and rage gripped me simultaneously. A warning growl was my response. I was perfectly aware that demons and the like often looked down on vampires and werewolves. They had never been human, and those of us who had weren't deemed worthy of respect. We walked in both worlds, human and other. They didn't. I couldn't help but feel they weren't giving us the credit we deserved.

Before I could spit a nasty retort at Falon, the sound of sirens destroyed the moment. Panic slapped me breathless, and I looked frantically to the open side door.

Falon made a frustrated noise but otherwise had little reaction. With a snap of his fingers, time stopped. It literally stood still. The sirens froze, a strange high-pitched sound off in the distance that didn't rise or fall but stayed one long, continuous ear-piercing note. The clock on the wall fell silent. I hadn't noticed its ticking until it was gone.

"I can't do this for long without dire consequences. Get out of here." Falon moved fast, sweeping past me to the living room where he stared out the front window. "I can buy you thirty seconds or so. Go, now!"

I was running before he finished. Superhuman speed carried me through the yard and across the street to my car. The atmosphere felt thick and resistant, as if I ran through water. Not so much as a leaf moved. It was as if the world had really stopped. Falon's power may have been limited, but it was immense.

It was a time warp. One moment the world was still, and the next I was speeding through traffic with Arys throwing question after question at me.

My hands shook on the steering wheel. I had to pause to catch my breath several times as I filled Arys in. He was quiet, listening intently as I spoke. His grave silence conveyed his unease.

I tried calling Kale again. Still no answer. "Dammit, Kale! Where the hell are you?" I growled to his voicemail. "You better have a damn good explanation for what I just saw."

"You should leave it alone, Alexa." A flash of angry energy accompanied Arys's warning. I felt it inside, a painful slap that melted away to a pleasurable sting.

I shook my head, refusing to argue with him on this one. "Something is going on, and I want to know what it is."

By the time we returned to The Wicked Kiss, I had called Kale six more times to no avail and heard as many snarky remarks from Arys in regards to my obsessive behavior. I parked in front of the main doors, taking no chances on getting jumped in the parking lot. Arys shadowed my every move between the car and the club.

"Wherever Sinclair is, he can take care of himself. You have more important things to do right now. Like stay alive." With a shake of his dark head, Arys steered me inside with a hand on my waist. "You have this tendency to taunt death, my love. It's frustrating."

"I do no such thing," I protested, enjoying the spark that jumped between us. "What you see as reckless behavior is me following my instinct. Give me some credit for not being dead yet."

"Maybe just a little."

I smacked him playfully, choosing to keep the conversation light. An argument about Kale was not on my agenda but finding him was. Sooner rather than later. I would give both Kale and Arys the benefit of the doubt for now. A vampire as old as Kale didn't need me to babysit him.

The crowd had thinned considerably since we'd left. I saw a lot of regulars littered about, both human and vampire. One lone woman occupied the dance floor. With her head thrown back, long brown locks flowing, she spun in slow, lazy circles. High as a kite.

People got off on a vampire bite in different ways. The pain and the rush of being bitten, screwed or both by a vampire was enough for most people. However, the real euphoria came from the bite of a vampire with power. They could manipulate the experience on a metaphysical scale as well as physical. It was bliss. Deadly, dangerous bliss.

Two female vampires and the array of human men falling all over them had claimed the cozy little lounge area tucked in beside the bar. Bodies littered a chaise lounge and love seat. I had to do a double take to make sure they weren't pushing the boundaries. This part of the club was public. Rules were rules.

A few jock guys sat around a table near the door loudly arguing sports. At first glance, they seemed to be in the wrong bar. Then I saw the bite one of them was trying unsuccessfully to hide with the collar of his jacket.

The rest of the crowd was made up of people mingling, drinks in hand, seeking to be or to have a playmate that likes to bleed. I had looked down on them once. Sometimes, I still did. I had no right; I was just like them. Power and blood were my drugs of choice, too. I just didn't have the shameless courage to flaunt it openly.

Shaz sat alone at the bar, nursing a beer, watching us make our way toward him. Jez was nowhere in sight. That left the back rooms. Would she go so far as to take a vampire back to a private room to get some answers for me? That couldn't possibly end well.

"Something is definitely up," Shaz greeted me with a grim smile. "I didn't get much, just that someone has the vampires in this city riled up. They're afraid of you. But, they're afraid of the one that wants you dead, too. After what you did to Bianca, I think they're feeling trapped."

Her name on his lips was like nails on a chalkboard. I wanted to cover my ears and scream. Instead, I pondered what he'd just said.

"So they're being forced to choose which one of us they'd rather live with. Me or the one who wants me dead. Rock and a hard place. I bet I made that choice really easy for them that night."

Several vampires had been present the night I attacked Bianca. They had felt what I'd done to her. That wasn't going to win me any votes.

Arys nodded knowingly. "They should be afraid of you, Alexa. But, they know the benefits of having an ally in someone like you. You've never done a thing to any one of them without reason."

"No," I trailed off, lost in thought. "I have been a known hunter of vampires. I have a bond with the most powerful vampire in the city. There is no reason for them to trust me."

My mind raced as I tried to put it together. I knew the one who was after me. I was sure of it. I thought back to a few months ago when a vampire had tried to stake me here in the club. What drove him to it was the belief that I would have power over him, something Shya had confirmed. I felt like I was missing a piece of the puzzle. So close.

"Let's go through potential suspects." Shaz held up a hand, ready to tick each one off on a finger.

Zoey? Only a year ago she had gone on a murderous rampage, seeking revenge on her father. Raoul's abandonment had left her crazed and broken. Murdering his lovers, she had put me on her list. The night it all went down, the night Raoul died, Zoey made herself my enemy. I spared her life only because of the twisted teenage love for her father that I still held buried deep inside. After calling an informal truce with her, she'd killed an innocent man, proving she couldn't be trusted. Still, I was certain she wasn't involved in this.

No, it had to be a vampire. I ran through a small list in my head, dismissing each one. What was I missing?

"Then perhaps we should start with your uh, friend, pup," Arys chimed in with a smirk that added sting to his words. "I'd think if anyone has a good reason to want Alexa dead, it's her."

Shaz locked his fierce green gaze on the brazen vampire. "It's not her. And if it was, I would kill her myself."

"Are you sure about that? It's not always easy to kill someone once you've gotten close to them. In fact, it can put you in an awfully bad position. Think you're ready for that?" Arys leaned on the bar, just close enough to Shaz to taunt him.

Tension flavored the atmosphere with something bitter and hot. Shaz wouldn't take his eyes from Arys. The two of them stared into each other, sharing a wordless exchange that I recognized from past conflicts. This wasn't the right time for them to go at each other.

"I get it, Arys," Shaz snarled. "We've already gone over this. I said I would deal with it. Now back off."

I cut Arys off before he could open his mouth again. Holding up a hand between them, I glowered. "This isn't helping. Can we stay on track? Or, should I just bash your skulls together and get it over with?"

"I think I'll pass on the skull bashing." Shaz turned a smile on me, and I melted just a little.

Before I could voice my own speculation, Jez appeared in the doorway separating the back hall from the club. Her golden curls were in disarray. With wide green leopard eyes and blood spatters from head to toe, she seemed to have stepped straight out of a horror movie.

The sight of her shocked me. I scanned her for injuries, unable to tell how much, if any, of the blood was hers. "What the hell happened to you?"

She glided towards us with feline grace. Her bright red lips twisted into a crazed smile. "So um, is it bad if I accidentally killed him?"

Arys laughed, a low, devious sound. I gaped at Jez, not sure what to make of the situation.

"Who?" That seemed like a good place to start.

"You know, I never thought to get his name." She shrugged and examined her bloody nails. "I got a little out of him before he got grabby. Once his hand landed on my ass without an invite, it was all over."

I was flustered but encouraged. "You got something out of him?"

Jez busied herself smoothing down her tousled locks. Now that playtime was over, the finicky cat came out to regain its composure. "Yep. It's a woman. He let it slip. He said that she put the hit out a week ago. A lot of vamps aren't biting. They don't want to get involved."

Now that was interesting and not at all what I'd expected. Whether it was fear, respect or indifference keeping the majority from getting involved I didn't care. I was happy to hear it.

"A woman. So, it could be Bianca." Arys tilted his head thoughtfully and gave me a pointed look.

"It's not!" The heat of Shaz's anger was sudden and scorching. It seemed to slap and tickle all at the same time. Potent with that heady werewolf energy, I couldn't help but react to it.

I watched Arys's gaze fall to the pulse beating steadily in Shaz's throat and realized I was reacting to his bloodlust. It rolled through me but didn't grab hold of my weak will. Arys may have been easing my burden, but I didn't like what he was thinking.

"I don't think it's her," I interjected. I succeeded in drawing Arys's attention my way. I shot him a warning look. "Seduction seems to be her thing. Not murder."

Shaz flinched at my words. His beer bottle suddenly dominated his interest. I knew he hated himself for getting involved with her. I wasn't going to add to that.

"No way. Definitely not her," Jez joined in with a laugh. "Not after the way you dropped her."

"What about you, Arys?" I couldn't help but speculate. "Are you sure one of your many ex-lovers isn't on some kind of revenge kick? It's happened before. And, trust me, that's getting old."

Arys tried to hide a smile but failed. "I can't help the effect I have. I'm like a drug, you know. I can't be held responsible for those who can't handle the high."

If Shaz didn't fit that description, it would have been funny. I ran through every female vampire I knew, eliminating them as I went, until I got to one that I had been quick to dismiss. Too quick perhaps.

I met Jez's gaze across the table, and we shared a thought. Maybe it should have been obvious. I didn't want to believe it.

Simultaneously we said, "Lilah."

## Chapter Twelve

I waited for some semblance of shock to hit me. It didn't. All I felt was the certainty that my hunch was right. I searched for a reason to rule her out, anything to discredit what my instinct insisted was the ugly truth.

Lilah had never openly threatened me or indicated in any way she saw me as a problem. In fact, she'd saved my ass in the past and even imparted a friendly warning about Shya. But, we had never been more than acquaintances. I knew very little about her other than the fact that she was a demon cursed into the corporeal form of a vampire. She still had power over other demons, though to what extent, I didn't know. So why me?

"What the hell did you ever do to her?" Jez gave voice to my thoughts. "You killed Veryl because he was blackmailing her. She should be one of your biggest fans."

"From what I know of Lilah, she isn't anybody's biggest fan," I mused. "Maybe she thinks I know too much about her. Or, maybe there's something in the files I swiped from Veryl that she doesn't want me to see."

We could speculate until we were blue in the face, but it wouldn't do a damn bit of good. No matter what the details, there could only ever be one reason she would want to get rid of me or anybody else.

"Power," Arys announced. "It's always about power. Especially with demons."

"Why wouldn't she just kill Alexa herself?" Shaz asked, holding up a hand to signal the nearest waitress for another beer. "Why send vampires that haven't been able to do the job?"

Nobody had an answer for that. I felt a desperate need to eliminate Lilah as a suspect. There was only one way to do that.

"I have to see her." I reached for my keys, an idea forming fast. "Chances of her being at the office are slim, but if she's not there, I may be able to find something there that I can use in a locator spell. Plus, she was asking me the other day about a missing item from Veryl's office. I wouldn't mind a chance to snoop around."

"I'm coming with you." There was a warning in Arys's eyes. He wasn't going to like this.

"You can't. If I go in there with you and she's there, it will be instantly suspicious. She may not even try anything if I'm alone. Not if she doesn't want me to know she's the one behind this."

"I can go in with you, Alexa," Jez volunteered almost gleefully. "You shouldn't go alone. Just in case."

Shaz shook his head and shoved his empty beer bottle aside. "Don't do it, Lex. Wait it out. Gather more information first. You can't just walk up to her and expect to chat it out."

"I can't just sit around waiting for the next attempt on my life either." I looked to Arys, expecting him to side with Shaz. To my surprise, he appeared to be contemplating it.

"Alright, go." It looked painful for Arys to spit the words out. "But, Jez goes with you. And, Shaz and I won't be far away. I want an open link to you the entire time."

I had expected a bigger fight from him. I was pleasantly surprised and relieved. Now that I understood more about our twin flame connection, I was able to understand our relationship in a new way. Our constant conflicts were often about the struggle for control. We both wanted it. We had the same need for it, and now I knew why. If what they say is true about the twins always being in conflict, then I guess we'd better get used to it.

Arys wasn't a fan of my tendency to rush into something. He wasn't so different though. If I didn't determine whether or not Lilah was the one behind the hit, it would eat at me until I did. Coming to her was something she wouldn't expect from me.

By the time Jez and I stood outside the office, I was buzzing with excitement. My goal was to come away from this confirming that it either was or was not Lilah. Walking around with a target on my back was stressful. The sooner I could put an end to it, the better.

Arys was half a block away with a less than enthusiastic Shaz. My pulse quickened as I pulled my power close, holding it ready. With Arys so close and the mental link between us wide open, the power flowed strong and plentiful. I didn't expect to find Lilah here, but I planned to be ready for anything.

I'd gotten pretty good at cloaking in recent months, but I had yet to cloak the presence and energy of another person along with me. Still, I was confident I could cloak Jez, too, with Arys's power blasting through me.

I held out a hand to Jez. "I hope this works. If anyone is inside, we can't have them sensing us."

Jez placed her hand in mine. Excited energy trickled from her to send a strange tickle up my arm. "I always thought Lilah was pretty sketchy, too detached, and her lack of emotion is scary."

"She's a demon. It just gets scarier from there. Ready?" I waited for her nod before pushing my energy out around us in a circle, cloaking us with a keenly focused thought. Jez gave a little gasp as my power encased her.

The main door to the office was locked, nothing the key wouldn't open. I hesitated, feeling for the heavy demon magic I'd seen Lilah surround the place in before. Nothing. Not hitting a demon barrier was a good thing, but it also meant the chances of her being inside were slim. I couldn't probe for her energy unless I dropped my circle and opened my energy up to her as well. Not happening.

An advantage to being a predatory animal was our innate ability to move silently. Hand in hand, we eased the door open just enough to slip through. My eyes easily adjusted to the dark. There wasn't a single light on inside, but the thin rays of light that crept through the windows kept it from being absolute black. Slow and cautious, we rounded the corner from the entryway into the hall.

Noise drifted toward us. It took me a moment to realize it was the sound of two people in the throes of passion. *Um, shit.* I glanced at Jez with my eyebrows raised, and she shrugged, urging me on.

The sound was coming from Veryl's office, or what had once been his office. The door was swung shut but not latched tight. About six inches of space allowed us a view into the room. My jaw dropped.

Lilah was sprawled on Veryl's fancy old desk. Her copper colored hair was in disarray and her head thrown back in pleasure. Standing between her legs, groaning with each thrust, was Falon.

I sure as hell hadn't expected this. I could feel Arys's questioning touch on my mind, wanting to know what was going on. I let him see what I was seeing, and his grim amusement came in response. Jez's expression revealed that she, too, found it funny. If she laughed and gave us away, we were screwed.

Too late. My power could hide me from a vampire, but it couldn't fool an angel, even a fallen one. Falon turned his head, finding us in his line of sight. Our eyes met, and my stomach dropped.

I pushed Jez backwards, toward the door. All we could do now was attempt to leave as if we'd stumbled upon them by accident, which in a way we had. That would have been easier if I hadn't cloaked our presence.

Falon never let us reach the door. The air rippled, and he was just there, his large silver wings iridescent and shimmering. How he'd managed to make himself decent so quickly was beyond me. His wingspan allowed him to easily and effectively block our exit. With arms crossed over his chest, he scowled at us.

"What the hell are you doing here?"

"I could ask you the same thing," I shot back. "But, I don't need to. I saw what you were doing."

Jez piped up, indignant. "I came to get something from my office. Got a problem with that?"

With a huff, she spun on her heel and marched down the hall to her office, following through with the bluff. I stood there staring at Falon, finding guilt in his pale eyes. I was willing to bet Shya didn't know his sidekick was sleeping with Lilah. From what I could tell, Falon wasn't happy with me discovering it.

"You didn't see anything," Falon warned, his tone low with menace.

I couldn't resist the urge to taunt him. "Oh, didn't I?"

I was keenly aware of Lilah's approach. I stepped back so I could keep both her and Falon in my sights. I didn't trust either of them.

She was as unkempt as I'd ever seen her. Her clothing had been hastily put together, and she wrestled her messy hair into a ponytail. Her flame colored gaze landed on me, and I could see her searching for the right words to explain away what we'd interrupted.

"Alexa, I'm sorry you walked in on that. Falon and I should know better than to allow such an indiscretion to take place. I'm sure you understand why this should be kept private." Lilah did a great job meeting my eyes. For a woman that was just caught with her pants down, she was smooth.

I squelched the urge to laugh bitterly. I wasn't keeping any secrets for her. "Honestly, I don't give a crap who you fuck. But, when you send people to kill me, that's when what you do becomes my business."

I was disappointed by her lack of surprise. Lilah nodded as if she'd expected me to know. Her neutral expression didn't change though her eyes darkened.

"You've done a good job of staying alive," she said, emotionless. It wasn't a compliment. "For the record, it's nothing personal."

Her lack of emotion was getting under my skin. I wanted her to be mad or aggressive. Anything that indicated she had a reason to want me dead. This calm demeanor of hers was pissing me off.

"It's personal now." I risked a glance at Falon who wore a mask of confusion. So, he wasn't in on her little plan to off me. Or, was he just a great actor? "I killed Veryl for you. You owe me answers. Why?"

Jez returned quickly, unwilling to leave me alone with the demon. I was grateful for her presence. She stayed back where she could observe the entire situation. Her pupils were large in response to the growing excitement. I could feel it, too, crawling over me like ants on my skin.

Lilah pursed her lips, her gaze unwavering. "You killed Veryl because you wanted to. I just gave you the reason you sought to justify it to yourself. I respect you, Alexa. I may even like you a little bit. But, you're a threat to me now."

Now? When had I become a threat to Lilah?

'Right around the time you gained power over vampires.' Arys's voice echoed in my thoughts. It startled me. I'd forgotten he was there.

I kept my attention on Lilah, acknowledging Arys with a thought but answering her.

"Then why the hell won't you try to take me out yourself instead of having others do it for you?" I was seething. Knowing I had placed a level of trust in her over the years made me feel like a fool. She had saved my ass in the past just to turn on me now. I would never understand demons.

"It's been interesting to see how you pull off staying alive each time. You're a worthy opponent." She dodged my question, answering it by doing so. Something was stopping her from killing me herself. Or, more likely, someone.

I found it interesting that Falon was so quiet. It wasn't like him to refrain from tossing in his opinion. His silence spoke loud and clear, telling me that his loyalties lie with Shya first and foremost, regardless of who he took as a lover. Whatever Lilah's issue with me was, Shya wasn't part of it.

The wolf rose up inside me to stare out at the demon. I was quaking inside, my power running hot and ready to be unleashed in a torrent. "You have no idea what an opponent I can be."

We stared into one another, each seeking out an unseen weakness in the other, anything to gain the edge without making a move. I was ready for her, braced for the heavy slap of demon tainted vampire power, but it never came. She wouldn't do it.

With a rustle of feathers, Falon disappeared, vacating before things got ugly. This way he could honestly tell Shya that he wasn't involved. I was tense, hoping Lilah would do something, anything to end this now.

"Let's just get this over with," I suggested, gesturing for her to take a shot at me. "You want me dead. Well, I'm standing right in front of you."

Lilah smiled, a small wistful tug of her lips that was gone as quickly as it had come. "I may be many things, but a fool isn't one of them. As long as Shya wants you alive, I can't be the one to kill you. Which just makes this that much more difficult."

"Are you kidding me?" I snapped. "Demon politics have you sending idiot vampires after me when we could just finish this here and now?"

She shrugged. So cold and unfeeling. She was likely the only vampire in existence that had never been human.

"I underestimated you. I won't make that mistake again. Like I said, this isn't personal. I have an agenda, and I refuse to allow you or Shya to interfere with that."

I had never wanted to see Shya more than I did right then. My hand strayed to the dagger at my hip, the one he had given me. It would kill a vampire with barest nick of the blade. It would work on Lilah.

She may not be willing to throw a shot, but that didn't mean I couldn't take one.

Lilah's gaze flicked to the Dragon Claw. "I may not have authority to kill you outright, but I can and will defend myself."

She wanted me to make the first move. That's all it would take to bypass whatever was keeping her from doing it.

I advanced on her, the Dragon Claw humming with power in my grasp. "Good to know."

Arys's warning echoed in my thoughts. 'Don't do it, Alexa. It's never so simple with demons. She'll lead you into a trap. Get out of there.'

'If I don't deal with this now, her hitmen will keep coming.'

'You can't simply act with someone like her. You must plan.'

Lilah watched me expectantly, an eager gleam in her eyes. All I had to do was make a move, the wrong one, and she would kill me. It was her loophole. If I brought it on myself, she was home free. As badly as I wanted to plunge my dagger into her chest, I knew it would be a mistake.

I held myself back despite the wolf's insistence that I eliminate the threat. As long as she couldn't initiate a fight, we were at a stalemate. There was no threat.

So, rather than attack Lilah, I decided to feel her out. Reaching out metaphysically, I touched her power, sensing the depths of it. It was rude and invasive but in no way an attack.

Right away, I felt the cloying hand of demon power clinging to her like a second skin. It felt murky and dark, absolute black. However, it was missing the deep abyss-like draw that Shya's power possessed. Lilah's was limited, confined by the barrier of her curse. I could feel it there, an invisible force binding her powers, and beneath it was the cool but familiar sensation of vampire.

Lilah could be a threat. No doubt about it, she had the ability to be lethal. I'd seen her drop a demon with just a command, but I wasn't a demon. I was a mortal and a threat. I had the advantage. I just had to find a way to keep it.

She was far too calm and casual for this situation. I couldn't handle her demeanor. She wanted me dead, and dammit, that was personal. I wanted her to be mad, to show hatred or spit a venomous word my way. The fact that she didn't find me worthy of any passion or emotion stirred a fire deep inside me. I wanted to destroy her.

A bored expression marred her face. She crossed her arms and gave me a look like one might give an annoying, yappy little dog. "Is that it? No showdown after all? Pity."

I stepped back toward the door. Arys was right. I needed time to think this over. Acting rashly would get me killed.

'Stop the presses! Alexa O'Brien has just admitted to herself that her lover is right about something. That's newsworthy.' Arys's self-assured chuckle filled my thoughts.

I ignored him, unwilling to acknowledge his gloating. I pulled the door open, half expecting to find Falon on the other side. He was long gone.

"Oh, we'll have our showdown," I said, waiting for Jez to exit the building first. I glanced back at Lilah. "If you're as big a bad ass as everyone thinks you are, you'll stop with the hits and take me on yourself. Either way, I'm coming back for you."

Jez hovered just outside, waiting anxiously for me to join her. I could feel Arys's obvious relief, but I didn't see how putting off the inevitable was a good thing. I wanted it over.

I was about to let the door slam shut when Lilah's next words stopped me in my tracks. For the first time since I arrived, her tone changed.

"Family is a funny thing, isn't it, Alexa? One minute they're dead, and then low and behold... alive after all."

Slowly, I turned to face her. I'd never fought so hard to keep my feelings from showing in my eyes. With a carefully constructed blank look, I pinned her with a dead stare.

"Your point?"

"It would be a shame if something happened to your sweet little sister. You've barely had time to catch up." She openly taunted me, knowing like every damn demon somehow knows, the right trigger.

I snapped. Human thought was gone. Rationale deserted me. The wolf burst forth in a territorial explosion of fangs and claws. Jez grabbed for me, but she was too late.

I lunged, hitting Lilah square on in the chest. We went down, sprawling with me on top of her. I succeeded in wrapping my hands around her throat. Before I could slam her head against the floor, she planted a foot on my stomach and sent me flying. I flipped over her, landing flat on my back in the hallway.

It crushed the breath from me, but I barely noticed. I was on my feet, lashing out with a blast of power before I could stop myself. A burst of swirling blue and gold exploded against Lilah. In the same moment, I was airborne, knocked off my feet by Arys.

He stood between the two of us, projecting an energy barrier meant to keep us apart. I already knew that with enough concentration I could break it. Could Lilah?

With a cold, calculating stare she scanned each one of us in turn. I half expected her to take a shot at Arys, but she was wary of him. Still maintaining her calm and cool exterior, Lilah spun on her heel and stalked out.

She paused at the door and set her deep orange gaze on me. Regret shone in her eyes. "I really didn't want it to have to be this way."

I watched her go, feeling a swell of mixed emotion rise within me. Not only did I have to stay two steps ahead of Lilah, now I also had to keep her from getting to Juliet. Dammit. Why couldn't it have been someone else? Why Lilah?

What made it worse was that I really believed her. It wasn't personal. There was something about Arys and I that threatened her. Why exactly, I didn't know. I intended to find out.

## Chapter Thirteen

The early morning sun was blindingly bright. Even with sunglasses, it was too much for my sensitive eyes. I squinted behind my shades, listening as a fireman explained the extent of the damage to my house.

The frame was still standing. It was strong enough for me to go inside and look around, but otherwise, there wasn't much left to salvage. Oh well. At least I still had the property.

I nodded to indicate that I was ready to enter what was left of my home. The fireman led the way, and I followed with my hopes up. I didn't expect much to have survived the fire, but I was keeping my fingers crossed on a few items.

The stench of smoke was thick. My lungs grew heavy as I tried to take shallow breaths. Everything was covered in a thick layer of soot. Every single surface was layered in black.

I walked through the house feeling numb. Numb was good. I had reached my emotional capacity for the week.

Everything was ruined. The television was a melted mass of crap along with every other electronic and appliance on the main floor. The framed picture of Shaz and me was shattered on the floor, burnt to oblivion. Logically, I knew the photo could be reprinted. Still, I couldn't help but feel like it was a bad omen.

My bedroom was what I wanted to see the most. I hurried down the stairs as fast as I could safely go. My clothes were soot-stained garbage. I didn't care about that. What I really needed to see was the locked box I kept in the bottom drawer of my dresser. I yanked the charred drawer open, fearful the box would be ruined or missing.

It was right where I'd left it. I easily found the key on the ring with my car keys. I could have wept with relief when I saw everything inside it safe and untouched.

I ran my fingers over the smooth surface of Kale's cross. I was ecstatic to see it was ok. Alongside it was the small velvet bag that contained an amulet from Lena. Through the bag, I could feel it, a little piece of stone that vibrated with deep earth energy, calling to my wolf.

I relocked the box and shoved it into my shoulder bag. Other than the picture of Shaz and me, these two things meant the most. Everything else could be replaced.

A brief look in the garage revealed a Jaguar that stunk to high heaven of smoke. A detail job might not be enough. Raoul's car spent a lot of time in the garage; I didn't drive it much. It had still smelled like him. His scent had clung to the interior, sealed inside because the doors so rarely opened. I hated that I liked it. That scent was gone now, burnt away with the rest of what had once belonged to Raoul.

A conversation with the fireman revealed that they couldn't determine where or how the fire had started. I knew, of course. Supernatural fire wasn't so easy to trace. He gave me some information about what my options would likely be in this situation. Rebuild the house starting with the salvageable framework still standing or tear it down and sell the property. I needed some time to think about it.

\* \* \* \*

A few days had passed since the fire. I had been lying low at Arys's house, pondering possible outcomes of both the Lilah predicament and the FPA investigation. If the FPA discovered Kale and I had killed Abigail Irving, what was I going to do about it?

There was also the matter of Kale's disappearance. I had yet to hear from him. He had been known to lock himself away with random women at The Wicked Kiss for days at a time, but this was different. I could feel it.

After leaving the remains of my house, I ventured out on a two-hour trip to the store. I was exhausted and looked forward to the escape I would find in sleep, but I needed to start reorganizing my life. New underwear was a good place to start.

Arys had been faced with the reminder that, though I was nocturnal, I was still a daywalker. He'd paced the house like a cat in a cage, spouting several reasons why I shouldn't go out alone even though the sun was up. Vampires and demons were trapped as long as the sun was in the sky. Lilah posed no threat.

I returned to Arys's house in the early afternoon. Dropping my bags in the kitchen, I abandoned them and headed for the bedroom. It wasn't going to be easy to stay with him. I adored every moment I spent with the man, but I was used to having my own space. A pang of sadness had me feeling sorry for myself. I missed my house.

Arys was buried beneath a mass of bright red sheets. It was too hot for anything heavier. His brow was creased in a frown, and he clutched the pillow tight in one hand. I hadn't been having the greatest dreams lately either.

I stripped down nude and climbed between the sheets. My dark vampire lay next to me, deep in the strange slumber of the undead. I stroked a hand absently through his silken hair, hoping to find comfort in touching him.

The window was so well covered that it was impossible to tell visually that the sun was up. I stared around the dark room, seeing nothing, my thoughts on overdrive. I contemplated what I should do with the remnants of the house. Selling the property and moving on was the best option, yet letting go of it was too hard to imagine.

I waited for sleep, begged for it. I slipped into that hazy in-between state and floated in limbo. Soon enough, I descended into a deep slumber, then my phone rang, jarring me awake. Arys stirred, and I rushed to silence it. I was hopeful that it would be Kale.

"Alexa, I'd like to see you tonight." Shya was the last person I had expected. He didn't waste time on phony pleasantries. "Midnight."

"This is about Lilah, isn't it?" A glance at the time on my phone indicated I had two hours until midnight. I didn't feel like I'd slept that long.

"Should it be?"

"No?" I wanted a chance to talk to him about Lilah but didn't think this was it.

He directed me to an old abandoned church a few miles down the road from his sprawling modern home. It sounded sketchy to me.

"Oh and Alexa," Shya stopped me before I could hang up. "Don't be late. Kale is depending on you."

He ended the call before I could respond. Well that answered one question. I took a deep breath and let it out slowly. "Fuck."

Arys rolled over and opened his eyes. "What did you do now?"

I couldn't even be offended, so I growled and punched a pillow before hurling it against the wall.

"I made the mistake of giving a shit about the dreamwalker. I didn't do anything though. Not really. I think Kale did something. I just don't know what yet. Something has Shya's panties in a twist."

"You underestimate the power you have over any man who is in love with you." Arys held tight to his favorite pillow in case I planned to snatch it, too. "Clearly he intervened on your behalf. The fool. He's just dragging you down with him."

I scoffed. "If I have that much of an effect on a man, then why is Shaz so detached lately?" It was unrelated. I wasn't sure why I said it.

Arys put his head in my lap and gazed up at me. "Shaz is confused and afraid. And, if he didn't love you the way he does, he wouldn't be either of those things. He's got to process what his role in this really is. Now," he sat up and threw off the blankets, exposing his glorious nudity, "let's get ready to go."

My gaze was riveted to him. Arys was beautiful. It was hard not to stare stupidly. "You're coming with me?"

"I'm not letting you go alone. That bastard demon is going to use Sinclair against you. Sorry, Alexa, but I don't think you always see so straight when it comes to him."

I buried my head beneath my pillow. Hiding my burning cheeks didn't alleviate the shameful truth. "Sometimes I really want to kick your ass." My muffled words brought a laugh from Arys.

"Come on, pretty wolf. Get up and get dressed. Unless you want to have a quickie first?"

His laughter grew when I threw my pillow at his head. Smacking it aside, Arys grabbed me around the waist and pulled me against him. His skin was faintly cool but warmed at my touch. He nipped playfully at my neck, and I sighed.

"What makes you so amazing? I mean, everything with Kale… how do you accept it like that? Like it's so easy."

Arys raised his head to look at me. His expression took on an intensity that held me transfixed. "I've spent over a century knowing I'd likely never know you. I've been waiting for you for a hundred years. Being with you is surreal. We were created as one. The moments that bring jealousy and pain, they're temporary. We are forever."

The weight of his words crushed the breath from me. Emotion quickly filled me to overflowing, and I had to blink back tears. Though Arys may not know it, he had just set me free from some of the chains I'd bound myself in.

"Thank you," I said softly, a catch in my voice. "For believing so deeply in something I still haven't been able to process. It helps to think there might be something bigger behind all of this."

Still, I had so many questions, and I was afraid of the answers. What was our purpose? And, would we find out before the power of our bond became too much for us?

Instead of pondering our fate, we prepared to meet the demon.

The abandoned old church wasn't much of a surprise. Shya had shown his penchant for forsaken holy buildings previously. Some twisted part of him seemed to enjoy conducting his business in desecrated places.

I took a moment to gather myself before leaving the car. A busted iron fence surrounded both the church and what appeared to be a small graveyard in the back, but my view of the presumed cemetery was obscured from where I sat.

"Feel that?" Arys asked, his eyes locked on the crumbling stone church. "That's some heavy duty shit."

"That's one way of putting it."

The smothering sensation of dark energy made it hard to breathe. I shielded tightly against it, but still I could feel it there, seeking a way past my guard. One thing was certain; Shya wasn't alone. It felt like he had a whole party of insanity going on.

During the drive over, I'd been a fit of nerves and fear. Now that I was here, I just felt ready. I couldn't speak for Kale, but I had done nothing wrong, and I wasn't walking in there acting like I had.

Out of habit, I checked my reflection in the visor mirror. Black liner around my brown eyes hid the lack of sleep and a splash of red lipstick made me feel a little bad ass. Skinny black jeans, a tight black strapless top and ankle boots with four-inch heels completed the look and boosted my confidence. I was suddenly glad I'd gone shopping. It sure beat pjs and sandals.

The beautiful old cross Kale had given me for my birthday hung around my neck. I didn't expect it would win me any brownie points with either Shya or Arys tonight, but I didn't care. It was the first time

I'd worn it. After how close I'd come to losing it, I wanted to take the chance to appreciate it.

Arys slid a hand up the inside of my thigh. I stopped him with a look. Lust had been burning in his eyes since he'd watched me bleed a gang member on the way here.

Mastering the bloodlust on a night like this meant not giving it the chance to master me. The feed had left me with that beautiful high, the one I was afraid to get used to. I didn't want to be bloodlust's slave, but I didn't want to kill indiscriminately, either. Arys would have gladly settled for any random person. I had insisted it be someone who had blood on their own hands. It wasn't realistic to think I could feed on the criminals and street vermin forever. Just wishful thinking.

"Come on, you animal." Giving Arys's wandering hand another shove, I gathered my power close and shoved the car door open. "Let's get this over with. No aggressive actions unless it's necessary. I don't want anyone to get hurt."

"He's a demon. Somebody is going to get hurt. From the way the atmosphere burns, someone already has." Arys joined me in front of the Charger and took my hand. "Be careful. Don't let anger do your talking for you. If he feels you've crossed a line with him, he's going to do all he can to intimidate you, even if it means using Sinclair to do it. Be prepared for that."

"What about you? Shya wanted you once. Maybe the both of us being here is a bad idea." I leaned into Arys, briefly seeking strength. I didn't dare take my eyes off the church.

He squeezed my hand reassuringly. "That is exactly where our advantage lies. You were already involved with him through Veryl before you and I met. It made sense for you to stay that way. Some alliances are worth the risk. As a pair, we intrigue him. He knows what we are. We can play that card if we have to."

We began the short walk to the church. It was dark. Only the faintest light glowed within. As we drew closer, noise reached us from the graveyard in the rear. So, that's where the party was.

"Why did you refuse to work with Shya? What did he offer you?" The closer we got, the quieter my voice dropped.

"He offered me everything. Protection, power, sex, an endless supply of victims. He would have given me anything I'd asked for. But, what he wanted most was my vow that you and I would stay out of his way. Since I don't know what our true purpose is, I refused."

"Why the hell would you not tell me this?" I hissed. "If I'd known, I would never have agreed to work with him."

"That's why I didn't tell you." Arys pulled me to a stop when we reached the perimeter of the church's property. He spoke fast and low. "It doesn't all have to be blood and death. You have power that puts you in a position to do a lot of good and to get as much from your arrangement with Shya as he gets from you. Hidden opportunities, Alexa. Seek them."

We stepped onto the church grounds, and immediately I felt the unrest in the earth. It had been a long time since anyone had attended services in this building.

A cacophony of noise drew us past the church. Chants, shouts and words spoken in other tongues created an eerie mess of sound. The glow of firelight cut through the darkness ahead. Arys released my hand seconds before we stepped into the light. I was not prepared for what I saw.

A tall iron fence surrounded a graveyard filled with old, worn headstones. A few large trees dispersed throughout gave it a splash of color amid the grey stones. At the farthest end of the graveyard, a bonfire burned. Several people formed a wide circle around it, many of them clad in dark robes.

Other small groups of people moved in the darkness, away from the firelight. It took me a moment to realize that most of them were engaged in various sexual acts. My attention was drawn to Shya where he stood just outside the circle. His wings were flared out behind him like massive black shadows. The firelight glinted off his skin, casting him in an orange glow. He was focused on something taking place near the fire, something everyone was watching.

The scent of blood and sex mingled into a tantalizing aroma. I'd never been so grateful to sate the bloodlust, especially when I saw what was going on inside the circle.

A young woman lay bound and naked on the grass. A blindfold covered her eyes. The demon thrusting into her from behind wore an expression of sordid ecstasy. His eyes were pure black, deep dark pools. The woman writhed and cried out in pleasure.

My mouth went dry, and I forced back a wave of nausea. What in the hell was going on here? I looked to Arys for some kind of unspoken support. The intrigue on his handsome face turned my stomach.

Shya turned slightly and met my gaze. His grim smile chilled me. He motioned for me to join him, and I refused by remaining rooted to where I stood.

Tearing my gaze from the disturbing scene by the fire, I scanned the others in the vicinity. I didn't see Kale anywhere. To reach out for his energy I'd have to drop my shields. I wasn't sure I was ready to do that yet.

Several of those present were demons, half a dozen maybe. Everyone else was human, a fact that disappointed and frightened me. I could almost hear all the flippant comments Jez and Arys often made about humans being just as evil as the rest of us if not more so. I knew it was true. A monster is a monster, regardless of the face it wears or the name given to it. We were all monsters in our own way. It was tragic really.

I stood there, a murderer with hungers and intents as ill as any, and I judged those around me. It wasn't that I thought I was better than them; I just couldn't bring myself to accept that I was one of them.

The force of the energy swirling and pulsing around us pressed against my shields, and I had to focus hard to keep them in place. I didn't think Arys was shielding at all. From the strange interest on his face and the huge pupils he was rocking, I'd have to say no.

The chant I'd been hearing grew in volume as the excitement of those around the fire rose. It gave me a bad feeling. It sounded like Latin. Coming to this party of the damned didn't seem like a great idea. *Dammit Kale, where are you?*

I watched with increasing unease as the fornicating couple quickened their pace. If this was what Shya liked to do in his free time that was fine, but I didn't want any part of it. As I watched, the sick feeling that this wasn't going to end well filled me.

Shouts, moans and cries filled the graveyard. I stood frozen, holding my breath. The demon having illicit sex with the human woman held my attention. Something about him triggered my wolf's wariness.

His movements were smooth, carefully calculated. He drove the woman into a frenzy until she was begging him for more. It was impossible to look away. Something big was coming, something other than the obvious.

Then I saw it: the flash of firelight on a blade. I didn't see him draw it, but the demon suddenly held a large knife in one hand. A surge of excited energy slapped against my shields and created a heavy pressure in my mind. The crowd was waiting for this moment.

The demon grabbed a handful of the woman's hair and violently jerked her head back. He slid that knife across her throat like it was butter. Blood poured forth, spattering the ground. The woman made a strangled sound and fell face down in the grass.

I was awestruck with horror when the demon soaked his hands in her blood before smearing it on his face and body. Horror turned to absolute disgust. The demon slammed the knife into the woman's chest and then reached in to tear her heart out.

He raised the bloody mass to his lips, and I looked away. I didn't want these images to live inside me forever. I would never be able to un-see this night. I hated Shya so much in that moment.

A shriek drew me back to the commotion near the fire. Several of the robed gatherers were dipping their fingers in blood and decorating their faces in wicked war paint. Their chant grew louder until I was fighting the urge to cover my ears.

From the fire, balls of flame shot into the sky. The chanters fell all over one another in a frenzy of sex. The demon walked around the fire like a self-appointed crimson god, drinking in the essence of sex, bloodshed and sacrifice.

Shya stepped away from the insanity and fixed his attention on us. I glanced nervously at Arys, wishing I could grab onto him for support but knowing Shya would see it for what it was: weakness.

Arys appeared completely unaffected by what we'd just seen. No emotion showed on his face. Sure, he'd had centuries to perfect his poker face, but it struck me as cold. Did he like what he just saw? Or, was he simply unfazed by it?

Shya stopped several yards away and leaned casually against a headstone. He beckoned to me with little more than a crooked finger.

"I knew you wouldn't come alone." Shya greeted us with a slight nod. Decked out in Armani or something like it, he gave us both a slow, appraising once over, scowling upon noticing the cross I wore. He held Arys's gaze longer than necessary. "Nice to see you again, Mr. Knight. I trust you're just here to observe."

With eyes narrowed, Arys pinned the demon with a scathing look. "I guess that remains to be seen."

I broke in before Shya could give voice to the spark of venom in his scarlet snake eyes. "I've seen more than enough stomach turning debauchery for one night, Shya. Can we skip ahead to the part where you make my life hell? It is coming, isn't it?"

I smiled so tight it hurt, not entirely feeling it but refusing to show any true emotion. Shya mirrored my smile with one of his own. There was nothing friendly about it.

"We're team players here, Alexa. You've always been a good member of the team, so I'll give you the opportunity to explain to me why I shouldn't destroy Kale." Shya held my gaze, watching closely for my reaction. "I have little use for those willing to double cross me. But, you would never do that. Would you, Alexa?"

A dizzying wave of shock and fear slapped me. I was momentarily speechless. "Not intentionally."

"Of course not." Shya's tone oozed with condescension. "And, I'm sure I would be correct in assuming that Kale's actions were entirely his own. You were in no way involved."

Now I was confused. What had Kale done? "I don't have a clue what you're talking about." I wanted to ask where Kale was but feared the answer.

Those red eyes bore into me as Shya tried to decide if I was lying. I could feel Arys's watchful gaze. He had to be curious now, thinking I'd gotten myself into trouble again. This time I was in the dark. I didn't know what was going on, but someone had better start talking.

"Alright. Then I suppose I should enlighten you." Shya made a small hand gesture, and the back door of the church swung open.

It was dark inside, revealing nothing. A moment later Falon appeared in the doorway. Son of a bitch. Did he follow Shya everywhere like a lost puppy or what?

Falon shoved two bound and battered forms ahead of him where they fell down the church steps onto the grass. The glow of the firelight landed upon them, and I saw that Kale and the dreamwalker, though alive, had certainly been subjected to abuse.

I lunged forward, intent on getting to Kale. Arys stopped me with a hand on my wrist in a vice-like grip. I tried to shake him off, but he held tight. I couldn't read his expression, though, the moment our skin touched, the power sizzled between us with a cool sense of displeasure.

Shya placed himself between his two beaten captives and me. I couldn't take my eyes off Kale. His face was a bloody mess. Bruises colored his skin in an assortment of black and purple shades. The way he leaned awkwardly indicated broken bones, most likely ribs. I knew without a doubt Falon had been the torture-happy fiend behind the physical abuse. I wanted to kill him.

"So it appears," Shya began with a devilish expression. "That Kale somehow got it into his head that he needed to save this young man from me. I can't imagine where he may have gotten that from. Can you?"

*No. Please no.* I concentrated on taking deep breaths. I felt lightheaded, like I may pass out.

"Please, Shya don't-,"

"That's enough!" He cut me off with an unseen force that shattered my shields. "It is not your place to decide who needs to be saved. I've always admired you for being a fighter, Alexa, but you will not interfere with my decisions. Since that wasn't already clear to you, I see I must make myself understood."

Panic crawled up my throat, choking off my reply. I watched with growing distress as Shya approached the dreamwalker. The kid looked up at him with little fear. He was already beyond it, ready to accept what came next. The need to do something filled me, but I had no power here. Not over Shya or Falon. I was useless.

Shya ran a hand lightly over the boy's hair. There was no reaction. The dreamwalker stared off toward the fire, as if he saw nothing of his reality. His short life had already been filled with the torment of his power. Wasn't that enough?

I sensed Shya's next move seconds before it occurred. I jerked away from Arys and almost fell in my haste. My shout of protest was cut short when Shya grabbed the boy's head in both hands and with immense strength, tore it from his body.

Blood and gore spattered Kale and the surrounding grass. Shya stepped back to survey his work before looking my way. An anguished growl built in my throat, spilling out uncontrollably.

"You didn't have to kill him!"

A flap of big black wings sent a ripple of energy over me that was like poison. Brief but potent, it burned me metaphysically, leaving me shaken and gasping for air.

"Yes, I did." Shya's eyes flashed with malice. "The boy was already a mental shell. This interference merely crushed what was left of him, rendering him useless."

There was no reasoning with a demon. The argument died on my lips. There was nothing I could say. The dreamwalker was dead because I had shown concern for him.

The party taking place around the fire was in full swing. Nobody had noticed what just happened, or if they had, they simply didn't care. How could it be that I was involved in a world so dark? So evil? I had never longed to be sitting at home with a family, a television set and two point five kids until that moment. Oh, to be normal and ignorant.

Ignoring the dreamwalker's body, Shya walked a slow circle around Kale. My guts tightened, and I thought I might be sick.

"Now comes the fun part." The demon stopped behind Kale, close enough to touch, but his deadly gaze was upon me. "You get to decide Kale's fate, Alexa. On my terms, of course." He paused, letting the horror wash over my face before he continued.

"You can watch while I kill him. Or, if you prefer, you can spare his life. On one condition." Like a reality TV show host, Shya paused for dramatic emphasis. "You take his place."

"What?" I said in the same moment both Arys and Kale shouted, "No!"

Our reactions must have been what he wanted because Shya chuckled. "Much like the wolf I handed over to you, I will do the same with Kale. He becomes your responsibility. In exchange for sparing his pitiful existence, you will accept his debt owed to me as your own."

Stunned was just scratching the surface of what I felt. This was beyond cruel. Shya was working an angle. Always a goddamn angle!

"There must be another way." I chose my words carefully, hoping I wouldn't make matters worse than they already were. "You know I can't pay any debt. I know you're pissed, Shya, but that's not fair."

"Not fair?" Falon spoke up like the obnoxious interloper that he was. "You very well could have traded places with *her* tonight." He indicated the desecrated corpse of the naked woman near the fire. Then he smiled.

I shot him a venomous look. "Funny to see you here, Falon. You know, with your dick in your pants and all."

We shared a brief moment, glaring in silence at one another. Shya watched us, noting the exchange.

"Nothing is fair, is it?" The strange lilt to Shya's tone set off warning bells in my head. "You are mortal yet, and still you reign over vampires and werewolves. Some may consider that unfair. It shouldn't be such a difficult choice. You are lovers, you and Kale, are you not?"

That was it right there. Shya's angle. I was the perfect mix of monster and human. Just enough monster to give me the power he desired, and just enough human for him to exploit my emotions to control me.

"No," I ground out through clenched teeth. "We're not lovers."

"Kale's devotion to you suggests otherwise." With a raised brow and a pointed look, Shya made it painfully clear that he knew he had me on this one.

I was uncomfortable with so many sets of eyes on me. I let my wolf stare out, into Shya. If I looked at Arys or Kale, I'd fall to pieces. "There must be another way. I'm not making some shady deal with you."

Slowly he shook his head. The depths of his red eyes were void of any emotion. Did Shya even feel true emotion? Doubtful.

"I'm afraid those are your only options. Don't worry, Alexa. I promise not to kill you. You are far more valuable to me alive."

My temper flared. I had underestimated Shya. I had fully believed him to be capable of such cold, calculated manipulation. Yet, I never gave him credit for how clever he was. I was backed into a corner, forced to commit to a choice that I would regret either way. Condemn Kale to death for doing the right thing, or owe Shya in his place.

"Alexa," Kale said my name like it was glass in his mouth. A cough racked him, and he spat blood. "Don't let him do this to you. Let him kill me. It's my choice."

"You heard the man," Arys's murmur was so faint, I wasn't sure if it had been said out loud or something he whispered in my head.

I rounded on him with a deadly glare, all fangs and claws. Neither of them was making this decision for me. I shoved past Shya and knelt before Kale where he sat broken and weary on his knees in the grass.

An uncharacteristic dullness shaded his beautiful brown and blue eyes. His energy was weak as if it had been stripped from him. Not only was that unbearably painful, it was psychically dangerous. He needed blood.

For the first time in weeks, I breached the unspoken wall we'd built. With a shaky hand, I reached to smooth the blood soaked hair off Kale's forehead. I lingered, running my fingers gently down his face.

"I'm not going to let you die. Not because of me. Don't ask me to make that happen."

"You need to walk away right now and let me go." He reached to touch the cross around my neck, and I jerked at the ice-cold caress of his fingertips as they grazed my flesh.

I felt Arys's light touch on my mind. He said nothing, but clearly made his presence known. I hated that this moment had to happen in front of him. I hated that it had to happen at all.

"I'm not doing that." I shook my head sadly. I wasn't ready to face these feelings. "I won't."

Weakened as he was, Kale still had no problem getting mad. "Dammit, Alexa. Don't kid yourself. We'll both regret it, you more so than I. Walk away."

His tone was firm. Serious. He just might hate me for what I was about to do. There was a good chance he wouldn't be the only one.

"I'm sorry, but your death can never be by my hand."

"I fucked up, Alexa. It's not your problem. Walk away."

"Stop saying that!" I stood quickly and clenched my hands into fists. My long claws cut into the palms of my hands.

I turned to Arys, finding him closed off. With arms crossed, he fixed me with a disaffected stare. He gave the impression that he didn't care. It was a lie.

'I have to do it.' I pushed the thought to Arys. 'I can't live with his blood on my hands.'

Arys merely stared, silent and grave.

Falon feigned a dramatic yawn. Checking his non-existent watch for the time, he loudly declared, "At this rate, the sun will rise, and there won't be a decision *to* make."

"Feel free to leave," I snarled. The pressure was mounting, and I was buckling beneath it.

"And miss this? Not a chance. I want to see you cave."

Shya held up a hand and gave Falon a look. To me he said, "Alexa. Your choice?"

One last try. I had to. "There has to be another way. You've made your point, Shya." I wasn't going to beg, but the temptation was there.

He moved fast, a blur of black. He grabbed Kale in a bone-shattering grip, holding his head at a dangerous angle. That was the only answer I was going to get.

"No!" My shriek echoed through the night. For a split second, all I could hear was the pounding of my heart in my ears. The fallen body of the dreamwalker was a very real example of how ruthless Shya was. I still didn't know the poor kid's name.

Shya released Kale and held his hands out in expectation. This was it, now or never. Kale stared up at me with a silent plea. I couldn't bring myself to give him what he asked for. If I didn't act now, I never would, and Shya would make my choice for me.

"Fine. I'll do it." My fate was sealed the moment the words passed my lips. "Now let me help Kale. He needs blood."

"By all means." If Shya's smile got any bigger, it was going to become the scariest thing I'd seen all night.

I watched him cautiously, unwilling to take my eyes from the demon. I reached for Kale, and he tried uselessly to push me away. It took great effort in his weakened state.

"No, Alexa. Leave me. I'll be fine." He slumped over on the grass, unable to stay upright.

I knelt close and pulled him into my arms. Anger flashed in his eyes, but he didn't have the strength to do anything about it. Shoving my hair aside, I bared my neck and offered it to him. His hunger sparked to life. Still, he resisted.

"Do it, Kale. You'll never make it out of here on your own if you don't. I'm not leaving you for the sun."

I had watched a vampire burn in the sun, and it had instilled a deep fear within me. When I rose as a vampire, as I was bound to, I'd vowed to never screw with sunrise.

His hunger was palpable. His reasons for refusing were likely personal, none of which mattered right now. I reached out to drape him in my heady power, luring him in like I had so many times before.

Kale's eyes widened, and I saw accusation in their depths. I might as well have been forcing a syringe filled with heroin on a junkie. Kale had a weakness for my blood and the power within it. What had weakened him before would strengthen him now, and I wasn't going to feel guilty about using my influence over him.

My eyes locked on Arys. He had moved closer, drawn by the power I'd encircled Kale with. The expression he wore was hard to read. The fire behind me was reflected in his blue eyes. I held his gaze, waiting for him to do something, anything to stop this. He only watched in silence as I offered my neck to Kale.

With a ravenous hunger, Kale pulled me roughly against him, exerting the strength only bloodlust commanded. He was lost in my thrall, a victim to my influence.

With that vicious hunger, he bit into my neck, tearing a cry from me. He pulled back and bit again, fast and deep. Panic thrilled through me in response to his animalistic assault.

I couldn't tear my gaze from Arys who watched with a hard set to his jaw. He didn't make eye contact with me. Instead, he watched Kale spill my blood. Arys's expression was guarded, and he had withdrawn his touch from my mind.

Kale drew on my blood and energy, which I freely gave. Pain throbbed from the wounds like fire racing down my neck into my back. As much as it hurt, there was a gratifying element to his bite. My power had wanted Kale for some time. In that moment, he was mine.

The chill of his mouth on my injured skin swept me up in a storm of desire. I didn't want to react to him like this, and certainly not in front of anyone else. His lust for me sprang to life, and I feasted upon his desire, responding to his hunger for my blood and body. At least Arys's presence kept me grounded; I was grateful for that.

Kale pressed against me as he fed. There was no mistaking the evidence of his growing arousal. The power swirled around us, taunting us with the promise of more. A delightful tingle started in my groin. I ached to have him nestled between my thighs again.

I was shaking and breathless. We fed upon each other in a sordid little tango. He drained my blood, and I feasted on his response to my power. However, blood loss had my head spinning; I had to stop him.

With both hands on his chest, I braced, ready to physically throw him off. "Kale, stop." My words were a lie. Even as I said it, I was entertaining thoughts of throwing him down on the grass beneath us and taking him the way I longed to.

Applause broke the spell holding us entwined. Kale jerked away from me as if my touch had burned. I collapsed on my hands and knees, digging my fingers into the earth in an attempt to ground my energy and get control of myself.

Falon clapped, slow and dramatic. My vision swam as I tried to focus on him. I was thrumming with the heavy charge of what I'd just done. Surreal.

Blood dripped from the bites in my neck as well as from my nose. Great. I'd never hear the end of this from Arys. I was afraid to look at him. Did he hate me for this? He had to understand that I couldn't simply let Kale die.

White noise roared in my ears. I stared at the ground and concentrated on the earth. Sharing power and blood with Kale was nothing like my union with Arys. They were worlds apart. Arys was part of me, but Kale was mine.

I shook my head, hating myself for feeling that way. It didn't matter now. Shya had made an agreement. He had to hold up his end. Kale was safe and that was what mattered right then.

The familiar touch of Arys was welcome when he picked me up off the ground. He held me upright until I was steady on my feet. Without saying a word, he smoothed the hair back from my face and swiped a gentle hand through the blood trickling from my nose. The dismay was heavy in his eyes.

Kale leaned back against a headstone, about as far as he could get from me without leaving the property. His eyes were wide and his pupils huge. Already most of his wounds from Falon's beating had healed.

"Impressive," Falon commented lazily.

I turned my attention to Shya. He was staring at Kale with interest. His gaze darted to me, and I knew by the intrigue on his face that my eyes were Arys's startling blue.

Shya stepped up close with a sweep of wings. He peered into me as if searching for something specific. I glared hard, biting back the nasty remark dancing on the tip of my tongue.

"I'd hate to have another incident with the two of you. In all honesty, I'm fond of you both." Shya referred to Kale with a dismissive gesture. "When you start being more trouble than you're worth, things get ugly. I'll consider this matter closed. However, I expect you will supply me with a dreamwalker, seeing as I am quite obviously still in need of one."

Staring into the cold red eyes of a ruthless demon, I was left between a rock and a hard place. This wasn't the time to argue his terms. It was ludicrous of him to demand that I find him a dreamwalker but refusal would get me killed.

Against my instinct, I nodded. "Fine. Whatever. Can I leave now?"

In a swift motion, Shya grabbed my hand, sealing the deal. His touch burned as flames rose up to engulf my arm. I shrieked. The pain was intense and unbearable. He released me quickly, and the fire vanished. Smoke rose from my arm. I stared in shock at the dragon burned into my skin. It wrapped around my wrist with its tail curled onto the back of my hand and its head rested on the inside of my forearm. It appeared to grip my arm with its clawed feet. Reptilian wings flared out from its back.

"What the friggin hell did you do to me?" I demanded, yelping again from the searing pain. It was leaps and bounds worse than Kale's vicious bite.

Shya stepped back, his expression grim. "I merely sealed the deal with my sigil. Bring me a dreamwalker, and I'll remove it. Try to cross me, and it allows me to find you and deliver justice. Don't worry. It won't burn for long."

He turned his back on us all and returned to the sordid party taking place around the fire. Cloaked by his massive black wings, he looked more like a monster to me now than he ever had. Falon had disappeared in silence. Good riddance.

I was left shaken and horrified. Staring at the burning, swelling dragon, I was torn between bursting into tears and raging after Shya in a fit of wolf's fury. Neither would bring me satisfaction, and the latter would leave me next to the dead woman by the fire.

Kale was gone. He was little more than a shadow moving through the graveyard.

Arys examined my arm, careful not to touch Shya's mark. With a frustrated sigh, he pulled me close and pressed his lips to my forehead. "Oh, my reckless wolf. And, you say you don't have a death wish."

## Chapter Fourteen

I stared up at the sign above the front door of The Wicked Kiss and sighed. Every night, every new twist in the chaotic tale of my life led me back here. Fuck it. It had whiskey.

It was late. The club was closed to the public for the coming day – sunrise was just a few hours away – but the building was by no means empty. The party never really stopped; it just changed.

I could feel the energy pulsing inside. I knew Kale would come here. He wasn't going to be content with what he'd taken from me. Before he was lost in a blood-drunk haze, I needed to see him, if only to make sure he wasn't going to do anything stupid.

Arys was furious with me in that severe, quiet manner that reveals a far deeper anger than if he'd just yelled. His refusal to accompany me inside served to emphasize further his seething rage. Despite my attempt to assure him I would be fast, he had muttered obscenities beneath his breath and slipped off into the dark to prowl for a victim to take the edge off.

I understood that need now. It was the only time I found peace anymore. Every time my world started to come apart, the promise of freedom in the kill taunted me. The pull was getting harder and harder to resist, and I was starting to ask myself why I bothered when madness held the promise of liberation.

The crowd had thinned down to a dozen or so. Those who would pass the day screwing and bleeding were already in the den of debauchery in the back. I did not intend to go back there.

The darkened atmosphere was welcoming, inviting me to slip through the shadows like so many others had tonight. We all sought something here. Escape from pain, hunger, loneliness. What we would never find was solace. Mine stood across the room, nuzzling the throat of a convenient redhead he had pressed against the wall.

Kale's head snapped up as he sensed me. I turned away quickly, cowardice quickening my pace. Sliding in behind the unmanned bar, I helped myself to a bottle of whiskey. Sure. Why not? Who needs a stinkin' glass anyway?

As the first swallow of whiskey burned its way down my throat, I risked a glance around. Kale's lady friend rubbed herself against him provocatively. I didn't want to watch, didn't want to feel the bitter bite of jealousy. He wasn't mine. I knew that on a conscious level, but deep within me, I didn't believe it. Wrong. So wrong.

Feeling my gaze upon him, Kale turned in time to catch me staring. *Shit.* With a stony expression, he grabbed the redhead's hand and led her through the club to the back hall. They disappeared beyond, and I burned with misplaced envy.

A few scorching shots of liquor hit me with a pleasant buzz. With the heat of the booze warming my insides, I embraced the false comfort it offered. Maybe it had been a mistake to come after Kale.

I was about to leave when he returned. He stormed up to me with anger burning in his brown and blue eyes. I greeted him with a raised bottle and a cynical grin.

"That didn't take long. Don't tell me you killed her. I don't even want to know."

He glared at me with darkness in his gaze. "You walk in here like my favorite blonde nightmare and expect me to even be able to think about someone else? What are you doing here, Alexa?"

The power sparked between us, lively and hot. I felt Kale's anger burning through me, and it brought a naughty smile to my lips.

"What does it look like I'm doing? I'm having a drink." I followed that with another swig of golden liquor. "If you're expecting me to apologize for saving your ass, then I'm afraid you'll be disappointed."

I fixed him with a steady stare, daring him to let me have it. This had been building for weeks now, since our night together. What happened tonight had pushed it too far, and now came the inevitable backlash. I was ready for it.

"You didn't save my ass," Kale fumed, his tone low and deadly. "You made an arrogant decision based on Shya stroking your ego. He's trying to appoint you as some kind of vampire queen, and you're letting it happen. You've gotten too power-crazed for your own good."

"That's bullshit." I was stunned by his allegation. "I couldn't stand there and watch him tear your head off, Kale. He put the choice in my hands, and I chose not to watch you die."

"Selfish." He spat the word in my face. Wild emotion fed his energy until it reached out to me with a stinging slap. "You don't want me, yet you think you have a right to decide my fate. It doesn't work that way."

His rejuvenated power smacked me, and I gasped. The surface sting gave way to a low burn that tickled its way down my spine.

"Is that what you want this to be about? Us?" I forged ahead with my defense. "It wasn't about us. It was about not letting Shya hurt you."

Kale leaned in close, his face inches from mine. "It was about us. I saw it in your eyes, that fear for me. A fear that only stems from love. And, love is nothing if not selfish."

"I did what I had to. I saved your life. I won't be sorry for that." My temper was starting to flare. His accusations were hitting some nerves that made me uncomfortable.

"I would rather have died."

At his confession, I went cold inside. My gut reaction was to shield tight, to block him from sensing how much his words had hurt me. Keeping it from showing in my eyes wouldn't be so easy. The best way to hide my pain was to allow it to become anger. The whiskey coursing through my veins helped.

Through clenched teeth, I snarled, "I'm sorry you'd rather be dead than have me show affection for you. If you need to hate me to make this easier on yourself, fine. But, I will not feel bad because you're not dead right now. You have no right to expect that of me." I pinned him with a reproving stare. "If you'd been the one to decide my fate, would you have let me die?"

For a moment I was afraid he'd say yes. I saw the hard set to his jaw and the ice in his eyes. With an exasperated, "Fuck," he shook his head, and his gaze dropped. "You know I wouldn't."

"Then don't you ever again ask me to watch you die." My voice trembled.

Silence fell between us. Kale slid onto the barstool next to me. As close as we sat to one another, we were worlds apart. I knew then with sobering certainty that we were forever changed, irreparably damaged.

"I can't live with the fact that you owe Shya in my place. It isn't right." Kale didn't look at me when he spoke. "Your other half must be waiting. So, why are you here drowning your liver in whiskey?"

"Because the alternative is messy." I picked at the label on the bottle I held as that truth fell from my lips. Booze was a poor substitute for blood.

Sitting beside Kale with his honey-drenched energy, I couldn't help but think about the night we'd killed Abigail. That night was coming after us now, with a vengeance. The memory steered my thoughts down that forbidden path to the night we made love in the rain. I was reminded of the deep satisfaction that could be found in the pleasures of body and blood. I blushed and turned away so he wouldn't see.

Awkwardness settled in to steal my words. There was a good chance I'd say something we'd both regret, so I bit my tongue and sipped my whiskey.

"I'm sorry about what happened with Shya." Kale broke the silence between us, with a gesture toward the dragon on my wrist. "It's not right that he marked you because of what I did."

I shrugged and held him with a watchful stare. "It's not right that you pulled a stunt that got us into a situation like that."

He stiffened, giving away so much in that small motion. I was sure, if I dropped my shields and let his warm energy wash over me, it would be flavored with pain and rage. The emotions lurked there in his eyes. Kale felt betrayed because I'd refused to give him the easy out that he sought.

How the hell was I supposed to feel guilty about that? My intent had been to save him. Maybe he didn't want to be saved, but he had no right to punish me for refusing to pull the trigger.

"I did what I did for you. And, the dreamwalker. It wasn't supposed to blow up in my face." With a deadly calm, Kale took my hand in his. He studied the dragon before running a finger gently over it. "I understand why you made the choice you did, Alexa."

A fiery tingle raced up my arm, and my breath caught. He had done all he could to avoid touching me in recent weeks. Now he caressed me boldly, stirring a part of me to life that I'd tried so hard to vanquish.

I knew how passionate Kale's touch could be. The way it felt to have his hands upon me, holding me tight while he buried himself inside me again and again. I felt the memory shining in my eyes and hoped he wouldn't see it.

"I think I understand," he continued. "I know your intentions were good, but I can't help but feel… betrayed. That run-in with Shya got pretty bad, and it worries me. What if it's worse next time?"

"It won't be; Shya got what he was after. Look Kale, I know nobody holds a grudge quite like a vampire." A growl laced my words. "But, I will not feel bad about this. I won't!"

Desperation tainted his heady energy. I gave up trying to shield against him. It felt so much better to let him in.

Kale's gaze dropped as if he couldn't look into my eyes when he said, "I wish we could take everything back and have it be the way it was before."

I stared at him with shock and dismay. His words hurt. "What gives, Kale? You've been a very willing participant so far. Don't you dare accuse me of seducing you. I'm not taking the blame for anything else tonight."

He released my hand suddenly, as if touching me was painful. "If only it had been as simple as that. This isn't lust. It never was."

No, it never had been. My anger deflated, and I no longer wanted the illusion of escape the bottle allowed me. I shoved it away with a sigh.

I didn't know how to react in this situation. I couldn't wrap my mind around the possibility that my choice to save him from Shya may have been the wrong one.

"So what do you want from me, Kale? I can't take it back. I don't even want to. And, I sure as hell won't kill you myself."

His eyes flashed with annoyance. "You can't take this seriously, can you? Never mind. I should know better than to expect you to understand."

He got up and turned to go. I grasped his wrist with more force than I intended. Our energy collided, creating a spark that lit up the area around us. Our eyes met, and the anger burning in Kale's enchanting gaze slipped away.

"I can't do this anymore," I blurted, pulling my hand back. Something in those amazing eyes led my thoughts down a forbidden path. "I should go."

"Let's go somewhere quiet." Kale took my arm and steered me along. "This isn't the right place to talk privately."

"In the back?" I dug my heels in. "Where you have your own private little playroom? No way. Bad idea."

"Not in my room. Just in the hall."

I let him pull me through the door that separated the club from the madhouse. We entered into a dimly lit sitting area furnished with a few bistro tables and two black leather couches.

A hallway branched off either side. One way led to the back of the building, to the bedroom where Shaz and I had killed Arys's sire, Harley. That had been a hell of a night. The opposite end of the hall led to the parking lot exit. That door was rarely used by anyone except those frequenting the back rooms.

The lounge area was empty; everyone was lost in his or her own private world behind the closed doors lining the hall. An array of differing energies swept through as if pushed by a sinister breeze. Fear, lust, hunger. That was just scratching the surface. Goosebumps broke out on my skin in response to the sense-stirring atmosphere.

Kale pulled out a chair for me at the closest table, but I shook my head. I couldn't sit still. Instead, I stood behind the chair, gripping it until my knuckles turned white. Kale perched on the arm of a nearby couch. He'd put a good six feet or more between us, evidence that the swarm of pulsating energy was teasing his senses, too.

"Now," he gestured for me to speak. "You have a lot on your mind. Let's hear it."

"I feel like I'm going crazy," I began, my words coming in a rush. An invitation was all I needed to let it all spill out. "It's like I'm breaking down, and I can't save myself from what's coming. Lilah put the hit out on me. My sister comes back from the dead. My relationships with men are all kinds of fucked up, and I can't help but think it's because I fucked my mother's lover. Where does Freud stand on that one?"

"You can't beat yourself up over that. It was a long time ago, and you didn't know." Kale said softly. "You're the strongest person I know. Strong enough to make a deal with a demon to save someone you care about. Weak people don't do that shit, Alexa. Weak people don't have hits out on them."

"I'll bet a lot of crazy people do." My lower lip trembled, and before I could censor myself, I was telling him everything: the twin flame revelation, Shaz's bad reaction to it, my internal conflict over my sister and why she had never told me she was alive.

Kale listened attentively, showing no emotion or reaction as I spoke. His poker face was good, not so much as a twitch during the twin flame stuff.

"I shouldn't be dumping this all on you. I'm sorry. It's been pretty overwhelming."

"Of course it has. That would be enough to break most people." His head tilted slightly, as Kale regarded me thoughtfully. "You aren't most people, Alexa. You can handle it. Besides, it's all good news for the most part. Your sister is alive, and now you know where your bond with Arys comes from. You should be happy."

My inner cynic wasn't too quick to agree. From the look on Kale's face, he didn't find any joy in what I had shared. Still, a silver lining could be found if I could look beyond the gathering storm clouds. It didn't all have to be bad. What I'd needed most was to get it off my chest, and now that I had, I was already feeling better.

"I will be happy. Eventually. Once the shock wears off."

A rush of thrilling energy came up like a sudden rain, stealing my words along with my breath. Desire fueled the immense force. The muffled sound of a woman's voice reached us. Shrieks gave way to cries of pleasure.

I shuddered, unable to refuse the call of such tantalizing energy. It piqued my interest, stirring my hunger to life. I did not want to react to it. Not here with Kale. Yet, I was pulled by a memory, knowing how easy it would be to blow the door down and devour the power of the vampire driving this dizzying wave.

I shook with the effort it took to hold myself together. I'd come a long way in controlling my power in past months. The hungers, the ache to wrap myself in the ecstasy of letting go... it seemed to grow by the day. As my power grew, so did my weakness. This double-edged sword cut deep. It was going to kill me; I could feel it in my soul.

"You're dangerous like this." Kale's voice was low and rough.

Trying to keep my cool was a challenge. I eyed him curiously. "Dangerous for whom, exactly?"

The roar in my ears grew like thunder rumbling in the distance. Drawing on the energy humming freely around us, I let it sweep in and through me. Kale's tension was palpable. He reached out to me metaphysically. The hypnotic pull of our hyped-up power mingled, dancing together.

"Dangerous for you if you keep that up." His voice was low, a sexy murmur. A shock of electricity raced down my spine.

"I'm not doing that on my own, in case you didn't notice." I was always ready to devour him.

His energy moved over me, making my knees as weak as my will. I could feel his battle between intrigue and apprehension.

"I'm serious, Alexa. Be careful." Heat emanated from him in waves. Fueled by emotion, his energy was dark and held the promise of violent passion.

"See what I mean," I threw both hands up in exasperation. "Crazy. You, me. All of us. Just fucking nuts."

Kale pushed away from the couch and came dangerously close. I backed up in response, trepidation driving my step. With the tornado of energy coaxing me to enjoy the promised delights, I was tapping some serious strength to resist.

"Crazy definitely covers it," he murmured. His eyes were twin pools of absolute black. Only the barest trace of color was visible.

The sound of sex grew louder in the otherwise quiet hallway. Kale's gaze went to my throat, lingering on the bites he'd left there. When his eyes once again met mine, the longing I saw in their depths was startling.

"I need to take off. Thanks for listening, Kale. I appreciate it."

I shoved past him, my eyes on the exit. It seemed so far away. How did the hallway get so impossibly long?

"So soon? Come to haunt me like the ghost of a memory I can't stop reliving and then leave me hanging?" His tone was low and deadly.

There it was, the dark side of Kale. The monster beneath the gorgeous eyes and friendly ear had emerged yet again. That evil, tormented side of Kale had led him to attack both Jez and me on separate occasions. Unpredictable and sinister, this creature was a result of several decades of torture at the hands of the one who'd made him.

Slowly I turned to face him. "We shouldn't be alone together. Not like this. It's not safe."

"No. It isn't."

I never made it another step before Kale had me pressed up against the wall. With a hand on either side of my head, he stood painfully close but not quite touching. I couldn't possibly slip past him without making it physical. Patience and restraint, I had to have them.

"Please," I whispered, careful to keep my tone neutral. "Don't do this. It can't always happen like this. Let me go."

He closed his eyes and pounded a fist against the wall beside my head in frustration. It was loud, echoing in the empty space around us. "Why didn't you let him kill me? You could have set me free."

When his eyes reopened, the pupils had shrunk down. In them, I saw pain.

I could offer him nothing. No words of comfort. No apology that wouldn't be a lie. So, I shook my head sadly and didn't say a thing. With a hand on the side of his face, I leaned in and brushed my lips across his.

Kale returned my kiss with a gentle passion that crushed me. Despite how dangerous he could be, I felt safe with him. Too safe. And, that made it risky.

With a ragged sigh, I broke off the kiss and said, "I'm setting you free now."

I gave in to the urge to slide a hand through his hair. I had done a pretty good job at burying my confusing feelings for Kale, but this made the wounds new again. Raw.

He stepped back, freeing me from his hold. I gave his hand a squeeze before turning toward the glowing red exit sign. "Goodnight, Kale."

## Chapter Fifteen

"You reek like booze. And Sinclair." Arys waited for me outside, leaning against my car with arms crossed and a sexy scowl on his face. "Sure you should be driving?"

Ignoring his jibe, I tossed my keys at him. "Feel free."

I hated it when Arys drove. He was a menace behind the wheel though he somehow managed to escape incident. However, driving would keep him from glowering at me in the dark while I drove, which made it an easy decision.

I winced when he peeled out of the parking lot with a squeal of tires. "What's the rush? It won't be sunrise for two more hours."

"Shaz needs you to give him a hand with your new wolf. When you didn't answer your phone, he called me. Sounds like Coby's losing his marbles."

I groaned as the worst-case scenario played out in my head. "He wolfed out in public a few days ago. That can't happen again."

"Better keep your fingers crossed then."

The drive back to town was spent in silence. I stared out the window as the scenery whipped by. Arys's discontent marched across my skin like an angry troop of fire ants. So, he was ticked about my choice to save Kale's ass. But, how could he expect anything less of me? Arys and I belonged together. That didn't mean I would never form bonds with or have feelings for others. Kale and I were friends. I wasn't turning my back on that.

Arys drove to the park on the edge of town. A concrete walking path wound through the grass and trees in a wide circle that led around a large pond complete with a fountain.

As I drew close to the gazebo at the park's entrance, I saw Shaz and Coby. The glow of a streetlight illuminated their silhouettes. Shaz stood stiffly, braced as if ready to pounce. Coby's hunched frame and arched back alerted me to exactly how close he was to the change. My pace quickened.

"Thank God you're here." Shaz's tension was palpable. He fixed me with eyes that were pure wolf. The strain of keeping Coby from losing it was showing. A sniff in my direction drew him right to the wounds on my neck. He looked from me to Arys but said nothing.

I crouched near Coby and gently pulled his shaky hands from his face. Claws protruded from his fingertips. His hazel eyes were wild, all wolf. He bared fangs, and a growl rumbled low in his throat.

"What happened?" I asked Shaz though my gaze was locked on the man about to burst into a wolf. Coby's energy ran hot. I focused on it, letting it flow over me. He was barely hanging on.

"We went to Lucy's Lounge to have a beer and shoot some pool. I think it all just overwhelmed him, being there with so many people. So many smells." Shaz shrugged as if it was self-explanatory.

In some ways it was.

A bar was filled with a wide array of human scents. Any one of them could trigger the wolf. Fear, pheromones, and sensuality all caught the wolf's attention and enticed the predator to hunt. This wasn't like the bloodlust; the change was confusing when it was new. If the wolf suddenly decided to break free and prowl after a particular enticing scent, it was nearly impossible to stop it.

Coby stank of fear, rage and wolf. His energy was a mess of ever changing vibes, taunting the vampire power lying in quiet wait inside me. I took a deep breath, focusing on the night air entering my lungs. I could feel the bloodlust lurking, anticipating the moment when the quaking wolf would push me too far.

"Coby." His head jerked at the sound of my voice. "You can control this. You have no choice."

His eyes were wide as he looked from me to Shaz with a whimper. "It hurts. I feel like I'm dying."

"That's because you're fighting it. You are the wolf, Coby. It can't hurt you." I waited, giving him a chance to believe that. I wanted him to handle this because I couldn't bear the thought of having to watch it destroy him. It would be my fault.

He backed away, his body contorting violently as he fought the change. It was hurting him, I knew that. It did hurt, even when giving in and allowing it to happen, but then the pain was brief and quickly became relief and even bliss. Fighting it was excruciating. Watching him stirred my wolf's sympathy.

"Alexa, do something." The touch of Shaz's hand on my arm pulled my gaze to him. He was trembling. Coby's frightened wolf was affecting him, too.

I'd used my power to manipulate the wolf before. I had forced Zoey, a hybrid trapped in wolf form, back into her human body. I didn't have time to think about the root of that power, the twin flame revelation or the events of the evening thus far. My wolf was in pain, and I reacted.

The moment I touched Coby, my wolf recognized him as mine. He was a part of me in a way that no other wolf I knew was. I sensed the connection of our wolves deep down inside me. Had Raoul felt this way towards me? As the one he'd turned, I had been unaware of our connection.

He growled and snapped but didn't pull away. I rested my hand against his forehead, bracing against the onslaught of energy pouring from him like an angry wave. He was on his knees before me, our eyes locked.

There was a roar of white noise in my ears. Pushing through the attack of emotion and pain in his energy, I concentrated on the wolf straining to break free. Coby's wolf was strong and desperate, anxious to give in to instinct and break free from the prison of his human form.

Everything around me fell away. The park, Shaz and Arys, all of it faded to black. All I saw was Coby. I grasped the energy of his wolf and forced it to bend to my will. I envisioned it lying quiet inside him.

Power went out from me, and Coby fell back on his ass gasping. When he looked up at me again, the fangs and wolf eyes were gone. The hand I'd touched him with shook slightly, and I was mildly breathless.

He gaped up at me, astonished. Extending a hand, I pulled him to his feet. Calling the power to manipulate his wolf had brought forth the hungers of that vampiric power. I released him quickly and stepped back.

Coby watched me with a strange expression, like he was wary. Then I realized he was looking past me to Shaz who was reacting to the power I'd called like a junkie hurting for a fix.

Shaz's eyes were wolf, frozen on me in a look of wonder and desire. His own energy grew frazzled. Not everyone could feel energy like this. Some were more tuned into it than others. However, this was a case of addiction on overdrive. Put someone who had never used drugs before in the presence of a powerful narcotic, and it would have little effect on them. Stick an addict in there, and they'll come undone.

I stared at Shaz in stunned silence. The glimmer in his eyes revealed something I had never seen before, the dangerous lust of the smitten blood whore. I watched as my worst fear for Shaz came to life. He eyed me like a pet waiting eagerly for attention, aching so desperately for it. I could have told him to get on his knees and worship me like a slave, and he would have done it if it meant riding the high he sought.

"Shaz?" I heard the hesitance in my voice, fear that this was about to get weird.

"Lex." He spoke softly, so low I barely heard it. He moved toward me with a staggered step.

"Are you alright?"

His hands were hot on my skin as he slid them up my arms, over my shoulders, finally burying his fingers in my tresses. Leaning in close he breathed deeply of my scent and sighed. "I'm afraid I'm losing my mind."

Desperate passion laced his touch. He kissed me with a drowning hunger. The bloodlust burst inside me, testing my control. With a groan, I tried to push him away, but he held tight. I didn't want it to be this way between us. It wasn't right.

Shaz pressed closer. I was quickly overwhelmed by his scent, so deliciously wolf and thrumming with that heady crimson. I couldn't do this. I wanted to bite into the soft flesh of his throat and bleed him so badly I ached, and knowing he wanted it too made the urge almost impossible to resist.

"Shaz, stop. I don't want to hurt you."

With both hands on his chest, I shoved. He stood his ground, refusing to budge. My precarious hold on control was slipping. Shaz was intent on seducing me. His mouth moved on mine with a feverish hunger.

"But, I want you to. I need it." He shoved his hands beneath the hem of my top to caress my bare belly.

I was humming with built up energy. I had everything Shaz wanted: the need for his blood and the power capable to take him to heights most could never dream of visiting. We were both slaves to our own personal drug of choice; in a horrific twist of fate, we were also just what the other desired.

Seeking a fix from one another was not only dangerous, but it was also stupid. We would find no saving grace in that; it could never repair what we had destroyed. That path only lead to the senseless pursuit of gratification until it consumed us. Arys's darkness threatened to devour not only me, but Shaz as well.

I could hear the beat of his heart, rapid and strong. It would take such little effort to spill his blood. Just one bite. The cold power of the undead swelled inside me. Shaz taunted my senses. He was all I could feel, see and smell. I wanted to taste him.

Shaz pulled back to meet my eyes, a challenge shining in his. In a foolishly bold move, he held my gaze and bared his neck in invitation. A growl cut the silence. I zoned in on the pulsing vein in Shaz's throat, and nothing else existed in that moment. I moved fast, my lips against his neck, fangs ready.

Before I could sink my teeth into my white wolf, I was violently jerked away. It was sudden and disorienting.

Arys's shout snapped me back to reality. "Alexa, don't."

My pulse thundered in my ears. Shock gave way to dismay. Shaz shook his head, his expression one of confusion and remorse.

"I was waiting for this to happen," Arys declared with a grim expression. "You two had to realize eventually that you are exactly what the other is craving in a fix. But, I'm not going to let it go down this way. You'll just kill each other."

"You won't let it go down this way?" Shaz spat scathingly. "I'm not a fucking charity case for you to step in and save, you condescending bastard."

His immediate fury alarmed me. Shaz wasn't known for his temper; he never lost it without good reason.

"Settle down, pup. I don't mean to step on your pride." Arys was unaffected. He merely regarded Shaz as if waiting for him to get it out of his system. "My concern is for Alexa. Would you prefer me to allow her to do something she'd regret for the rest of her life?"

The muscles in Shaz's clenched jaw twitched. Crossing his arms over his chest, he shook his head but didn't speak. He was pissed at himself, not Arys. I could relate.

I jumped in before Shaz decided to get snappy again. "Can we not do this right now guys? I'm not in the mood for the macho bullshit. Although, maybe if you were both shirtless and lightly oiled, I could warm up to it."

I did not succeed in getting the tight smile from Shaz I'd been hoping for. Arys raised a dark brow as if considering my idea. "It's not a bad plan," he said with a wink. "Something to consider."

Shaz looked from Arys to me, his gaze trained on my neck. I swallowed hard. I knew what was coming. Instead of directing his inquiry to me, he spoke to Arys.

"Those bites, they're not from you, are they?"

"No. We've had a bit of an interesting night ourselves, pup." Arys made a sweeping gesture, indicating that I should take over.

"We've had a hell of a night, Shaz." I showed him the dragon burnt into my flesh and recounted the earlier events of the evening.

Shaz listened patiently while I spoke. While describing the demon sacrifice I'd witnessed, Coby shuddered and muttered, "Sweet Jesus." It was a scary new world for him, for me as well, as far as demon sacrifices go. I wouldn't forget this night any time soon.

"So you allowed this to happen, Lex?" Holding my wrist, Shaz examined the ugly demon brand. His disgust was thinly veiled. "You accepted it for Kale. I don't even know what to say to that. Frankly, the only word that comes to mind is stupid."

The bitterness that dripped from his words was alarming. I jerked my hand from his grasp, recoiling in shock. His judgment stung.

"That's harsh, Shaz. But, thanks for letting me know what you really think." I turned to leave, calling back over my shoulder. "It wasn't so long ago that you were begging me to spare the life of your forbidden lover, or have you forgotten already?"

I had fully expected Arys to read me the riot act about my decision to save Kale. I had not expected Shaz to be so ruthless and hypocritical. They acted like abandoning Kale to Shya's personal punishment was the obvious, easy choice to make. Kale and I may have crossed the line in our friendship, but he didn't deserve to die because of it. And, I would not allow either of them to make me out to be the bad guy for sparing him.

## Death Wish

\* \* \* \*

The scent of burgers on the barbecue was mouthwatering. The sun dipped low over the horizon in a burst of pink and orange decorating the western sky. It was gorgeous, and I marveled at the myriad colors. I savored every sunrise and sunset these days.

The low murmur of male voices came from the deck where Shaz and Coby manned the barbecue. After the insanity of the previous night, I was in great need of a normal evening. Things had been strained between Shaz and me since I had stormed off last night. Despite the obvious awkward tension, we were doing our best to fake smiles in all the right places and pretend that we weren't falling apart.

"He's cute." Kylarai leaned in close to breathe the words, her grey eyes on Coby. "But, does he ever talk?"

We sat side by side in lounge chairs on the lawn below the patio where Shaz and Coby stood. Watching the sunset, we sipped strawberry daiquiris and anticipated Shaz's amazing burgers.

"Not really. Although, we didn't have much of a chance to talk the night my house burned down. He wolfed out in town last night. It's been hard for him."

"Aw, how tragic." The little smile playing about Kylarai's lips was nice to see. Since Julian's death about a month back, she'd been slowly overcoming her grief. She needed time to heal, of course, but seeing her smile was both a gift and a relief.

Tonight was the perfect night for a barbecue and a run. I couldn't wait to shed my human skin and be wolf. After spending the majority of my time surrounded by vampires, it was heavenly to be here with my wolves. It felt like home.

I gazed longingly past the fence to the farmer's field beyond. Just a short jaunt across it was the tree line, the entrance to the forest that we called home. Kylarai's house was perfectly situated on the edge of town, the ideal place for a werewolf to have the best of both worlds.

After debating with myself over whether I was too lazy to get up and get a refill or not, I left the comfort of the lounge chair and climbed the deck stairs to the kitchen door. Shaz followed me in, sliding the door shut behind us. I gave him a quizzical look as I opened the fridge to hunt down the daiquiri pitcher.

"What's up?"

"Coby is a pretty nice guy once he gets talking. Very reluctant with the wolf stuff." Shaz leaned on the counter, watching me. "I think he'll be fine. He just needs to accept that he's a wolf now. It's always denial and resistance in the beginning."

I nodded, pouring the delicious strawberry concoction into my glass. "Coby can handle it. The fact that he's still sane works in his favor."

Shaz's gaze was drawn to the faint vampire bites on my neck, and my stomach turned. I looked away, but it was too late. I caught the judgment in his eyes before he could hide it. Falon, Juliet, and now Shaz, I was getting pretty tired of that expression.

I forced a smile and turned to go back outside. Shaz stepped in front of me, blocking my path. He pulled me against him, and his musky wolf scent filled me. Holding me close, he nuzzled me, rubbing his face softly alongside mine. Though genuinely affectionate, his actions displayed dominance. Without saying a word, Shaz had made it clear that he was the Alpha male and that he considered me to be his. I felt his wolf's claim over me, and I bristled.

He didn't want last night to come between us, but our dilemma just wasn't that simple.

"I love you, Lex."

I touched the side of his face and nuzzled him back. "I love you, too."

Before he could delay me further, I pushed by him and disappeared outside. I knew there was more he wanted to say. This wasn't the time or the place to bring up personal issues.

Kylarai was seated at the table in the far corner of the patio. I slid into an adjacent chair and tried to smile pleasantly when Coby set a tray of cooked burgers before us. He avoided my gaze, glancing at Ky instead. Shaz joined us a few minutes later, and successfully, we all faked our way through dinner.

"So Coby, what kind of work did you do? Is it something you'd like to continue?" With a little shrug and an embarrassed smile, Ky added, "I mean, when you get back on your feet."

"I sold insurance, and I hated every moment of it. Being the suit and tie sales pitch guy never did fit me so well." Coby was so soft spoken that his low voice was almost a murmur. "I kind of always wanted to be a tree hugger. An environmental activist or something, you know? I doubt it pays well, but it would be rewarding."

*Death Wish*

Kylarai gripped her burger tight, causing it to drip sauce onto her plate. She stared off wistfully toward the forest. "I used to fantasize about working for Greenpeace. Unfortunately, that didn't happen. I ended up in law instead. Not even juicy criminal law. Just boring old divorce court nonsense."

Coby studied her, his hazel eyes taking in her delicate mannerisms as she tucked a strand of dark hair behind her ear. "You must get a bird's eye view of how ugly things can get. It must at least give you a new appreciation for love. I mean real love, the kind that would never end up being a fight over a house or kids."

"Well… I can't say I know a lot about that. Not firsthand anyway." A shadow passed behind Ky's eyes, but it was gone as quickly as it came.

"Me neither."

A moment of strange quiet settled over us. I watched two sparrows flittering in a tree in the yard. They made me long to be one with them, an animal of the earth, a part of nature. I longed to be wolf.

Shaz picked up the conversation by telling Coby a little about our past in this town. He carefully edited out some details about Raoul and Zoey. The way Shaz told it, we lived a sitcom life with laughter and joyous times. I paused, my burger momentarily forgotten as I stared at him in wonder. Was his story for Coby's benefit, or did Shaz really remember it that way?

Maybe I saw things all wrong. Perhaps it wasn't as bad as I remembered. Yeah… right.

"Anybody else as eager as I am?" Shaz was drawn to the forest, his gaze locked on the beckoning expanse of trees in the distance.

"Yes." I felt the wolf pacing inside. I was done with going through the human motions of supper and drinks. It was time.

Coby grew nervous. His anxious energy prickled along my skin. "I don't know if I can do this."

"You can." Shaz gave him a friendly pat on the back. "The beauty of it is that you don't have to fight it right now. It feels better when you can just let it happen. I promise."

I understood what Coby was going through. The change made you vulnerable. I met Shaz's gaze. "We'll go on ahead. You guys can catch up."

Leaving Coby in Shaz's capable hands seemed like the best plan. He was already a nervous mess. Having Kylarai and I present wouldn't help. In the beginning, when I'd first changed, I'd been alone. It took a long time to get comfortable with other wolves.

Hoping to avoid adding to Coby's distress, I descended the deck stairs and disrobed beneath the raised patio, out of sight. Kylarai joined me, stretching her lithe frame before dropping to the ground. She was wolf before her paws touched the grass. The change came much easier over time. Embracing it, I savored the way it felt as the wolf burst forth. It took only seconds for my body to re-knit itself into wolf form. A brief explosion of pain quickly faded away to bliss.

I trotted along behind Kylarai as she slipped through the open back gate and into the field. The sun had dropped low enough to give us the cover of near dark. We made our way toward the trees, pausing here and there to sniff at the scent of another animal or check out the gopher holes littering the field.

My thoughts were simple when I was wolf. I could easily allow the human side of me to fall away, and I was happy just to be.

We had just blended in amid the trees when I cast a glance back toward the house. It was tiny in the distance, just one of many that backed onto the field. My keen eyes easily spotted Shaz's white fur. An ash brown wolf flanked him. Coby would be just fine. I was sure of it.

I launched into a light run. Raising my nose to the wind, I breathed deeply of the scents of the forest. Fertile earth, fresh pine and an assortment of other smells filled my nostrils. I was home.

We lingered near the clearing in the middle of the woods, waiting for Shaz and Coby to catch up. It didn't take them long. Coby's eyes were wide and alert, but otherwise he seemed comfortable in his wolf skin. He paused to sniff everything as he went. The new scents and keen senses could be overwhelming at first, but they were intriguing.

The scent of coyote was fresh. They'd passed through not long ago. They had a tendency to avoid us, so we didn't come across them often. For the most part the local coyotes lingered on the other side of town, creeping only close enough to be heard at night when they raised their voices in yips and howls.

Hoping to ease Coby into our world, we playfully stalked small night critters. Following the scent of a field mouse, I tracked it to where it hid in the long grass, hoping to go unnoticed. I pounced playfully, a few feet from the mouse, sending him scurrying away as fast as his little legs would carry him. He was a cute little thing, beady eyes and all.

## Death Wish

I wouldn't dream of hurting him. The little mouse was in no danger from me; I preferred prey that could fight back.

Shaz led a small hunt when we came across a relatively fresh deer trail. I had little interest, but I followed along, slinking through the trees as we tracked the big buck. He was an impressive beast alright. The rack of antlers atop his head was massive. Tall with long legs, he was a gorgeous creature.

I hung back, watching as the others encircled the deer. Kylarai was an ace hunter. She had a way of gliding up alongside her prey without being noticed until it's too late. Her brown hide was barely visible as she stalked the buck. Shaz paused on the opposite side with Coby, waiting for Kylarai to make the first move.

For a moment, everything stopped as we waited for Ky to pounce.

A twig snapped in the distance, mere seconds before the scent of humans reached me. Immediately alert, I met Shaz's green eyes, finding alarm in their depths.

The shotgun blast was as deafening as it was shocking. For a split second I couldn't tell where it hit. Then the deer dropped and began to flail. A strangled sound came from the buck as he thrashed helplessly.

A second shot rang out and something grazed my flank. I'd never known hunters to be in these woods. My heart pounded in my ears. I could barely hear the sound of paws hitting the ground furiously around me as we ran with supernatural speed.

As the adrenaline faded, the pain grew in intensity. By the time we reached Kylarai's backyard, every step I took hurt. It could have been so much worse; a near miss was nothing to laugh off. It hurt like a bitch. I collapsed on the grass, embracing my human form. The wound was ugly, a large, deep puncture that bled profusely. I felt lightheaded but I'd had worse.

"Are you ok, Lex?" Shaz wasted no time resuming human form. He lifted me carefully in his strong arms. "Looks like it just grazed you a good one."

"I'll be fine. It just hurts like a mother fucker." I groaned and clung tight to Shaz. Burying my face in his neck, I concentrated on his familiar scent. "Last thing I need is to get taken out by hunters. Lilah would love that."

He carried me inside, down the hall to the bathroom, while Kylarai ran ahead to turn on lights and wet a towel with warm water. Shaz held me while she cleaned the wound.

"I cannot believe that just happened." Ky's eyes were wide with terror. "That was too close." Reaching into the bathroom cupboard for rubbing alcohol she added, "It's an ugly gash, but it's not as deep as all the blood made it look. Let me clean you up, and you should be fine."

I didn't feel exactly glamorous sitting tight in Shaz's arms while Ky cleaned and bandaged a wound on my ass. How embarrassing.

"Since when do we get hunters this close to town?" I wondered aloud. "I hope that's a one-time thing."

"That scared the hell out of me when that deer dropped. For a second I'd thought one of us had been hit." With a shake of his blonde head, Shaz grimaced. "Thank God it wasn't worse than this."

"This was not how I wanted to introduce Coby to our world." I groaned when Shaz gingerly set me on my feet. Pain shot through my leg and rear end. "We need to let the others know. They need to be careful. It could still be dangerous out there."

I limped my way back down the hall to the kitchen where Coby paced near the dining room table. He'd gotten dressed in jeans and a dark hoodie. The anxiety rolled off him in thick waves.

Shaz swept past me, disappearing outside to fetch our clothing. I leaned on the kitchen counter, using it to hide my nudity from the already uncomfortable Coby. He glanced at me with unease.

"We've never run into humans out there. Never." I didn't think I was reassuring him.

Coby seemed to be trying to look anywhere but at me even though most of my nakedness was hidden behind the counter. Nudity was second nature to me when I was with other werewolves. He was still adjusting.

"That was pretty damn scary. I mean, the guns were terrifying. I've never run like that in my life."

Shaz returned with our clothes, and I slipped my t-shirt on, struggling a little with the tight fitting jeans. They were not ass-wound friendly.

With a gentle hand on Coby's shoulder, Shaz attempted to calm the nervous wolf. "It was an isolated incident. We're safe here."

"I know." Coby nodded. "I'm just trying to process what just happened. I knew life was about to get dangerous, but I had no idea what to expect."

"That's the thing. You never know what to expect."

"If it's not vampires and demons, it's idiot humans with fucking guns." I swore up a storm as I helped myself to an iced tea from the fridge.

Kylarai emerged from her bedroom, clad in a long robe. I envied her comfort. My ass throbbed, and the jeans were not helping. I wanted to get back to Arys's house, to my own robe.

"Well, that was a rush," Ky said, her soft features set in a grim expression. "As long as nobody starts a wolf hunt out here, we're safe."

I nodded, lost in thought. An uneasy feeling grew in the pit of my stomach. It seemed to be a random run in. They'd been hunting deer, not us. Still... I couldn't help but feel a little uneasy.

"I'm going to drive Alexa back to Arys's place. Do you mind if I leave Coby here for a few minutes?" Shaz asked Kylarai. "I'll be right back for him."

"No, of course not. He can hang out here for a bit." Ky gathered her hair into a ponytail before giving me a quick squeeze. "Take it easy."

I wasn't too keen on being chaperoned from place to place, but Arys had been adamant that I not be alone. Trouble really had a way of finding me lately, but I didn't need a babysitter, dammit.

Getting into the small confines of Shaz's Cobalt was both physically and emotionally painful. I was pretty sure we were about to have a conversation neither of us would enjoy.

"Are you ok?" Shaz asked as he backed out of Ky's driveway. He gave his head a little toss to flip a stray lock of platinum hair out of his eyes. That one little action made me melt, and I had to stifle a sigh.

"Yeah, it's all good. Nothing a little time won't heal." Unlike other things.

"That's not what I mean." He glanced over briefly, long enough for me to see that look in his eyes. It was the same look he'd given me the night he'd discovered Arys and I had slept together. The night he showed up at my door and said those dreaded words, 'We need to talk.'

I stared at him expectantly, studying his profile, my gaze lingering on his strong jaw line and the curve of his lips. Did we have to do this now? Couldn't we just continue to sweep it under the rug?

"I'm sorry about last night," Shaz continued. "I shouldn't have been such a dick. How are you doing? With the whole Shya incident? Arys said you haven't slept since."

"Oh he did, did he? Vampire has a big mouth." I frowned. They had taken to discussing me behind my back, an annoying habit. "I'm fine. I'm just not ready to relive it in my dreams yet."

Shaz winced. "That bad, huh?"

"I can say this much, if you ever think you're a monster, attend a scary ass demon ritual, and you'll feel a whole lot better about yourself." I shuddered as an image of the savage demon orgy flashed through my mind.

"That's reassuring."

We drove along in silence for several blocks as Shaz took the long way around town to Arys's house. I waited patiently. I knew Shaz well. Whatever he wanted to say, it would come out. Shaz wore his heart on his sleeve. Emotional and sensitive, he was everything I wasn't. And, I loved that about him.

His grip tightened on the wheel. He ran a hand through his hair once, then twice, his most obvious tell. Finally, he blurted, "I want to be the one you choose in the end. We belong together, Lex."

"In the end?" I stammered, trying to grasp what he was saying.

"I can't shake this feeling that things are going to get worse between us before they get better. I've been in love with you for years. We're just getting started, and already we're falling apart." Shaz stopped the car at a red light and took the opportunity to squeeze my hand. Pain tainted his energy, thick and stifling. "We can't go on like this forever."

My pulse quickened, and I sat up straighter in my seat. A sharp throb shot through my leg, and I made a pained sound. "What are you talking about, Shaz?"

"Come on, Lex. How long can we all keep playing musical beds for before it blows up in our faces? Three is a crowd, and five is just getting downright nasty." He made a face of disgust. "Not to mention however many lovers Arys has on the side that neither of us know about."

"None," I said, uncertain of my feelings regarding this conversation. I was an unwilling participant. "The only ones messing around on the side are you and I. Believe it or not."

Shaz was quiet, his lips pursed in thought. "I'm surprised. Doesn't seem like his style."

I took a deep breath, bracing myself, hoping I wasn't making a mistake with what I was about to say. "You know, Shaz, you're the only one currently involved with someone outside the three of us."

He stiffened and took the next corner sharp enough to make the tires squeal. "Yeah, I guess that's true. I'm the bad guy here. I can't stop punishing you for what happened with Kale."

"I noticed. Why is that exactly?"

We turned onto Arys's street. I thought he might not answer. Shaz pulled the car to a stop in front of the house and turned to me. The emotion in his eyes was raw and strong when he said, "Because I can't punish you for Arys."

The silence was deafening. It had been no secret that Shaz wasn't happy about my relationship with Arys. Hearing his confession made it painfully clear how deep his feelings were. He would never be ok with what Arys and I shared.

I didn't know how to respond. I was shocked by his confession. And hurt. Hurt that he would hold this inside for a year, letting it fester into something too big to control.

"So Bianca is my punishment for something that has never been within my control?" My voice cracked, and I cringed inwardly. "That hurts, Shaz."

He looked away from me, out the driver's side window at the dark house across the street. "I thought it would make me feel better. Like I'd evened the score. All it's done is make me feel like shit."

"Well, that makes two of us." I couldn't tear my gaze from him. He wouldn't look at me, and that made the suffocating sensation inside me grow.

"I know you and Arys belong together." Shaz's voice caught as if he wrestled with his emotions. "But, I spent so many nights lying awake at Raoul's, listening to him have his way with you, wiping your tears after, the entire time wishing you would look at me the way you looked at him. And now, I'm reliving it with the vampire."

I felt myself deflate. His solemn words crushed me. "I've always loved you, Shaz. I didn't always know it though. Raoul was a teenage dream. A foolish nightmare I was torturing myself with. Arys is part of me. He is my other half. And, you and I should both know that if I am anything, it's my own worst enemy. I adore Arys, but I need you."

"But for how long?" He turned to pin me with jade green wolf eyes, stormy with emotion. "How long can we play this game for three? I get it. I do. It's like he and I are black and white, and you're the shade of grey that links us. I feel like I'm part of this whether I want to be or not."

"You don't have to be," I murmured. I couldn't help but think of Kale and his plea for me to set him free. Maybe it was time to set Shaz free, too. "I love you, Shaz, but I don't want to imprison you. You deserve more. I want you to be happy."

His shoulders slumped. Again, he ran a hand through his hair. I hid a smile, knowing he wouldn't understand it.

"You make me happy, Lex. I know I have a role to play here. I don't want to let you down. I don't really know what I'm trying to say. I just wanted to apologize for last night, and to tell you that no matter what happens, I'm still here. I'm still yours."

The intensity in his eyes was both startling and reassuring. We were both fighting so hard to keep things from coming between us. But, we couldn't win that battle as long as he was seeking a fix from Bianca.

"I know that, Shaz." That wasn't what I wanted to say. Rather than risk an argument about Kale or further discussion about our ill-fated triad with Arys, I simply smiled and reached to stroke a hand down his face.

I shared his desperation, the need for the assurance that everything would be ok. It wouldn't though. There was no happily ever after for us, at least not the way we wanted.

## Chapter Sixteen

I clutched a takeout cup of my favorite coffee and stared expectantly at the entryway. Any moment now, Shya would sweep through the doors of The Wicked Kiss. After avoiding my attempts to reach him for the past three days, the demon had decided to grace me with a few minutes of his precious time.

The last few days had been blessedly quiet. After the talk with Shaz the night of the barbecue, I had fallen into Arys's bed and slept a luxurious twenty-four hours. For that one day, I escaped into my subconscious where for once, everything was calm.

Things had been unusually quiet since. There had been no further attempts on my life from Lilah's vampire flunkies, and I had yet to see her again. However, that was only a matter of time, hence the need for Shya and I to have a little talk.

I sat alone at the bar though Shaz was in the building. He was taking security detail a lot more seriously since we'd discovered who was behind the hit. Arys was prowling the city for the vampire who had set fire to my house. He wouldn't be deterred despite my protests.

I was starting to feel more comfortable in The Wicked Kiss than I did anywhere else these days. Funny considering not so long ago it scared the hell out of me. That was before my definition of scary had been redefined.

I never saw her heading my way. Not until she was almost upon me. I swung my gaze away from the entryway in time to see Bianca closing in on me. I tensed, ready to get up and face her. At the last moment, I decided to stay seated. She wasn't a threat. That didn't mean I wanted to hear what she had to say though.

Bianca didn't dare take the barstool next to me. She stood a safe few feet away, forcing a cool, collected demeanor. She was nervous. Good.

"I know I'm the last person you want to see right now," Bianca began, meeting my eyes with the false confidence of a woman who knew damn well she was playing with fire. "I just wanted to tell you that for what it's worth, there's never been a time I've fucked him when he hasn't called me by your name."

Her brazenness ticked me off, but her words were like water on the flames. I couldn't help but feel a grim sense of satisfaction.

"Why the hell are you telling me this?" I stared into her with the intensity of the wolf. "I didn't kill you. Why make me reconsider?"

"I'm not your enemy. I just wanted to make that clear."

She stalked away before I could correct her. Vampires were always working an angle. If hers was to state that she had no loyalties to Lilah, she could save it. If the vampires in this city were forced to take sides, I sure as hell didn't want Bianca on mine.

A small smile played about my lips. I sensed the truth in what she said about Shaz. It didn't make his actions any less painful, but it added some sweetness to the sting.

Smirking to myself, I turned on my stool and found myself face to face with Shya. I jumped, spilling coffee on the bar in front of me.

"Goddammit, Shya!" Heat crept up my cheeks as I reached for napkins and furiously wiped up the mess.

The demon looked me over with crimson snake eyes, taking in my long loose locks and simple jeans and t-shirt attire. He appeared no different than he ever did. Clad in a pricey suit, his jet-black hair slicked into place, the only things missing were his wings.

"I don't have much time." Like usual, he wasted no time on small talk. "I trust you wish to discuss Lilah."

"I do." I nodded, glancing about to ensure nobody lingered close enough to eavesdrop. "Were you aware that she put out a hit on me?"

"I was. And, I forbade her from killing you." Shya shrugged as if he couldn't see the big deal.

I sipped my coffee, wishing it were blood or whiskey. "That hasn't stopped her from sending others after me."

"I knew you could handle them. You've proven me right."

"They burned my fucking house down! With me inside." I wasn't impressed with Shya's flippant attitude.

He watched me closely, noting the rise and fall of my tone, the tight grip on my coffee cup. "Yet here you sit. Alive."

"Fine, forget it. I'm not talking in circles with you tonight. I just want to know why Lilah wants me dead and what I can do about it."

Shya's gaze dropped to the dragon etched into my flesh. It began to itch and burn. I sat stiffly, refusing to scratch it like I wanted.

"Lilah wants to break the curse that holds her in a corporeal form. With her power angelically bound, Lilah, a goddess of the underworld, becomes a run of the mill vampire." The demon scanned the vicinity curiously. "A vampire. A creature that you have power over. You can keep her from breaking the curse, so of course she wants you dead."

I chewed on that for a minute, letting my gaze wander over the crowd on the dance floor. Lilah was desperate. I had seen it in her eyes the night she gave me the Dragon Claw. Desperation would drive people to do crazy things. Demons, likely more so.

"Makes sense," I acknowledged. "Where do you stand on all this?"

Shya's lips twitched. The haughty way he held himself and the amusement perpetually dancing in his eyes made him appear entertained and disaffected, yet a subtle shift in his energy betrayed his unease. Despite always surrounding myself with my best shields around Shya, I could feel it.

"Lilah's curse is best left intact."

A man of few but effective words tonight; I could respect that. "Why exactly do we not want her to break it? Give me something here."

"Brush up on your demonology. Lilah is the firstborn granddaughter of Lilith, the first human to become a demon, a powerful bloodline. Free of that curse, she'd resume her rightful place as a dark goddess."

Shya tapped his fingers on the counter. He spoke as if he were in a rush, the white rabbit realizing he was late.

"I know who Lilith is," I replied, watching him anxiously pick at an invisible thread on his sleeve. "I thought that story was a myth. So, why don't we want Lilah to reclaim her throne? Stop being such a damn demon and spit out something I can work with."

Shya's eagerness to leave was obvious and annoying. The bastard had burned his mark into me, yet he couldn't give me ten minutes of his uninterrupted time? Bullshit.

"Goddess of Chaos." He slammed a fist down on the bar. "Should be self-explanatory."

"You have more power than she does. Right now. You want to keep it that way." I wasn't asking; I saw one of those opportunities Arys had warned me to watch for, and I took it.

The demon eyed me suspiciously, one finely sculpted brow raised. "Yes."

"Then tell me how to kill her."

A frown marred Shya's smooth features. "Killing her would only destroy her physical body."

Oh hell, I groaned inwardly. Demons never ceased to astound me. Something came to me then; Lilah had handled Shya's dagger gingerly.

"That's something she doesn't want either. She was wary of the Dragon Claw."

"No, if her body is destroyed, she would return to her angelic cage."

I was confused. "I don't get it. That sounds like a pretty good place for her to me. So why don't we just send her there?"

Shya leaned in close, invading my personal space. He smelled like cinnamon and sulfur. "No. Eventually she would manipulate a weak angel; she would return to destroy us. Do you understand? Even angels cannot destroy a demon as powerful as Lilah. They can only contain her. We should bind her here, where we have control."

"A weak angel," I whispered, more to myself than to Shya. "Like Falon?"

"Falon?" Shya repeated, his eyes on the front entry behind me. He didn't get another word out before a commotion broke out in the lobby.

Shouts rang out, and the atmosphere became chaotic and frenzied. Several patrons stopped to see what was going on, but more continued to dance in oblivion. I got to my feet to check things out at the same moment my sister appeared in the doorway.

Two heavily built men in dark suits flanked Juliet. Each of them wore a gun at the hip. One carried what looked to be a heavy-duty taser. Shaz was at Juliet's side, speaking in low tones. She ignored him, striding toward me while he kept pace with her. One of my other security guys lingered in the entry, blood streaming from his nose.

I turned to see what Shya made of this, but he was gone. The stool where he'd sat was empty. Only his fading scent remained. *Figures.*

"Nice to see you again, Ms. Fitzgerald," I greeted her with a brittle smile. "I trust this is not a personal visit."

So, the FPA had sent my own sister to bring me in for Abigail Irving's death. Nice move. Very well played. I knew it had been too much to hope we could resume a familial relationship. We had been dead to one another since that night over a decade ago.

"I'm sorry, Alexa." Juliet held her hands out in an apologetic gesture. In tight jeans and a cropped leather jacket, she looked both trendy and dangerous. "I thought it best if I came for this. I don't want anyone to get hurt."

Shaz stood off to the side, looking helpless and angry. I knew this was going to get ugly. Besides, I wanted no part of any organization that would send one sibling after another. I was suddenly grateful Shya and Veryl had gotten to me first.

"I'm sorry you thought this was a good idea." I crossed my arms and waited calmly. I was not going without a hell of a fight.

"We know you killed Abigail. You and Kale Sinclair." Juliet held a hand up to her companions who were looking eager to get the ball rolling. "We're here to officially detain you."

"Sorry, little sister. I'm not going to make this easy for you." I reached out with my power, feeling for Kale's energy in the building and finding it. He shouldn't be here.

One of Juliet's partners stepped forward, threatening to get too close. He slapped the taser against his open palm and glowered down at me from his six foot five height.

"We don't have to take you alive," he barked. "One wrong move, and I will take you out."

I laughed then and gestured for him to come closer. I'd slash his throat open before he could blink.

"That's enough out of you, Agent!" Juliet snapped. She was clearly the one in charge here, and she wanted her people to remember that. "Back up and shut your mouth, or go wait outside."

Agent Asshole stepped back beside the guy who was smart enough to stay quiet. Juliet shot him a dark look before turning back to me.

"Alexa, this doesn't have to get violent or ugly. I don't want that." Her dark eyes were pleading. I'd seen her turn that same wide-eyed expression on our parents to get what she wanted, and it had usually worked.

"Have you stopped to think for just a second that maybe Abigail Irving wasn't such a team player after all?" I asked. "She was a double agent, Juliet."

A flicker of doubt crossed Juliet's face. She was following orders without asking questions. Definitely the Juliet I remembered. I had always been the rebellious one. She'd been Mom and Dad's perfect little princess.

"I have to bring you in, Lexi. If what you say is true, we'll find out. We'll get to the bottom of it. Nobody has to get hurt."

"Stop saying that. If you really came here thinking I'd come quietly, then you don't remember me at all. I haven't changed that much." I gathered my power tight, ready to use it if I had to. *Please don't make me,* I prayed silently.

"Where is Kale Sinclair?" Ignoring my firm refusal to co-operate, Juliet continued as if she were in charge. But, she was forgetting that she was in my club. "We know he's here. I've got men on the back exit. There's no escape."

"He's busy right now. I'll get him." Spinning on a heel, I strode toward the back hall, gritting my teeth.

Agent Asshole made as if to come after me. Juliet stopped him with a hand, indicating that the other agent should accompany me. Without a second look at him, I crossed through the back foyer and down the hall, headed for Kale's room. When we were a safe distance down the hall, I slammed a foot into the side of the agent's knee as hard as I could. He let out a scream that I quickly silenced with punch to his throat.

He crumpled immediately, sliding to the floor unconscious. I swiped the gun from the holster at his hip and checked the chambers. Wooden bullets. They had definitely come prepared to take on a vampire. Or, a werewolf that would rise as a vampire upon death. Crap.

I sprinted the rest of the way to Kale's room and banged on the door. I would have burst in if I hadn't been afraid of what I'd find inside.

I kept up the incessant banging until the door swung open suddenly; I almost fell inside, into Kale's arms. The scent of blood and sex was overwhelming. Kale's robe did little to hide his nudity. The three naked brunettes huddled in his bloodstained bed didn't help. If the FPA hadn't just stormed my club, I'd be more actively disgusted at what I saw in Kale's room.

"Alexa, hello. Come to join the party?" Kale snickered and reached for me. His pupils were huge. He was high as a kite.

"Oh for fuck's sakes." I slapped his hand away and punched a hole in the nearest wall. It didn't help, but I needed to blow off some steam. "The FPA is here for us. Because of Abigail Irving. You need to get dressed right now and pull yourself together."

To Kale's credit, he sobered noticeably. "The FPA? Here? Son of a bitch."

"They've got wooden bullets and people at each door. I'm not sure how long we should play along. We're going to have to take them on; I'm not letting them take me out of here."

Kale picked up his pants off the floor and let his robe drop. I turned away with an embarrassed blush but not before catching an eyeful. This was no time for unwelcome flashbacks, but they came unbidden.

I left the room, unable to take Kale's nudity or his giggling playmates a second longer. He caught up with me when I was halfway down the hall. The FPA agent I'd knocked out was struggling to get to his feet, and I threw another punch followed by an elbow as we passed.

I emptied the gun of bullets and dropped the empty weapon beside its owner. I considered killing him and every person Juliet brought with her. But, sending her back to her boss with that kind of news wasn't what I wanted. I didn't want to harm my sister. I just wanted her to go away and leave me alone.

"You really have no idea who she is, do you?" Shaz's voice was loud in the unusual quiet.

The band had stopped, and my remaining staff was ushering patrons out the door. Shawn hung back, well away from the scene taking place near the bar. Making a peace sign, he subtly let me know he was ready if I needed him. Despite the trouble I'd had with vampires, Arys included, they made great allies.

"It's ok, Shaz." I announced our presence. "Everything's cool."

Kale swept past me to walk a slow circle around Juliet and the remaining agent. He looked amazingly well put together for a man who'd been naked just a minute ago. Leather duster over a dark shirt and pants with his hair in disarray, he looked exactly the way he must have felt, like he'd just banged and bled a few humans.

Juliet turned slowly as he made his way around her. She stood ready to defend herself, unwilling to pull her gaze from the vampire looking her over like she was a tasty new treat.

Kale's honey-sweet power was running high and heady. I couldn't let that distract me; I wasn't able to hold my shields in place and use my power.

"So you've come to police the supernatural for the human government." Bemusement shone in Kale's mismatched eyes. "I'm surprised that for an O'Brien, you're such a fool."

My jaw dropped in surprise. So did Juliet's. Her eyes narrowed.

Drawing a stake from inside her jacket, she faced off with Kale. "You murdered a government agent."

"Come now," Kale admonished. "We both know this is just a play the FPA is making to introduce themselves to Alexa with a bang. They fear her. And rightfully so."

"This is about justice for a dead woman," Juliet's snarl was low and deadly. Her wolf paced behind her eyes.

Agent Asshole pulled his gun, aiming it at Kale's chest. "Where the hell is Kellum?"

"Agent Easy?" I quipped, jerking a thumb toward the back hall. "I put him to sleep. He'll be fine. Might have a bit of a concussion though."

A vein pulsed in the agent's forehead, and his finger tightened on the trigger. I let the energy flow down my arm to pool in my hand. If he shot Kale, I'd make that agent wish he'd never been born a thousand times over before I killed him.

Someone must have sounded the alarm because several dark clad agents came in both the front and back doors, surrounding us on all sides. They were all human except for Juliet. Interesting. I was willing to bet the FPA saved their big guns and used the humans as disposable soldiers.

Juliet looked from Kale to me, deciding which of us was a bigger threat. Right then, it was Kale. He was eyeing her with a predator's stare, likely imagining if she'd taste as good as I did. A shiver crept up my spine at the thought.

"We can do this peacefully." Juliet's tone was strong and fierce, but I could sense her unease. "Come willingly, and we can avoid a lot of trouble."

"You overstep your bounds, wolf. Humans have no place in the affairs of monsters. Your choice to represent them will come back to haunt you," Kale promised.

With a shrug and a smirk, Kale lashed out with a kick that Agent Asshole never saw coming. It caught him in the temple, and he dropped to his knees. Kale grabbed the agent's arm and twisted. The snap was audible. The agent's gun dropped to the floor with a clatter.

Everyone moved at once. Three agents swarmed Kale, including Juliet. He turned to take on those with guns first, leaving his back exposed. Juliet saw her brief opportunity and went for it.

I caught her wrist in a bone-crushing grasp. Using the momentum from my swift action, I followed through with a shove that sent her sprawling. But, Juliet was no easy opponent. Both highly trained for her position and having the natural abilities of the wolf, she was on her feet instantly, ready to take me on.

"Don't do this, Lexi," she pleaded. Despite the emotion in her voice, the wolf in her eyes was a stranger, and it wanted a fight.

We were the only two moving in slow motion. As we stared into one another, our companions were locked in combat. A blur of white-blonde was all I could see of Shaz as he took down an agent waving a gun. A shot was fired, hitting the lights over the dance floor. A shower of sparks cascaded down around us.

Kale was throwing off FPA agents like they were children. Using both physical strength and metaphysical power, he had little problem fending them off. For now. Eventually, someone was going to get hurt.

"I'm not going to be treated like a criminal by an agency that would use my own sister against me. Think about what you're doing, Juliet."

She flipped a long curl out of her face and clenched the stake tightly. "I'm doing my job."

Talking it out like long lost family made whole again just wasn't going to happen. I spared a glance at Kale, finding him overrun with agents. Where were they coming from? I let loose the blast of energy I'd been holding. It slammed into the agents, taking several of them down.

I nodded to Juliet. "Fair enough."

For a split second, there was only us, my sister and me, and the memories of the night everything had changed for us. And, then time resumed its regular pace, shattering the dark cloud of nostalgia. We were never going to get that back. Those young girls we'd both been, they had died that night. We weren't the same anymore. That was painfully clear when I blocked Juliet's first hit.

She was a good fighter. Gone were her days of scratches and hair pulling. She knew how to throw her body around, how to take a hit and to throw one, but after so many years on the mean streets at night, so did I.

I knocked the stake from her hand with a kick. She used the opportunity to grab my ankle and twist. I went down hard on the floor, twisting along with her to avoid a broken ankle. Jerking my foot from her grasp, I threw a psi ball at her to gain the seconds needed to get to my feet. Another shot went off, and an agent dropped, holding his leg and screaming.

Juliet was ready for me with a fist that I narrowly dodged. We danced then, a back and forth game of hits and blocks, trying to catch the other off guard. She was spry and light on her feet. More than once, she caught me by surprise. I wasn't above using metaphysical assistance to push her back and knock her feet out from under her.

I kept expecting her to come to her senses and call a stop to this madness. What drove her wasn't simply a desire to do her job. It was having me in front of her after so long, and finally being able to unleash her anger over what Raoul did to us. She wanted me to pay for being his lover.

Seeing fangs on my sister was unnerving. I didn't want to hurt her, but I wasn't giving in either. Shots went off, and this time one of my vampires fell, injured but not dead. I couldn't allow anything to happen to Kale or Shaz. I was going to be forced into admitting defeat.

Juliet rushed me again, and this time she had claws. No deal; I wasn't willing to kill her, so this had to stop now. I rounded on her with a high kick. It hit her square in the forehead, and she went down. I got on top of her, pinning her with my weight and a push of power.

"Tell them to stop!" I demanded. "Now."

She stared up at me with angry wolf eyes. I could feel her hesitance. With a hand on her throat, I gave her a shake. "Dammit, Juliet. Can't you see that our people are going to die over a dead woman who was a goddamn traitor? Stop them."

Rationale battled passionate, righteous fury behind Juliet's dark eyes. "Enough!" She shouted, and like magic, every agent took a defensive stance but obeyed her command.

Shaz and the few vampires who had come to our aid dropped back, watching me for direction. Kale wiped blood from the corner of his lip. A dead agent lay at his feet. Well, that was really going to help our case, wasn't it?

I groaned inwardly before standing up and pulling Juliet to her feet. "You want to watch me suffer. I get that. Really, I do. So you win. Let's go."

Juliet pulled away from me, her eyes downcast. "It's not like that. I have a job to do."

"Let me save you the family drama." Kale stepped forward with a confident swagger. Every agent's gun was trained on him, but he paid them no mind. "You don't want Alexa. You want me. And, I'll go with you right now without any further trouble if you leave her out of this."

Agent Asshole practically threw himself at Juliet in protest. He clutched his broken arm to his chest. A sheen of sweat glistened on his brow and his breath came fast. "Hell no. She was at the murder scene."

Kale set his sights on the agent, and the power just oozed from him. "I acted alone. I killed Abigail Irving, and I loved every damn moment. You only want me."

The heady allure of vampire power was so strong that I almost believed him. A human like Agent Asshole didn't stand a chance under that kind of persuasion. He nodded, dumbfounded and silent. Juliet appeared uncertain. I wanted to protest what Kale was doing, but I couldn't form the words.

"Just you?" Juliet repeated, a glimmer of hope in her eyes. Taking in one of us would be better than neither. "You freely admit this?"

"I'll freely do anything you want me to. As long as Alexa is left alone." The seductive lilt he spoke with was like a hand sliding down my spine.

It seemed to have a similar effect on Juliet because she nodded and gestured to her men to grab him. I watched in shock and awe as Kale stood quietly, willingly allowing them to cuff him. The restraints they used hummed with magic, and that's when my internal alarm went off.

"No," I shouted. "You can't take him. He hasn't done anything. Irving was a fucking traitor." I shoved an agent aside so I could get close to Kale. Placing both hands on his face, I stood on my tiptoes and whispered, "What are you doing?"

"You saved my ass. Now I'm saving yours." Taking advantage of our close proximity, Kale pressed his lips to mine. The kiss was brief but intoxicating. He tasted like blood and honey, waking my hunger. Draped in his saccharine pull, I ached for him.

I wasn't content to keep my mouth shut and let him take the fall for me. We had both taken Abigail's blood. She had been our victim.

"Juliet, be reasonable. You're a pawn to a political agenda. That's not the Zelda Fitzgerald I heard you talk nonstop about." It was desperate; appealing to the girl she'd once been was my last resort. We were both sporting some ugly cuts and bruises. Now that we'd scrapped it out the way siblings do, there was nothing else for us to do.

Her eyelashes fluttered, and she looked away, suddenly unable to meet my eyes. "I'm not Zelda Fitzgerald."

"No, you're Juliet O'Brien," I mimicked our father's tone. "So start acting like it."

She did look at me then. With the stubborn fury that was neither werewolf nor woman but simply O'Brien, she waved a hand dismissively. "Get him out of here, boys."

Agent Asshole jammed his gun into Kale's back and gave him a shove. "You heard the woman, bloodsucker. Try anything, and I'll bury a wooden bullet in your heart before you can blink."

"You're not taking him without taking me," I protested, my voice rising in panic.

Kale let the agents push him along toward the door. He spared a parting glance at Shaz with the command, "Grab her."

Shaz didn't need to be told twice. He intercepted me before I could follow. I struggled against him, but he over-powered me. I could have fought him off with a slap of a psi ball, but I could never do that to him.

I watched helplessly as the FPA agents ushered Kale out of the building. Juliet lingered though she slowly edged toward the exit.

"I have never felt as betrayed by anyone as I do by you, right now." I spat the words at her. "We're family, Juliet. We were."

With a shake of her head, Juliet had the nerve to look hurt. "Lexi, you can't be trusted. You work with demons and share power with vampires. I just want to do what's right."

"You mean what the FPA tells you is right. They have you brainwashed."

"I'm not sure that I'm the one who isn't seeing things as they really are."

That burned. I wanted to run after her, to tackle her like I had when I'd caught her reading my diary. Shaz's arms tight around my waist prevented that.

"I'll be coming for him, Juliet. I can find you and the FPA. I will. You tell them I'm coming." My shouts grew absolutely venomous as I thrashed in Shaz's grip. "That vampire is mine. I claim him, and I will answer for him. If the FPA touches one hair on his head, sending you in here tonight will be the greatest mistake they ever made."

She gave a curt nod before disappearing through the exit without a look back. Only after she was long gone did Shaz let me go.

I spun around to face him, ready to cuss him out for restraining me. The crestfallen expression he wore stole my words. The patrons and staff that remained dispersed, leaving us alone in front of the bar.

"You lied to me, Lex," Shaz accused. "You said it was over with him, but it's not. I saw the way he kissed you. The way he looks at you. Hell, I just watched him take the fall for you."

"It is over. I haven't been screwing him. Not since the one and only time." I could not believe he was doing this. It was ballsy and rude, not to mention uncharacteristic.

Shaz's jade gaze dropped to my wrist. "You made a deal with a demon to save Kale. He just handed himself over to a bunch of lunatic humans to save you. It's so not over with you two. You and I both know that love can exist just fine without sex. In fact, in some ways, it's stronger."

I swallowed hard. He was right. Shaz and I had loved each other for years before we were ready to take it to the next level. Still, Kale was different.

"I would do the same thing for you or Jez or Ky." I ran my tongue over my lips, tasting blood and Kale. I needed to hunt. The bloodlust lurked beneath the cloak of my fury, waiting for the right moment to strike.

"I know," he replied quietly, "but would it be for the same reasons?"

Vulnerable. My white wolf was in pain. We were both in pain, but his pain made him enticing. Too enticing.

"You fuck another woman and call her by my name, but you're questioning why I make the choices I've made?" My voice broke, and I was suddenly overwhelmed. The dam barring the wave of emotion threatened to break. I wasn't ready for that. "I have to go. I need to kill something."

My pulse pounded in my ears. My stomach twisted, and the vampire's hunger filled me. I needed to feel a victim's struggles while I spilled their blood, and that victim could never be Shaz.

I hightailed it out of there like the devil himself chased me. Shaz called my name, but he didn't stop me. He knew the risks as well as I did, and Arys wasn't there to keep us from crossing the line this time.

The parking lot was empty and eerily silent. Part of me hoped Lilah would take a shot at me tonight. I needed to blow off some steam. I had no destination in mind. Giving myself over to the growing darkness inside me, I let the bloodlust be my guide.

## *Chapter Seventeen*

It was getting easier to give in. When I just quit fighting, the entire process went a lot smoother. Though I hated myself afterwards every damn time, in the moment, it was bliss.

Like so many times before, I slipped into that zone that was pure predator. The tangy aroma of blood tickled my nose. It filled my mouth, warm and pulsing with life. I drank in both blood and energy, seeking all my victim had to give. Perhaps choosing one of Kale's bimbos was in poor taste, but she had come out the back door into the parking lot at the wrong time.

I sat on the ground, leaning against the building. I stared at the dead woman, and she stared back at me, her eyes open and lifeless. The gaping wound in her throat mocked me. I was a killer, and Juliet was justified in wanting to stop someone like me.

Some might say Kale's playmate knew what she was risking by coming to a place like this, and they would be right. I didn't let vampires kill in my club, but it still happened. Yet, I couldn't even keep my own rules. Pathetic.

For a long time, I sat there, listening to the traffic on the streets beyond the club. The high began to ebb, and reality crept back in. I couldn't accept that the FPA had Kale. What would they do to him? Kill him? Worse? I had to do something.

A few hours remained before dawn. I needed to get back inside, clean up and slip Shawn a handful of cash to take care of the body. I was supposed to meet Arys back at his place for sunrise. Until then, I had a few things to think about.

The club was almost empty. A few staff members lingered. Most of the rooms in the back hall were occupied. I could feel the mix of human and vampire energy. And Shaz. I could feel his wolf though he was nowhere to be seen. My stomach dropped.

With a few words to Shawn and the instruction to help himself to the cash from the register, I went to the washroom to wash the blood from my hands and face. It wasn't as bad as I'd expected. Getting better at this whole blood-hungry killer thing wasn't something I could get excited about.

I stood there staring at my reflection in the mirror. My eyes were the deep brown I'd always known them to be. It was more unnerving than if they'd been Arys's enchanting blue. When I saw him within me like that, it was easier to blame my actions on the undead power rolling around inside me. Brown eyes. It was all me.

I left the ladies' room and took a left into the back hall rather than a right toward the heart of the club. I shouldn't do this. I told myself to stop, but one foot in front of the other, I drew closer to the door that beckoned me.

I knew what I'd find, knew I didn't need that truth branded forever in my mind's eye, yet I couldn't turn back. No more hiding behind closed doors and words left unsaid. I reached the door marked with the number six, and my hand trembled on the knob.

Pushing the door open, I took in the scene before me, and everything began to spin. A tangle of naked limbs, the scent of sweat, and a startled shout all hit me at once. I stared in open-mouthed horror at my white wolf and his illicit lover as he scrambled to pull the sheets over them. But, it was too late.

Reality was a cruel mistress. I felt like the rug had been pulled out from under me. This was too much. This was where I surrendered. White flag. I'm done.

Shaz's jade green eyes were locked on me. He sat there frozen, utter surprise etched on his face. His platinum hair was a mess. Red lipstick smears painted the corner of his mouth in a mocking shade of scarlet. Matching stains adorned his bare chest and neck. I didn't want to see this, didn't want to feel this knife twisting in my gut.

Apple cinnamon scented candles lit up the room, but they did nothing to disguise the telltale scent of sex, blood and shame. My stomach turned painfully, and I thought I might be sick.

Like the tragic emotional scene in a movie, everything seemed to slow down. I opened my mouth, but no sound came out. There he was, naked in her bed with her atop him, clutching the sheet as if it would hide the truth.

Shaz sat there looking guilty. Bianca watched me expectantly, waiting for my reaction. Maybe she expected me to finish her off this time, like I'd promised. Our eyes met, and I saw the deep-seated satisfaction she couldn't hide. The tiniest hint of a smile tugged at her lips.

Deeper than my own pain was the sorrow of my wolf. That part of me didn't understand how he could do this. I backed up until I hit the wall. I tried to form words, needing to say something.

"Alexa, wait! Please, let me explain." Shaz sprang into action, shoving Bianca aside.

I held up my hands and shook my head. "Stay away from me."

Unable to contain the tears, I ran. I didn't stop until I reached the parking lot. I collapsed on the pavement, hysterical sobs building inside me. Blood red tears stained my hands. Knowing Shaz would come after me if I stayed, I got to my feet and continued moving. Maybe Arys was right. Maybe it was time to burn The Wicked Kiss to the ground.

I left my car behind and just walked without a destination. I headed south, away from the downtown core. The agony cut like shards of glass against my insides. I couldn't do this anymore.

Shaz and I, we were over.

If I'd doubted it before, what I'd seen tonight had only confirmed it. Maybe it had started with Shaz needing a fix, but it had evolved. Now he was lost, consumed by his need to hurt me and to justify it to himself. This wasn't the Shaz I knew. He had changed, but so had I. And now, here we were. Broken.

I left the busy downtown district behind and with it, the raw, painful truth. I intended just to walk as far as I could possibly get without further thought. That's all I wanted, to get away, as far away as possible.

The vampires that jumped me had other plans.

Six of them swarmed me, each coming from a different direction. Lost in the gut-wrenching pain of my heartbreak, I hadn't sensed their approach. Lilah couldn't have chosen a better time to send her people after me. They were on me so fast that I didn't stand a chance.

A large fist met my face and stars exploded behind my eyes. I went down immediately, but two of them dragged me to my feet. I struggled against them, but the blows kept coming until I couldn't tell how many of them were hitting me. If any of them had power, they didn't use it. This was a good, old-fashioned beating.

"She doesn't seem so tough," a gruff voiced vampire said to his buddies. "This is a little disappointing."

"Aw look, Colin, you made her cry." A chorus of laughter followed.

I reached for my power with the intent to use it on the guys holding me, but my concentration was scattered, and my vision swam. I'd taken so many hits already, I could barely focus. Lesson learned. Never underestimate the power of a group beating.

The taste of my own blood filled my mouth. I was not going down this way. I lashed out with a metaphysical attack on the two holding me. It threw them both off their feet. However, one pulled me off balance, and I fell to my knees. A psi ball in each hand, I hit two more. I could scarcely keep track of who was where. The remaining two rushed me, wrestling me to the ground. My head smacked the pavement, and everything began to darken.

I expected the blows to rain down upon me, but they never came. A sharp cry came from one of my assailants. It was followed by shouts and commotion. I blinked to clear my vision, finding myself looking up at a man with great silver wings. Aw, shit. Not another fence rider. How could this help me?

But sure enough, he was smacking the vampires around like they were dolls. The swell of his power was stifling and heavy, just like Falon's. With a groan, I rolled over, trying to catch my breath as I got to my feet.

My head pounded, a throbbing so intense it hurt to open my eyes. A strong hand on my arm sent a surge of panic through me. I found myself staring into sympathetic, gold-flecked green eyes. It took a moment for it to sink in that he wasn't trying to hurt me.

"You're alright," he said, his voice soft and soothing. "Let's get you cleaned up."

I spat blood and swiped a hand across my face. Between the tears and the smacks, my face was a mess of blood. I probably looked like I'd been hit by a bus.

Three of the vampires were dust. The others were long gone. I took a few shuddery breaths and gazed at my rescuer. He was tall and lean with a muscular build and silver wings similar to Falon's. That's where the similarities ended. This angel had gentle eyes and a mouth that was made for smiling. His hair was short and thick, a light brown that could have been dirty blonde.

"Please don't tell me you're a friend of Falon's," I muttered, finding my teeth intact. Thank God for that.

The angel grimaced. "Hell no. I'm not affiliated with that sorry bastard. Come on. I know a little watering hole nearby. We'll get you washed up and order a round of shots."

He led me along down the quiet street. I was puzzled for sure. An angel that wanted to do shots? Well, he was fallen.

"Thanks," I said, calming as the adrenaline slowly began to fade. "You really saved my ass there."

"I'm surprised you couldn't save your own ass. You are the vampire wolf, are you not?"

"Vampire wolf," I laughed. "That's a good one. I guess you could say that. It's been a long night. I was kind of taken by surprise."

"I'm Willow." He offered me a hand, which I accepted.

"Alexa."

"Ah, the protector of mankind."

"Excuse me?"

"Your name. That's what it means. The protector of mankind."

His words struck hard and sunk deep. I hadn't known my name meant something so profound. After taking a human life tonight, hearing it felt like a slap in the face.

"If only that was true." I smiled bitterly and my face hurt.

Willow tilted his head, studying me. "It could be."

We stopped at an abandoned building with darkened windows, but when Willow pulled the battered wooden door open, light and music spilled out onto the street. A small weathered sign read Woody's Pub.

"I love this place." Willow's smile became mischievous as he ushered me inside, his wings disappearing from sight.

I really wasn't sure what to expect from this guy. I had very little experience with his kind, and what I knew of them was not good at all. Still, he'd saved my ass, and so far, Willow was nothing like Falon. A relief, to say the least.

The pub was relatively small. Most of the patrons were middle aged and older. A TV hung from the ceiling in a corner broadcasting a sports channel. Willow pulled me along, my hand clasped tightly in his much the way a protective parent might hold onto a child.

Without hesitation, he pushed through the door to the ladies' room. A woman stood at the sink washing her hands. She caught sight of Willow in the mirror, then my battered face, and her jaw dropped. She pursed her lips in disapproval before hurriedly drying her hands. Her eyes met mine, and I waited, expecting her to say something. Another glance at Willow had her rushing for the door.

"Is bursting into the women's washroom something you make a habit of doing?" I asked when we were alone. I busied myself wetting disposable hand towels with warm water.

"Not usually," he laughed softly. "I never expected it to be occupied. This place isn't known for having a lot in the way of female clientele."

My face was a mess. Blood ran from my nose and lip. My left eye was bruised deep purple and swollen. Small bruises decorated my chin and forehead. Wincing in pain, I dabbed at the blood staining my skin.

"Here," Willow reached to take the wet towel from me. "Let me help you."

With a gentle hand, he turned my face toward him and began to clean my wounds. It was comforting and inviting. Though he was a stranger to me, I felt safe with him. Protected.

I perched on the edge of the counter, trying to figure out this fallen yet protective angel. I studied him closely. Long thick lashes framed his beautiful eyes. His skin was flawless and smooth. He smelled faintly of rain on a summer night. Though he was casually dressed in jeans and a long sleeved t-shirt, he had an ethereal glow. I could feel the light in him, a quality Falon didn't have.

"Good thing your kind heals fast," Willow mused, reaching for fresh towels.

"Thank you for helping me," I said softly. "Oddly enough, getting my ass kicked has been the best part of my night."

Willow carefully buried the bloody towels in the bottom of the garbage. I made a useless attempt at finger combing my hair. It was pointless really.

"Let's go drink. Then you can tell me all about it."

## Death Wish

A few minutes later we were sitting across from one another at a small round table, several shots of tequila placed between us. I eyed the shot glasses warily. Tequila had not been my friend in the past.

"You first." He slid a shot to me along with the saltshaker. A tray of limes sat within reach. "Take the shot and start talking."

Simple enough. What did I have to lose other than sobriety? All the booze in the world wouldn't erase my evening. I skipped the salt and went right for the tequila. Like always, it tasted how I'd imagine floor cleaner would taste. With a shudder, I choked down the shot and reached for a lime. It didn't take long for the brutal liquor to hit me.

"Where should I start? With the lover I just caught in bed with another woman? Or the sister that works for the FPA who just took one of my best friends into custody?"

Willow tossed back his shot like a champ. "Start at the beginning."

It was easy to open up to him. As the shots kept going down, the words kept coming. Before I knew it, I was telling him everything. Raoul's secret past as my mother's lover, my bond to Arys, issues with Shaz and Juliet, Lilah's hit on me and the woman I'd killed that very night. It all came spilling out.

I sat there in a small, seedy bar, confessing my every sin to an angel, but talking to someone who wasn't a part of my inner circle was liberating. Willow was a keen listener, commenting and questioning in all the right places. His eyes held no judgment, not once.

After a good hour of pouring out my deepest feelings and darkest secrets, I was both drunk and carefree. Sure, it may be temporary, but I'd take it. The tequila hangover I'd have later was going to be brutal, so I might as well make the bender worth it.

"So, what do you think?" I asked finally. "Am I broken or what?"

Willow leaned forward on the table, his hands clasped. "No more than the rest of us. I think you're stronger than you give yourself credit for. You can handle what happened tonight, and you can handle what's yet to come."

I ran a finger over the dragon etched into my wrist. "I wish I could be so sure."

"It's not supposed to be easy to do what's right. That's what makes it worthwhile. You could have given in long ago. Instead you fight the darkness of your vampire." He spoke with such certainty.

"You were never meant to be together. Twin flames rarely live the same lifetime. They aren't meant to. Too often, they destroy one another. The intensity of their bond is too great, and it consumes them."

"How is that supposed to be making me feel better?" I laughed drunkenly, unable to let the weight of his words sink in just then.

"Because the two of you have a purpose. Withstand the hardships of your bond, and you'll be defined by the good you do. Not the bad."

Maybe he was right. The mistakes I'd made, they didn't define me; I wouldn't let them. There was a reason for everything. I had to believe that.

"I wish I could do something about that." Willow's gaze fell to my wrist. "There was a time when I could have abolished it."

"What's your story, Willow?" Curiosity got the best of me even though I had planned not to ask. "How can you be fallen and be so amazing?"

"My story is hardly worth telling." He shrugged and reached for another shot of tequila. "I'd much rather talk about you."

"I'm sick of talking about me. Sick of being me. Sometimes." Tequila burned its way into my stomach, and I made a face. The lime did little to take the edge off.

Willow frowned. "You don't mean that. Everything you've faced has led you to this moment. Right where you're supposed to be. Trust it."

Before I could respond, we were rudely interrupted by a grey-haired, overweight drunk. He stumbled into our table, slurring an apology. His bloodshot gaze landed on me, taking in my battered appearance.

His lips peeled back into a slimy grin, revealing several missing teeth. He gave Willow a smack on the back and chuckled. "Looks like the little lady stepped out of line. You do what you gotta do, ain't that right, pal?"

Willow was on his feet throwing a punch before I could blink. The drunk took a fist in the jaw and went down, out cold. I gaped in surprise at the angel as he shook his fist and cursed.

The bartender shouted for us to take it outside. Slapping a few bills down in front of him, Willow grabbed a bottle from behind the bar.

"Let's get out of here. A walk by the river with a bottle of cheap wine sounds about perfect right now." For an angel Willow was a pretty wild guy.

It had been ages since I walked in the river valley. The river divided the south side of the city from the rest. We descended the stairway leading us down, away from downtown to the quiet beauty of the river.

Willow popped the cork on the cheap sparkling wine, taking a long swallow before passing it. Producing a pack of cigarettes, he lit one up and took a long drag. I held up a hand in refusal when he offered it to me. I couldn't help but laugh. Willow was a heck of a guy.

"Alright, now spill it," I said when we were seated on top of a picnic table, staring out at the dark river. "Tell me how an angel falls."

He was silent for so long that I thought it was his refusal. Lighting another cigarette, he let out a plume of smoke and fixed his gaze on the water. "There are so many ways. Many reasons why. My sin? I fell in love with a whore."

Like Falon, Willow didn't give off an energy vibe I could easily feel when his power wasn't in active use. But, seeing the pain in his eyes, he didn't have to. I swallowed the bubbly wine; it tasted faintly of strawberry. I could say nothing that would be an appropriate response, so I respectfully waited for him to continue.

"Christina was special. She had a heart of gold, as they say. In the end, she'd been more concerned about my fall from grace than her own well-being. She wasn't just a woman who slept with men for money. She was a lost soul able to still find hope in every sunrise who believed people were better than they were ever given credit for." He paused, and I pushed the bottle into his hand. His lips twitched in a half smile of thanks. "I knew what I was risking by letting myself get involved with her. But, it was love. That love cost Christina her life."

"I'm sorry, Willow. I can't imagine what you've been through." Now it was my turn to regard him with sympathy. An angel forbidden to love a human. How tragic. But, I knew well that there is no choice in love. We are all its slaves.

"I just wanted to save her. Instead, I condemned us both." Willow tossed his cigarette butt and reached to light another. "That was a year ago. And now, I'm just another fallen angel with grey wings and blood on his hands."

I accepted the last of the wine, wondering how the heck we'd polished it off so fast. My head was spinning. I'd had more than enough, but I drained the bottle anyway.

"Silver," I said, having to put more effort into the one word than I should have. I was so going to regret this come hangover time.

"Excuse me?" Willow raised a brow.

"Your wings. They're silver. And beautiful."

"And you're slurring like a first class wino," he chuckled, "but thank you."

An easy silence settled over us. We stared out at the bright city lights on the opposite shore as they sparkled against the night sky. More than a few times, they bled together as my vision swam. I needed to sleep it off, but I couldn't tear myself away.

Dawn was two hours away yet. It was nice, sitting there inside the illusion of a quiet, beautiful night. But, illusion it was; the visual of Shaz and Bianca drifted up from the depths of my memories where I'd shoved it. I felt ill. Booze and betrayal don't mix well.

"Can you forgive him?"

"I don't know." A chilly breeze rolled in off the water. I shivered, certain it wasn't merely from the cold. "I'm not sure I can I ever look at him again and not see what I saw tonight."

Willow nodded in understanding. He gave me a studious look again, head tilted as if he were choosing his words carefully.

"I know how painful it is. The woman I loved slept with men for money. A lot of them. Even now, I don't understand how she could do it. But, I know one thing: she loved only me. Not them." His hand was warm against mine as he patted it gently. "Does he love her?"

I bit my lip and closed my eyes. My chest tightened painfully. "I don't know. He might."

"You already know the answer. Deep down, you know. So, does he love her?"

I opened my eyes to find him staring at me expectantly. He was right. I did know.

"No. He doesn't love her." Saying it didn't make me feel any better. Knowing it changed nothing.

"Then you have a choice to make." Willow offered me an encouraging smile. "But first, go home and get a good sleep. You look like you need it."

*Death Wish*

Before we parted ways a few blocks from The Wicked Kiss, Willow extended an open invitation to contact him any time I needed a friend or just a gut-punching drink.

"A friendly warning, Alexa," he gestured to the dragon on my arm. "Demons and angels have clearly cut lines and rules they have to follow. But, some fall in between. Fallen angels, vampires, shifters and so on, they are shades of grey, able to bend rules and command parts of both worlds. It's why Shya does what he does. He needs those shades of grey. Watch out for him. And, don't hesitate to get in touch if you need to."

"I'm not sure how I could ever return the favor." I was touched by both his warning and his offer. "But, if I can ever do anything..."

"I'll let you know."

I was in no shape to drive. I also wasn't up to telling Arys about my night. Not yet. I needed some time alone. Since I had no home to call my own, I was left with little choice. I'd stay in Harley's old room at The Wicked Kiss.

Shaz's car was gone from the parking lot when I returned. Letting myself in the back entry, I double checked the door lock behind me and headed for Harley's room. I grit my teeth as I passed the room where I'd caught the two of them. To my relief, I felt no sense of Bianca or anyone else inside.

When I stood awkwardly in the middle of Harley's room, I sent a text message to Arys to tell him I wouldn't be home at dawn as planned. He'd be pissed that I didn't call, but I didn't want to have that conversation.

The strangeness of sleeping in the same room where Shaz and I had killed Arys's sire was quickly replaced by stomach turning nausea. Oh, damn you, tequila.

I soon fell into a dizzying sleep. Thanks to the ass-kicking booze, I fell past the point of dreams into the black abyss of liquor-induced slumber.

## Chapter Eighteen

It was evening by the time I rolled down the short stretch of highway to Stony Plain. Several hours of drunken sleep had left me feeling like a zombie. My head throbbed, and I felt both hungry and nauseous at the same time. A deadly combination. The entire drive home was spent swearing up and down I'd never touch tequila again.

I made a brief trip through a drive-thru for coffee and a yogurt cup. I really should get something in my system. If I didn't pull myself together, I would be no help to Kale.

"Aw, crap." The sight of Shaz's little blue Chevy Cobalt parked in front of Arys's house brought the curses streaming from my lips. Couldn't he just leave this alone? I didn't want to look at him right then let alone talk about it.

I half-heartedly considered driving right by and going to Kylarai's for a shower and meal instead. It had been home once. She'd welcome me with open arms, and I could use a friend right now.

Feeling like death and in great need of a hot shower, I made the decision to suck it up and go inside. I would face the music, but that didn't mean I had to dance. With a firm hold on my tongue and the nasty things I wanted to spit in wounded fury, I sidled up the walk and opened the door.

It was quiet. The inside of the house was draped in darkness. Leaving the afternoon sun behind, I stepped into the veiled cover of Arys's house. Right away, I could feel it. Energy hung heavy on the atmosphere, remnants of power that stank of bloodlust, desire and pleasure. What the fuck?

Letting the door slam, I swept through the kitchen to the living room. Shaz was asleep on the couch with a light blanket draped over him. He stirred at my approach. The scent of a fresh wound drew my attention to the vampire bite on the inside of his wrist. Along with the spiced up residual energy in the house, it wasn't hard to put it all together. This had to be a bad dream.

Arys was a dark shadow in the hall as he emerged from the bedroom clad in a robe. "What the hell happened to you?"

Shaz blinked a few times, his jade gaze taking in my bruised face. "Lex?"

I didn't have the energy to be as furious with them as I was. Something had clearly gone on here, something that involved bloodletting between my two lovers, without me.

I shoved by Arys with my focus on the shower. "I'm not speaking to either of you right now."

I slammed the bathroom door and peeled my clothes off. Bruises decorated my body, but like my face, they had healed substantially while I'd slept. Another day and it would be as if it had never happened. The worst of it was the killer shiner, nothing sunglasses couldn't take care of in front of humans.

From beyond the door, I heard Arys say, "Well that went better than I expected."

It was impossible to enjoy the hot shower. Knowing they were out there waiting for me put the pressure on. I should have gone to Kylarai's.

I took my sweet time shampooing my hair and soaping my sore body. I didn't turn the water off until the hot tap ran cold. Ranting and raving to myself beneath my breath, I wrapped a towel around my hair and slipped into Arys's room where I dressed in yoga pants and a black tank top.

I should have been a number of things as I returned to the living room: angry, jealous, betrayed... Instead, I was just weary.

They both began to speak the moment I stepped into the room. I held up a hand to silence them while deciding whom I could stand to look at.

"Please, both of you just shut up and let me talk." My voice was surprisingly calm. "The last twenty-four hours have really sucked ass. The FPA has Kale, and I got my ass beat by a gang of vampires. A fallen angel got them off me, the only reason I'm standing here right now."

I let my gaze sweep over each of them in turn. They each sat on opposite ends of the couch. Shaz's hair stood up on one side from the way he'd slept. His t-shirt was rumpled. Fatigue and guilt shone in his eyes. He clearly hadn't slept well.

Our eyes met, and the sick sensation of betrayal began to gnaw at me again. I saw my pain reflected in his eyes. It was hard to look at him.

"Coming back to the two of you and the metaphysical stink in this place is not an improvement on top of everything else," I continued, my gaze landing on Arys. "You want to tell me what the hell went on here? Or, do I even want to know?"

Arys was completely unruffled. He leaned back, arms folded across his chest. He regarded me with the wariness of one regarding a venomous snake, cautious and bracing for the unpredictable.

"Shaz came here when he couldn't find you. He needed a fix. I'm not one to say no." Arys shrugged, daring me to get mad.

"Maybe you should start," I snapped.

"It was just a feed, Alexa. Nothing more."

"Isn't that what Bianca is for?" I glared daggers at Shaz. "To meet all your nasty little needs?"

Shaz fidgeted and squirmed, like he couldn't get comfortable. "Not anymore. It's over with her, Lex. I mean it. The look on your face when you opened that door, I'll never forgive myself."

"Oh," I drawled sarcastically. "I guess that makes it ok then."

"Alexa, watch your mouth," Arys scolded. "You might say something you'll regret."

My temper flared. "You've been incredibly helpful, haven't you? Conveniently so."

A storm of emotion crashed over me. It was more than just anger or hurt. It was everything together in an overwhelming tornado of pain and fury. All I really wanted to do was cry. I hadn't really had the chance yet. However, Arys was sitting there with a cocky know it all expression and a challenge in his eyes. He was the perfect target for my rage.

"Do you think it makes me happy to see you in so much pain? To be able to feel it and know there's nothing I can do to take it away?" Arys asked, maintaining his calm, cool demeanor. "I told you I wanted to kill her. You refused. The pup has fucked up, but you could have stopped it."

"Are you out of your mind?" My temperature rose steadily until I was flushed with heat. "I'm not taking responsibility for what he's done."

"Then take responsibility for refusing to be what he needs." Flippant and self-assured, he oozed arrogance. He thought he was right. Unfortunately, he usually was. "The two of you could be feeding your hungers together. Your refusal is selfish ignorance."

I couldn't recall ever wanting to slap him as bad as I did then. I had a tirade ready to unleash on him. The need to vent everything was strong. Then I realized it was exactly what he wanted. Arys knew if I used up my fury on him, I wouldn't lay into Shaz.

Suddenly, I didn't want to rant and rave anymore. Having a willing outlet ruined my mood. I sat heavily in the leather recliner chair perpendicular to the couch. With my head in my hands, I cried.

Crystal clear tears streamed down my face. I tried unsuccessfully to wipe them away. They came in a torrent as everything I'd been burying inside over the past month exploded forth.

Shaz broke first, unable to sit and watch me cry. He sank to his knees before me on the floor and dared to lay a hand on my shoulder. "Lex, I'm so sorry."

I froze at his touch. All I could think about was how his hands had been all over her. "Don't touch me."

He jerked back as if I'd burned him. In some way, I had. Numbness crept in to make me feel detached. I heard myself hollowly say, "I think you should leave."

"No," he shook his head desperately. "I need to make this right somehow. I need you to know how sorry I am."

Shaz reached for me again, stopping himself when I stiffened. I was falling apart inside, and I didn't want him to watch it happen. "I want to believe you. I do. I just can't look at you right now."

I couldn't. Seeing the agony in his jade orbs caused the last of my strength to crumble. I longed for the forest, ached to be wolf. Leaving my human body wouldn't erase the pain, but the union I shared with nature only as wolf was healing. Raoul's house was gone. It was time to move closer to the forest.

Shaz waited another minute before walking out. I hated myself for throwing him out, but it was best for both of us. I had to fall apart and put the pieces back together before I'd be ready to face him.

I listened to his car pull away with a squeal of tires. He was upset and rightfully so. I turned to Arys to find him watching me with a mixed expression of intrigue and dismay.

"You wanted that all along, didn't you?" I asked bitterly. "For him to come to you willingly."

Arys inclined his head in a nod. "Of course. But, it's not my intention to cross any lines with you. He came to me before, Alexa. You knew this could happen. Would you truly rather he seek out the thrill with someone else over me?"

"No." I felt like a pouty child, but wasn't I entitled to my feelings? "I trust you with him. I don't like being left out of it though. Feels too much like him with her."

"Fair enough. I apologize, but I assure you I would never take it farther than a quick bite. Not with him. He needs to be in a controlled situation, which I can provide for him."

Arys made a good case. If Shaz was getting off on the bite of a vampire I trusted and loved, it would keep him away from The Wicked Kiss. I'd accept it, but I didn't have to like it.

"Just another damn junkie. Like me. Like all of us." Tears continued to roll down my face though the sobs had subsided.

I wiped them away angrily. The war between rage and pain continued inside me. Arys let me have my moment of angry tears. He really did understand me better than I gave him credit for.

I had to go back to the bathroom to blow my nose and splash some cold water on my face. My eyes were bloodshot from crying. I stood in there for a few minutes, regaining my composure. I pushed my damp hair back from my face and concentrated on deep breathing. I could do this; I had no choice. I'd had my heart trampled before, and I'd come out stronger for it.

When I returned to the living room, Arys was standing in front of the window, gazing out at the sunset. It was the most light I'd ever seen come through the window into his house. The sun was deep enough over the horizon to pose little threat. Its final beams were accompanied by dashes of orange and pink.

Much the way the moon drew me, so did the sun. Sunset in the forest was heavenly. It kissed goodbye to the day with the promise of night lurking so close.

"I don't mean to gloss over what you've been through in the last day or so, but what do you plan to do about Lilah? Did you talk with

Shya?" Arys continued to stare out the window, squinting against the sun's final rays.

"I did. He bailed out when the FPA showed up. The only thing I can do about Lilah is find a way to bind her. To keep her from breaking the curse that holds her. The good news is Shya doesn't want that curse broken either. I have an ally."

"An ally you can't trust."

"I can trust him on this. I'm sure of it." I shrugged. "Regardless, I can't deal with Lilah until I get Kale back from the FPA. I told Juliet I was coming for him. I meant it."

Arys rounded on me with the furious outburst I was expecting. "Like hell you are. You are not putting yourself in danger for Sinclair. He can take care of himself."

"Save it." I waved a hand dismissively. "I don't need your permission, Arys."

His temper had an uncanny ability to go from cool to raging hot in mere seconds. I knew him well enough to expect it. I concentrated on staying calm. If we both flipped out, this would get ugly.

"I wasn't so keen on your ridiculous choice to take his debt for Shya, but now you're really not thinking." Arys's voice rose steadily. "You'd be doing the entire world a service by binding Lilah. You can't sacrifice that for Kale."

"The FPA is issuing a challenge. They need to know I won't be controlled like my sister. If I leave him there, they'll kill him. Or worse." A shudder racked my body. I didn't want to imagine what they could be doing to Kale.

Arys scowled, looking at me as if I were an idiot. "They won't kill him. As long as they have him, they have something you want. They won't waste that. If you walk right into their hands, you'll just be giving them what they want from you."

"I'm not leaving him there," I insisted. A fight with Arys had not been on the agenda. However, if he was going to pursue it, I'd be happy to put him in his place. A conflict between the two of us was never less than fiery.

"You've lost your mind." Arys's eyes flashed dangerously. "You're going to do something reckless, like usual, and torture Shaz and I by making us watch you die for him."

That did it for my calm composure. The pressure had been mounting for days now. I snapped. "You wouldn't be such a hard ass about this if I hadn't screwed him. It happened once, dammit, and it's never happened again."

My intent was to storm out. I needed a good run on all fours. I needed escape. Arys had other ideas. He grabbed my arm as I stomped past him and jerked me around to face him.

"You think you know it all," he spat the words in my face. "This isn't about you fucking him. This is about you loving him."

"Oh, this again." I laughed bitterly. I tried to pull free of his grasp, but he held tight. "So Kale and I could screw until we're blue in the face, and it wouldn't bother you as long as there were no feelings involved? I call bullshit. I need to leave."

"Wrong. You need to remember who you are and what you're capable of." He kissed me then, a hard, angry press of his lips to mine. "You can't always let emotion drive you. To stay alive, you must also listen to logic."

Just one kiss got my heart pounding. I gazed into his dark blue eyes, falling into their depths. "Logic left the building a long time ago. I'm not going to keep having this fight with you."

"If you won't accept my feelings and opinions as valid, then you have no choice." The blue of his eyes slowly bled across the whites, going all wolf. It was no less terrifying this time than any other. "You are my other half, and I will not let you keep making decisions that threaten both of us."

"Don't try to control me," I muttered, my wolf rising to the surface. "You should know better by now."

"Ah, there's my girl." Arys grinned, revealing fangs. "I can handle your tears, but I prefer your temper."

"Is that so? I might make you regret those words."

"Do what you must, my love, but I'm not letting you go in after Kale."

There it was. Challenge issued. Arys looked so damn sure of himself, so prepared to do what it took to bend me to his will. It had always been this way with us. The peace only lasted so long. *Conflict would follow the twins always…* It echoed in my mind, a dark reminder that the odds were not in our favor.

The two of us had faced off over many things, big and small. One of the biggest issues we'd faced was my choice to seek help from Arys's sire, Harley. It was a dangerous and probably dumb move. It had set Arys off in ways I didn't care to remember. However, I had learned a few things from Harley that had saved my ass since. I wasn't sorry. Nor was I sorry that I'd killed him after.

If I was sorry for any of it, it was only that the death of his sire had hurt Arys. Of course, his little trip down memory lane with Harley hadn't been so easy on me. Catching the two of them in bed bleeding a naked woman was one image I'd rather not have burned into my memory forever. Still, the image of Shaz and Bianca was worse, much worse.

As I stared into Arys's inhuman eyes, I was faced with a choice. I could lose my temper and give him the fight he was seeking, or I could find another way around it. I'd had more than enough conflict for one week; that wasn't what I needed from him right now.

No, what I needed was a brief reprieve from all of it. I kissed him without thought or hesitation. Pouring the raw emotions into it, I devoured him. Arys didn't miss a beat. Kissing me back hungrily, he slipped his tongue between my lips. He tasted faintly of blood. Shaz's blood.

I groaned, but it wasn't because I didn't like it. Tasting Shaz on Arys sparked a fire low in my core. Sliding my hands into his disheveled hair, I pulled him against me with a ravenous need.

The frenzy driving me caught Arys up in its pull. I needed a release, some kind of rapture to chase the pain into the shadows if just for a moment. Arys was quick to comply with my demand for him to satisfy my need. His hands were on my hips, and his lips found the ticklish spot on my neck.

I tugged at his robe, peeling it off him like I was unwrapping candy. I couldn't get to what was inside fast enough. Running my hands over the hard expanse of Arys's chest down to his stomach, I captured his shaft in one hand. Eliciting a moan from him brought a smile to my lips.

Dropping to my knees before him, I took him into my mouth with an eager flick of my tongue. He said my name like it was both a curse and a blessing.

Arys threaded a hand into my hair, grasping my head with a demanding affection. Heat raced to my groin. I took great joy in his response to my careful manipulations. The power and control I had over him was intoxicating. Only when his hand tightened painfully in my hair did I stop.

I backed him up against the couch so he was forced to sit. While he watched, I stripped off my clothes then wasted no time climbing onto his lap. His arms went around me, clutching me tightly to him. He buried his face in my neck as I slid down his hard length. A sigh of relief escaped me.

I set the pace atop him. I hungered for control, something I didn't feel I'd had a lot of lately. This man was mine, and I was going to take from him what I needed. That kind of control was dizzying, erotic.

"Think you can shut me up, huh?" Arys murmured, his mouth hot against my skin.

"It's working so far, isn't it?" I silenced him with a bruising kiss. Arys was a smooth talker who could talk his way out of or into anything. He was used to being in charge. But, not this time.

A growl rumbled low in his throat, and I laughed in delight. I could feel the wolf creeping around inside him, unable to break free. It wasn't real, merely an echo of my own wolf. Still, it was as dangerous as any caged beast.

He gripped my hips in an attempt to guide my rhythm. I shoved his hands away, pinning them at his sides. With a shake of my head, I smiled wickedly. Having him inside me didn't free me from the emotional turmoil I carried, but it did lift me up on a wave of euphoric, glorious ignorance.

The sound of our moans and cries filled the room. I pushed Arys to the limit. He brought me to climax again and again before finding his own release.

The sexual energy surrounding us was potent and spicy. I leaned forward to rest my head on his shoulder while I savored it. He said nothing for a long time. He just held me.

Finally, he whispered, "Let's just stay in tonight. You should rest. Take some time to think."

"Sounds like a great idea. I just need to do something first."

"Does it involve being wolf? Because I can feel your beast inside me in a desperate way."

"It does." Reluctantly, I got to my feet and gathered my clothing. I didn't want our tryst to be over because it meant going back to reality. The wolf wouldn't wait though. I'd had my moment of bliss, and she demanded hers.

*Death Wish*

    The short trip across town to Kylarai's was all it took for everything to come crashing back. I just couldn't shake it. The loss of Kale, my sister's betrayal, Shaz and Bianca, it all ate at me.

    I followed the small town streets to Ky's. The wolf within sought the forest and the relief it provided from the human world. Such bittersweet freedom.

    Leaving my car in the driveway, I ran around the house to the backyard. I pulled my clothes off as I went, dropping my keys near the steps leading up to the patio. If Kylarai saw me streaking through the early dusk like a bat out of hell, she would know something was up.

    I leaped into the air, coming down on all fours as wolf. The shift was fast and fluid. It felt, for just a moment, like true liberation. Everything was so much simpler as wolf.

    I ran as if I could escape, but there was no escape, only acceptance.

    Speeding across the stretch of field separating Kylarai's backyard from the forest beyond, I was accompanied by the fading sunset. It did not cease in its beauty for my heartbreak. Its color never dimmed. The world would go on regardless of my place within it. For the first time I began to feel like I belonged in the dark.

    Weaving in between trees, leaping fallen logs and brush, I pushed my body as hard as possible. My muscles burned and my lungs heaved. I ran blindly, having no destination. I couldn't flee the truth; it clung to me.

    If Arys was my darkness then surely Shaz was my light. He'd kept me grounded, sane, until now. I needed him. If that was selfish then so be it. Long before I had met Arys, I had formed a special connection with Shaz. He meant so much to me. How would we get over this?

    Shaz had said we would be ok. After everything went down with Kale and then finding Shaz playing with the vampires at The Wicked Kiss, he had promised me we would get through this. Yet, I felt so betrayed.

    I'd made my share of mistakes. I was no one to tell Shaz what he could or could not do. But, I had promised it was over with Kale, and as screwed up as that whole situation was, I had stuck to my word.

    I couldn't help but think the twin flame revelation had something to do with this. Shaz had been remorseful up until he found out what Arys and I really were to one another. It had driven him into the arms of another woman. He had been mine, but a matter of brutal seconds had changed everything.

Lifting my voice to the wind, I howled. Mournful and eerie, the sound of my pain echoed through the treetops. Again and again, I cried out my misery to the forest.

Miles away in the distance, Shaz echoed my heartbroken cry.

## Chapter Nineteen

I watched Shya pour six sugar packets into his tea. Gross. He totally just ruined it. He was oblivious, sipping from it like it was perfection.

His crimson eyes settled on me. "I apologize for the other night. Skipping out on you wasn't my intention."

I glanced around the near empty Tim Horton's coffee shop. Nobody sat within earshot of our conversation. "Did you mean to leave Kale and me for the FPA to drag off?"

"I had no way of knowing what would happen. Kale should have done a better job of covering your tracks after the Irving kill. He isn't usually so careless." Shya gave me an appraising glance, one that indicated he blamed me for Kale's blunder.

"So that's it? The FPA has him, and you won't do anything about it?" I had expected this from the demon, but the shrug and smirk accompanying his response surprised me.

"I'm not a babysitter, Alexa. I can't bail my people out of every screw up they get themselves into." He tapped another sugar packet against the table before opening it and adding it to his tea. "Besides, Kale hasn't been the sharpest tool in the shed lately. Falling in love has made a fool of him. Perhaps some time with the FPA will do him some good. Frankly, I'm just happy they didn't get their hands on you."

I stared into my coffee cup as I censored myself from spitting out a nasty retort. I understood why Kale meant so little to someone like Shya or Arys. So, why the hell couldn't they understand why he meant so much to me?

"What will they do to him?" I was afraid of the answer, but my imagination wasn't helping.

Stirring more sugar into the tea, Shya clinked his spoon against the cup repetitively. I had to fight back the urge to rip the utensil out of his hand. He studied me intently, noting everything from my expression to the way I fidgeted with a napkin, folding and refolding it.

"They'll start by torturing as much information as they can out of him about anything and anyone. I'd imagine they would start with you and your vampire, as well as me and what I've been up to since the FPA saw me last. Then they'll either kill him or recruit him if he doesn't manage to escape them. It's unlikely though not impossible."

"Fuck," I muttered, crushing the napkin in my fist. "I can't just leave him there."

"I'd call it even and walk away if I were you. You both took a fall for the other. Sentimental, sure. Romantic, perhaps. Ultimately, pointless. It's done no good for either of you." With a shrug and a shake of his dark head, Shya frowned. "Your attention should be on Lilah right now. She's not the type to give up. And, I can assure you, her attention is very much on you."

I drank down some of the hot coffee, needing the caffeine fix but finding it hard to enjoy. "What's that supposed to mean?"

"It means she's more desperate than ever to break the curse. She's lying low, staying out of touch. But, she's not staying idle. I can promise you that. We must bind her, Alexa."

"How?"

"I can do the binding, but I'll need you to strip her power first. Your power over vampires makes you the one person with the best chance of success."

That was suspicious. "Why can't you do it?"

"She's my queen." Shya stiffened, appearing uncomfortable. "A binding is disrespectful but it won't harm her. I can't do that. You weaken her enough, and I can effectively bind her. It will render her powerless, but it will only be temporary. It should buy us some time."

"Time for what?"

"To figure out what she needs to break the curse and make sure she never pulls it off."

I pushed a hand through my long hair and stared out the window at the traffic. I didn't want to do it. I didn't want anything to do with Lilah or her curse. Now I had no choice because of the trouble she was bringing my way. Besides, I couldn't turn my back and let her break the curse if I had the ability to stop her. Willow said my name meant 'protector of mankind'. If Lilah returned to her dark goddess throne, all of mankind would suffer for it. It couldn't happen, not if I could stop her.

"Fuck," I repeated. "I miss the days of hunting down idiot vampires. I don't have the stress capacity for this shit."

"With great power comes—"

"Yeah, yeah," I cut him off, holding a hand up to stop his clichéd comment. "I know."

Shya drained his teacup. In a motion almost dainty, he ran a finger along the rim. "The night of the full moon. That's when we do it."

"That's in three days. It's also a risky time for me. You know, the whole werewolf thing." I waited for his response, but he only stared blankly at me so I continued. "The wolf will be really strong. I've never denied it on a full moon night." I purposely left out the fact that I couldn't tap my power when in wolf form. That would be revealing a weakness to a demon; I wasn't going to blunder into such a mistake.

"You can though, correct? The change isn't dependent on the moon."

"No. I can shift at will. The moon, it encourages the change. It calls to the wolf. I can resist it, but for how long I'm not sure."

I'd seldom been in such a predicament when it came to the wolf or the full moon. I'd been doing this for enough years to be where I both wanted and needed to be when the moon was full, in the forest where I belonged.

"Then I guess we'll have to find out." Rising to leave, Shya added, "All magicks are at their strongest during the full moon. We need to do it that night. Be at my place before midnight. I'll get Lilah there."

I stood too, abandoning the last of my coffee. "Then there's no reason why I can't go after the FPA for Kale tonight."

"I'd advise against it."

I fell into step beside him. "I can't leave Kale there. He wouldn't leave me."

The demon threw his head back and laughed, a sound so chilly in its intensity that it made my skin crawl. "And, here I recall you being so insistent the two of you are not lovers."

"We're not." I shrugged it off. No point trying to explain it to him.

Shya held the door open for me, waiting for me to pass through. It was a polite gesture, but it also put a demon at my back. When we reached the parking lot, he stopped me with a light touch on my shoulder. Again, my skin crawled. Damn demons.

"I want to send Falon with you if you go. Don't argue. I know he's difficult, but the FPA has nothing in their arsenal that can harm him. He can protect you."

I pursed my lips thoughtfully, searching his snake-like eyes for the real reason. "Or, he can spy on me for you. Make sure I'm not striking any deals with the FPA that you should know about."

"That too." The dazzling smile he flashed at me wasn't without its charm. He seemed to be eternally pleased with himself.

"I think I'll pass." I headed for my car before he could stop me. "I'll see you in three days."

I was prepared for Arys's adamant refusal upon returning to the house. So, when he met my announcement with a shrug, I was more than a little stunned. We stood in the kitchen. He watched me closely as I cleaned up after making a sandwich.

"What's your deal, Arys? What happened to the fight you promised to give me over this?"

He swung the fridge door open and pointed at a splash of ketchup spilled on a shelf. "Did you plan on using this later? Or, is this just how you are?"

I wanted to be offended, but I couldn't stop myself from laughing. "Hey, rudeness. Just because your refrigerator has never had food inside it before doesn't mean you have to be anal about it. I was going to clean it up. Eventually."

Living together was not something either of us had been prepared for. Funny, considering we were part of one another. Unfortunately, our bond didn't translate well into day-to-day living situations. We were both very much the lone-wolf type. If I didn't find a place to live soon, we would drive each other crazy.

"I've decided it's not worth fighting with you." He jumped back to the original subject. "Like the ketchup splatters in my kitchen, your stubbornness is part of who you are. I want to protect you, but I don't want to change you. So, if you want to go get Sinclair's sorry ass, all I can do is support you."

My eyes narrowed, and I paused partway to the fridge with a wet sponge in my hand. "Hmm… smacks of suspicious."

"Let's be honest. You'll go whether I want you to or not. So fighting about it with you is irrelevant and a waste of time." He watched me scrub the ketchup mess with a satisfied grin on his handsome face. "So, when do we leave?"

"I knew it." I shook the dirty sponge at him before throwing it in the sink. "Always a catch."

"Sorry, sweetheart but we share some serious power. Time to start acting like it."

"Fair enough." I knew he was right. It had taken time to accept and adjust to the power we shared. After a year, I was just finally feeling comfortable with it. Still, our union had sparked a firestorm in the paranormal rumor mill, and most of what they said about us was true. Now, we had to be ready to prove it when push came to shove.

I couldn't be certain how much the FPA knew. Juliet had always known I was born with strange abilities. If they didn't know about twin flames yet, they soon would.

"I'm supposed to meet Jez and Brogan at The Wicked Kiss in an hour. We need to do a locator spell to find the FPA. Apparently, they move their base a lot."

Arys nodded, frowning at the ketchup-stained sponge in the sink. "They have a base in each major city. They keep it small enough to move often but big enough to serve their purpose."

"Then let's go. I'm eager to see the life I could have led."

It was still early. The Wicked Kiss was nearly empty when we arrived, just the staff, but Shaz was absent. I wasn't expecting to see him, as we had yet to face one another, but it had to happen. Still, I just wasn't ready.

After failing to find a good quiet space where Brogan could concentrate and have room to make a salt circle, we settled on the ladies' washroom. Jez perched on the counter, watching Brogan pour the circle. I leaned against the door, ensuring nobody entered until we were done.

"You've got something of Kale's, right?" Brogan asked, getting comfortable inside the circle.

"I hope this counts. He gave it to me for my birthday, but it was his mother's." I passed her the cross, feeling anxious when it left my fingers.

"Perfect."

Jez pulled a tube of lipstick out of her purse and began to apply it to her already fire engine red lips. "Hey, Alexa. Tell me again what the hell you're thinking taking Arys in on a rescue mission for Kale."

"What can I say? It's complicated. Arys doesn't want me to do this, but he understands why I need to."

She shook her head of golden hair. "Poor Kale. I wonder what they've been doing to him. I'm almost afraid to find out. I don't trust the government. Monsters. Worse than we could ever be."

I made a face, sick at the thought of the hell Kale could be going through at my sister's hand. "I'm sure I'm not one of his favorite people right now. He wanted me to let Shya kill him. He told me that he wanted to die that night."

I could still see his face in my mind, the resentment in his eyes as he threw himself away from me before tearing out of the graveyard.

Jez turned from the mirror to face me directly. Surprise shone in her deep green eyes. "Did he really expect you to make the choice to kill him? He can't possibly think you would. You two have this crazy, star-crossed lover thing going on. It's kind of beautiful really."

"Beautiful?" The word felt wrong. All wrong. "It feels like a sin."

"That's because it's tragic. Your love isn't meant to be, yet it still exists. So, a part of you always yearns for it." Jez pinned me with a gaze filled with the pain of one who knows. "What makes it beautiful is that it's strong enough to survive the fact that it's wrong."

I stared at her intently, searching her for the source of such profound pain. We'd all loved and lost before, but she'd never mentioned anything so soul-breakingly painful.

"You sound like someone who knows."

In a blink, she buried the pain I'd seen, going on as if it had never been there. "We'll go spring him out of the pen. It'll be fine."

Brogan watched our exchange with a sympathetic frown. "Love's a real bitch, isn't it? The last man I fell for, I mean really fell hard for, was married. I didn't know until eight months into the relationship. He'd been leading a double life. Boy was he lucky I'm a white witch."

"Men, women, vampire, human," Jez muttered sourly. "It doesn't matter. Someone lies, cheats or generally fucks up, even when it's meant to be. Love is a sadistic bitch."

"So does that mean you're not seeing Zoey anymore?" I steered the conversation in a lighter direction with a wink and a knowing smile.

Her demeanor changed immediately. Smiling coyly, she fluttered her long lashes. "Oh, I'm definitely seeing her. Seeing a lot of her." She blew a kiss at me through the mirror.

Brogan let out a low whistle, and I laughed. I wanted nothing more than for those I loved to be happy. Still, I couldn't help but worry a bit; Zoey was a lunatic. Although, I might hardly be the right person to throw around words meaning crazy.

We fell quiet when Brogan indicated she was ready. Her earthy energy rose up to warm me. It had a soothing quality that reminded me of Lena. I held my breath while watching her do the spell. What was I going to do if this didn't work?

Eyes closed and brow creased, Brogan whispered Latin words I couldn't understand. A gentle breeze swept through the room, lifting her blonde hair but touching neither Jez nor me. The cross lay before her, untouched. It began to glow with a faint light.

All at once, both the wind and the light vanished. Brogan's eyes opened and she nodded. "I can feel him but it's difficult. It's been masked. I used the cross as an amulet by channeling the energy I was picking up. We should be able to use it as a tracker of sorts."

"Damn," Jez whistled. "Impressive, Brogan."

"Thanks. It was nothing big though." Despite her genuine modesty, the young witch beamed.

She held the cross out to me, and I accepted it gratefully. It hummed with energy, Brogan's and if I concentrated hard, Kale's, too. The cross was linked to him now. Fascinating.

"Well," Jez hopped off the counter and gave her golden locks a toss. "Let's go give the government hell."

I walked out of the bathroom and straight into Shaz. He was lurking in the hall outside the door, waiting for me. Arys leaned against the wall a few feet away, his arms crossed and his stance casual.

"Are we good to go?" Arys asked.

I nodded, my heart in my throat. "Yeah. It's all good."

Pushing away from the wall, Arys inclined his head toward Shaz, giving me a pointed look. "I'll wait for you in the lobby."

Jez and Brogan followed him, leaving Shaz and me alone to stare at one another awkwardly. I didn't know what to say. I knew if I waited until I was ready for this conversation, it would never happen. I could never be ready for this.

Shaz's jade eyes were filled with remorse and sorrow. He seemed at a loss for words, finally spitting out, "Alexa, God, I'm so sorry."

He was. I genuinely believed him though it didn't make this any easier.

"I accept that. And, I want to forgive you. I just…"

"I know. Trust me, I know." He ran a hand through his hair and glanced in Arys's direction. "I didn't think I'd ever get over the two of you being together. I know it's not the same situation. Not even close. Still, I know what it's like."

Whether he meant to or not, he threw a guilt trip at me with that one. Fair enough. I couldn't argue that perhaps the way my relationship had developed with Arys had been wrong and unfair to Shaz.

"I know you do," I admitted, finding it hard to swallow around the lump in my throat. "I never gave you enough credit for how well you handled everything with Arys and me. I'm sorry for that."

"Don't." He ran his hand through his hair again, noticed his nervous tell and stuffed both hands in the pockets of his jeans. "Don't make this about who messed up more. I've had time to think about everything, do a little research. I know how important a twin flame union is. No more guilt about Arys. Ok?"

Absolute relief filled me, but had it come too late to save us?

Shaz continued. "I have no reason or excuse for what I've done recently. It was selfish and I'm sorry. If I could take it back, I would."

"Thank you. For all of it. It means a lot."

"I need to make things right between us. I hate what I've become. This is not what I pictured for myself when I fought Julian for Alpha. I need to get my shit together. For me and for you." He reached out to take my hand. His palm was hot, his energy scattered. "So, I'm leaving town for a while."

I stared at him, dumbfounded. "What?"

"I'm not going anywhere until you've dealt with Lilah. I'm your wolf, and I'll back you with her and with the FPA. Then I'll go. Just until I can clean myself up. Be me again, you know?"

Shocked was one way of putting what I felt. "Where will you go?"

Reaching to stroke a hand down the side of my face, Shaz shook his head. "I don't know yet. I think I need to be wolf for a while."

I had longed to run away on four legs and leave the world behind, but I hadn't done it. Now, Shaz was going to leave me, and the thought cut deep. I couldn't be selfish; I had to let him go.

"Then you should do what you need to do." The words didn't come easy. I wanted to sink to my knees and stare numbly at nothing while I fell apart inside.

Every time I thought it couldn't get any worse, it did, but I had no time to fall to pieces. I had to confront my sister and whoever else would be at the FPA to greet me, so I took a deep breath and held myself together.

Shaz pulled me into his arms and pressed a kiss to my forehead. I was stiff in his embrace, afraid to sink into him the way I longed to. Would he ever feel like mine again?

"I guess we should go," he said somberly. "Everyone is waiting."

"You're coming with us?"

"I told you, I'll be at your side through this. I know part of you must hate me right now, but I love you, Lex. Nothing on this earth could ever change that." He gave me another kiss before releasing me. His lips were warm against my temple.

I caught his hand for just a second, squeezing it affectionately. "I hopelessly adore you. Despite everything."

"I know." He sounded so defeated.

I owed him the same devotion and forgiveness he had shown me when I didn't deserve it. With a steady hand but a shaky voice, I said, "We'll be ok."

## Chapter Twenty

"This is it," Brogan announced. "I'm sure of it."

The cross hummed in agreement in my hands. The five of us were piled into my Charger, sitting outside the abandoned Charles Camsell Hospital in the northwest side of the city. The hospital was at the center of several ghost stories and tales of horror told by the locals, stories I had dismissed in the light of day. Now that I was sitting outside the building in the dark feeling the sinister vibe rolling off the place, I was forming a newfound respect for it.

"A scary old mental hospital?" Jez was aghast. "Oh hell no."

"This place gives me the creeps," Shaz murmured, his gaze fixed on the crumbling structure.

The sensation of being watched by several sets of eyes hidden within the building got my skin crawling. It had once been an aboriginal tuberculosis sanatorium with a reputation for vile acts and cruel experiments. Most of the ground floor windows were boarded up. A fence wound the perimeter of the property, but it was open in several places, hardly anything that would keep anyone out.

Graffiti covered the walls and fence. Everything from gang names to satanic symbols decorated the place. It did nothing to ease the foreboding look and feel of the hospital. I so did not want to go in there.

"Why the hell would the FPA want to set up shop in there?" I wondered aloud.

"Simple," Arys spoke up. "Who would ever dare to bother them here? Other than you, of course."

"Of course."

The hospital was huge, seven or eight floors high. Not a single light could be seen from outside. The government had to be out of their tree to think it was ok to set up shop in a place like this. It crawled with a deep, dark energy I could only describe as malevolent.

"Where do we even begin?" Brogan sounded reluctant. "Should we all go in? It feels bad in there. Scary bad."

"It does," Arys agreed. "It feels like they're waiting for us."

"They?" Jez echoed.

"The spirits. They know we're not all human. They're intrigued." Arys was looking a little intrigued himself. Perhaps too intrigued.

"If we all go in, it could seem too aggressive," I spoke up. "I want this to be as peaceful as possible. There are two people in there I care about. I'm not looking for a fight."

Arys met my gaze with a spark of excitement in his blue eyes. "Someone should wait outside. It would be wise to leave two people out here. If we run into trouble in there, having backup would be nice."

"Volunteers?" I asked.

"I'd be happy to wait out here." Jez raised a hand. "This place scares the ever loving crap out of me."

"Ditto. I'll stay here, too." Quiet and apprehensive, Brogan volunteered with a small wave.

I left my car keys with Jez but kept my phone with me. I stared at the Dragon Claw, unsure whether bringing it would be in my best interest. In the end, I left it with Jez. Having that kind of weaponry on me wouldn't help my attempt to come in peace. The FPA was made up mostly of humans. Any supernatural help they may have inside wouldn't be more than the three of us could handle... I hoped.

"Aw hell, let's get this over with."

"Call or text me if you need us," Jez called after us as we left the car. "If you're not out in an hour, we're coming in after you."

"If I'm not out in an hour, call Shya." I wasn't sure he'd be much help, but it was all I could think of.

Arys and Shaz were on either side of me as we approached an opening in the fence. The tiny hairs on the back of my neck stood on end, and despite the leather jacket I wore to hide the dragon on my wrist, I broke out everywhere in goosebumps. Something horrifying dwelled in this place.

The closer we drew to the hospital, the thicker the negative energy became. I shielded hard against it, but it slapped against my shields, seeking a way in. Shaz shivered slightly in the warm night air, but Arys seemed entirely unaffected.

We crossed the expanse of lawn, and I searched the upper windows for the beings I felt watching us. I saw nothing.

We reached a small side door. It was locked, but Arys had no trouble getting in. He went first, and I followed with quickly growing trepidation. My instinct screamed at me to turn back. Only the steadily humming cross kept me going.

"Feel that?" Arys's voice echoed inside. "The energy in this place is wild. The FPA probably has no idea how massive it is."

I paused to take in our surroundings. My eyes easily adjusted to the dark. I still would have given just about anything for a light. We stood in a long, white hall. It was littered with broken boards, fallen beams and glass. Graffiti marred the walls, but it was messy and hard to make out.

"It's insanely cold in here," Shaz said in a loud whisper. "It feels like we're being watched."

"It feels like something is trying to shove its way inside me." With gritted teeth, I pushed back against the unwelcome spirit. It was a human spirit and no match for me.

"They're attracted to us," Arys mused, "because we are so in tune to them. They can feel it." His vampire energy was lively and hot. He was vibing off the building and its long deceased occupants.

"Are you enjoying this?" Shaz muttered in disdain, picking his way along behind me through the debris. "Good Lord, this place is a health hazard."

"I am actually." The low chuckle that echoed around us was creepy, even for Arys. "Don't worry, pup. I imagine the FPA have had the asbestos cleaned up. Otherwise, they wouldn't be making this their Edmonton home base."

"That's reassuring."

We reached the end of the hall where the elevator was. In a sketchy building with no power, it wasn't a viable option. I glanced around, looking for the stairs. As I passed the elevator, the doors slid open.

I shrieked and jumped straight into Shaz who swore. Arys's laughter quickly turned my fear into anger.

*Death Wish*

"If you can't stop being creepy, then stay down here while we go up," I snapped at the smirking vampire. "The fact that you're enjoying this place is really making my skin crawl."

Arys sobered, his smile fading. "I'm a vampire, Alexa. Are you not used to it by now? This place reeks of death and power. I feel at one with a place like this. It's… comfortable."

A stray beam of light made its way through a broken window to slant across Arys's face. His pupils were huge, drowning out the color in his eyes. He was right at home here while I was ready to run screaming back the way I'd come like a soon-to-be victim in a horror movie.

I felt the shadows all around me, slinking about in the darkest corners and crevices. The energy here did not entice me. It terrified me. I wanted nothing to do with it.

The dark and the light, as twin flames, this was where we differed. It was unsettling to see the absolute darkness in Arys's eyes, and I saw it clearly. The way I felt in the forest, being one with the earth and all it encompassed, that's what Arys felt in a place like this. The realization was harsh and a little sad.

"This is starting to feel way too much like a scary movie," Shaz laughed, a high nervous unnatural sound. "Are you sure the FPA has a base in here?"

I clutched the cross necklace tightly between my fingers. Focusing hard on the pendant, I searched its energy for its link to Kale. It was hard to ignore the pressing negative entity outside my realm of focus. The spell Brogan created continued to hum, steady and stronger now that we were inside.

"Yes. They are here. And, I wouldn't doubt that they already know we are, too."

We pushed on, moving as fast as we could in the pitch-black stairwell with rusty barbed wire wound around the handrail. As good as my vision was in the dark, it wasn't as good as Arys's. We reached the second floor and found what appeared to have been a laboratory of some kind. Fewer windows were boarded up here. Right away, I saw the old bloodstains on the floor.

I backed out of the lab, toward the stairs. "Higher," I whispered. "This isn't the floor."

Something horrible had taken place in that lab, something that promised to reveal itself if we didn't leave. My heart pounded in my ears. I was beyond scared. An unseen threatening force far outweighed a physical threat like a vampire group beating. I don't do ghosts, and I sure as hell don't do pissed off ghosts with a serious need for vengeance.

Shaz stuck close to me as we made our way up. He was oozing fear as well. Arys must have been drowning in it. Fear was a lovely intoxicant. Unfortunately, not for the one feeling it.

We bypassed the next few floors, stopping when we reached the sixth. We were much closer now, though we still saw no sign of habitation by anything alive. Entering the hall of the sixth floor, I gasped when I felt a tug on my hair.

"Please tell me one of you just grabbed my hair."

"Nope," Shaz's response was accompanied by Arys's amused, "Sorry, love. Not me."

"Don't touch me," I hissed at the spirit that lingered too close for comfort. It darted in close to grab my hair again before fleeing. I proceeded to curse up a storm that left Arys chuckling like an immature teenage boy. "This isn't funny, dammit!"

The sixth floor housed several rooms, each of them containing beds with restraints. My stomach shriveled as I passed the rooms, glancing into each one with fear of what I would see. I knew the government was getting their hands dirty in places where they didn't belong, but this was just ridiculous. The unrest here was violently disturbing.

I paused in the middle of the hall, listening carefully. It was faint, but I could just barely make out the high frequency squeal given off by electricity.

"They're upstairs. The top floor. They have power up there."

I was ready to stop stumbling around in the dark. The debris was potentially deadly. Even with keen eyesight, it was impossible to see every fallen board, nail or shard of glass.

A blood-curdling scream rang out. It was followed by the slamming of a door at the far end of the hall. My heart thundered so hard in my ears that I thought for sure it would burst. Shaz moved in close to me, reaching to grasp my hand. His palm was clammy and cold. Panic flowed openly from him.

Arys was already heading down the hall toward the sounds. Shaz and I exchanged a glance before following him slowly. I was keenly aware that we were also being followed. A look back revealed nothing, but I felt them there, creeping along behind us.

"I can't understand why anyone would willingly walk into this place." Shaz gripped my hand so hard it hurt. The bones in my fingers began to grind together, and I winced.

With my free hand, I pulled my phone out to check the time. We'd only been in there for ten minutes. It felt like forever. I couldn't wait to get out. I noted that, though there was no clear reason for it, the signal was almost dead in here. Fantastic.

Arys stopped at the end of the hall, peering through the window of the closed door. He didn't hesitate before grabbing the knob and turning. I felt the sudden urge to shout at him to stop. It was too late.

I stopped dead in my tracks. A grey mist burst from the room to cover Arys. The mist pulled apart into separate shapes. Several figures circled him, reaching out with wispy tendrils of energy to touch him.

"Are you seeing this?" I whispered to Shaz, scared even to breathe for fear of attracting the unwelcome attention of those things down the hall.

"Oh, yeah."

Arys stared into the room before turning to look at us. His eyes were solid black. The heavy energy was really getting to him. He was vibing off it and clearly enjoying it.

"You're not going to believe what's in this room." Without another word, he strode inside the room with the ghostly figures trailing after him.

Continuing on down the hall couldn't possibly be a good idea, but I did it anyway. Shaz tugged on my hand as if trying to stop me. I could feel his wolf's unease. The wolf didn't understand ghosts nor did it want to.

Another scream rang out. It turned my legs to jelly. Each step that brought me closer to the room was harder to take. I forced myself to turn the corner and peek inside. I felt the blood rush from my face. Vertigo hit me and I lost my balance. I would have hit the nasty, contaminated floor if it weren't for Shaz.

Arys stood in the doorway watching the ghostly scene play out before him. A woman lay strapped to the bed. She was a spirit, re-enacting her horrific death. The ghosts dispersed from Arys to take their places and play their roles. One of them, a doctor, smiled at me before reaching for a phantom tool that no longer truly existed.

He approached the bed with his macabre little medical saw raised high. Nurses stood off to either side, watching intently. Their faces showed little expression. They felt nothing as they witnessed yet another murder. How many times had they watched something like this take place?

The air seemed to have been sucked from the room. I felt like I was suffocating as I watched the doctor turn on the rotating blade and lower it to the imprisoned woman's forehead. I couldn't look away, couldn't do anything but listen as the blade sliced through her flesh and into the bone beneath.

She screamed, that same scream I'd heard twice already. The nurses moved in to hold her as she flailed, straining at her bonds. The doctor didn't let up as blood spattered his hands and face. Only when the woman lay dead and still did he stop. Then the scenario restarted, and the entire thing began again.

I shook my head, my mouth open in a silent scream of my own. I couldn't watch that again. Holding tight to Shaz's arm, I dragged him with me away from the door. Arys turned to us with a strange sort of half smile tugging at his lips. The dark power in this building was affecting him in a bad way.

"Arys, we've got to get out of here. This place, it's not good for someone with power like ours." I tried to appeal to his sense of reason, but I could see that it was long gone.

He advanced on Shaz and me with a predatory gait. "There's something very bad here. I know it's dangerous, and yet, all I can think about is which one of you I want to bleed first."

Oh, great. This was just what we needed.

I gathered my power, ready to use it on Arys if I had to. The act of tapping my power drew the attention of the spirits inside the room, and they all turned to gaze at me as if I were interrupting their gruesome scenario.

"Arys, we have to get upstairs. You need to keep it together. You don't want to hurt us."

My pleas fell on deaf ears. He was lost in the rush of the hospital's influence. His voice was low and smooth, seductive. "I always want to hurt you, my wolf. I've just had many years to practice restraint."

"This is not the time nor place to lose your mind," I growled, my fingertips dancing with gold and blue energy. "I have business here. Enough of this horror movie shit."

The last few words echoed in the silent hall. Where my fear ended, my fury began. I was ready to knock Arys on his ass if he couldn't control what the place was doing to him. I was here only to make demands of the FPA, not to be harassed by dead people that I did not kill, and most certainly not to fend off Arys.

"Let's go," I said to Shaz, jerking a thumb toward the exit to the stairwell.

Arys remained where he was, outside the door to the room of terror. He watched us ease away. Amusement danced in his eyes. "I'll give you a head start."

"Is he fucking serious?" Stunned horror filled Shaz's face. He was all fangs and claws as the wolf surfaced in response to the threat.

"Come on." I didn't waste time. I knew a crazed vampire when I saw one. I ran for the stairs with Shaz hot on my heels.

The sudden and total absolute black as we ran up the decrepit staircase was blinding. I tripped before reaching the first landing. I fell down on one knee in the glass, dirt and hospital debris. A spider web brushed against my face, and I fumbled to get it off me. Shaz grabbed my arm and dragged me to my feet. Wearing heeled boots had been a bad idea.

We were rounding the corner of the landing when Arys caught us. He grabbed me from behind, jerking me off my feet. My hand slipped from Shaz's, but I shouted at him to keep going.

Never in all the time I'd known Arys had he ever treated me so viciously. He slammed me back against the wall, causing broken plaster and drywall to rain down around us. Something thumped into the side of my head, but I was too busy fighting off the power drunk vampire to pay it any attention.

Pinning me to the wall, Arys went for my throat. A burst of power went out from me. It threw him off his feet, and he crashed into the stair railing before tumbling down the steps to the floor we'd just escaped. It didn't slow him down for long. He got right back up, lunging up the stairs.

I threw an energy barrier up between us. He hit it hard enough to stumble back, but it held. I stared at my lover on the other side, wondering what had happened to him. Arys had always proven to be the stronger of the two of us, the rock. I had never seen him manipulated by a force bigger than he was. This building housed things darker than I had imagined, things dark enough to affect my vampire.

Arys sneered at me from the other side of the invisible barrier. Gliding his hands over its surface, he smiled. "This is amusing."

Gripping the railing, I backed up the stairs toward Shaz, keeping my eyes on the vampire. I knew we could turn our shared power on one another, though I didn't know to what extent.

Arys dissolved my barrier by simply pulling my power into him, making it his. Like a rabid animal, he came at us again. Before he reached us, there was a bright flash of light. It stopped Arys in his tracks.

Falon appeared on the stairs, separating Arys from Shaz and me. With a small gesture, the angel effectively held Arys frozen in place.

"Twins," he sighed dramatically. "Always their own undoing."

"What are you doing here?" I lacked the ability to sound annoyed with him. Much as I hated to admit it, I was glad to see the asshole angel right then.

"Saving your ass from your other half, apparently." Falon marched past me to the upper landing where the secrets of the top floor awaited. "His power is rooted in darkness. The evil here seems to like him. It's probably better if he doesn't come any further."

Falon pulled open the heavy door at the top of the stairs and motioned for me to hurry up. Shaz didn't need to be told again. He ushered me up without hesitation. I glanced back at Arys.

"I can't just leave him." Splitting up didn't seem like a great plan. It never worked out well for people in the movies.

"Spare me the romantic drama and get your ass moving," Falon snapped with a loud flap of wings for emphasis. They settled in against his back to hug his body tightly. "I have better things to do than babysit Shya's prized werewolf. Let's get this over with."

Just that fast, I was no longer glad to see the cocky prick. The remnants of my fear melted away in the face of my sudden rage.

"Better things to do? Like the woman who's trying to have me killed? I'm aware that Shya doesn't know about your fuck buddy."

"Are you going to blackmail me, Alexa? You'd better be careful."

Shaz tensed beside me but he remained silent. He had never dealt with Falon before, and he didn't need to start now either.

The only thing that kept me from slapping Falon's smug face was the ghostly apparition that appeared behind him. It was a soldier. He moved to block the doorway, as if he would keep us out. The FPA set up their base on a floor haunted by military mental patients. Fitting.

"Your vampire will be fine." Falon walked through the soldier without so much as acknowledging him. "I'll get him on the way out. How many vampires is that in your collection now? Just two?"

I followed him, shuddering as the soldier's ice-cold energy passed through me. I clenched my teeth. "What's your problem with me, Falon? Really."

Being stuck with Falon hadn't been part of my plan for the evening. Of course, not a damn thing that had taken place so far had been part of the plan. I hated leaving Arys in the stairwell, but he was out of control. Still, I felt secure with Shaz at my side; we could handle this.

Falon seemed taken aback by my serious question. He'd been expecting more vulgar language. Frankly, so had I, but I wanted to know. He'd had a problem with me from the moment we'd first met.

The seventh floor was much quieter metaphysically than those below. The wing we were in was without electricity, but I could see the glow of lights far in the distance. The hallway was clean and empty. It was like stepping into a whole new building, though I could still feel the murky promise of evil far below my feet.

We made our way toward the light, passing through several sets of large, heavy double doors along the way. When I'd given up on getting a response, Falon said, "Nothing personal, O'Brien. I just don't like your kind."

"What kind is that?" This from Shaz who was watching the angel the way a cat watches a bird seconds before it pounces.

"The kind that walks the line. Those who exist in between. Vampires. Werewolves. Even some lesser demons. Those who were once human but have been changed. Unnaturals." There was bitterness in Falon's tone.

"Got a reason for that?" I couldn't keep the snarky edge out of my question.

"Don't need one."

Oh, he had one. That much was clear. Actually, I didn't need him to share; it really made no difference to me.

As we pushed through the next set of double doors, an ear splitting alarm went off. The hall immediately filled with men in uniform, guns drawn. Several of them shouted in surprise as they took in Falon's silver wings. I raised my hands to show I was unarmed. Shaz did the same. Falon merely smirked.

"Hold your fire, boys. Coming through." Juliet pushed through the men until she stood before us. She did a double take on Falon but smoothly recovered. Her gaze landed on me, cool and calculating. "Alexa, I wish you hadn't come."

## *Chapter Twenty-One*

"Yeah well I'm not real thrilled to be here," I replied. "The haunted house from hell to get up here was a blast though. That's a heck of a way to keep people out."

"It usually works." Juliet gave my male companions a once over. She wasn't comfortable with Falon's presence if her furtive glances in his direction were any indication.

"I just want Kale," I announced, drawing her gaze back to me. "Just let me leave with him, and I'll go without any trouble."

Her dark curls bounced when she shook her head. "I'm sorry, Lexi. I can't do that. He murdered an agent. We can't let him get away with that. How would that make us look?"

"He murdered a double agent," Falon spoke as if he were already unbearably exasperated with the situation. "He did you a favor. Now if you'll just scamper along like a good little wolf and fetch him, we'll be on our way."

Juliet flinched and more than a few men present exchanged a questioning look. Had Falon just revealed something about her they didn't know? The FPA must be run by idiots.

"I'm not authorized to release him to you or anybody else." Her tone was flat, her expression hard. "I suggest you all leave. Don't come back."

I laughed in disbelief. "Not a chance. I'm not leaving without him."

"Please, don't make this difficult. It's out of my hands."

"Then let me speak to someone with a little more clout than you."

I faced off with my sister, seeing a stranger instead. We had been birthed by the same woman, raised in the same house as children, yet none of that mattered now. The world had taken us away from each other, molding and shaping us. Now we were alike in DNA only. I didn't know her anymore. Our utter estrangement was so hard to swallow.

"Please," Juliet repeated, a trace of desperation in that one word.

"I'll take it from here, Agent O'Brien."

The man's voice cut through the strained silence. The cluster of armed agents parted to allow him through. He stepped up beside Juliet with the air of one who was used to being in charge.

Tall with dark brown skin and piercing brown eyes, he was clad in a grey suit. His hair was cropped short, and he didn't bother to hide the gun on his hip. He jacket was open to reveal the holster. If it was supposed to intimidate me, it wasn't working.

Ignoring Juliet, he thrust a hand at me. "I'm Agent Thomas Briggs. Nice to finally meet the infamous Alexa O'Brien."

I accepted his hand, hoping that playing nice would get me farther than starting out with a scathing remark. "Nice to meet you, Agent Briggs. I trust we can come to some kind of amicable understanding."

Placing a hand on each hip, Briggs surveyed the situation. "There is no need for conflict. Especially between family." His gaze strayed from me to my sister. "Please tell me, Ms. O'Brien, what can the FPA do for you?"

I found his choice of words odd. "I just want Kale Sinclair."

"Out of the question. Anything else I can help you with?"

Dismissed, just like that. Hell no. "No. I'm here for Kale Sinclair, and I am not leaving without him."

"I'll have my men escort you out then."

Falon snapped his fingers and every FPA agent present was frozen in place where they stood. "I don't think so. The vampire is one of ours. We are entitled to him regardless of his so-called crimes. The next move I make will be to blind every human in this building. Care to reconsider?"

Briggs strained for his gun. He was fixed in place, held by Falon's sheer will. Despite how much I loathed the fallen angel, I was developing greater respect for his abilities.

"Let's not be hasty." Briggs regarded the angel with venom in his eyes. "There is no need for violence."

"There is also no need for your human government meddling in affairs that are none of your concern." The air around Falon grew warm with his pulsating power. It was low, subdued, but heavy enough to alter the atmosphere.

Briggs had the decency to look wary as Falon walked a slow circle around him. He wasn't ready to give up control just yet though. "We have ways of dealing with demons."

"Then it's a good thing I'm not a demon."

Juliet and I shared a look. She shifted uneasily from foot to foot. Falon's power had only been projected at the humans.

"Alright, Falon," I said. "That's enough."

"Not until he tells me something I want to hear." Falon shot me a dirty look. "Besides, I'm the one calling the shots. Not you."

That was a fabulous united front to show the FPA. I rolled my eyes and weighed my options. Fight, bargain or leave. I didn't see any other choice. Falon was readying for a fight, but I wasn't yet willing to take that path.

"Agent Briggs, I'm not leaving without my friend." I shoved Falon aside so I could meet the agent's gaze directly. "So either this can get nasty, or we can come to some kind of agreement. Choose carefully."

Briggs glared daggers at me but seemed relieved that I wasn't allowing Falon to blind them all. Yet. "You can't just walk in here demanding things of the FPA. I don't give a damn who or what you are. There is nothing you have that we want badly enough to grant Sinclair his freedom. He's a menace."

"Wrong answer." I shrugged and motioned for Falon to do whatever he wished.

He never so much as moved, but every man surrounding Briggs began to cry out as they were struck blind. Briggs remained unchanged. He was steadfast in his decision, I had to give him that.

"Do what you will. It won't get you any closer to the vampire. He's behind lock and key that even you won't be able to get through."

Panic seeped from Juliet. She wasn't as calm and cool as her superior. "Sir, surely there is some way we can reach a compromise."

I gestured for Falon to release the agents from his hold. He resisted at first, giving me a strange look I couldn't read, but then he freed them.

A few men pointed their guns at him. That was pointless. A bullet wouldn't harm an angel. Surely, the FPA wasn't so poorly informed. Men that frightened so easily when faced with the supernatural should not be trying to police it.

"Trust me, Ms. O'Brien," Agent Briggs directed his comment to me. "You wouldn't want him now. Cut your losses and move on."

I lunged at Briggs, finding myself immobile as Shaz held me back. "What did you do to him?" I shouted, my voice echoing throughout the vast hall.

Though the top floor held far less ghost activity than the rest, I felt a surge of electricity crackle around me as several spirits drew close, lured by my outburst. They didn't scare me now. All I could think about was what had happened to Kale.

Agent Briggs smiled the smile of a man that fears nothing. Bastard. "He's still alive. If such a thing can be said about a vampire. His sanity isn't holding up as well as his body during the interrogation process, I'm afraid."

"Where is he? I want to see him." Seething, I felt the power wash over me with my anger. I knew when my eyes changed color; I could feel the rise of vampire power within me. The hovering ghosts pressed closer, and I lashed out at them with a push of energy to drive them back.

Briggs rested his hand on the butt of his gun in warning. "You're not stepping foot inside this facility without being cuffed."

"Fine." I held my wrists up in offering. "Cuff me."

Briggs gestured for Juliet to do the honors. She looked uneasy as she pulled a set of cuffs from her back pocket and approached me.

"Don't be a damn fool," Falon snapped. "Sinclair is on his own from here on out."

I ignored him. Nobody was asking him to stay. He was here on Shya's orders. Not my problem. Shaz released me, but he stood ready to grab me again if necessary.

"I'm sorry, Lexi," Juliet whispered as she locked the magic-enforced cuffs onto my wrists. "I have to."

"In case you're thinking about pulling anymore tricks," Briggs warned. "I should inform you that I have men on the ground with your two lady friends. Let's all be on our best behavior so we can all go home alive. Shall we?"

The FPA had another way in and out of the building. Of course. I was willing to bet it involved more powered elevators and less poltergeist activity. I should have left Arys with Jez and Brogan. I knew both ladies could hold their own, but it was my fault that they had to now. If anything happened to either of them, I'd be coming back for Briggs.

The cuffs locked into place, and my eyes widened. They acted as a metaphysical mirror, reflecting my power back at me. To use it would only bounce it back at me. So, they weren't such idiot humans after all. Impressive. And, a little frightening.

Briggs waited until the agents had covered my companions and me on every side before turning to lead the way down the hall to where the light was brightest. "I'll show you that Sinclair is still alive. Then, I'll have you escorted out. Unless of course you are really willing to negotiate?"

"You had to get me in cuffs to spit that out?" I sneered. "Can't help but notice I'm the only one wearing them."

Briggs pointed at Falon and Shaz each in turn. "He can't be held by them, and he's not a threat that a gun can't take care of. Humor me, Ms. O'Brien."

The agent oozed confidence though remained respectfully wary. He was likely a man that was damn good at his job. Devoted to the cause, whatever that was. I suppose I should have been honored the FPA found me threatening enough to require precautions, but I was just a little disappointed that I wasn't as threatening as Falon, one they could not hold.

I followed along like a cooperative little wolf as Briggs took us to a door marked Sector One. Inside was a large office complete with a wall of monitors and a lengthy desk filled with computers manned by various agents. They didn't so much as glance up at our entry.

I scanned the monitors mounted on the wall, finding shots of various parts of the hospital. Every entry and several main halls on other floors were covered. The stairwells were curiously without coverage. A blind spot. Somewhat careless of the FPA, but I'd retain that info for later should I need it.

They had watched our arrival obviously, waiting for us to blunder our way through the haunted maze below. Meanwhile they'd been sending men down to Jez and Brogan. Big Brother had been one step ahead. Like usual. The fact that my sister was one of them really made it sting.

Beyond the control room lay a hall to the right and one straight ahead. We turned to the right and passed several small personal offices before reaching a series of several larger rooms. I was willing to bet the rooms were soundproofed.

"So," I said, feigning casual. "Why the top floor? Is there a particular reason? Seems like secret ops is more of a basement thing."

Briggs ignored me, striding along like a man on a mission. Juliet dropped back to walk beside me. She kept a carefully neutral expression, but I could feel her discomfort.

"The basement is where the morgue is," she said. "Everything from the ground floor up is child's play compared to what's down there."

I was both intrigued and wary. "Interesting. I'll bet you don't get a lot of unwelcome visitors in a place like this."

"Not usually. Curious civilians occasionally."

We stopped outside a door where two agents stood guard. Briggs exchanged a few words with them, and they stepped aside. Briggs turned to me before opening the door.

"Only you. Your friends wait here with my men."

I shook my head and met his dark eyes directly. "I'm bringing my wolf in with me. Trust me when I say he's the only thing keeping me sane while I'm in this building."

I stared at the agent with vampire blue eyes and hands humming with power I couldn't use. Since parting from Arys, my control had been slipping. It wasn't the building though; it was the cocky suits that thought they could govern my actions.

I had a stare down with Briggs. Neither of us blinked or looked away. I wasn't sure what he saw in my unnatural gaze, but finally he nodded. "Only the wolf."

As Briggs opened the door, I cast a warning glance back at Falon. He leaned back against the opposite wall and crossed his arms. His response was a big phony smile. Bastard.

Agent Briggs led the way into a large, dimly lit room. Shaz and I followed with Juliet and two other agents at our backs. The room was relatively bare, housing only a table with a coffee pot and Styrofoam cups. Three chairs sat lined up before a large pane of glass, which I quickly realized was a two-way mirror.

Apprehension filled me as I feared what I might see on the other side. It was dark now, but I knew Kale was in there. I saw no access to that room from the one where we stood. The agents standing guard outside closed the door, sealing us into the tiny room.

Briggs reached for a light switch on the wall but stopped mid-motion. "I trust you know this isn't going to be pretty. I must warn you, if you try anything or hurt any of my people, you'll never make it out of this building alive."

"Spare me the Hollywood movie dialogue. I'm not here to read from a script." I was snappy and anxious.

Shaz gravitated closer to me, not quite touching but ready for anything. I motioned for Briggs to get it over with. I was ready to wrestle him out of the way to flip the switch myself, cuffs and all.

I wasn't ready though. Not by a long shot.

Briggs flipped the switch, bathing the room on the other side of the glass in bright fluorescent light. I heard a gasp, unaware it was me. The interrogation room beyond the glass was so white, the walls, the floor, even the table and chairs off to one side. What wasn't bright white was stained crimson. Blood painted the floor in places. Splatters decorated one wall like crude abstract art. In the center of it all was Kale.

He hung suspended from the ceiling by heavy-duty shackles, and his head fell limply. From where I stood, I could see that those shackles dug painfully into the flesh of his wrists. His feet touched the ground but just barely. Bruises and cuts decorated every inch of his body. One eye was swollen shut, the other badly bruised. The side of his face was caked in dried blood.

He was naked and beaten. And, I was livid. The rage that filled me was like nothing I'd ever known. The need to kill was fierce, and I threw myself at Briggs without thinking.

Like the amazing partner he was, Shaz wrestled me back before I could make a huge mistake. I couldn't do the damage to Briggs that he deserved. Acting rashly wouldn't help Kale. I knew it logically, but the wolf within didn't give a damn about logic. She just wanted to kill Briggs.

"Hold her back if you want her to stay alive," Briggs warned, drawing his gun.

"How could you treat him like that?" I shouted, my voice rough with wolf. I didn't fight Shaz, instead letting him hold me tight. An accusatory glare at Juliet was wasted. She wouldn't meet my eyes.

"Lex, chill out," Shaz's voice was calm and soothing. "If you lose it now, you won't be able to help him."

Kale's head came up suddenly as if he sensed me. The soundproofing ensured he couldn't hear my tirade. Did he know I was here?

"If anything, we've gone easy on him, considering what he did to Abigail Irving." Briggs shrugged. Kale was nothing to him, not a person with feelings or several lifetimes of knowledge. Kale was just a piece of meat to treat as such.

"You have your head so far up your ass you can't see the light," I growled. "You can't employ anyone linked to the supernatural and expect them not to betray you. Abigail, Shya and anyone else." I looked pointedly at Juliet out of spite. "There is no harnessing the supernatural."

Agent Briggs and I exchanged a long look. He knew there was truth in my words. I could see it in his eyes. Like so many others here, he was following orders and not about to argue that with me.

"What's he worth to you, Ms. O'Brien?"

There it was, the million-dollar question. So many ways I could answer. I felt Shaz's tension as he waited for my answer.

"I'm willing to negotiate. Name your price." I watched Kale through the glass, aching to go to him, aching from seeing him like that. His abuse lit a fire inside me that would not be extinguished until I made the FPA sorry they had fucked with someone I cared about.

"There's only one thing we'd be interested in receiving from you."

Everyone present was dead quiet, watching the exchange. Shaz's hold on me loosened just slightly.

"And what might that be?"

"Your service."

Laughter broke the silence. My laughter. Was he just fucking with me?

"You're kidding, right? I just told you the supernatural can't be trusted. Why should I be any different?"

Briggs found no humor in the situation. His eyes narrowed, and he waited for me to quit cackling before replying. "Because we have your sister."

I hadn't expected much from the FPA, but this was a new kind of low. "Seriously? You're threatening my sister? The sister that I believed was dead for ten years? The sister who came into my club and took Kale?" I laughed bitterly. "Try again."

Juliet flinched. A pang of guilt shot through me, but I shoved it aside. I would always love Juliet, but I couldn't let them think they could use her against me. If that meant giving her the cold shoulder, so be it.

"What do you really want from me?" I cut to the chase, refusing to play games. Looking at Kale's battered form was beginning to weigh heavy on me.

Briggs cleared his throat. "Information."

"On Shya," I filled in the blanks. "I can't help you. He doesn't tell me a damn thing." My mind raced as I rushed to find something that would appease him. "But, I do have some files I swiped from Veryl Armstrong. They're heavily encrypted, and I haven't been able to get into them. I imagine that means there's something worth finding in them."

"Files that belonged to Veryl Armstrong?" Briggs was intrigued. That was a good thing. "And, you'd be willing to hand them over without even knowing what's on them first? That could be risky."

"It could," I agreed, "but I'll do it."

"Of course, you could be lying. You may know there's not a damn thing on the files worth having."

"Ask Juliet if I've spoken anything but the truth. A werewolf can smell a lie." I dared him to call my bluff. Briggs was stiff and hard to read. I hated him.

"She's not lying, Sir," Juliet confirmed. She still wouldn't look at me. It hurt as much as it ticked me off.

I pulled away from Shaz and made my way closer to the pane of glass. Raising my cuffed hands, I touched the cold, smooth surface, wishing I could reach through to the other side. Kale's gaze swung my way, landing on the mirror on his side. He knew I was here. I was sure of it then.

"He's not the vampire you share power with," Briggs asked curiously, "so why's he so important to you?"

I didn't turn to face him. I couldn't take my eyes off Kale. "It's irrelevant."

A door on the far side of Kale's prison opened. I caught a glimpse of guards outside that door and a familiar face caught my eye. Bianca. The bitch worked for the FPA. Unreal.

A look at Shaz revealed total shock. He hadn't known. Good Lord, I hoped he hadn't revealed anything to her about me that he shouldn't have. She'd be wise to stay far away from my club. Next time I faced her, she would die.

The door closed, cutting off my view. A scantily clad brunette strutted her way through the room to stand before Kale.

"What the hell is she doing?" I demanded, staring in shock as the woman began to slip out of what little she wore.

A knife was strapped to her stocking covered thigh. A few thin cuts marred her wrist and stomach. When she stood half-naked before Kale, she pulled the knife from its sheath and slid it across her forearm. A thin line of blood welled up. She dipped a finger in it then rubbed it along Kale's lower lip. He couldn't resist licking the tiny smear.

She sauntered away, her bare breasts bouncing provocatively. After fetching a chair from the table, she sat down ten feet away from Kale and taunted him. Making shallow cuts, she played in the blood, rubbing it over her breasts and down her stomach. It didn't take long for Kale to bare fangs and begin uttering threats. This was vampire torture at its finest.

I was a twisted combination of horror-struck and enticed. My bloodlust awakened, driven by my desire to make someone hurt. I turned to face Briggs with a wicked glare.

"Make her stop. Now." My tone was quiet, almost a whisper, but it was deadly.

Whatever Briggs saw on my face must have been enough. He hit the intercom and shouted, "Sylvia, that will be enough for tonight."

Silvia hesitated, staring at the mirror even though she couldn't see us. Maybe she hadn't known she was being watched. One of the agents in the room with me leered openly at her nudity. She took her sweet time slipping back into her bra.

Just when I thought she'd exit the room, she glided up next to Kale and pressed her cut arm to his lips. When he bared his sharp fangs, she pulled away so he snapped at empty air. Her arrogant laughter filtered through the wall intercom.

I pounded both fists against the glass in anger. The pane didn't budge beneath the force. Sylvia didn't know it yet but she had just guaranteed herself a date with a vampire that wouldn't go easy on her. I'd seen horrific things in Arys's memories, but all of them were better than she deserved. My wrath demanded to be sated.

My sanity slipped. The cuffs were keeping a lid on my power, but they couldn't keep my four fangs hidden or muffle the snarl that spilled from between my lips. I eyed the three humans each in turn, trying to decide whom I wanted to taste first. The need to feel warm human blood dripping on my tongue was overwhelming.

An image flashed behind my eyes, sudden and startling. The bright red of my Charger beneath the streetlights, a flash of golden hair, an angry shout. Then blood, pumping hot from the artery.

I watched through Arys's eyes as he slaughtered the agents outside. Somehow, he'd escaped Falon's hold, unless the angel had simply released him.

I fought back the image and the hunger it drove crazy within me. Knowing it was Arys's bloodlust feeding my own made it easier to regain control. Regardless, it was time to go.

"I'll bring you the files on a flash drive," I told Briggs, forcing my gaze away from the pulse beating steadily in this throat. "You and your people will then leave me and my people alone. We are not your enemy. Keep me on your watch list if it makes you feel better. I assure you, I have no interest in interacting with the FPA as either an enemy or an ally. Understood?"

Agent Briggs appeared undecided. Information was the most valuable tool these organizations possessed. He was taking a gamble and so was I. Neither of us knew what those files could mean to either of us. I was taking a chance that no matter how bad it was, it would be worth Kale's life. Briggs now had to decide if he felt the same way.

"Certainly," he said at last. "We will arrange a time and place to exchange Sinclair for the flash drive. It's best that you don't come back here."

"I'm not leaving him here like this." I gestured angrily to bloodstained room. "I can have the files for you in a matter of hours. Tonight even."

Briggs was stony faced, his eyes emotionless. "We'll be in touch within seventy-two hours. Take it or leave it."

I felt helpless. I'd never believed I would be leaving here without Kale, but with Arys running amok outside and no access to my power, I had very few options.

"You're making a mistake, Agent," I warned.

Briggs banged on the heavy-duty door, and the agents standing guard outside opened it. "The only mistake I'm making, Ms. O'Brien, is allowing you to walk out of here at all. My men will escort you. We'll be in touch."

It took all my strength to turn my back on Kale and walk out of that room. Briggs disappeared down an adjacent hall, but Juliet remained. Falon was gone.

Several agents ushered us to an elevator. I observed carefully as an agent provided both a voice and fingerprint sample to a scanner before the elevator began to move. Juliet waited until we had stepped out a secure exit at the rear of the building onto the grounds outside. Then, she pulled me aside and removed the cuffs from my wrists.

Low and hushed she whispered, "I'll do everything I can to make sure they don't hurt him anymore, Lexi. I promise."

The emotion I'd carefully concealed in front of Briggs erupted like a volcano. "Don't call me Lexi. That's what my sister called me. You are not my sister."

I shoved past the agents with Shaz at my side. Without a backward glance I added, "Tell Briggs that if he has a problem with the dead agents you'll find out front, he can take it up with me. Nobody else."

I walked away to the sound of agents on cell phones, calling for back up. Useless. Arys was long gone. I couldn't sense him anywhere. By the time Shaz and I reached the car, I was fighting back tears, screams and maniacal laughter. This had not gone as I'd anticipated.

Jez and Brogan sat on the hood talking in low tones. Three dead agents lay sprawled near the car. Thankfully, both ladies were unharmed.

"I don't know about you, but we had a blast," Jez greeted us sarcastically. "Your vampire is long gone, by the way."

"Are you two ok? Did anyone try to hurt you?"

"Nah. Arys went after them. I thought he may try for us, too, but he didn't stick around long once they were dead. What the hell happened inside? Where's Kale?"

"Let's get out of here, and I'll fill you in."

I reached out to Arys, flinging open that mental door between us. 'Have you lost your mind? Where are you?'

He felt distant. His thoughts were scattered and rushed. He resisted my presence in his head. 'Go home, Alexa.'

He shoved me out with an abruptness that left me feeling dizzy. I was never letting Arys near that old hospital again. This did not sit well with me.

The drive back to The Wicked Kiss wasn't a happy one. My sister was now my enemy. The FPA was a menace I didn't feel would go away after one transaction. I needed to stay alive for the next three days if I wanted to see Kale again, but to do that I had to successfully bind a demon during the full moon.

I was so screwed.

## Chapter Twenty-Two

I paced the length of Arys's house like a caged animal. From the kitchen, through the living room and down the hall, and then back again.

After exchanging a few words with Brogan regarding the possibility of Veryl's files being magically secured, I had parted ways with my companions. Shaz had strongly insisted on coming back to Arys's with me. My insistence that he go home to Coby had been stronger.

The clock ticked down the minutes until dawn. It wasn't far off now. Where was my vampire?

I spent a restless half hour at my new laptop fighting with the locked files. I made a few backup copies, which I stored online before copying them to a flash drive. I also emailed a copy to Brogan who had promised to take a look at them. Handing the files over to the FPA may come back to bite me in the ass, so I had to find out what was on them, preferably before they did.

I didn't have the patience to stare at the computer screen. The closer sunrise drew, the more uneasy I became. Arys was more than capable of taking care of himself, but I was still worried.

To stop myself from pacing an indent in the carpet, I occupied myself with a shower. I stood beneath the hot spray for a long time. It was so hard to relax lately. I was wound tight and fearful of when I would break.

The sound of my phone had me rushing to turn the water off and grab a towel without slipping. With my hair dripping, I clutched the towel to my chest and reached my phone seconds before it went to voicemail.

"I can't stop thinking about you." The sound of Shaz's voice coaxed a sigh from me. "Has Arys shown up?"

"Not yet." Securing my towel in place above my breasts, I returned to the living room and peered out the window. "That place did something bad to him. I've never seen him like that."

"Is he going to be dangerous when he turns up? Should I come over?" The hopefulness in his tone was crushing.

I understood his desperation to make things right with us. If only it were that simple.

"It's alright. I can handle him. Stay home and get some rest. I think we both need it."

I could sense his disappointment on the other end. I was disappointed, too. I kept waiting for a chance to mourn the destruction of the good thing we had once shared. Already, our relationship was in shambles, and we were left to pick up the pieces. Still, I felt we could salvage something eventually.

"Thank you, Shaz, for being with me tonight. You were there when Arys failed me. When I would have failed myself."

There was silence on the line as he gathered himself. When he spoke, it was thick with emotion. "It confirmed what you both said about me. The role I play. I'm starting to understand how we all fit together."

"I'm glad. I'm still trying to do that myself." The towel began to slip as I made my way down the hall to get dressed. I almost fumbled my phone when I grabbed for it.

"I don't want to leave you. I feel like I have to." The misery in his words was gut-wrenching. "Tell me not to go, Lex."

I sat heavily on the edge of Arys's bed, a hand over my mouth as I bit back the anguished cry that threatened to break from me. One deep breath, then another. What I wanted and what I felt had to happen were two different things. I owed him honesty. I owed it to both of us.

"I wish I could, babe, but I think you should." I couldn't believe I was saying this. "It will be good for you to get away for a while. To do what you have to do. I want you to be happy, and to do that, you need to make peace with yourself."

Abandoning the wet towel, I slipped into a pair of pink cotton panties and pulled my robe on. The menial task did nothing to take my focus off the somber man on the phone.

Shaz swore softly. "I feel like I'm abandoning you. Like I'm running away from the things I've done."

"If you were running away, you wouldn't have stuck around long enough to tell me. You're a good man, Shaz. You just made a few mistakes, and they pale in comparison to mine. If getting out of Dodge is what you need right now, then you should do that."

Did I want him to leave town? Hell no. But, this wasn't about me.

"You know, Lex, I can't remember a time when I wasn't head over heels in love with you." He laughed softly, and the sound of it warmed me. "I was a smitten kid happy just to be your friend. I never thought I'd be yours."

I had many fond memories of my friendship with Shaz over the years. It had always meant so much to me. "You weren't much of a kid. You were eighteen when we met. Only three years younger than me. So wise beyond your years."

"What we had then, that friendship, I don't want to lose that." He stifled a yawn. It made me yawn in turn.

"We won't. I promise." Returning to the living room, I peered out the window at the sky. The stars had disappeared from sight. "Get some sleep. You sound tired. We'll talk later."

"Don't do anything crazy without me. I love you."

"And, I love you, wolf boy. Sweet dreams."

After ending the call with Shaz, I stood there staring at my phone longingly. I would never forget the things we'd done recently to hurt one another, but I could forgive. And, I would move forward.

Try as I might to remain calm, each minute that brought sunrise closer increased my worry. Arys should be back by now. I padded into the kitchen and rummaged through the pantry until I found the chocolate bar I'd stashed for a stressful moment. Maybe the taste and sensation of chocolate and caramel melting on my tongue wouldn't change anything, but it was a special joy all its own.

A cold wave crashed through me seconds before I heard a sound at the front door. Relief quickly followed. My dark vampire was home.

Abandoning the chocolate on the counter, I moved quietly toward the front porch. I hung back just inside the kitchen, waiting with building trepidation. The last time I saw Arys, he wasn't functioning at full sanity. I let my power flow forth to fill my hands with the crackle of raw energy.

Arys entered with the silent stealth of a true predator. A human never would have known he was there. I took a few steps back, placing me in the middle of the kitchen. When he crossed the threshold, there was fire in his eyes and an arrogant smirk on his handsome face.

"Alexa," he practically purred my name. His energy ran high. It felt thick with blood, darkness and hunger. Hunger for me.

I stared at him, wide eyed and cautious but also curious. I never saw him move from the doorway, but he was suddenly there, pulling me against him with a forcefulness that both alarmed and excited me. The power I held ready fell flat; he'd extinguished it as simply as blowing out a candle.

His tongue plunged between my lips to explore my mouth. Demanding and insistent, he kissed me with such aggression that his fangs cut my bottom lip. Trying to err on the side of caution, I placed a hand on his chest and gave a gentle push. He refused to be budged.

"Arys," I pulled back from his kiss and tried to get him to meet my eyes. "Where have you been?"

He didn't answer me. Instead, he stared at me with a deep, drowning desire. He moved fast. Grabbing my wrists, Arys spun me around so my back was to his chest and pushed me against the table. With one hand, he pinned me in place, the other reaching beneath my robe.

I gasped when he hooked two fingers in my panties and jerked them roughly down my legs. My robe easily slid aside for him to expose me. A strange concoction of fear and arousal sprang forth. The wolf within me was excited by his fierce aggression, but the human side of me was afraid of death at the hands of my lover.

The heat of his mouth against the back of my neck starkly contrasted with the cold drops falling from my damp hair. Arys slid a hand into my wet hair, holding my head so I couldn't turn to look at him. His teeth were sharp against my skin, scraping along my neck but not yet puncturing.

It was all happening so fast. Was I going to let him take me like this? By force like an animal?

A shiver crept through me. He fumbled to free himself from the confines of his jeans. Despite my apprehension, a surge of heat pooled between my legs.

I couldn't move because of the way he held me pinned. I struggled to turn around to face him, but he held firm. With one strong hand, he grasped both of my wrists, crushing them together as he forced them above my head. He was hurting me, dominating me like a possession rather than a person. Not so different from the way he'd treated the victims he'd taken to his bed before killing them.

Memories flashed through my mind, surfacing from the depths of my subconscious. Arys's memories surfaced in bursts of blood-stained images, visions of Harley and Arys terrorizing faceless, nameless men and women.

Unease gripped me. Maybe I shouldn't allow this to happen.

I gasped as Arys buried himself inside me. Something awoke within and I snarled. The dark laugh that spilled from him taunted my desire. I was drawn to the darkness in Arys, always drawn in. He held me down on the table, completely at his mercy, and against my will, I loved it.

Arys's powerful thrusts forced me to cry out. The free hand he stroked along my hip slipped down between my thighs to the sensitive place there.

The power overtook us, growing to catch us up in the dizzying flow. A sinister element tinged it. It called to me, tempting me to look further into the abyss, to step closer to the edge.

The act that consumed us had nothing to do with love. It was downright rough and dirty sex.

My claws left deep gouges in the tabletop. Arys's name was a constant cry as I spun headlong into the promise of ecstasy.

He never gave me a chance to catch my breath. Releasing his vice-like hold on my wrists, Arys turned me to face him and lifted me onto the table. Stepping in between my legs, he reclaimed my body with his.

He leaned in to kiss me, and I slapped him across the face. It was impulsive and instinctive. My claws left bloody red scratches on his cheek. Mischief gleamed in his eyes. He bared fangs at me in a cocky grin.

"Is that all you've got?" He taunted before shoving my arms down and kissing me with a heady fervor that left me breathless.

Even the wolf couldn't stay mad at him. He oozed sex appeal and a sensual masculinity I couldn't deny. I clung to him as together we raced toward paradise.

I sensed the bite was coming. I was eager for it when Arys went for my neck with the aggression of a rabid dog. My pained sound only encouraged him. The scent of blood and sex filled the room, an aroma that had come to be both heaven and hell for me.

The sensation of his lips and tongue on my wounded neck combined with the blissful pleasure between my legs easily drove me over the edge. I fell through a cloud of euphoria, becoming entangled in a sticky web of darkness. It threatened to devour me, to cover me in shadows until I was no longer the light to Arys's dark but one with it instead.

I pushed Arys away. I needed to clear my head. The orgasmic rise and fall of energy was suffocating. He resisted but eventually stepped back, watching me closely.

My hand went to my neck. It wasn't bad. The bleeding had already slowed. I tugged my robe back into place and hopped off the table. I wasn't sure how to feel about what just happened.

Buzzing with an overload of energy, I cast a wary glance at Arys. "Wanna tell me what that was all about?"

His midnight blue eyes shone with remnants of our power, though the insane sparkle had thankfully faded. "Did I hurt you?"

"Yes, but not the way you're thinking." I bent to retrieve my underwear, slipping them back into place. A large bruise on the inside of my thigh caught my eye. "Tell me what happened to you at the hospital. You really freaked me out."

With a sheepish grin, Arys pushed a hand through his disheveled hair and dropped his gaze to the floor. "I'm sorry about that. I'm not sure what happened. Something in the hospital set me off."

"You think? It's not funny, Arys. You could have hurt Shaz or me. Or worse. There was serious evil in that place."

"I'm aware of that." He turned away, disrobing as he headed for the bedroom. "Whatever is in the basement, it's evil and it's pissed."

He disappeared from sight. I was forced to follow him to continue the conversation. I leaned against the doorframe, watching his fine, naked form slide between the sheets. He patted the bed beside him, but I knew how he worked. I knew that look in his eyes.

Remaining rooted to the spot, I crossed my arms and frowned. "That's all you've got to say? It would have been nice to have you at my side when I faced the FPA. They cuffed me, you know. It was the only way they would let me see Kale."

"Cuffs can't hold a werewolf," he scoffed. "Settle down, Alexa. I can feel your brimming anger like hot needles. I had no control over what happened to me in the hospital. Whatever is in there, it manipulated me. It was the power of the dead. I couldn't resist it. But I'm fine. We're all fine."

Arys regarded me with a haughty expression. I sighed and shook my head. Power, blood and death, the combination was capable of doing bizarre things to a person. I'd seen it with Arys, Kale and even myself.

Trying to reason with him right now was senseless. I was just grateful he'd come down enough to resist tearing my throat out.

"Arys, the cuffs the FPA used were magically enforced. If I used my power, they reflected it back at me with a negative charge so I couldn't re-absorb it. You can't dismiss these people as harmless government idiots. They have resources that can be used against us."

He seemed to ponder this revelation. The small bedside lamp light glinted off his jet-black hair, creating a blue sheen. The sheets were pooled haphazardly in his lap, inviting me to seek out what lie beneath.

I had to give myself a shake. The subtle but strong pull of his allure sought to draw me in again. I couldn't shield against him. Not when I could always feel him inside.

We stared at one another in silence. I could see him turning it over. The FPA had been a silent threat, so silent that I hadn't believed the rumors of their existence until I saw them for myself.

Simultaneously we said, "You can't go back there."

I laughed and Arys scowled. He was trying to downplay what the old hospital had done to him, but I wasn't buying it. Not after seeing it with my own eyes.

"Works for me." I ignored the seductive gaze he turned on me and kept talking as if oblivious. "If I never step foot inside that place again it will be too soon. I'm not sure what was worse, the FPA torture chambers or the dead people on the way up."

"So what did they want from you? Something you couldn't give them? Is that why you weren't able to spring Sinclair from his prison?"

I saw him try to hide it, but his satisfaction was written all over his face. If I were Arys, I would have been satisfied, too. It still irritated me.

"The agent I dealt with accepted my offer of Veryl's files. In fact, he was quite intrigued when I mentioned them."

"You can't even get into those files. If you hand them over and they find something they shouldn't, you'll be the one paying the price." With his head tilted studiously, he rubbed a hand over his chin. "Is that really a risk worth taking?"

"Don't ask me questions that you don't want the answers to."

The black tinted energy leaked from Arys like an oil spill, murky and thick. I was careful not to react, wary of setting him off again. It was going to take some time for him to come down entirely from the rush the hospital's dark energy had given him.

Arys reclined against the mountain of pillows stacked against the headboard. Folding his hands beneath his head, he fixed me with a look that directly contrasted the casual appearance he exuded.

"I didn't wait this long to find you just to watch you gamble your life away over another vampire. Be careful, Alexa. I'd hate to have to kill Sinclair to cure you of your recent bout of insanity."

I gaped at him in shock. "I'm going to pretend I didn't hear that. You're not yourself right now, and I'm not in the mood to fight with you."

He beamed a perfectly creepy Cheshire cat smile at me. "But, you're so sexy when you're pissed. I thought you were really going to let loose when you threw that slap." He chuckled, and the sound made me weak in the knees. "Come here, my wolf. Show me the fire inside you."

Immediately I wanted to go to him, to crawl over the bed to him and climb on top. I resisted with great difficulty. Arys was manipulating me with his intoxicating thrall, pulling me in like he so easily did his victims. I didn't trust him, not with the predatory way he was looking at me.

"I'm not your victim, Arys, and I won't be threatened." I took a few steps toward the bed. "I'll deal with the FPA however I feel is best. Got it?"

With a raised brow and a twitch of his lips, Arys nodded. "As you wish, your highness. I'll sit back and watch you figure it out."

Conflict. Always some kind of conflict. Now that I was more aware of it, I saw how embedded the battle had always been in our relationship. Arys and I had been butting heads long before we'd shared a bed. It was always in us, the inability to maintain the delicate balance of what we shared.

It would follow us always. I feared the day it would escalate from petty arguments to something that would truly put us at odds. It had happened once before, six months ago when I'd killed Arys's sire. Things had gotten pretty bad. I couldn't shake the sense of foreboding that gripped me, telling me it would get worse yet.

I shoved the unwelcome feeling away and focused only on the current moment. Worry about a time that had yet to come was useless, so I gave in to the lure of the mesmerizing vampire instead.

The desire to have him inside me again was fueled by his drowning blue gaze. Arys crooked a finger, beckoning me to come to him.

"I believe we were just getting started."

## Chapter Twenty-Three

"I don't like this, Lex." Worry filled Shaz's jade eyes. "There's got to be another way."

"I don't like it either, but I need you to do what you do best: Be Alpha and take care of our wolves."

We stood on the deck in Kylarai's backyard. The sun had set an hour ago. The stars were peeking out through the dark veil of the night sky. The moon spilled silver light down upon us. That beautiful light would grow in its brilliance as the night went on. I ached to run down the deck stairs to the grass below, to plunge my fingers into the earth and be one with the beast inside. Instead, I would be spending the full moon with demons.

Shaz's jaw was clenched, and his eyes were all wolf, the green obliterating the whites entirely. "What if you need me? Have you ever gone a full moon night without being wolf? It just sounds so dangerous."

"No, I haven't. All I want to do right now is tear my clothes off, drop to all fours and tear across that field at top speed." I sighed, a sound of self-pity. "Arys will be with me though. It'll be fine."

"Or, he'll make it twice as hard for you because he relies on you to keep the wolf at bay."

Shaz was skeptical and rightfully so. The power of my wolf lived in Arys due to our bond. More than once, it had exceeded his control. The wolf couldn't manifest through a vampire into a physical form. Arys relied entirely on my shift to ease the burden of the beast that lived deep within him.

"Or, he could wolf out," I acknowledged as my gaze strayed to the glass patio doors.

Kylarai, Coby and Zak sat around the kitchen table enjoying drinks and small talk. Ky's laughter carried through the glass panes as she cracked up at something Coby had said. She sipped from a teacup and reached to touch his arm, peering at him from beneath her long lashes. She was flirting with him.

I smiled, turning back to Shaz so she wouldn't see me. "It will be easier for me to deal with Lilah if I know you are here. Safe."

"But, I won't have the same assurance about you." He wouldn't meet my eyes. Instead, he stared out at the tree line in the distance.

Shaz was conflicted, torn between his obligation to me and to himself, but I didn't want to be an obligation. I needed him, but I could survive without him if it meant seeing him discover himself and find freedom from the dark world I'd drawn him into. I could let him go if I had to. As much as the wolf inside fought and snarled against that decision, she too knew that love sometimes meant letting go.

"You don't need to worry about me, Shaz. Put yourself first for a change. Be wolf with the others and be happy. You're far too beautiful to go giving yourself worry lines." I gave him a playful nudge and swallowed the sudden burst of raw emotion.

He captured my hand, raising it to his lips. Pressing a kiss to my palm, he breathed in my scent as if afraid he would forget it if he didn't memorize it now. We stood there with nothing more to say. Kylarai's laughter was the only sound, muffled by the closed patio doors but musical just the same.

I smiled, but it hurt to do so. I didn't want to leave my wolves, especially Shaz. I wasn't arrogant enough to believe everything would go off without a hitch tonight. A demon with a price on my head wasn't going to be easy to subdue, particularly if I really was all that stood between her and the freedom from her curse.

Death held more terror for me now than it ever had before. Because of the blood bond I'd formed with Arys, I was guaranteed to rise as a vampire upon my mortal death. I had grown to fear that transformation so desperately that I'd asked Shaz and Kylarai a few weeks ago to kill me if I became little more than a bloodthirsty maniac. Arys was not aware of my request nor did I want him to be.

"I should go," I forced the words out.

With a nod, he released my hand, hesitating just a moment before he pulled me into his arms. Tucking my head under his chin, I closed my eyes and savored the comfort of his embrace. It reminded me of a time when we had been so close that people assumed we were lovers before we'd even kissed. Things had changed, but I could still feel that connection between us, buried under the rubble of our broken romance.

When he let me go, I felt like something was missing. My wolf leaped against my insides, demanding to be freed. It was getting harder to resist.

I turned to go, my hand on the patio door.

Shaz's voice followed me. "Be careful, Lex."

The scent of coffee and werewolf hit me when I stepped inside. Shaz remained on the deck, staring out at the night. After wishing the wolves at the table a nice night, I headed for the front door with Kylarai hot on my heels.

"Are you ok?" She asked in a soft whisper when we stood alone on the front step. "The tension between the two of you is suffocating."

"I'm fine. I just wish I could stay."

"Liar."

"Ok, I'm lying." Trying to hide anything from the mother hen of the group was hopeless. She knew both Shaz and me well. She was the big sister neither of us ever had. "I'm not fine. I'm coming apart inside and doing my damnedest to hide it."

The confession felt good. Keeping everything buried was hurting me, not helping.

"You've never been very good at hiding your feelings. It's one of the things I love most about you." Kylarai's grey eyes shone with warmth. She gave me a tight hug that crushed the breath from me. "We need to have some quality girl time. You don't have to bear every burden alone."

I nodded and bit my lip, trying to hold back my next words. "Shaz is leaving town, Ky. I don't know how I'm going to survive without him."

Her smile faded, and she gave a solemn nod. "I know. He told me. I'm so sorry, Lex. Maybe it will be for the best. Give you both a chance to sort things out."

"I know," I sniffled, cursing the few stray tears that had escaped. Clear and human, they mocked me in ways blood tears did not.

"He's leaving because he loves you, Alexa. Because he wants to be the link to the light that you need to battle Arys's darkness. He knows now what that means."

"How is that possible when I don't even know?"

Ky shrugged and pushed a blonde lock out of my eyes. "He has faith. And, so should you. Everything happens for a reason. Your link to Arys, your love for Shaz, it all has to mean something. Remember that."

She was right. Staying strong would carry me through. That's what I needed now. "Take care of each other tonight, ok? I've got to go."

Arys was waiting in my car. I got in, started the engine and backed out of Kylarai's driveway without a glance in his direction. I didn't want him to see the pain I fought down inside. I had to change my focus. Tonight's rendezvous permitted no room for crippling emotion.

I could feel the weight of his gaze as I drove. The vampire was a clever creature though, and he knew better than to ask whatever questions were dancing on the tip of his tongue. He allowed me to pretend everything was fine and dandy until we reached the outskirts of the city.

"Might as well head down to the Avenue. It's still early but hunting down a snack shouldn't be too hard." Arys sounded uninterested. Bored.

The Avenue was a strip just off the downtown core, known for being a fast paced, highly frequented red light district. It was my hunting ground of choice when the demands of the bloodlust became too much. I wasn't proud of the things I'd done there, but it was my best alternative to mindlessly slaughtering innocents. I just didn't feel quite so bad about spilling the blood of a man that used and abused fifteen-year-old girls.

"That's not what you really want though, is it?" I eased the Charger to a stop at a red light and glanced his way. "You like them with enough innocence to make it wrong. Don't you?"

A wicked smile tugged at his lips. "You've seen my memories. You tell me."

"If I wasn't here, you'd be hunting one of the prostitutes. Or, maybe some random passerby that captures your attention. Someone that you can play the game with. Someone you can draw in, work into a frenzy, and devour."

I wasn't wrong. His silence confirmed that. The differences between the two of us were becoming more apparent all the time. Since

I'd learned we were twin flames, I had been looking harder at each of us, seeking evidence of the light and dark we were both said to possess, and I was finding it. True to the yin-yang description, we each held a little of the other inside.

"Ladies choice tonight," Arys said with a wink. "How's that sound?"

"Fantastic," I replied, my tone thick with sarcasm.

I pulled the car into the parking lot of a small, vacant church. We quickly joined the rest of the creatures of the night, prowling the streets for the perfect victim. The Avenue was not where I wanted to be. The stink of car exhaust and the filthy city streets made me long that much more for the clean earthy scent of the forest and the wolves that should be running at my side. Not being there with them, it felt so wrong.

We passed a row of abandoned buildings complete with smashed windows and graffiti. Dark stains marred the concrete in several places. The screech of tires echoed a few blocks away. Loud rock music poured out of a sketchy bar at the end of the street.

Arys captured my hand in his as if we were just a regular couple out for a stroll. "Your wolf feels wild tonight. Dangerous."

His fingers were cool between mine, maybe more so because of the heat rushing through my veins. I burned with the wolf. Arys was hinting his concerns but not asking. Good man.

"I'll be fine," I tried to say with cool assurance, but it came out through gritted fang teeth. My fingers were tipped with deadly claws, and I had to concentrate hard on the human sights and scents around me. "I'm not sure I can do this. The bloodlust is buried so deep tonight. I can barely feel it at all."

The three nights of the full moon, before, during and after, were the few days of the month when I was free of the vampire essence rooted deep down in my core. As grateful as I was for that, it wasn't going to work in my favor tonight. I was about to face the vampire demoness that wanted me dead, and I had to be ready to bring it hard if need be. The wolf could potentially cripple me.

Arys stroked his thumb along my finger. "I can always feel it. Some nights worse than others. I need to do this, but you don't have to."

"I know. You're still not choosing though." I squeezed his hand and smiled up at him.

I was nervous about being present for Arys's kill when I myself was free of the bloodlust. It felt too much like being an accomplice of my own free will. When the bloodlust drove me to kill, I wasn't making the conscious decision. That didn't make it ok, but it made it easier to live with myself afterward.

We passed the loud bar and rounded the corner, coming upon a small group engaged in some kind of conflict. Shouts rang out, and the thud of fists on flesh was audible. A young prostitute stood off to the side, trying to avoid the melee. Her thick makeup did nothing to hide her youth. She looked like a kid playing dress up.

"Nobody touches my girls for free." One man shouted into the face of another, holding him tightly by the collar. "I hope you got a good feel because I'm going to break every one of your fingers."

They looked up as we approached, ready to send us on our way if we dared to do something stupid, like intervening. I took in the sight, making a quick decision. Pimp or john. Both?

I gave Arys the slightest nod. Immediately I felt the change in him as he slipped into full-on predator mode. The pimp barely had time to sneer, "What the hell are you looking at?" before Arys was on him.

Arys grabbed the greasy sleaze in a death grip, sinking his deadly fangs in a motion so fast it was hard to follow. The pimp shrieked and flailed to no avail. The john looked on in horror, as if unable to believe what he was seeing. Then he turned and fled down the street, cursing up a storm.

The woman backed up a few steps before crumpling in a dead faint. I stood there transfixed, knowing I should help her but unable or unwilling to tear my eyes from the feasting vampire.

Arys was in his element. Blood sprayed, and the tangy aroma reached out to taunt my bloodlust to life. It sprang forth with a fervor that rocked me. Just moments before it was nonexistent, but watching Arys flick his tongue over the wounds before sinking his fangs once more was bringing me to my knees.

A groan drew my attention to the fallen hooker. She rolled over and attempted to get up though her insanely high heels made that difficult in her woozy state. I moved to help her, grabbing her arm. She peered up at me with frightened brown eyes. My gaze went to the bloody cut on her forehead, and it was all over.

I dragged her close and bared my massive fangs. She screamed, a high piercing sound that hurt my sensitive ears. She lashed out, striking me repeatedly in the face as I struggled to pin her arms. She smelled like blood and cheap perfume, and I wanted her.

I fought for her throat, overpowering her with my superhuman strength. The next hand that slapped my face belonged to Arys. Everything became a blur as he wrestled the woman from my grasp and shoved her away, shouting at her to get moving if she wanted to live to see another night.

"Alexa!" He shook me until my teeth rattled. "Have you lost your mind?"

He smelled like blood and death but felt like power. So much power. I leaned into him, seeking the thrill of the connection we shared. I kissed him with dark intentions, aching for him to take me to a higher level of ecstasy. Tasting the blood on his lips had me clawing at him like a lunatic, which given the circumstances, I was.

He kissed me back, plunging his tongue into my mouth with a hunger to match my own. My larger fangs sliced his lip, and the taste of his blood had me ready to tear my clothes off right there in the filthy street.

"Alexa, stop. We have to go. You fucked up." Arys pushed me into motion, forcing me to keep up with him as he dragged me down a darkened side street in a circle back to the car. I protested his forcefulness, finding it hard to see through the fog in my brain.

I did fuck up. I was the worst kind of killer, one who would do under influence what I wouldn't allow others to do. And, I had no control over it. Right then, I didn't give a damn. I was raging with the hunger for human life and the aching need for my other half. I wanted to find release from the desire. Only Arys could give that to me.

We reached the car, finding it as we left it. Nobody was lurking around the small church at this time of night. I tugged at his jeans, unable to give voice to what I wanted. He stared at me as if I really had lost my mind.

"Do you see now?" He asked. "My darkness is growing inside you. The balance is shifting. You're in danger."

"Please," I murmured, ignoring his unwelcome warning. "I need you."

Arys gazed at me with lust in his deep blue eyes. And something more. Worry. Love. Regret. Then he gave in to the pull, and we fell into the big back seat of the Charger like two smitten teenagers.

After shedding only as much clothing as required, I climbed onto his lap and rode him like I was running a race and the finish line was in sight. Arys clung to me, holding me as if he feared I would disappear. Pressing his face into my hair, he breathed deeply of my scent and sighed.

Feeling him inside me as our power swept through us, I was transported to a place where light and dark didn't exist, where we were simply one, the same shade of grey.

After the thrill of climax subsided, rationale began to creep back in. I collapsed against him, my head resting on his shoulder. Reaching out a shaky hand, I drew a crooked heart in the fog on the back window.

"Why can't we stay this way forever?" I asked, expecting no answer. "It isn't fair."

"Nothing is fair, beautiful wolf." Arys stroked my tousled hair. "Don't make the mistake of thinking that means it isn't worth it."

We sat there for what felt like just seconds but was sadly much longer. I was racked with guilt over what I'd done to the prostitute. I could have killed her. Or turned her. Acknowledging that Arys was right about his darkness consuming me was hard. I didn't want it to be true.

## *Chapter Twenty-Four*

"You brought your other half. How nice." Shya was less than impressed to see Arys at my side. "I expected as much."

"Did you really think I'd let her come here alone?" Arys sized up the demon with blatant scorn. "I don't know what you're up to, but I do know you can't be trusted."

Shya waved us into his large, open, modern home. "Please join me in the back. It's far too nice a night to stay inside."

He led us through the living room and adjoined kitchen, out the large double doors that opened onto the backyard. I was relieved to be outside, preferring it to the suffocating confines of the house. Though it was open and large, Shya's house was so white washed that it was hard on the eyes. Besides, being indoors on a full moon night felt like being caged, so I gratefully drank in the sight of the impressive backyard.

The patio was adorned with a black and white furniture set. The upper floor of the house extended out above the patio, giving it a protective cover from the elements. A glass-topped table sat in the center, laden with food and drinks. Right away, my gaze was drawn to the scarlet-filled champagne flutes.

A stretch of fragrant, green grass separated the patio from the pool. It was inviting with its crystal clear water shimmering beneath the silver glow of moonlight. Beyond the pool, the vibrant lawn stretched as far as the eye could see. Shya certainly had a fine piece of property. It was trendy and luxurious. Perfect for hosting a party, which he seemed to feel he was doing.

"Help yourselves to anything you like." The demon indicated the display on the table. "Lilah should be here before long. We need to time the binding just right. It must be done at midnight."

Arys picked up a champagne glass, sniffing its contents before returning it to the table. "Blood?"

"I aim to please."

The yip of coyotes broke the quiet. They were far away though their voices carried. It caused the animal within to stir restlessly. I needed to be furry, and I needed it now. The bloodlust's reprieve earlier had been brief. Much too brief.

I ignored the elaborate table display. "So what's the plan? I've got to warn you, I'm not feeling entirely confident that I can hold the wolf back."

"You have no choice." Shya's smile vanished. His crimson eyes were ice cold. "Hold yourself together until I bind her or else we fail, and you will likely die. How's that for incentive?"

Arys frowned but said nothing. He walked a slow circle around the pool. His gaze traveled around the entire backyard as well as every entry into it. I was so happy to have him with me; I was a nervous wreck and was sure it was obvious.

"Follow my lead, Alexa," Shya continued, "and everything should go off without a hitch. Then we shall both be free of the threat she poses."

The doorbell rang and I jumped. My heart leapt into my throat. Shya clasped my left hand in his, trailing a warm finger over the dragon etched into my flesh. I shuddered, unable to repress the reaction to the snake-like slither of his power crawling over me.

"Trust me." Then he was gone, striding through the house to the front door.

"Arys, I can't do this," I whispered. My hands trembled and I fidgeted anxiously.

He was at my side in an instant, watching Shya warily. "You can and you will. You have to. Remember, there is no other creature on earth like you. Show them why they fear you."

His smooth as velvet voice was soothing, infusing me with confidence where before there had been fear. Our connection was as strong as ever. I focused on it humming through me until my fingers began to tingle.

An unnatural breeze bathed me in a cool wind seconds before Falon appeared beside me. It didn't startle me this time. I was beginning to get used to the fallen angel's sudden appearances.

He grabbed my arm and leaned in close. I could feel the urgency about him. "Keep my secret, and I'll owe you a favor." His breath was warm against my ear. He held firm, refusing to let me pull away until I responded.

We both looked up at the sound of Shya's voice. He was heading back our way with Lilah in tow. She was dressed for a fight in cargo pants, a tank top and army boots. Her flame colored hair was tied back in a braid, and her eyes sparkled with devious delight.

Falon's grip tightened painfully. For some reason, he was desperate to keep Shya from finding out about his sexcapades with Lilah. This might be a deal worth making.

"Fine," I hissed, shaking him off. "I'll keep your dirty little secret. For now. Don't make me regret it."

He quickly put distance between us, taking a seat on one of the comfy looking lounge chairs. His silver wings shifted to accommodate him. Leaning back, he feigned casual so well I almost bought it.

Shya oozed arrogant confidence when he stepped back onto the patio. He swept over to the small sofa adjacent to Falon and perched on the arm. Lilah stopped at the threshold, her orange eyes scrutinizing each one of us in turn.

"Alright, Shya, what are you up to?" With hands on her hips, Lilah glared daggers into the smirking demon. So, she didn't trust him either. That was reassuring.

"I told you, my dear. I would deliver the wolf straight into your hands. Did I not make good on that promise?"

I felt Arys tense beside me. Somehow, I remained calm despite the bombshell that had just dropped. It was too soon to assume what was the truth and what was a lie. I had no choice but to give Shya the benefit of the doubt.

Lilah met my eyes briefly, and I saw uncertainty in her gaze. She refused to acknowledge either Falon or Arys. "What's the catch? Last time we spoke you were adamant that I wasn't even to look at her the wrong way. What could you possibly need so badly that you'd be willing to give up such a prized piece of your collection?"

I bristled at that but remained unaffected – I could take a few insults – I had bigger concerns.

"You know what I want." Shya's entire demeanor changed. He was suddenly the slick businessman.

The two demons shared a look, and something passed between them. A peal of laughter rippled from Lilah. "It's never going to happen, Shya. Nothing in this world or the next could convince me to hand you that kind of power."

"Not even if I have valuable information that could help you break the curse? Information that you will lose if you kill Alexa and turn your back on me."

The yip of coyotes far off in the distance taunted my wolf. Demons weren't part of my world; I didn't belong here with them. Escape. That's what the wolf cried out for. Release. I swallowed hard and tried taking a few calming breaths. I could do this; I was fine.

Lilah looked at me, and her eyes narrowed. I met her stare steadily, daring her to make a move. I'd be happy to tear her throat out. It might not kill her, but it would hurt like a bitch, and I would enjoy doing it.

"I'm here because you promised me a deal I couldn't refuse," Lilah's voice grew thick with anger. She sauntered up to Shya, glowering down into his smug face. The air pulsed with the suffocating heat of demon power.

"And, I will give you one." If Shya was anything but coolly amused, it didn't show until he rose to face Lilah head on. Staring into her with a burning hatred in his red eyes, he grinned. "I have the key to breaking your curse."

"Bullshit," spat Lilah.

I held my breath. Watching the two of them attempt to stare one another down, I couldn't help but feel that I wouldn't like where this was going. I was right.

"It's Alexa."

My heart stopped. My mouth went dry, and I had to replay those two words in my head several times. Did I hear that correctly?

Lilah recovered quickly while I stood there dumbfounded. She looked skeptical but wasn't too quick to dismiss it as bullshit. The weight of her gaze was heavy. My cheeks burned. I felt like I'd just been betrayed, but I didn't know what the hell was going on.

I exchanged a look with Arys who stood ready to defend me. The promise of chaos hung on the air. I reached past the wolf who paced inside me to the power rooted in my core.

"Go on." Lilah crossed her arms and tapped a foot impatiently.

Shya looked incredibly pleased with himself. "What is the one thing that you need most in order to escape the curse?"

"I'm not playing this game. Get to the point."

"The blood of a divine creature," Shya continued, dismissing her angry retort. "The most obvious would be an angel. It would also be nearly impossible. That leaves very few possibilities. However, other divine creatures exist, others who belong to the light. One of which is within our midst."

A dramatic pause got Lilah thinking and left me sweating. Falon sat up straighter in his chair, listening attentively. Every person present turned to study me. I felt like a specimen on display, which put me on the defensive.

"I can't believe you never figured it out." Shya openly mocked the puzzled vampiress. "Alexa is a White Flame. Against the odds, she's been united with her twin. She doesn't live under the shapeshifter curse. She's gifted."

Lilah's eyes widened, and she took a step toward me. "She's one of the Hounds? How can that be? They were all destroyed."

My hands danced with blue and yellow energy. My patience had run thin, and the wolf was ready to chew its way out of me. Vampires and demons had been discussing me as if I were no more than an object for years. I'd had enough. Now, I was readying for a fight.

"Not all of them." Shya caught my eye and winked as if this were some joke we were both in on. "Living as a vampire has sheltered you, Lilah. The Hounds can never be thoroughly destroyed. You should know that."

I couldn't hold back anymore. "What the hell are you talking about? I won't be discussed as an object when I'm standing right here."

"Hounds of God." Falon broke his silence, drawing everyone's attention from me to him. "Shapeshifting was originally a punishment, a curse twisted by both angels and demons. The Hounds of God were those shapeshifters that were not cursed but gifted. They battle evil rather than become it. Legend would have you believe the Hounds no longer exist but they do. They are chosen. There are stories of Hounds dated as recently as the 1600s."

I tried to absorb what I was hearing. Lilah was eyeing me up in a whole new way. All it took to make me feel like an ignorant young mortal was spending time with those who had outlived me by thousands of lifetimes.

"So you see," Shya came to stand between Lilah and me. "Alexa's blood is the key to breaking the curse that binds you. Had you succeeded in having her killed, your best chance at freedom would have died with her."

Understanding settled in Lilah's flame colored eyes. She nodded knowingly, her gaze darting from me to Shya. "Now you want to exploit my folly for your own gain. I bet you're quite proud of yourself."

"Indeed, I am." Shya rubbed his hands together like a gleeful child. "You know my terms. They haven't changed."

Was this for real? I couldn't tell who Shya was screwing over anymore. It appeared to be me. I rolled a psi ball in my hands as I considered smashing it into the back of Shya's head.

"No." Lilah was firm. "You ask too much."

Shya's rage was sudden and furious. The power rose up around him to burn with the intense heat of an open flame. The dragon on my arm pulsed in response.

"Helping you reclaim your throne entitles me to as much. Make me your second-in-command or remain forever as you are, an outcast queen with no people or kingdom to call your own, answering to a werewolf with more power than you will ever see again." Shya was seething. So was I. The bastard was playing Lilah and me against each other. He would side with whoever could give him more.

I reached deeper, allowing more power to spill over me. I wasn't going out without a hell of a bang. Arys shot me a warning look, which I pretended not to notice. I was panicking. All I could do was be as ready as I could.

"You pathetic, insipid, power-hungry worm." With the grace of the undead, Lilah gravitated closer. Jabbing a finger into Shya's chest, she grinned maliciously, revealing fangs. "You can only dream of having power like I had. Your collection of rare and wonderful creatures won't bring you what you seek. You will always be underworld scum unworthy of even cleaning my boots. I'd spend eternity in this form before I'd consider making a deal with you."

There was a boom like thunder. Shya's huge black wings flapped once, driving Lilah back. Despite her limited demon power, she was unafraid. I'd once seen her drop a demon with no more than a word. The fact that she didn't seem able to do it to Shya indicated he was far more powerful than she would admit.

Her gaze slid to me, and the sparkle of intrigue within had my wolf in fits. "You and I can help each other, Alexa. Neither of us needs to be bound by Shya's manipulative deception. Help me regain my full power, and I can remove his mark from you."

Tempting but not good enough. Shya terrified me in all his dark glory, yet he was nothing compared to what she would be if she escaped the curse, I was certain.

Now it was my turn to talk. I had very little to say. The wolf was fierce, ready to fight her way out of my body. It fed my growing anger.

"Both of you can go right back to hell where you belong." I threw the psi ball so it exploded between them. A giant crack opened up on the patio and a breeze began to stir.

"Hey!" Shya shouted, reaching as if to grab me. "Watch it. I paid a pretty penny for this house."

Lilah used the small distraction to rush me. I met her attack with a shoulder to the midsection and used her momentum to throw her over my body. She hit the concrete with a heavy thud but didn't stay down for long.

"I really didn't want it to come to this," she said, swiping her bleeding elbow on the hem of her shirt, "but I won't let a goddamned mortal stand between me and my freedom."

She came at me with a backhand, which I deflected, but followed up too quickly with another swing, which I missed. The physical impact was bone jarring. The mix of demon and vampire power that she slammed into me lifted me off my feet. I came down hard on the grass beside the pool. It crushed the breath from me, but she allowed me no time to recover.

Lilah sprang, landing on top of me, knocking me back to the ground. Her ice-cold fingers wrapped around my throat and squeezed. Before I could blast her, Arys was there, dragging her off me. The two of them traded blows, and I used the brief reprieve to get to my feet.

Shya and Falon remained unmoved, watching the scene play out before them with carefully veiled expressions. Shya tipped his head in Lilah's direction and nodded. After his little ploy to use me for his own gain, he still expected me to work with him. I wanted nothing to do with him or his plans. Unfortunately, I didn't have a lot of options.

Arys did all he could to keep Lilah's attention from me. He carefully deflected a burning ball of energy, retaliating with one of his own. She was a blur, moving fast to avoid it while delivering a roundhouse kick with those massive boots. Arys caught her leg and shoved, knocking her off balance. She hit the ground and rolled, back on her feet just that fast.

I was ready when she came at me again. I crooked a finger, inviting her attack. It caused her to falter, to question my motives. It was all I needed to reach out for her power. My intent was to take it, make it mine and tear it from her. The vampire energy within her easily bent to my will, but her demon power ran over me like a lake of burning hot lava.

I screamed as the demonic force slammed through me. I couldn't contain or control it. It tore through me quickly, leaving me dizzy and nauseous. When Lilah pounded her elbow into my head, I fell to my knees, my body contorting as the wolf tried to break free.

"Don't you do it, Alexa." Shya's voice sounded muffled and far away, like he was under water. "Finish this first."

With clawed fingers, I dug at the earth beneath me. It hurt to hold the wolf back. Arys was at my side, fighting Lilah off with both power and fists. A cry became a howl as I fought the wolf. I had to overcome it. If I turned wolf my power would be locked inside me. I couldn't tap it unless I was human. No, not human. Vampire. Much as I hated to admit it, my power was all vampire.

Lilah met each of Arys's blows with a counter attack. She hadn't wasted the years of her curse; she adeptly used his strength against him. Pulling him in close, she twisted her body, lifting Arys off his feet. She slammed him hard against the concrete patio, knocking him senseless.

Her boot hit my face with enough force to make my vision go black. I tasted blood. I blinked several times until everything swam back into focus. Shya could feel free to come to my aid any time now, but if I held my breath on that one, I'd die waiting.

I struggled to get up while fending off the attacks. I slashed a hand tipped with claws across her midsection, digging deep into her flesh. It would have been a fatal wound on a mortal, but it was enough to get her to back off. Shya may have been a disgusting liar, but he was right about one thing: Lilah wasn't willing to risk the death of her vampire form.

"For a demon as old as you are," I spat blood. "You're not very bright. You were never on my radar, Lilah. Not until you started gunning for me."

I drew myself up to my full height, wincing in pain. I gasped for breath while Lilah examined her wound. It was bad. With a little more force, she would have had to hold her insides together.

"It was only a matter of time. I may not have known you're a Hound, but everyone knows you're a White Flame. It's no secret. I figured I'd get a jump on you before you came after me. There's only room in this city for one vampire queen. Since it's all I've got left, I'm not about to share the title."

"I don't want any goddamn title," I snarled, my voice rough with wolf.

Lilah took a step back, then another. She shook her head, and her long braid moved like a snake. "You don't have a choice. It's you or me, and every vampire in this city knows it. Hell, even those two dipshits know it." She gestured to Falon and Shya with disdain. "Sorry, Alexa, but a twin flame union never occurs without a damned good reason. A reason that never bodes well for the underworld."

The perils of my life began to make sense. Shya's interest in my power. Lilah's desire to kill me. Falon's utter hatred for me. They feared Arys and me.

The realization was as numbing as it was startling. There was no time to pick apart the why and how of it all. I wasn't feeling like something to be feared, but if there were a time to rise to that challenge, it would be now.

"Have it your way then, Lilah." I shrugged, "but I plan on walking out of here tonight. If I have to send you back to the cage the angels made for you, then so be it."

Surprise flickered over her face. She glared daggers at Shya before meeting Falon's eyes. He dropped his gaze, refusing to acknowledge her silent plea. Falon may have enjoyed the fun times, but his loyalty lay with Shya.

"Oh, I see how it is." Lilah gazed around at each of us in turn. Then she sprang for me.

I reached for Arys who was looking edgy with solid blue wolf eyes. I clutched his hand, seeking and finding that deeper connection between us. We were stronger together. With my free hand, I hit Lilah with a psi ball that exploded against her chest. It launched her backwards, into the pool with a splash.

"Shya, feel free to step in any time," I growled, watching the waves lap the edge of the pool.

"Strip her power, dammit," came his venomous reply.

Arys pulled me close and forced me to meet his eyes. His hands were shaky and feverishly hot. He gripped me so tight it hurt. "You need to finish this. Fast. You've got to let the wolf out."

The power spilled from him in buckets. It crashed through me so hard and fast, it felt like I'd grabbed a live wire. I fell to my knees, and Arys pulled me up, murmuring words of encouragement. I had no time to adjust to the influx of Arys's power; a torrent of water rained down around us as Lilah rose up from the chlorinated depths.

Her hair was plastered to her head, and her eyes were solid black. She was like something straight out of a horror movie. Her dark beauty captivated me, but she left me more than a little scared.

Releasing Arys's hand, I stepped forward to meet Lilah. My hands were alight with dancing, golden blue flames of power. It surged through me with enough pressure to blow the top of my head off if I didn't channel it properly. No time to worry about that now.

With a wild war cry, Lilah hit me with a shot of raw power that tore a yelp from me as it threw me into Shya. I crashed against one of the wings he spread to stop my flailing form. It was like hitting a brick wall, albeit one layered with the softest feathers I'd ever touched.

I regained my balance quickly. Projecting a strong enough shield around me took my full concentration. It was difficult to hold, but it deflected the next blast she sent my way.

The power flowed through me, growing in strength as I opened myself up to it completely. Everything around me fell away. All I saw was my prey: Lilah.

I advanced on her slowly, finally feeling no need to rush. Now it was about who wanted it more. She may have had thousands of years of ruling the underworld as her driving factor, but I had several people who relied on me and a purpose I had yet to discover. Nobody was taking that away from me. Not tonight.

Trading power blows wasn't going to work. Arys said I was reckless, and what I was about to do might be just that, but I was going to do it anyway.

When just ten feet separated us, I dropped my shield and hit her with a blast of power. I had no intent to harm her, merely to stun her. Lilah cocked her head in confusion, wondering why I didn't really let her have it. I held up both hands and gestured for her to bring it on.

*Death Wish*

Suspicion shone in her black eyes. Still, she took the shot. Instead of attempting to block the writhing mass of energy she threw, I grasped it and pulled it into me. Lilah's power wasn't so different from mine. The strange combination of demon and vampire roiled about like a small tornado as it swept through me. The vampire energy I could feel and touch as if it were my own. I grasped it tightly, bending it to my will.

I had no command over the demon magic slamming through my core. Lord, how it burned. The limitation of her curse was all that kept me alive right then. I focused hard on the link between Lilah and me. I drew on the stream of energy, intent on maintaining the connection between us.

I knew how to force the power into someone until they overloaded and their heart burst. Since I wasn't able to kill Lilah, I opted to try the opposite. I decided to pull it into myself until, with any luck, she had nothing left to give, just as Shya suggested. Even a demon trapped in a physical form would need rest at some point. The tricky part was to channel it through me and back out, straight into the earth, before it killed me, something I had yet to try on such a grand scale.

My heart thundered in my ears; everything sounded muffled and far away. I struggled to align my energy with hers so I could keep it flowing between us; it took everything I had.

The fire began in the pit of my stomach and spread throughout my limbs. I stumbled but kept moving toward her. Closer proximity made it easier to maintain my grip on the energy. When I was almost touching her, she jerked back, realization settling in.

"No way," she hissed. "You won't do it. It's suicide." She tried to cut the link between us, to stop the stream of power flowing from her. I held tight, refusing to let her wrench it from me.

I could barely breathe for fear that taking a breath would break my precarious hold on her power. My voice was low, barely audible. "If I die, I'm taking you with me. I'll be back as a vampire. And, you'll be a prisoner of angels. I still win."

It became a metaphysical tug of war as we each sought to gain and keep control. When Lilah failed to tear her power back, she shoved it into me with a fierce intensity that dropped me to the ground.

I knelt on the cool grass, gasping for air. The roiling mass of vampire and demon energy filled me to capacity. The pressure inside me grew unbearable, and I shrieked. I channeled the massive force through me, forcing it into the earth. Simultaneously, I continued to draw Lilah's power in, cycling it through me despite the growing sensation of being on fire.

Arys drew near and the pain dimmed. A resurgence of strength filled me. Sucking in a deep breath, I knew it was do or die. I jerked hard on the line between us, causing her to stagger. An immense wave of raw energy pounded through me, and I fought to push it into the earth beneath me. There was a rumble, and the ground seemed to move. Lilah lost her balance, falling on her ass with a dazed expression.

The connection between us broke. It was all I could do to keep the flow moving through me until I'd driven it all into the earth. My chest ached and my vision blurred. Blood dripped steadily from my nose. The pain in my head was enormous. Maybe I had failed. Maybe it had killed me after all.

I was vaguely aware of Shya's dark form swooping in. Latin spewed from his lips, words and phrases unknown to me. The murky sensation of pure demon power rolled over me, and the dragon on my wrist itched. Arys reached for me, asking questions a mile a minute. I couldn't focus on any one thing.

Now that I was weakened and free of my vampire side, the wolf saw its opportunity and took it. I tugged at my clothing to no avail. The change took me, a split second of gut-wrenching pain, and then, bliss, I was wolf.

## *Chapter Twenty-Five*

I fled Shya's backyard as if the flames of Hell licked at my heels. I cleared the perimeter of his property and continued through the neighboring farmer's field. Shya's rural location had likely been chosen for privacy during unsavory events, but it was my saving grace just then.

The wolf was in charge. After fighting it off all night, it felt wonderful to let go and just run. I raised my voice to the night and cried out to the moon. The unfamiliar smells reminded me that I didn't belong here. And, I was alone. I ached for Shaz.

'Come back to me, my wolf.' Arys's smooth as velvet voice danced through my mind. 'Never have I feared so much for you.'

'How was that for reckless?' I couldn't resist goading him. I trotted along through the field until I came across a rabbit carcass left behind by the coyotes.

'Reckless is putting it lightly, but it was a smart move. You did it. You weakened her so Shya could bind her.' He couldn't hide the swell of pride in his thoughts.

'I didn't do it alone. I would have burst into flames if you hadn't been there.'

'That's not what I want to hear right now. Come back, Alexa. It's not over yet.'

No, it certainly wasn't. I still had Shya to deal with. The evil bastard had been willing to use me for his own gain. I shouldn't have been surprised. He was a demon. It's what they do. Kale, the dreamwalker, and me: we were all expendable to Shya and others like him.

I hated him with a deep-rooted passion. Clever and charismatic, he was a force to be reckoned with. Though I couldn't see his mark in wolf form, I could feel it there, a metaphysical brand etched in my flesh.

I turned back toward Shya's house, my fury growing with each step. The quick change to wolf after such strenuous exertion had done wonders for me. I felt energized instead of drained, like I could take on Shya as well and win, but I wasn't about to let my ego talk me into getting my ass kicked. Shya could be dealt with, though it would take outsmarting him rather than mere aggression.

There was no sign of Lilah when I slunk through the yard up to the house. Shya and Arys were in one another's face, talking in hushed, angry tones. Falon watched with a grin, finding the conflict entertaining. They all looked my way as I approached. For a fleeting moment, I wondered how easy it would be for a demon to recover from a torn out throat.

"Congratulations," Shya beamed, a serpentine smile contorting his face into something I would later see in my nightmares. "You proved yourself to be the better vampire."

I stopped where the grass met the concrete patio. Fixing the demon with a blank stare, I pledged a silent vow to myself that I would not let him manipulate me anymore. I wasn't meant to be part of his world, and I wouldn't let him ruin me.

I stared at him until he edged away from Arys. "Forgive me. Would you like a robe or something?" Shya snapped a finger, and Falon disappeared into the house with a scowl.

My clothes had been ruined in the shift. That hardly ever happened anymore, but since I'd just bought them, it was a greater annoyance. Falon returned with a beautiful black silk kimono with an orange dragon emblazoned on the back. He shoved it into Arys's hand before returning to his lounge chair.

'What does he want for it?' I directed to Arys. 'My soul?'

"She doesn't trust you," Arys spoke for me. "With good reason. What do you expect in return from her?"

Shya maintained a neutral expression though amusement shone in his eyes. "For that? Nothing. Consider it a gift."

Arys held the kimono out like a curtain to shield me from the demon and fallen angel. I shifted back to human form, feeling naked and exposed regardless. I slipped into the robe, almost sighing as the exquisite material slid over my bare skin. When it was secured around my waist, I let Shya have it.

"What the fuck was that? You were going to sell me out to Lilah like I'm a goddamn commodity. I knew you were skeevy, but you are a real piece of work. I'm not making the mistake of working with you again. On anything. Count me out. From now on, I don't work for you, with you or for your so-called agenda. I've got my own agenda."

The seriousness of my proclamation was destroyed by Falon's low chuckle. I shot him a look that oozed venom. Shya ignored our exchange.

He crossed his arms and observed me coolly. "I hope your agenda includes the dreamwalker you owe me. A deal is a deal, Alexa."

That's it? That's all he had to say? Of course it was. I wasn't going to get an apology or explanation.

"What do you need a dreamwalker for anyway? Another power play?"

Shya shrugged. "See now that's something I can only share with those who are willing to work with me."

"Fair enough."

"I was just discussing that very thing with your vampire here." Shya gestured to Arys who glowered. "We all stand to gain a lot more if we can work together. I'd advise you to play nice, Alexa. The two of you have an awful lot of power. That kind of power earns you friends and enemies. However, it's never wise to allow it to turn friends into enemies."

He never so much as threatened me nor did he exude any menace, yet the promise was there, Shya's unspoken guarantee that I would be sorry for cutting the puppet strings.

"We were never friends." I was ready to leave. Engaging in further conflict with demons tonight didn't appeal to me.

Arys stuck to my side protectively. I stepped through the patio door to exit through the front of the house. I thought Shya might just let us go. Not without a last parting shot.

"You know you can't save her." Shya's voice followed us, his words for Arys alone. "You're running out of time."

Arys stopped but gave me a gentle push, urging me on. He turned to Shya with a deadly calm. "So are you. Isn't that why you're so desperate to hang on to her? She doesn't belong in the darkness with people like you and me. You know that. And, you know one day she may come for you."

I stopped dead in my tracks. My skin prickled at what I was hearing.

"She'll never remain mortal long enough to be a problem for me." Shya nodded curtly. "You've seen to that. Haven't you, vampire? Your selfish blood bond has tipped the balance. Eventually her flame will burn out, and with it, the purpose you both share."

I tugged on Arys's hand, needing to flee Shya's unwelcome words. "Let's go. We don't need to listen to this."

Arys hesitated, his jaw clenched. The negative charge of his anger made the temperature rise. "Don't even think about it, you smug son of a bitch."

Shya laughed then, a cold, foul sound that I felt in my bones. With hands spread wide in a gesture of mock innocence, he said oh so calmly, "It would be a shame if Alexa joined the world of the undead sooner rather than later."

Arys snapped. Breaking away from me, he lunged at the smirking demon. I grabbed for him and missed. He landed a well-placed punch that brought a gush of blood forth from Shya's nose. Falon intervened before he could throw another.

Falon shoved Arys in my direction. I caught hold of his arm before he could go after Shya again. "We are leaving right now," I insisted, dragging him to the front door.

Shya wiped at his nose, his eyes never leaving me as I put distance between us. "Don't worry, Alexa. Once you become a vampire, your blood will no longer break Lilah's curse. We all win."

Delusional. I was staring into the eyes of a madman. I couldn't possibly vacate Shya's house fast enough. Nobody would win as long as Shya was manipulating us for his own gain. Maybe I couldn't stop him, but I didn't have to play the part he'd written for me.

I was near hysterics by the time we were in the car speeding away from the house of hell. The calm strength I'd exuded fled, leaving me vulnerable to the fear that waited. I shook in the passenger seat while Arys drove with the aggression of a man on the warpath.

"I'll kill him," he swore, slamming a hand against the steering wheel. "Somehow I will find a way to send that sorry bastard back to hell where he belongs. I won't let him hurt you."

"Arys, this isn't your fault. I know you're blaming yourself. I made the choice to be bonded to you by blood. I knew what that meant."

"No, you didn't." The light from the dashboard cast a green glow on Arys's grim expression. "You didn't know everything about us then. What we are. How the blood bond would affect that. I never told you. It was selfish and arrogant of me. Now you're paying the price."

I stared at him, ignoring how fast the night flew by out the window. "If you hadn't bonded me, Harley would have. He almost did."

"I wish I'd let him." Arys's confession was like a small bomb being dropped in my lap.

"How can you say that?" My voice trembled. "I am part of you. It's better this way. We didn't know the risks, but we will find a way to manage them."

He was silent. Staring stonily straight ahead, Arys's lack of reaction spoke for him. My jaw dropped as it began to sink in.

"You knew," I whispered. "You knew it would tip the balance between us."

I waited for him to deny it, praying he would. When his response didn't come fast enough I had to fight back the urge to shake him.

"Yes. I knew," he said at last.

I was at a loss for words. Arys had knowingly put me at risk just so no other vampire could claim me. "Why?"

"It was selfish. I'd waited so long to find you. You were already mine in every other way. I never planned to do it. I didn't want this for you. Shaz suggested it, and I saw an opportunity to bind you to me beyond this mortal life you live. And, I took it." His voice became gruff, thick with remorse. "I'm sorry, Alexa."

I squeezed my eyes shut. With my head in my hands, I fought back the bitter sting of tears. How many more secrets were being withheld from me? I was starting to feel that everyone I knew had a secret that would shatter my world.

Sucking in a deep breath, I let it out as an exasperated sigh. "If Harley or someone else had blood bonded me, it would still have tainted me with darkness that doesn't belong. I will not hold this against you. I can't. I have too many broken relationships with people I love."

"If Harley had done it, I would be free of blame. And, I could have killed him to set you free."

I felt betrayed. It was so hard not to. Though I loved Arys in ways I could not describe, I was painfully aware that he too had endangered me simply because he had wanted something. I said I wouldn't hold it against him, and I meant that, so why did part of me feel that was a lie?

As the rush of the evening faded, my head started to ache. I'd channeled an amazing amount of power without my brain exploding, a small miracle. A migraine was a small price to pay compared to the alternative of lying in a smoldering heap of fur at Lilah's feet.

Arys glanced over, his gaze heavy with the weight of his concern. "I hate watching you do that to yourself. The headaches and the nosebleeds… it's harming you. The power is too much."

I turned away. Staring out the window was the best way to avoid those midnight eyes. "Let's not have this conversation again."

The Charger's interior grew tense. I fidgeted with the hem of the silk robe. I'd had more than enough thrown at me for one night. Arys and I might be faced with eternal conflict, but a reprieve was necessary at times.

The atmosphere grew increasingly strained as we left the rural roads behind and entered the city. He wasn't going to let it go – I could feel it – so I wasn't surprised by his outburst.

"It's killing you, Alexa. Slowly but surely, it is devouring you. The power, the bloodlust, all of it." His voice rose to an ear battering level. It took a lot for Arys to really lose it. The trace of fear in his heavy, irate energy made it impossible to respond with anger.

"I know, Arys. It's not the vampire blood bond. It's us. Willow said twin flames always destroy each other. The strength of our bond is too much for either of us. Whatever we exist for, it's not meant to be easy."

His fingers tightened on the wheel, and his foot got heavier on the gas pedal. "Looks like I'm not the only one keeping things to myself. You didn't think that little tidbit of conversation was worth sharing?"

"Despite how much you seem to enjoy a good fight, I didn't think it was worth arguing about." I slid a sidelong glance his way, drinking in the sight of him.

With that perfectly messed black hair, those entrapping eyes and the hard set to his jaw, I couldn't help but swoon a little each time I looked at him. The sensitive side I'd discovered beneath the rough, passionate exterior drew me like a moth to a flame. It was the yin yang effect. The light buried within the darkness.

Our duality filled me with relief and encouragement. Neither of us was wholly light or dark but our own mix of both. Arys believed he was a creature of death and darkness, but light dwelled inside him waiting to burst forth. I wondered which of us would be most surprised when it did.

We jerked to a stop at a red light. Arys met my gaze, and his angry retort died on his lips. Whatever he saw in my eyes, it changed his tune.

"We fight. We fuck. We forgive. It's what we do," he teased, sliding a hand over my silk covered thigh. "Seriously though, it's killing me to see what this is doing to you."

I covered his hand with mine. That simple touch conveyed the depth of our connection. "The last year has changed you so much. I'm not sure you see it. It's quite beautiful."

He held my gaze, and we fell into one another. We shared something special, something that blood and death could never take from us.

The startling honk from the car behind us broke the brief spell. Arys hit the gas, and we sped through the intersection. My phone rang, blasting out the *Austin Powers* theme song. Arys chuckled, and I shot him a dirty look.

I fished the phone out of my bag. "You've really got to stop changing my ring tone. That could get embarrassing in public."

"That's the plan." He expertly deflected my attempted slap without ever taking his eyes off the road.

The call display revealed a number I didn't know. I answered with suspicion in my voice. I recognized the voice on the other end immediately, and my mood soured.

"Ms. O'Brien, this is Agent Briggs. I'm calling about Kale Sinclair."

"I hope that means this is about meeting to make our trade."

"It's not. This is about a missing vampire. Sinclair escaped."

My jaw dropped. My initial reaction was to be impressed. Something in the agent's voice made me wary though. "What happened?"

"He escaped us, leaving at least twenty of my agents dead. I wasn't on duty at the time so I didn't witness the incident myself, other than what I've seen on the security footage. Our efforts to locate him have been unsuccessful." Briggs sounded bitter.

A lump formed in my throat, and I swallowed hard. "What about Juliet? Is she ok?"

"She's fine." Briggs cleared his throat, and his voice dropped a few octaves. "I'm sure I don't have to tell you how dangerous he is."

"After several days and nights of torture at the hands of humans playing God, I'd imagine it would be enough to drive anyone a little nuts," I spat, growing enraged. "He's not your concern anymore. If you send your people after him, if you do a damn thing to him, I'll be more than a blip on your fucking watch-list radar. Is that clear?"

There was a slight pause before Briggs replied, his tone forced. "Crystal. However, I can't allow a potential security threat to call the shots for me. I suggest that you find him before we do."

He hung up before I could reply.

\* \* \* \*

I searched every place I thought Kale might be. His classic Camaro still sat outside The Wicked Kiss, right where he'd left it the night the FPA took him in. Nobody inside the club had seen him recently, which was a relief. If he were on a bender, walking into The Wicked Kiss would turn him into a bloodthirsty version of a kid in a candy store.

A brief stop at his house revealed no recent trace of him. His energy lingered around the place, but it was faded. He hadn't been there.

As dawn drew closer, I had no choice but to go home and wait for dusk to continue my search. Arys didn't say a single snarky thing. He humored me, going through the motions of assisting in my search, and I adored him for it.

We returned to Arys's to find Shaz waiting there for us. He sat on the hood of his car staring at his phone. His blonde head jerked up at our arrival. I hadn't expected him. Warmth filled me, and I was eager to throw myself in his arms.

Until I noticed the bags piled in the back of his car.

I got out of the Charger and stood there awkwardly. Along with several duffel bags, he had packed the guitar he loved but rarely played. Edging closer to Shaz's Chevy, I spied a framed photo lying on the passenger seat. It was the same one, of us as wolves, that Kylarai had given me. *Oh God, no. I can't do this.*

Shaz put his phone away and came around the car to pull me into his embrace. I was numb. Arys gave him a pat on the shoulder and swept by us, into the house. Had Arys known Shaz was planning to leave today?

My white wolf kissed my forehead, and it felt like goodbye though he had yet to say it. "Will you come for a drive with me?" He asked, his voice betraying the pain he was trying to hide.

Unable to speak, I nodded and let him guide me into the car. I had to pick up the photo to avoid sitting on it. Clutching it in trembling hands, I stared at it in disbelief. How did I let this happen to us?

"Tell me what happened tonight." Shaz maneuvered the car through the quiet streets of Stony Plain. "I was worried about you. Considering your lack of clothing, I gather you couldn't resist the change."

I recounted the evening for him as best I could, but I struggled to talk about it simply because I didn't care anymore. I left out a few things, like Shya's threats. I didn't want to say anything to affect Shaz's decision to leave.

All I could think about was the heavy scent of him tickling my nose and how he was about to walk out of my life for God only knew how long. What if he didn't come back?

Shaz beamed a bright smile at me, but it didn't reach his eyes. "I knew you could handle her. I'm proud of you, Lex. You've always been so strong. It's one thing I've always admired about you."

"Strong? No, that's not me. Just stubborn."

We drove across town and stopped at the same park where Coby had almost wolfed out a few days ago. Shaz and I had shared an emotional moment there soon after Arys and I had united our power. Shaz had told me he loved me, and I had pretty much begged him not to hate me. That had been one year ago; time had gone by so fast.

"I thought we could sit on the bridge and watch the sun rise." He gestured to the fading stars. "It won't be long now."

The park was empty except for us. The playground stood vacant and dark. It would be hours before children would grace it with their brilliant, happy presence. Without them, the swing sets and jungle gyms seemed so forlorn and out of place.

We passed the gazebo. The path beyond it led in a wide circle around a large pond complete with a giant fountain spewing water in the center. When the midday sun shone brightly, a rainbow could be seen dancing in that fountain. I longed for it now. The darkness of early dawn felt cold and bleak. Though I was primarily nocturnal and content with it, I wished for the sun's golden rays to warm me.

As we walked along the path beside the pond, I wrestled with the many questions I was dying to ask him. Finally I settled for, "Where will you go?"

Shaz slipped his fingers between mine, clasping my hand tightly. "I don't know. Not yet. I might head for Jasper. Spend some time in the mountains. Just get away from it all."

"I'm sure that's just what you need." I nodded, feeling awkward and hollow.

We rounded a slight bend and crossed a miniature bridge with a bubbling stream flowing beneath it. The sound was comforting, a trickle of nature's beauty despite the ugliness that lay ahead. Glancing over the bridge into the water below, I spied coffee cups and chip bags destroying what should have been pristine, untouched by the filth human hands could bring. I stifled a heavy sigh and concentrated on simply putting one foot in front of the other.

Shaz led me to the big arch bridge that was the main focal point of the entire park. From twenty feet above the water, the pond's bottom could not be seen, and I wasn't sure how great the depths were.

We sat together on the edge, our arms looped around the metal railing. I waited for him to say something because I could not. I wasn't ready to cry yet.

This bridge already held somber memories for me. I had come here with Raoul's letter a year ago. Its contents had tortured me while I shed my tears into the water below. I suppose this place was as good as any for goodbye.

"I hate myself right now." Shaz sat stiffly beside me. His anguish was palpable. "I'm sitting here wishing you will beg me not to go, but I know you won't. You'd never stand in the way of what's best for someone else, even if it hurts you."

"Because I love you, Shaz." My voice was breathy, barely there. I didn't have the strength for the words this moment required.

"I know." His voice conveyed both anger and grief. "I don't deserve you, Lex. Not after what I've done. And, don't tell me it's no worse than what you've done. What I did was out of spite. There's no justification for that."

I swung my legs and gazed into the murky depths of the pond. The sky was gradually lightening; shade by shade, the night was slipping away.

"It's over. We need to move forward."

Shaz gazed at me thoughtfully, a sheepish grin lighting up his gorgeous face. "Remember the night you came home to Raoul's to find Belle there with him? The night you decided you were done with him for good. We sat in the backyard on the porch swing drinking whiskey."

"Yeah, I remember." It had been years ago. It felt like a lifetime.

"That night was the night I knew I was head over heels in love with you." A soft laugh accompanied his confession. "I think I loved you from the moment we met, but that night, I knew it for sure."

The night he spoke of had been hell for me. Kale and I had run into trouble, and then I'd returned to Raoul's after getting my ass kicked to find him playing with Belle, the pack tramp. Shaz had been the only thing that kept me from clawing her eyes out that night.

"You know I'd forgive you anything, right?" I squeezed his hand with a sudden desperation to never let go. "Even doing something stupid with an FPA spy."

He nodded and averted his eyes. "I wouldn't blame you or Arys if you decide to take her out. I've never felt like such an idiot."

That special moment of in-between fell upon us. To the west, the sky remained dark with the final touch of night. Upon the eastern horizon, a golden glow began to grow. Night and day shared the sky. That brief moment was so often overlooked but poignant and beautiful.

We sat in silence, holding hands and watching the sun chase the moon from sight. I would have given just about anything to make time stop, trapping us forever like that. I was torn between the desire to cry and the need to never shed a tear, to simply numb it all out. I doubted my ability to function without this man. He had always been there, but now he was leaving.

Dumbfounded. That's how I felt when the sun was high in the sky, and I realized time had betrayed me. Shaz stood and pulled me up with him. Wrapping his arms around me, he nuzzled my face with his, and then the dam broke.

The sudden onslaught of tears crippled me. I slid a hand into his hair and held him close. Silent sobs wracked my body. I had wanted to save my tears for after he'd gone, when I was alone. So much for that plan.

"Aw, Lex. Please don't cry. It's killing me to do this. I have to. So I can be what you need when I come back." Shaz swiped a thumb through my tears. They were crystal clear drops, a small blessing in such an excruciating moment.

"Go and do what you need to do." I sniffed and choked on a sob. "I'll be ok. Promise you won't worry about me. Focus on what's best for you. No matter what."

He kissed me, a tender press of his lips to mine. I threw my arms around his neck and let my passion pour forth. If this were our last kiss, it would be a damn great one.

When at last our lips parted, I was as ready as I would ever be to watch him walk out of my life. I couldn't shake the deep-rooted fear that he may never return.

"I should get you back to Arys's." Shaz turned to go, but I remained rooted to the spot.

"I think I'm going to walk. I just need some time alone. It's fine, really."

"Sure. I get it." His gaze dropped to our joined hands. "I should go. I don't want to, though."

I gave him a playful shove and forced a brittle smile that felt as if it would shatter any second. "Go on. Get out of here. The mountains await you."

Still, he wouldn't go. He shifted his weight from one foot to the other, staring uncertainly across the park. "This is the part where I ask you to come with me, and you tell me that you can't."

A fresh wave of tears threatened to spill from my eyes. "In a perfect world, we'd have been out of here a long time ago. You know I can't do that. Not with Lilah and my sister."

"And Arys," Shaz added, nodding knowingly. "Yeah, I know. I could never ask you to turn your back on everything. You're needed here."

He kissed me again, and I breathed deeply of his scent. Pine and wolf with a hint of cologne. My wolf.

"Stay safe," he whispered, resting his forehead against mine. "I love you, Lex."

His jade eyes glistened as he lingered momentarily, but he ultimately forced himself to turn around and walk away.

"I love you, too, wolf boy."

I sat back down on the bridge, hugging my knees to my chest. I stared straight down into the water, unable to bring myself to watch him drive away. The sound of his car starting got my heart pounding.

Only when it had faded into the distance did I let myself completely fall apart.

## Chapter Twenty-Six

Whiskey scorched a fiery path down my throat. I slammed the empty glass on the bar and contemplated a refill.

Josh had given up on keeping me out from behind the bar. He served the patrons and more or less ignored my presence. I made a mental note to give him a raise.

I didn't want to be at The Wicked Kiss. I could feel Shaz's absence like a punch in the gut. Three days wasn't much, but it felt like ages since he'd left. The hunt for Kale was my only distraction from the gnawing ache.

The vampire hadn't made an appearance, which was starting to make me nervous. If he didn't turn up soon, I'd have Brogan do another locator spell. I hated asking her for favors; involvement with me had gotten her mother killed, and I didn't want to endanger Brogan, too.

But, I also didn't want to hunt Kale like an animal. Maybe he came out of that scary ass hospital in need of some alone time, or maybe they'd driven him too far. Either way, I had to find him, to help him if I could.

Kale's past had left him damaged. The vampiress who made him had subjected him to horrible things, gruesome things that he wouldn't talk about. Kale had fought hard to leave that time in his life behind, but he had always walked a fine line between sane and ape-shit crazy. I suspected the FPA had made him snap. That frightened me. I'd seen Kale go a little nuts; I didn't want to see him at full madness capacity.

The FPA claimed to manage supernatural threats. Thus far, their only interest in the supernatural seemed to be recruitment, threats, torture and death; the FPA had proved to be shady and dangerous. I trusted them about as much as I trusted Shya, maybe less. They would be watching me, and I would be wise to return the gesture. Know thy enemy and all that jazz.

I bypassed the cheap whiskey and grabbed the pricey stuff. The golden liquid went down deliciously smooth. Swirling it in the glass, I watched Crimson Sin with disinterest. The lead singer was a werewolf, which almost explained why the band was willing to play regular shows here.

"Is this seat taken?"

I was surprised to see Willow sliding onto the bar stool across from me. Drumming his fingers on the counter, he peered past me to the wall of booze at the back of the bar. His wings were hidden from sight. He was casually dressed in jeans and a t-shirt with a ball cap covering his hair. Nothing about his appearance indicated his true nature.

"Willow, hi. I wouldn't have expected to see you in a place like this." I held up the fine whiskey in offering. "Can I get you a drink? It's on the house, of course."

He continued thoughtfully, eyeing the liquor selection. "How about some tequila?"

The thought of tequila turned my stomach, but I shoved a tray of limes toward him and reached for a bottle, grimacing at the nasty little worm in the bottom. Depositing the bottle and a shot glass in front of him, I hunted for a saltshaker. He waved dismissively and took his first shot without it.

"So," he gazed appreciatively at the tequila bottle. "Word on the street is that you and Shya forced the genie back into her lamp, so to speak. She must be pissed."

"I stripped her power so Shya could bind her, but only after he offered her my supposedly divine blood to break the curse. She shot down his demand for more power, and that was that." I shrugged and sipped my drink. "He had to be lying, but she didn't seem to think so."

"About your blood? No, that was the truth. You're the light of a twin flame union and one of the legendary Hounds. That is divine in a sense. It's pure and good, even if you yourself are not."

I pondered this, turning it over and dismissing it as ludicrous. "I'm not good. Not even close. I have blood on my hands. Innocent blood."

"Join the club." Willow clinked his glass against mine and tossed back the strong booze.

"How do you do that?" I blurted without thought. "How do you talk like that, as if you've accepted it? You don't deserve to be labeled as one of the bad guys, Willow. I do."

He chewed on a lime and regarded me thoughtfully. "I fell in love. Knowing that love, for even a short time, it was a gift. I don't regret it. The repercussions are worth it."

I was certain that his lady love would have shared his sentiment. It was endearing and inspiring. Willow had faced heartbreak beyond what I could imagine. Though he sat there drowning his sorrows as surely as most drunks did, he still believed his love was worth his misery.

"Anyway," he smiled and held up another shot in a gesture of cheers. "I thought I'd come by and share a friendly drink or ten with you. Figured you could use it."

"You wouldn't be wrong." I clinked my glass against his and savored the mind-numbing nectar. A roaring drunk might not have been the most responsible way to deal with my feelings, but I could either numb them out or go on a blood bender.

A small commotion near the door drew my attention. The strong sense of werewolf reached me. I watched the cluster of people in the entry with growing curiosity. Justin broke free of the throng and headed my way.

Justin was a tall, insanely well-built vampire. Dark skinned with deep brown eyes that glittered with constant bloodlust, he was one of the baddest vampires I knew. Intimidating was an understatement, which was what made him perfect for running security now that Shaz was gone.

He had openly pledged his loyalty to me when I had asked him if he wanted a job, but I never would dream of any vampire in this city bowing down to me as if I were a queen. Poor Lilah was so desperate to regain an army of minions to do her bidding that she was willing to settle for coercing the undead, most of which were little more than useless blood junkies barely existing from night to night.

"Alexa, there's a wolf here insisting she needs to see you. Says she's your sister." Justin's gaze traveled over Willow dismissively before settling on me. "Is that the same sister that dragged our boy Kale out of here? Want me to get rid of her?"

I groaned and spewed out my favorite cuss words. "No, let her in. Alone. Nobody comes in with her. And, stay in sight. Just in case."

Justin tipped his head in acknowledgment and spun on his heel. "You're the boss."

"Little sister has big balls to come back in here after her last visit," Willow observed. He slid a few stools away, dragging his booze and limes with him. "Pretend I'm not even here. Unless you want me to go?"

"No, that's fine. Stay. It's cool." My eyes were fixed on the door. Yes, Juliet certainly did have some serious nerve coming back in here. Still, she was an O'Brien; I wouldn't expect anything less from her.

Juliet entered, pausing until she spotted me. Her long, leggy frame moved in graceful strides across the room. Why couldn't she have been the short one? In yoga pants and a bright blue top, she looked both casual and lethal.

"Can we go somewhere and talk?" She didn't bother with a phony greeting and cut right to the chase.

I stared at her with a carefully neutral expression. Peering into her dark eyes, I was both saddened and infuriated. "I think here is just fine. Go ahead. Talk."

Irritation flashed across her delicate features. She glanced around at those within the vicinity and then shot me an exasperated look. "Alright. Alexa, be reasonable. We're sisters. So we've taken different paths in life? That doesn't change what we are to one another. I'm sorry for my role in what happened with Kale. I promise you, I had no part in what they did to him."

She wasn't lying. I guess that should have been reassuring. I was beyond upset with her. I was torn between wanting to smack her and wanting to hug her.

"I still can't believe you never told me you were alive. It stings, Juliet. You're a government drone now. I can't trust you. And, that hurts too."

"You can trust me. I am not your enemy. I'm your sister, dammit. I have busted my ass to keep the FPA off your tail, but there's only so much I can do." With a frustrated sigh, she sat heavily on the stool Willow had vacated. "I wanted to tell you I was alive. For a long time they wouldn't let me. Then after so much time had gone by, I couldn't bring myself to do it. I was afraid."

"Afraid of what?" I spun the whiskey glass in a slow circle, needing to keep my hands busy. It was all I could do not to fidget with my hair.

"Afraid of this." Juliet threw her hands in the air. Snatching the glass from my hand, she tossed back the contents and scowled. "It's not supposed to be like this, Lexi. We were sisters before we were anything else. Please try to remember that."

There was a cheer from the crowd gathered around the stage as the band's guitarist addressed the audience. The noise level grew substantially as they launched into another hard rock song. It gave me a much needed second to decide how to respond. I wrestled with my head and my heart, neither in agreement.

"That's all I think about every time I look at you," I confessed. "It scares me to see the kind of people you're involved with. The FPA has changed you."

"Raoul Roberts changed me. That's when our paths were clearly drawn. He took everything from us. I did the best I could with what I had to work with." Her chin jutted defensively, and she visibly shut down. "We are on the same side, Alexa. We just don't operate in the same way."

"You've got that right," I scoffed, unable to censor the bitterness. "I don't torture innocent people, and I don't give my loyalty to anyone who does."

With a toss of her dark curls, Juliet stood abruptly. "I came to apologize. For everything. I'm sorry. I hope one day we'll be able to put this behind us. You're still my big sister. I love you."

She was gone before I could utter a stunned response. I watched her disappear through the crowd and out the door. Mentally, I kicked myself. I was being stubborn. Not so unlike how I had been with her as a kid.

Juliet was the baby and adept at working it to her advantage; she could bat her eyelashes and get our parents to fall for anything. As kids, she would do all she could do stick it to me, yet at the end of the day, she needed me, her big sister. It was my duty to take care of her, and I'd done my best despite how often I wanted to strangle her.

The urge to go after her struck me. I denied it. I wanted nothing more than to find peace with my sister. I knew it would happen, but I just had to accept that our reconciliation wouldn't happen tonight.

*Death Wish*

Willow waited until Juliet was long gone before sliding back onto the stool across from me. He took in my clenched fists, deep-set frown and sad eyes. He could have made a forced attempt to cheer me up or offer a word of ill-timed advice. When he did neither, my respect for him grew.

Pointing to the stack of bottles behind me he said, "So what's the scotch like in this place?"

\* \* \* \*

*February 19, 1867*

*It's been more than a decade since I last visited Alice. The wicked witch didn't look a day older than the last time we spoke. Either she ages well, or she has one hell of a deal with the devil. I'm willing to bet the latter.*

*She laughed when she saw me, her black eyes sparkling viciously. "Still seeking answers, vampire?" she asked, holding out her hand for money. "Come now, let us look."*

*She sat me down at her table and pulled out a mirror. She placed it between us and waved a stick of incense in my face. I was annoyed by the pungent smell and impatient for her to finish with the theatrics.*

*"I shouldn't have come here." I started to rise, but she stopped me with a look.*

*"You went away." She nodded knowingly. "You thought you could escape what haunts you. Where you go, it goes."*

*I had spent seven years in Europe. Could she have guessed that? Doubtful. I stared at her, intrigued but wary. "Yes. I find myself seeking her face in every crowd. In every city in this world."*

*Alice made me close my eyes, demanding that I focus on the scent of the horrid incense and wipe any thought from my mind. I waited, filled with skepticism. What had I been thinking in returning to the old fraud? The sudden sting of a knife jabbing the end of my finger tempted me to open my eyes as she dripped my blood onto the mirror's shiny surface. She began to hum, a strange lilting note that continued for several minutes. Then it stopped, and the silence grew heavy.*

*"You will not see her face until time reveals it to you. Seek not your other half but yourself." Alice's voice took on a low, unnatural*

timbre. *"Darkness taints your twin flame union. It seeks to destroy you both. It waits for her birth like a lion eager for the hunt."*

My eyes flew open. Panic seized me as her words echoed in my ears. Alice stared at me with eyes glazed in a milky white film. The atmosphere grew hot with an energy so old and powerful it hurt. Alice was no longer present. Something else spoke through her lips.

*"Vampire, you are burdened by death. A burden you will share with her. As you draw closer to the purpose you share, the darkness draws closer to you. Beware. Ready yourself for that day. For what will come. For the day you kill her. You will destroy one another."*

Those words reached deep inside me, touching something sacred that I had yet to understand. I shook my head, unwilling to believe what I'd heard.

Alice waved a hand over the mirror, drawing my gaze. *"Look,"* she commanded.

Fog rose up from the surface of the glass, slowly dissipating. As it cleared, an image formed. I saw us as if through another's eyes. A flash of blonde hair, the hint of a smile, the most beautiful laugh I have ever heard. She was cast in shadow. I could not see her clearly.

The image changed. I watched myself grab her violently. I shook her as she fought me. She slapped my face, and I bared fangs at her. She said something then, something almost inaudible though I heard it as if she had shouted.

*"You know you have to do it,"* she whispered. *"It's ok. I'm ready."*

I wanted to shout at my future self, to beg him to stop. I watched myself pull her close and bite into her exposed neck. I watched myself kill her.

*"No!"* I stood up so fast the chair I'd been sitting in flipped over. In a sudden rage, I grabbed the mirror and smashed it on the floor. Then I lunged at Alice.

It was over rather quickly. I left Alice strewn across the table in a bloody heap. I should never have gone there. I should never have come back from Europe. I'm horrified by the vision in the mirror. What does it mean? Surely, nothing can be predestined for certain. Can it? I won't let it happen. Alice's vision will not come to pass. There has to be a way to alter the future. And, I will find it.

My pulsed pounded through my veins. Reading his journal had brought memories of Arys's life to the surface, even the memories that I had buried deepest in my subconscious. I looked up from the last entry in Arys's journal to study him.

He sat across from me on his favorite recliner. A sketchpad sat on his lap; with pencil in hand, he was immersed in his drawing.

I didn't want to interrupt him with questions or comments on what I'd just read. His artistic flare had been just as surprising as everything else about Arys. Spending so much time at his house had allowed me to witness it for myself. I was content just to watch him work.

He was shirtless, clad in soft blue cotton pajama pants with his hair damp from a recent shower and an expression of deep concentration, Arys was a treat for the eyes. I strained to see what he was drawing but couldn't make it out from where I sat on the couch.

"So you've finally finished reading that damn thing, huh?" He didn't look up from his work, but a grin played about his lips. "I was starting to think you never would. I imagine you have something to say about it."

"I do. I understand why you didn't tell me about our connection sooner." I stroked the old, yellowed pages of the journal, holding it protectively. "You hoped you'd find a way to change what you saw. If you did, I'd never have to know the truth. Too bad things didn't work that way."

Arys did look up then; wearing a pensive expression, his smile vanished. "Yes… too bad. That's why I dragged you to Lena for answers. I was praying she would tell me something different, something to prove Alice wrong somehow. Instead she confirmed what I already knew, for the most part."

Seeing the shadows in his eyes, I knew I could never tell Arys about the strange certainty I'd had in the past that I would die at his hand. Never.

"We can't make assumptions. You saw one thing in that vision. There has to be more to it. Things change, and even if they don't, there's a reason for them. All we can do is take it a day at a time. We have a purpose, Arys. There is a reason for what lies ahead. Whatever that may be."

Sure, I was afraid of what Alice had shown Arys, afraid because I felt it to be true. However, it was what came after that frightened me more. When I would rise as a vampire and become another insatiable menace of the night. That's when the balance we shared would tip. That's what Shya wanted.

"Right," he sneered. "We just have to try not to destroy each other in the meantime. No big deal."

I laughed, trying not to share his dark outlook. Someone had to keep things light. "So far so good. Lena and Alice knew things about us. They can't be the only ones. Maybe there's someone else, someone who can clarify things. There is so much we don't know yet."

"Perhaps it's better that way."

"All I know is that I'm ready for a few low key days of lying around, doing absolutely nothing. I just want to enjoy the here and now." I set the journal aside and stretched languorously, hoping to change the subject. "I'd like to spend the next two days in bed."

That brought back the sexy smile that lit a fire in my belly. Arys raised a dark brow and gave me a suggestive look. "Meet you there."

I held his gaze for a moment, wondering if I could make it down the hall before him. I sprang off the couch and darted from the room. Arys was faster, springing ahead to block my path. I tried to playfully body check him out of my way, but he grabbed me around the waist and tugged me off balance. We both tumbled to the floor in a giggling heap.

A bit of rough wrestling on the carpet resulted in burns on my knees that were not nearly as fun to receive as one might think. I knocked him down and made as if to run away, when he caught my ankle and sent me sprawling. I laughed until I cried, needing the rejuvenation that came from a cleansing laugh.

When Arys was least expecting it, I shoved his head against the floor and bounded for the bedroom. This time he didn't catch me. I was spread out in the middle of the bed when he appeared, shaking a finger at me.

"That was a cheap shot." He rubbed the side of his head. "Nice one. Now get naked so I can ravish you."

I didn't need to be told twice. I was eager for intimacy, seeking to escape the upsets of the past few days. Hell, the past several weeks even.

Slow and sensual, our lovemaking possessed a passion unlike anything we'd shared before. In search of freedom from the future that claimed us, we clung desperately to one another. We moved together with the natural grace of lovers entwined deep beyond the physical realm.

I held Arys close as he adorned my face in feverish kisses. Nothing was going to take him from me. I had lost so much, but I would not lose him. If finding our purpose meant fulfilling that vision in Alice's mirror, then maybe I didn't want to find it.

Guilt racked me at the thought. I couldn't deny my purpose, whatever it was. It was a key component of my existence. As trapped as I felt right now, ultimately it would set me free. If I had the courage to see it through...

I ran my hands over Arys's body, savoring every part of him, the way he felt, his invigorating scent and the taste of him as he claimed my lips. I found heaven in his arms, the only place I felt I belonged these days. Dying by Arys's hand wouldn't be so bad, not in comparison to the many horrible alternatives.

Hours later, I slipped from the bed with the intent to make coffee. Arys was restless, tossing fitfully in his sleep. I ran a hand through his hair, and he murmured my name but never woke.

Glancing around for something to throw on quickly, I spotted a folded black t-shirt on top of the dresser. No sooner had I grabbed it than the achingly familiar scent of Shaz wafted up to assault me. I slipped into the shirt, biting my lip against the tears that threatened. No way. No damn tears.

So, he'd left me something filled with his wonderful, masculine wolf scent. Nothing worth crying over. Yeah, right.

I busied myself making coffee. I couldn't sleep, so I flipped through the local newspaper, browsing the real estate section. With mug in hand, I took the paper into the living room and settled on the couch. Arys's fallen sketchpad caught my eye.

Curiosity coaxed me to pick it up. I turned it over to find a pencil sketch of myself. My breath caught and I sputtered coffee. Arys had finely depicted me with eyes lowered and a half smile. My hair blew in an invisible breeze. What shocked me though were the two precise fangs peeking from beneath my lip. Arys had drawn me as a vampire.

It was startling to see even as a simple sketch. Wolf fangs were bigger, vicious and had taken years to get used to. This was different. Foreign. I didn't like it.

I dropped the sketchpad onto the seat of the recliner, staring at it dumbstruck. I adored Arys; I'd go to hell and back for that man. Judging by everything I knew about twin flames, I likely would. But, this was too much too soon. This was one horror that I wasn't ready to face yet.

# *Epilogue*

"Alexa, it's beautiful. It's so open and spacious. Oh, look at the skylight! This house is a dream." Kylarai strode through the house gushing. I followed along smiling and nodding.

It was a gorgeous house, no doubt about that. A large spiral staircase greeted us upon stepping into the foyer. Every room was massive and state of the art in terms of architecture and appliances. The backyard had a small fenced off pool and an elaborate lawn with room for a flower garden. It was a dream, alright, Kylarai's dream.

She had accompanied me on my home buying excursion. I had decided to sell Raoul's property to someone willing to rebuild on it. My time there was over. I was starting anew.

Arys and I could not co-exist for much longer within his small bachelor-sized bungalow. Bonded didn't mean we could stand to be in each other's space twenty-four hours a day. We each needed our own space. I had to find a place that felt like it could become home.

I was also working on a small condo apartment purchase in the city. Stony Plain would always be my home, first and foremost, but having a backup pad in the city seemed like a necessity since I spent so much time there.

A year had passed before I'd touched the money Raoul had left me. I was using it now to start fresh: a new house, a new part of town and a new attitude. Kick ass or die. I planned on kicking ass.

"I don't know, Ky. It looks a little too picket fence-y for me." I shot a friendly smile toward the real estate agent lingering nearby, ready to offer me several reasons why the place was perfect.

"But, it's so beautiful." Ky's grey eyes sparkled as she took in the enormous kitchen with a vaulted ceiling.

I snickered and nudged her. "It would definitely be a nice upgrade from that little house you have now."

"Would you like to see the upstairs?" The realtor asked. "I'm sure you will find it just as impressive."

I jumped in before Kylarai could force me up the stairs. "No, thank you. Could you show me something a little less high-maintenance? Preferably on the edge of town if possible."

A few minutes later, we were following the real estate lady across town in Kylarai's Escalade. I caught her sneaking covert sidelong glances my way. Her brow furrowed, and she fiddled with the radio.

"Go ahead and ask, Ky. I know you want to."

Her face fell, and sympathy flooded her eyes. "I'm sorry. I suck at poker face. How are you doing? He's been gone for two weeks now. It must be hard."

"It is hard. It was hell those first few nights. I cried like a lovesick teenager." I grinned, showing her I was fine. I wasn't though. Not really. I missed Shaz so much it was all I could do to hold myself together. "It's getting better though. I'm happy that Shaz is doing what's best for himself. He needs to."

"Ok, good." Kylarai nodded a little too enthusiastically. "I'm glad to hear that. You know I'm always here if you need to talk."

"I know." I reached to pat her shoulder affectionately. "Thanks. I love you a lot, you know."

"The feeling is mutual."

"Is it also mutual for Coby?" I teased.

Her cheeks grew pink, betraying her. "Why whatever do you mean?"

"Nice try, lady."

Kylarai thought I didn't know she'd been sneaking over to Shaz's apartment to visit Coby. I was pretty sure Coby had been making himself comfortable at her place, too. Last I'd heard, Jez and Zoey were still getting cozy, as well. I was genuinely joyful for them. I wanted my friends to be happy and in love. Nothing else took the place of love.

We passed the golf course and took a left on the edge of town. I shook my head, not certain that I liked what I was seeing. It was mostly a stretch of farmland along the back road between Stony Plain and the neighboring community.

## Death Wish

We passed a rickety old house on the same property as the old cemetery where I'd once killed a trespassing werewolf. Then we hung a right into a driveway lined with thick foliage. The cemetery was close, but a patch of trees so thick it was almost forest blocked the burial grounds from sight.

The house was of average size with two floors and an attached garage. On one side of the property lay the forest thatch and the cemetery; the other side opened onto a farmer's field with more trees far off in the distance. A spark of hope flickered to life inside me. So far, the place had potential.

I eagerly followed the realtor inside. The house wasn't nearly as large or fancy as the last one we'd viewed, but it had a cozy feel to it the other had been missing. The front door opened into a long hall. Directly to the right, a set of stairs wound around a corner, disappearing on the way to the basement. A few steps down the hall revealed a second staircase, which wound its way to the upper level. Continuing straight ahead, the hall led into a large kitchen and living room.

The kitchen wasn't a chef's dream, but it was complete with all appliances and island seating. A set of sliding doors led to the backyard, which I could see held a furnished patio and luscious green grass. Nothing fancy out there, but it had plenty of space.

The living room was on the small side, but the gas fireplace beneath the TV nook gave it a cozy feel. I flashed a smile at Kylarai who looked less than impressed. Following the real estate agent upstairs, I was overjoyed to find a large master bedroom with a Jacuzzi tub in the attached bathroom.

It was a three-bedroom house with a partially finished basement, a little more space than I needed, but I was sure I could utilize it. We walked around the property outside, and my interest continued to grow.

"I think I really like it," I said, trying to judge the distance from the yard to the forest far beyond. It was a fair jaunt away, but a wolf could do it in a minute or two. The thatch of trees next to the house provided enough space to be wolf in my own backyard. The only house nearby was on the other side of the graveyard. Perfect.

"As you can see, the cemetery is hidden from view completely. It's owned by the town, and they go to great lengths to ensure it's well-kept and undisturbed by rambunctious teens." The realtor continued her sales pitch though she already had me. "If you have any questions or concerns, I'd be happy to address them."

"Thank you. I think I'd just like to take another walk around, if that's ok."

"By all means. I'll give you a few moments to think it over." She disappeared around the house to the front, leaving me to ponder what looked like a promising decision.

Kylarai gazed out on the field behind the property line. "Well, it's no dream house, but it really is ideal for a wolf. You can do so much with this yard. It would give you something to focus on this summer, too. Something positive and relaxing."

Birds fluttered about in the trees above us. I watched them fly from branch to branch, singing merrily amongst themselves. Traffic could be heard on the road out front, but it was sparse and muffled. The seclusion here appealed to me.

"Is that an offer of help I hear?" I wandered over to the patio to peek into the empty flowerpots that lined the edge. "You know I'm no good at the whole home decor and plant life kind of thing."

"Of course. I'd love to help. We can take a trip to the greenhouse on the highway and pick out flowers." Kylarai chattered on about plants, spitting out names I didn't know.

I knelt to plunge my hands into the vibrant green grass. The earth reached out to me, humming with an immense power that spoke of life and harmony. Concentrating, I could feel the energy of the nearby graveyard. It caused the fine hairs on the back of my neck to stand on end but held little true power or elements of danger.

Saying goodbye to Raoul's house hadn't been easy simply because it hadn't been by choice. That chapter of my life was now closed, as it should be. Still, so much lay ahead.

I had just begun to discover the source of my power and what it might mean to those that opposed me. Lilah hadn't been seen since that night at Shya's. Jez said there had been no sign of her around the office. She had gone off somewhere to lick her wounds and regroup. Powerless or not, a demon of her caliber wouldn't be gone for long. At least, not long enough.

Kale was still missing. Try as I might, my search was beginning to seem futile. Brogan's second locator spell had failed as well. I didn't even know if he was alive, though I couldn't shake the deep-rooted sense that he was. Somewhere.

I had meant what I said to Shya. I wouldn't be doing his dirty work anymore. Somehow, I would find a way to not only avoid delivering him the dreamwalker he sought but also keep him from getting his hands on one.

I thought often of the dreamwalker that the demon had killed in front of me. He was just a kid, a nameless one at that. Nobody deserved that kind of fate. I wanted to help people, those with power who so easily fell prey to monsters like Shya or the FPA. It wouldn't be easy, particularly with the demon's sigil on my arm.

I rose and wiped the grass and dirt from my hands. I was feeling good about my decision. We returned to the front yard where the agent stood chatting on her cell phone. She quickly ended the call at my arrival and smiled expectantly.

Clinging to the past was easy; letting go was hard. I had to move forward. This house was the right place to start.

I held out a hand and sucked in a deep breath. *Here goes nothing.* "I'll take it."

*Trina M. Lee*

Check out www.TrinaMLee.com for news and information on the upcoming sixth book in the Alexa O'Brien Huntress Series.

*Death Wish*

## About the Author

Trina M. Lee has walked in the darkness alongside vampires and werewolves since adolescence. Trina lives in Alberta, Canada with her fiancé and daughter, along with their 3 cats. She loves to hear from readers via email or twitter.

For news and book information please visit:

www.TrinaMLee.com

14463940R00169

Printed in Great Britain
by Amazon.co.uk, Ltd.,
Marston Gate.